FACES

E. C. BLAKE

DAW BOOKS, INC.

__DONALD A. WOLLHEIM, FOUNDER__
375 Hudson Street, New York, NY 10014
ELIZABETH R. WOLLHEIM
SHEILA E. GILBERT
PUBLISHERS
www.dawbooks.com

First Printing, July 2015
1 2 3 4 5 6 7 8 9

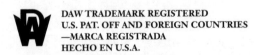

*This book is dedicated to my sister-in-law, Laurel Stein,
with thanks for her encouragement and insight.*

◆ ◆ ◆

Acknowledgments

There are four people I need to acknowledge, and they are always the same four.

My agent, Ethan Ellenberg, was the one who recognized the possibility in the premise of *Masks* when I first submitted it to him in the form of a brief synopsis. He encourage me to make that my next project. He was, as usual, right.

My editor, Sheila Gilbert, as is her wont, immediately saw the weaknesses in the submitted version of *Faces* and made exactly the right suggestions to make the book stronger. Any remaining weaknesses are, alas, my own.

And last, but absolutely not least, gratitude and all my love to my beautiful and intelligent wife, Margaret Anne, and lovely and talented daughter, Alice, for being willing to put up with a husband and father who types entire worlds into being, while keeping him constantly reminded that despite those acts of creation, he is not, in fact, God.

Finally, my thanks to all the readers who have told me how much they've enjoyed Mara's adventures and how fond they are of her. I'm rather fond of the girl myself.

ONE

Shelter from the Storm

THE DEAD LAY ON THE BEACH, row upon row, the snow gently wrapping their disfigured forms in shrouds of purest white, hiding the horror, hiding all differences. Had she not known how they were arranged, Mara could not have told which were Watchers and which members of the unMasked Army.

Except for the smallest corpses. There had been no children among the Watchers.

She stood, Keltan to her right and the Lady of Pain and Fire to her left, on the hillside landward of the gathered corpses. Keltan's presence warmed her. No one else had dared come close to the Lady and the wolves clustered around her feet. The survivors of the unMasked Army . . . though "army" seemed far too grand a term for what had been whittled down to no more than eighty fighters and perhaps two hundred men, women, and children in all . . . huddled together in small groups across the rows of dead from the Lady. Edrik stood with his wife, Tralia, both of them supporting Edrik's grandmother, Catilla, commander of the unMasked Army. Hyram was there, too, his arm protectively around the shoulders of Alita, the dark-skinned girl who had been rescued with Mara from the wagon taking them to the mining camp. Two other girls who had been in that wagon, Prella and Kirika, held each other close. Chell's men who had survived . . . about fifty in all . . . stood with their prince and their captains on the seaward side, where the sinking sun turned them into faceless silhouettes as though they wore the black Masks that had crumbled away into dust from the Watchers' faces when they'd died.

Whatever words were to be said over the dead had already been said by the surviving members of the families . . . those families where *anyone* survived. Not far from where she stood, Mara saw three corpses gathered together: man, woman, and young daughter. An entire family wiped out.

A family like mine once was.

Among those corpses lay that of Simona, the baker's daughter who had been the fourth girl rescued from the wagon with Mara.

No tears dimmed her vision. Her ability to weep, like so much else, seemed to have been stripped away from her this day. Instead, her grief coiled, with her anger and fear, somewhere deep inside her, down where the nightmares lurked, the nightmares created in her mind whenever she used her Gift of magic to kill, whenever she absorbed the magic of those who died in her presence.

Though she had killed few if any of those on the beach before them now. The Watchers had killed those of the unMasked Army. And the deaths in turn of those Watchers, and the psychic burden they imposed, could be laid directly at the feet of the Lady in white fur by her side.

"The burial ceremonies are complete?" the Lady said now to Mara, in a voice only she—and the wolves; she saw their ears flick at the sound of their mistress' voice—could have heard. The Lady had stood upon the hillside, watching silently, while the corpses were gathered and laid out.

"Yes," Mara said.

"So." The Lady raised her hands. In Mara's Gifted sight, they began to glow brighter and brighter, until they seemed like twin suns come to the beach. She knew that those around her who were not Gifted, like Keltan, saw nothing at all. She still found that hard to believe.

The Lady made a pushing motion. Mara saw a ball of white fire spring forth from her palms, spread into a towering wall of flame, and sweep across the beach. As the fiery wave passed, the bodies vanished, dissolving into white dust that the flame pushed ahead of it into the sea.

One instant, the corpses were there. The next, they were gone, and the snow fell onto empty, level ground, already softening the human-sized blotches of bare stones where the bodies had lain an instant before.

Mara heard a kind of collective gasp from the unMasked Army and the men of Korellia, followed by renewed weeping from those whose loved ones' remains had just vanished. She'd gasped, too, but for a different reason: for the first time she had seen *where* the Lady obtained her power. This close to her, she had sensed its flow.

Most Gifted could only use magic collected and held in containers of black lodestone, the strange mineral that attracted magic to itself. But the Lady of Pain and Fire, the Autarch, and Mara herself could draw magic directly from other living things, including people, though the Autarch's power was limited in that he required those people to be wearing magical Masks for him to access their magic.

The Lady had just drawn magic from the wolves.

Mara looked down at them. They grinned back at her, tongues lolling.

"I see you glimpse the truth," the Lady said softly to her. "But this is only the beginning of your understanding. Once we reach my stronghold . . ." She looked out to sea, and frowned. "But first, we must reach it." She glanced at Keltan. "Boy."

"Keltan," he muttered, but she hardly seemed to notice.

"Tell Catilla we have to leave at once. The storm is returning."

"But you stopped it," Mara said.

"No. I only quieted it, locally, for a short time."

"But didn't you start it in the first place?"

The Lady shook her head. "The land of Aygrima has magical defenses, established centuries ago. That ancient magic created this storm. It will last for however long those who crafted that magic decreed it should last." She spoke to Keltan again. "If we are not off this beach before full night, there will be more deaths. We must move *now*."

Keltan frowned, glanced out at sea, froze for a moment, and then dashed off without another word. Mara followed his gaze, and saw what had given him pause.

The sun was vanishing, but not yet falling below the horizon: instead, it was being swallowed by a rapidly rising line of black clouds, whose towering peaks it outlined in flame as it disappeared behind them.

"I'm not sure they *can* be off the beach before the storm comes back," Mara said, turning to the Lady. "Can't you quiet it again, at least for a time?"

The Lady shook her head again. "I came down to the shore holding as much magic within myself as I could, and I drew much more from the dying Watchers, but I also used a great deal destroying the remaining Watchers and cleansing the beach." *And destroying Chell's ships*, Mara thought, glancing at the crippled *Defender* lying heeled-over and broken-keeled on the beach, and uneasily remembering the gleeful fury with which the Lady had savaged it. But she didn't mention that out loud.

"The wolves provide some, but they are not inexhaustible," the Lady continued. "No. I can do nothing more against this storm, or stop the rising seas that will soon lash this beach. But as I have said, I have prepared food and shelter a short distance away, to see us through the night. After that. . . ." She pointed into the hills. "We are three days' journey from my stronghold, and that is three days as *I* travel. It may be a week with this ragtag bunch, and the journey is difficult."

Mara felt a surge of anger. "Then leave without us, if you're so worried. Save yourself. What do you care about this 'ragtag bunch'?"

The Lady raised an eyebrow. "I need them," she said. "I need people. And, as I have told you already, I need *you* in particular. If I—if *we*—are to overthrow the Autarch, then we must all help each other." She looked across the now-empty beach at the unMasked Army, and Mara, following her glance, saw Edrik already beginning to chivvy people inland. Beyond Edrik, the water, almost calm a few moments before, now tossed restlessly against the shore, and out to sea, the waves advanced in white-capped rows growing ever larger.

The final blazing sliver of sun vanished behind the rising clouds, plunging them into shadow. A wind even colder than before swirled the snow across the beach.

"I will use my magic as I can to make the journey easier for them," the Lady said, "but I cannot remove all hazards or discomforts."

Mara stared out across the beach, at the weary, crying children being urged to their feet, at the weeping widows and walking wounded turning their backs on the rising sea to start the long, uncertain journey inland. "Is there anything I can do to help? This suffering . . . it's all my fault."

"It is the *Autarch's* fault," the Lady said sharply. "Don't forget that. And don't forget that he *will* pay. Now that I have *you*, he *will* fall, as hard and fast as his father." She took a deep breath. "And, no, there is nothing you can do to help. I have no magic you can use, and I do not think you are willing to deliberately take magic from your companions."

Mara shot a horrified look at her. "I'll never be willing to do that. It's . . . I don't dare."

"Really?" The Lady smiled slightly, the expression revealing deeper lines in her face than were usually apparent, so that for the first time Mara had a hint of her true age. "I can see we have a great deal to talk about . . . and a great many misconceptions on your part to clear up. But all that must wait." The wolves, sitting or lying at ease all around them, suddenly rose to their feet as one animal. "We are moving at last, and I must lead the way." She turned, tugged the hood of her white fur robe into place, and strode higher up the hill. She did not move like a woman of at least Catilla's age, and as she stood, slim and erect, at the crest of the hill, waiting for those below to follow her inland, she might have been taken for no older than Mara. Like the Autarch, she seemed to have the secret of perpetual youth.

Like the Autarch, Mara thought, chilled by more than the wind. She knew how the Autarch had extended his life: by draining magic from the Child Guard and, through the newest version of the Masks, from many others. So how was the Lady achieving the same effect?

Mara had a lot of questions for the Lady of Pain and Fire. But first, of course, they had to survive the night. *What did she mean, she's prepared shelter? How? And what kind of shelter?*

Despite her questions, she didn't follow the Lady to the top of the hill. Instead, she went downhill, in search of Keltan.

She found him gathering the belongings of a woman who cradled a squalling infant in her arms. "Lost her husband," Keltan grunted as Mara came up. "Needs help."

Mara nodded, then turned to the woman. "Let me carry the child for you for a while," she said, holding out her arms.

But the woman glared at her, hatred plain on her face even in the fading gray twilight. "Don't touch her."

Mara gasped. "I—"

"Don't come near her, you . . . you monster!" The woman could barely choke out the loathing-filled words. She turned and strode blindly toward the hill where the Lady waited, clutching her infant to her breast.

Keltan, still carrying the woman's bundle slung over his back, paused beside Mara. "She didn't mean it," he said. "She's just upset . . ."

"She meant it," Mara said. *And the worst of it is, she may be right.*

"I thought you'd stay with the Lady," Keltan said. "What are you doing down here?"

"I don't want to walk with the Lady," Mara said. She wished she could take Keltan's hand, but they were both full. She contented herself with walking beside him. Side by side they trudged toward the hillside through the snow, the wind swirling it around their feet and biting through the flimsy coat she wore. "I want to walk with you. With someone ordinary."

Keltan shot her a glance. "Thanks . . . I think."

"You know what I mean." Mara sighed. "The Lady—she wants me for something. She wants me to become like her, I think. To help her over-throw the Autarch. But if I do what she wants . . . Keltan, I don't want to be a monster. I just want to be a girl."

"You *are* a girl," Keltan said. "I've kissed you, remember? Definitely a girl." He shook his head. "But if you mean you just want to be an *ordinary* girl . . . Mara, I'm sorry, but you can never be that. After what you've done . . . after what you've seen . . . you'll never be ordinary. You never have been."

Mara said nothing. Her life in Tamita, before her failed Masking, seemed as dim and distant as a pleasant dream, one that had vanished upon waking, leaving behind only a faint sense of well-being . . . and long-ing. Had she ever really been a carefree child, playing barefoot in the streets, sitting on the city wall and watching the crowds in the Outside Market, sneaking out at night with Sala for a secret swim, secure in the knowledge her mother and father loved her and she had a hot supper and warm bed awaiting her every night?

Now her father was dead, and maybe her mother, too. She'd seen so much death, had *caused* so much death, had done things she would never have dreamed possible less than half a year ago, things she wouldn't have believed if they'd been in one of the tales she'd enjoyed reading as a child. Everyone wanted to use her, to turn the powerful abilities she had never wanted to their own ends: the Autarch, Catilla, Chell, and now the Lady of Pain and Fire. None of them seemed concerned with what *she* wanted, or needed, or longed for. They just saw her as a tool, a tool they would use until it broke.

But if I break, she thought, *with the power I have to rip magic from the living, to kill and destroy . . . how many more will die?*

Keltan was still looking at her. "Mara, you're *not* a monster," he said in a low voice. "You never will be. You never *could* be."

How would you know?

The wind blew harder and harder, and the snow flew past more and more thickly. *Never mind people dying on the beach*, Mara thought. *They'll be dying in their tracks if we don't find this shelter the Lady promised.*

She couldn't really see anything at all anymore except the bent back of the man in front of her, carrying a huge bundle while his wife struggled along beside him with a toddler in her arms. The small boy's white face stared at Mara over his mother's shoulder. She knew it had to be her imagination, but it seemed as if he were blaming her for his misery.

They had been trudging away from the beach for half an hour, while the last light faded from the overcast sky, when suddenly the column stumbled to a halt. "What's going on?" Keltan asked Mara.

"No more idea than you." She craned her head to try to see, but the snow and darkness defeated her. But she heard shouts, being passed down the line, resolving, as they came closer and closer, into "Shelter to the right! Camp for the night!"

The man in front of them received the shout but didn't bother to pass it over his shoulder to Mara and Keltan. Mara heard it anyway, and felt as if a weight had been lifted from her shoulders. "Thank goodness," she said to Keltan.

Keltan didn't look convinced. "What kind of shelter could there be out *here*?"

They found out soon enough, as the column turned right. Beneath a tall bluff that blocked the worst of the wind, which roared through the trees at the top of the cliff, they found four long, low, windowless structures, with rough log walls and roofs of branches, ranged around and revealed by the flickering flames of a giant bonfire. Their shapes reminded Mara uncomfortably of the longhouses of the mining camp. Smoke from holes cut in their roofs mingled with the smoke from the bonfire, chased up the face of the bluff by tumbling sparks until the wind finally caught it and ripped it to shreds.

"How did the Lady do all this alone?" Keltan said. "Magic?"

But Mara, peering through the falling snow and flickering shadows, shook her head. "No," she said. "Or at least, not entirely. She *didn't* do it alone. Look." She pointed.

"Who are *they?*" Keltan said, voice suspicious, as he saw what Mara had spotted first: strangers, men clad in furs like the Lady's, though gray and black rather than white (*rather like her wolves*, Mara thought), some still busily chinking the gaps in the logs on the buildings with a paste of some sort, while a few laid additional boughs on the roofs.

"I don't know," Mara said, as surprised as Keltan. She'd somehow thought the Lady had been living in lonely isolation for all the years since she'd been driven from Aygrima—but why should she have been? Why *shouldn't* she have followers or subjects?

Or slaves? she thought uneasily. *Does she draw power solely from the wolves?*

That was an uncomfortable thought.

Already, people were beginning to divide up among the four long structures. Edrik, Tralia, Hyram, and Alita were in the thick of it, directing families and couples to two of the huts, single women (Prella and Kirika among them) to another, men to the fourth. "I'd better help," Keltan said. "And find the woman this bundle belongs to." He gave Mara a quick smile and hurried off.

Mara hung back, watching. It all seemed to have very little to do with her, though of course she needed someplace to sleep that night, as well. The thought of going inside the longhouse to face the accusing faces of the other single women, though—especially Prella and Kirika—didn't appeal to her.

Something nuzzled her gloved hand. Startled, she jerked it away, then looked down to see one of the Lady's wolves grinning up at her. It trotted a few feet, then turned and whined.

Hardly believing she was doing it, Mara followed the animal. It led her through the camp, children watching wide-eyed as she passed, men and women drawing back. Their hostile expressions gave her no hope of being forgiven by the bulk of the unMasked Army any time soon.

The wolf guided her between two of the longhouses. Behind them stood a large tent, its white walls flickering orange from a fire inside. Smoke rose from the center of its roof. The wolf pushed through the closed flap, and Mara followed.

She found herself in a cozy canvas-walled chamber, floored with rough-woven brown cloth, warmed by a fire in a stone-lined pit dug at the very center, and further lit by an oil lamp hanging from one of the two stout poles holding up the tent, each the trunk of a tree so freshly cut that sticky sap still oozed from where the branches had been stripped away. The fresh scent of pine mingled with the smoke.

On either side of the fire pit, bedrolls lay open on piles of green branches. At the far end of the tent, on a red-upholstered folding bench wide enough for two, sat the Lady, still wearing her white furs. The smoke rising from the fire half-shrouded her, and the heat made her appearance wavering and uncertain. Six of the wolves rested at her feet; the wolf with Mara made seven. She wondered where the other six were. The Lady's left hand rested in the ruff of the wolf at her feet; her right hand toyed restlessly with an amulet of gold and crystal hanging from her neck. She smiled at Mara. "I thought you might be more comfortable here with me than in the shelters with the others."

Mara rounded the fire, and as she did so, the wolf that had led her to the tent joined the others at the Lady's side. "Can you communicate with them?" she said, staring at the animals.

The Lady's smile widened. "Oh, yes. And see through their eyes." She raised her own eyes to Mara. The firelight struck red sparks from them. "How else do you think I knew the unMasked Army was on its way? I have long kept watch on Catilla's pitiful band of would-be revolutionaries. It has been clear for years . . . *decades* . . . that they would never pose a threat to the Autarch, though at least, I supposed, they have provided a refuge of sorts for those who somehow escaped Masking. But I admit I was startled when the Watchers suddenly descended on the Secret City and drove them out." She studied Mara. "I did not know, then, that it was your doing."

"I didn't—" Mara began.

The Lady raised a placating hand. "You didn't mean to. Yes, I know. And yet you *did*. And I am thankful for it, for it brought you to me." She ruffled the silver mane of the wolf at her side, whose red tongue lolled as it watched Mara through amber eyes. "Though for a time, I thought I had lost you. I knew you had left Tamita—in rather spectacular fashion—and knew you had fled to the coast with Prince Chell, but my lupine spies do have some limitations, and following a boat out to sea is, of course, beyond them. Once you sailed into the night from the village where you stole your craft, you were beyond my ken." Her hand tightened on the wolf's fur. "I was not happy about that, and so I was delighted when I saw you arrive among the remnants of the unMasked Army with the prince . . . and considerably less so when you sailed away again. By that time, of course, we were already on our way to the coast. My consolation, had you not returned, would have been that at least I would return home with the survivors of the unMasked Army. My village—the one that gave me succor when I made my journey through the mountains as a girl—is dwindling. An influx of fresh people is just what we need. But to my relief, you reappeared. The rest you know."

"The rest I do *not* know," Mara said. "How did you even know I existed?"

"The Secret City is not the only place I've watched closely over the decades," the Lady said. "The mine of magic is another. Aside from the handful of magic-collection huts scattered around Aygrima, it is the sole source of magic for the Autarchy. I have long understood that if I am ever to move against the Autarch, it is the first place I must strike. As it happens, I was not watching it when you arrived. I *was* watching it when it was almost leveled by an explosion—an explosion contained by magic. And I was watching as you returned to the Secret City. It was absolutely clear what had happened, crystal clear that you have been Gifted, as I have been Gifted, with the ability to use all colors of magic, and to draw magic from living things." Her left hand again caressed the mane of the wolf. "I knew I had a potential . . . ally, if only I could make contact with you."

"If you're so powerful," Mara said, "why didn't you just stroll into Aygrima yourself and present yourself at the Secret City?"

The hand in the wolf's fur tightened into a fist for a moment, then relaxed. "I cannot enter Aygrima," the Lady said. "The Autarch has guarded the borders against me. Or rather," her mouth twisted into a moue of distaste, "he stands on the shoulders of giants to do so. He has neither the skill nor the power to create such magics himself. But centuries ago, when magic first came to Aygrima and the first powerful Gifted arose, they learned much about its use that we have forgotten." Her right hand returned to the amulet at her neck. It obviously meant something to her, but Mara had no clue what. "Magic is in the very ground of Aygrima," the Lady said softly. "Diffuse, too diffuse to be of use even to me—to us. But black lodestone dust is everywhere, and even those minute particles draw magic to themselves. And taken in total, across all the miles and miles of plain and forest and mountain and valley that make up Aygrima, the power is immense. The ancients learned to craft that magic into vast spells that could be activated at need. The Autarch cannot create such spells himself—no one can in these days—but he knows how to trigger them. As I told you on the beach, it was such a spell that summoned the storm that prevented your prince from sailing away with the unMasked Army. No doubt the Autarch gave the means of activating the spell to the commander of the Watchers he sent north to the Secret City. A scout probably saw the unMasked Army boarding the ships and reported back, and the commander called up the border magic to ensure his prey did not escape.

"Sixty years ago, the first thing the Autarch did when he returned to Tamita after having forced me out of Aygrima was to aim the magic protecting the borders directly at *me*. If I enter Aygrima anywhere, by sea, by land—even by air, if I could manage such a thing—I will be struck down by the land itself, crushed in an instant as easily as you would slap a mosquito."

Mara shivered. "Then I don't see how—"

"The magic is not aimed at *you*," the Lady said softly. "You *can* reenter

Aygrima. And at the place in the mountains where I will show you, you can destroy the ward that keeps me out. Then, together, we and my followers and the unMasked Army can march south to overthrow the Autarch."

Mara stared at the woman in the folding chair. "March south. Against all the Watchers he can throw at us, all the magic he has stored in the Palace? I don't know how many fighters *you* have, but the mighty unMasked Army is down to a few handfuls." She shook her head. "You're crazy."

The Lady's eyes narrowed and Mara shivered; it seemed the temperature in the tent had suddenly dropped. "You had best hope not. Because neither you nor all those with you whose survival now depends on my power and generosity have any choice in the matter." She straightened suddenly, lowering the hand that had been fondling the amulet. "You should sleep." She glanced to the right. "Your bed is there." She stood. "I will return later. I must ensure that all is well in the rest of the camp." Pulling her furs more closely around her, the Lady moved to the tent flap, the wolves rising as one animal to follow. They stopped and glanced back at the same moment the Lady did, one hand poised to push open the canvas. "Sleep well," she said to Mara. "If you can." And then she swept out.

The wolves trailed her one by one. The last of them turned and looked at her. Its amber eyes caught the red light of the fire, casting it back in red sparks identical to what she had seen in the eyes of the Lady itself.

If she's telling the truth, Mara thought, *those* are *her eyes. Or can be.*

And then the wolf nosed through the tent flap, the canvas closed behind it, and Mara was alone.

TWO

A Wolf in the Night

MARA, warm beneath wool blankets and exhausted beyond mea-sure, fell asleep in moments. But in the middle of the night, the nightmares from which she had been blessedly shielded while at sea found her once more.

It didn't matter that she had seen them all before: that naked, headless Grute, the slaughtered Warden, the broken-necked Watcher, the blood-soaked Guardian Stanik, the ground-entombed horsemen, and her mur-dered father were all familiar sights. The horror they brought with them remained unabated, and she fought her way up from sleep like someone struggling through thick mud, carrying with her a scream that burst from her throat the moment that, at last, she woke . . .

. . . and found herself staring into the eyes of a wolf.

The fire in the tent had burned down to little more than embers, and so the light was dim and red, but there was still more than enough for her to see those eyes, the pupils so wide they looked pure black, and the shaggy, furred face that surrounded them. The wolf whined, then pushed its muzzle into Mara's side. She put a tentative hand on its head, between its ears, and the wolf, with a contented sigh, sank down onto its belly and rested its chin on her blankets.

Mara blinked sleepily at it, the terror already fading. Then she looked beyond it and saw another set of glittering eyes: the eyes of the Lady, lying wide awake on her blankets on the far side of the tent, surrounded by several sleeping wolves.

Mara slipped back down into slumber.

She had no more nightmares that night.

◆ ◆ ◆

When she woke, it was still dark in the tent, but not *as* dark; a faint gray light made it through the canvas, more than enough to show her that the Lady was gone, once more out and about in the camp, she supposed, her wolves at her side . . .

. . . though not *all* of her wolves. The one that had come to her in the night remained. Its head lifted as she stirred, and she found herself looking into its eyes once more. In the growing light, she could see that they were amber, the same color as those of the wolf that had guided her to the tent the night before and been the last to bid her farewell when the Lady had gone into the camp. Was it the same animal? She couldn't be sure, though it had a similar blaze of white fur on its chest. But she found its presence comforting: oddly enough, since it could rip out her throat anytime it chose.

"You wouldn't do that, though, would you?" she said out loud, rubbing the wolf's ears. It . . . *he*, she realized, looking closer . . . whined, and his tail thudded against the ground. "You're just a big puppy dog."

A big puppy dog full of magic through whose eyes the Lady of Pain and Fire can spy whenever she chooses, she reminded herself. But she was still glad the beast was there.

A few minutes later she pushed through the tent flap, the wolf at her side, emerging into a camp beginning to bustle as fires were stoked, break-fasts prepared, and preparations made for the day's journey. The snow had piled into deep drifts around the shelters and lay thick and white every-where else, but the wind had died and the sky was a pale blue above the dark ridges of the forested hills all around. It took Mara only a moment to spot the Lady at the eastern edge of the camp, conferring with one of the men she had brought with her, presumably discussing the trail ahead. Like Mara, she had a single wolf with her; Mara wondered where the others had gone. Scouting, perhaps.

A little more exploration took care of the next important item on her to-do list: find the latrine. Much more comfortable, albeit considerably colder, she went in search of Keltan.

She found him kneeling beside one of the fires, toasting bread on a stick. "That smells wonderful," Mara said as she came up beside him. He glanced up, and flinched a little as he saw the wolf. She dropped a hand to the wolf's mane. "Don't worry, he's harmless."

"Right. Harmless." Keltan shook his head, then turned his attention back to the toast. "The bread is a week old. It smells better than it tastes. But if you're hungry, you're welcome to it." He took the stick out of the fire and held the bread out to her. "Alas, milady, I fear we're fresh out of butter and honey. No deliveries this morning."

Mara laughed. "I'll get by." She took the bread gingerly, tossing it from hand to hand to cool it. "But what about you?"

"I've already had one piece of stale bread. I'm fine."

Mara bit into the bread. It certainly was stale, but she was hungry enough not to mind. "Are we really that short of food?"

"Yes." Keltan glanced over his shoulder toward where the Lady still stood talking to her man. "Do you know where she's taking us?"

"A village of some kind. Up in the mountains," Mara mumbled through a full mouth. She chewed and swallowed. "Could be up to a week's travel, she says."

Keltan made a face. "Lots of really hungry people before we get there. Lots of really hungry *kids*."

The toast had never tasted all that great. Suddenly it tasted like sawdust.

"Did you . . . sleep all right?" Keltan asked softly.

Mara knew what he meant: he was well aware of her nightmares. She nodded. "Not at first. But then . . ." Her hand went to the wolf's fur again. The wolf rolled his eyes to look up at her. "The Lady sent this big fellow to me. And the dreams just . . . went away."

"I don't understand." Keltan regarded the wolf. "What *are* they? They're not like any wolves I've ever seen."

"I think the Lady . . . *made* them, somehow," Mara said slowly. "I don't know everything she uses them for. But I do know they hold magic—magic the Lady can use. *And* she says she can look through their eyes when she chooses."

Keltan's own widened. "You mean she could be looking at me *right now*?"

"She is," said a voice behind them that made them both jump. Mara turned to see the Lady of Pain and Fire staring down at them. "But not through the eyes of Whiteblaze there . . . *this* time." She chuckled. It sounded rusty, as though mirth were not something she was accustomed to displaying, or possibly feeling. "Mara, you and I will both walk in front today. I may need to use magic to clear our trail, here or there. I would like you to see how I do it."

"I'm coming with her," Keltan said, getting to his feet.

The Lady's silvery white eyebrow arched above her left eye. "Are you? And who are you, again?"

"His name is Keltan," Mara said.

The Lady's right eyebrow lifted to match the left. "Keltan? That's the name of the Autarch's—"

"It's not my real name," Keltan said wearily. "I don't use my real name."

"He's my friend," Mara said. She reached out and took his gloved hand in her own, giving it a squeeze. He squeezed back.

The eyebrows came down in a frown. "I see." The Lady stared at Keltan, her ice-blue eyes not that different in shade from those of the lone wolf still accompanying her. For three breaths she said nothing, then she suddenly looked away. "Very well, if you wish. Come now, both of you. Full day is upon us and we should already be on our way."

Despite her urgency, another hour passed before the ragtag column of refugees and stranded Korellian sailors left the campsite in the wake of Mara, Keltan, and the Lady. The Lady's wolves—and her villagers, a dozen sturdy men, armed with swords and bows and wearing metal-studded leather beneath their furs and cloaks—ranged ahead and behind, in the uneasy company of scouts appointed by Edrik from the ranks of the un-Masked Army and sailors from Chell's contingent. Edrik, along with Chell and his captains, walked in the second rank behind the Lady, Keltan, Mara, and her new lupine companion, Whiteblaze. Catilla and the few other truly elderly people among the unMasked Army rode on toboggans pulled by dogs that had come with the villagers: ordinary dogs, not the wolves of the Lady, though the dogs themselves, with their sharp-pricked ears and curling, bushy tails, were definitely on the wolfish side.

Heavy snow clogged the trail, and the refugees made slow work of it, trudging up ridges, carefully descending slippery inland slopes. Always, the upward slope was longer and steeper than the downward. Children tripped and fell and cried. Men and women walked mostly in grim silence. The Lady's followers broke the trail ahead, so that at least there were footsteps for Mara and the Lady to follow, but the snow dragged at her booted feet nonetheless, and the wind bit at her cheeks. She tried to remember the date, and failed. Surely spring could not be far away . . . though, this far north and climbing toward the mountains, who knew how long it might be delayed?

Still, though they moved slowly, they moved steadily. As the day wore on, the new snow on the trail grew less. "Storms from the sea spend themselves quickly against the rising land," the Lady explained when Mara commented on it. "Even magical ones, apparently. By tomorrow, we may see no signs of fresh snow at all." She glanced up to the right, where the first peak of the all-but-impenetrable range that marked the northern border of Aygrima loomed. "The real hazard lies up there. This much snow, this late in the year . . . let us hope it stays in place."

They halted that evening in a small valley at the very foot of that towering peak. Here there were no prepared lodges, but fortunately the wind had calmed. As stars pricked the clearing sky, the refugees set about erecting whatever crude shelters they could, using the trees on every side and the tents and other materials they had brought with them from the Secret City.

Fires blossomed like red flowers, and soon the camp had settled into place. Before doing anything else, the Lady's select group of villagers had erected the tent she and Mara shared. Keltan had left Mara to help Hyram set up the tent *they* shared . . . though watching Alita with Hyram, the way they touched at every opportunity, the way they spoke softly, heads close together, Mara suspected Hyram wished he was sharing with Alita and Keltan was on his own.

It made no sense to be jealous. Hyram had made it clear he felt nothing for her anymore, not since her foolish actions had brought the Watchers down upon the Secret City. She suspected his interest had only ever been because she was new and mysterious when she'd arrived at the Secret City. But she remembered those weeks and felt a faint pang all the same.

Followed by Whiteblaze, who had clung to her heels all day, Mara approached the Lady's tent, but paused with her hand on the flap, feeling a strange vibration in the ground beneath her feet. Whiteblaze whined, hackles rising. *What . . . ?*

She didn't finish her thought. "Avalanche!" screamed a voice, and she jerked her head up.

High above them, the slope of the mountain peak was *moving*, billowing clouds of white swallowing what had looked like a solid sheet of ice seconds before. A wall of swirling snow hurtled toward them at unbelievable speed. The ground shook. Behind her, in the camp, people shouted and screamed, but she stood frozen in shock, staring at her imminent death.

It never arrived. A wall of red fire rushed past her, enveloping her for an instant in powerful magic that made her gasp, and raced up the slope. The magical flame had an angular shape, like the prow of a boat. It slammed into the base of the descending mass of snow, and in an explosion of flying snow and clouds of steam the avalanche divided, splitting and rumbling away to either side of the glimmering red apex of the fiery barrier. Trees far to her left and right thrashed and broke and disappeared beneath tons of snow, but right where she stood, where the camp stood, nothing changed.

The thundering descent of snow and ice quieted, slowed, stopped. Though shouts and cries and sobs still rang out in the camp behind her, to Mara it seemed for a moment as though utter stillness had descended. She stared up the slope. Half a dozen of the Lady's followers had been working in the trees, harvesting firewood. Every one of them had fallen to his knees, ax or saw dropping from limp hands into the snow.

Whiteblaze whined, looked up at her, and wagged his tail.

Mara turned around and saw the Lady standing perhaps thirty feet behind her, arms spread wide, palms upraised, eyes closed. The six wolves with her had all lain down on their bellies. Their heads rested on their outstretched paws. Their eyes were closed.

Mara felt a chill that had nothing to do with the frigid air or the near-escape from white death. Her question had been answered. The Lady of Pain and Fire had not only drawn magic from her wolves, *she had drawn it from her villagers*. Just as Mara had done at the mining camp, she had ripped magic from their living bodies.

The Lady's eyes opened. She took a deep breath. Her gaze met Mara's. She smiled. "As I said . . . you have much to learn."

Mara turned away from the Lady to stare back up at the men from whom she had drawn magic. When Mara had done it involuntarily in the mining camp, everyone had collapsed, unconscious. But the villagers, though they certainly looked dazed, were clearly still awake. Not one of them had fallen prostrate. Already they were gathering their tools, climbing to their feet. In another minute they were back at work as though nothing had happened.

The sounds from the camp had turned from screams of terror to shouts of relief. Mara turned around and looked back down at the huddle of tents and lean-tos. Mothers hugged crying children, men engaged in agitated conversation, and everywhere faces were turned up slope, looking at the Lady . . . looking at her.

Looking at them with both with fear . . . no, she realized suddenly: not fear, *respect*. Their expressions were not those of people afraid of a monster, but those of people grateful to have been saved by someone stronger than themselves.

If the Lady of Pain and Fire is not a monster, Mara thought, *then even if I am fated to become like her, I may not become one, either.* The thought seemed to release something deep inside her, something hard and tight and cold. It opened and warmed. And suddenly she knew what that strange new feeling was.

Hope.

Mara turned to face the Lady once more. "You're right," she said. "I have a lot to learn." She paused. "Will you teach me?"

The Lady smiled. "My dear child. Did you really think I would not?" She strode forward, the wolves flowing around her feet. "Come inside, and I will begin."

Mara stood aside as the Lady approached. The wolves did not enter the tent, instead scattering, as if given a secret signal, spreading out in all directions and vanishing into the fading light, all but Whiteblaze, who remained at Mara's feet, tongue lolling, eyes fixed on her face. The Lady swept aside the tent flap and went inside. Mara moved to follow, but paused as she heard a shout from behind her. "Mara! Mara, are you all right?"

She felt a flash of irritation. *Not now.* She turned to face Keltan, dashing up the snow-covered slope toward her. "Of course I'm all right," she called back. "Why wouldn't I be?"

He skidded to a halt and stared at her. "Why? The avalanche—"

"The Lady stopped it."

"I know, but . . ."

"Keltan, I'm fine. Go back down to your tent. Help Hyram. I have to talk to the Lady."

Keltan's face, a pale blotch in the twilight, frowned. "Hyram doesn't need any help. The tent has already been set up. I thought we could eat together—"

"No," Mara snapped, then softened her tone, feeling guilty. "Sorry. Keltan, I have to talk to the Lady. I have to find out how she did what she did. She knows how to control this power I have. I have to learn from her."

Keltan took a step back. "I . . . I see."

"Good. Thanks." The guilt grew. "I'll come down later. We'll talk then. I promise."

He nodded, but she only glimpsed it out of the corner of her eye as, burning with eagerness to talk to the Lady, she turned her back on him and pushed into the tent, Whiteblaze at her side. There was a moment's silence from outside, then she heard his footsteps crunching through the snow again, heading downhill.

The Lady once more sat in her place at the far end of the tent, her eyes on Mara, smiling. "I did not cause the avalanche," she said, "but I almost wish I had. You have the hunger now. I can see it in your face. You hunger to learn to control the extraordinary Gift you have been blessed with, the Gift we both share."

"Gift?" Mara walked toward the Lady. "To me it's seemed more like a curse."

The Lady made a disparaging gesture. "Nonsense. It is absolutely a Gift. Without my Gift, I would not be here now. Without my Gift," a wave, which somehow took in the aborted avalanche outside, "*none* of us would be here now." She pointed at Mara with the same hand. "And without your Gift, *you* would not be here now. Were you an ordinary unMasked, you would have died in that mining camp when the rockbreakers exploded. Were you ordinary, you would never have been rescued from it in the first place. You would be Masked in Tamita, a part of your soul being drawn out from you every day to feed the false youth of that monster on the throne, to keep him alive long after he should have followed his father to worms and dust."

"You draw magic from these followers of yours," Mara said. "How is that different?"

The Lady's eyes narrowed. Her fingers touched the amulet around her neck. "It is different," she said, "because I am not the Autarch. They have given themselves to me willingly."

Mara blinked. "What?"

The Lady leaned forward. "You will see, when we reach my home. But for now, know only that I take nothing from them that they have not volunteered to give."

"When I . . . do that," Mara said softly. "When I take magic from those around me . . . it . . . hurts." Hurt was a sadly inadequate word to refer to the agony that had coursed through her. "Ethelda said it was 'un-filtered magic,' that it burned for that reason. Does it . . . does it hurt *you?*"

The Lady frowned. "I did not know this Ethelda you speak of, but she was a Healer, was she not?"

Mara nodded. "She Healed my face." She touched the skin of her cheek, unmarked by the scars that marred the features of Alita and Prella and all others whose Maskings had failed. "She saved my life. And my sanity."

"Then clearly she was an unusually perspicacious member of her profession. But you must understand that even the best Healer is still a prisoner of her preconceptions, shaped by her training within the Masked regime of the Autarch. And the Autarch does not want anyone to know the truth. He does not want anyone to know that he survives by draining magic from those around him, from the Child Guard in particular and, increasingly with these newest Masks, from everyone else. More to the point, he does not want anyone *else* to arise who has that ability. He wants—*needs*—all the magic he can get to stave off advancing age and protect himself from the threats he imagines all around him. So of course he has made it clear to those beneath him that anyone who comes along with the same kind of power he secretly wields must be destroyed, must be hounded out of the kingdom . . . as was I." The Lady spread her hands. "Your Ethelda clearly understood some of the former, but, ironically, seeing the manner in which the Autarch uses his power only strengthened her belief in the truth of the falsehoods the Autarch has spread to maintain his leech-like attachment to his sources of magic."

The words seemed to wash over Mara like a wave from the ocean. "I don't understand," she said.

"Come, sit with me," the Lady said. She moved over, and after a moment's hesitation, Mara sat beside her on the red cushions of the folding bench, her hip pressed close to the Lady's, warmer than Mara would have expected, as though the Lady burned with some hidden internal flame. The Lady put her hand on Mara's knee. "Child," she said. "The Autarch has lied, and those lies came to you through Ethelda. There is nothing evil about the power I have—the power *you* have. You *can* draw magic from living creatures without harming them, or yourself." She pointed at Whiteblaze. "Does he not look healthy?"

"But when I do it," Mara said stubbornly, "when I draw magic from other people . . . it hurts. Every time. As if it's wrong. As if it's . . . bad for me. And Keltan . . ." She glanced at the tent flap, already regretting her words turning him away. "He collapsed. He wasn't the same for . . . days. I did something to him . . ."

The Lady put an arm around her shoulder and pressed her too-warm cheek against hers. "That wasn't because what you were doing was wrong, child," she said, an indulgent chuckle in her voice. "It was simply because you were doing it badly. Because you lacked knowledge, and experience, and training."

Mara didn't know what to think. She wished she could talk to Ethelda, but Ethelda was dead, slain by the Watchers who had attacked them on the beach, her body blown away into white dust by the Lady's cleansing fire. The Lady had saved everyone who survived by drawing magic from her villagers before she reached the beach, and from the wolves and from the Watchers themselves once she was there. How could that be evil?

"How can magic be evil?" the Lady said, her words echoing Mara's thoughts so exactly that Mara pulled away and shot her a startled look. "It's simply something that exists, like clay or wood. It's something that some people can use, and some cannot, just as some people can shape clay or wood to make beautiful objects, and others cannot, no matter how hard they try. Something that some Gifted people—people like you and me— can use much more effectively than others, just as some potters or carpenters are more skilled than others. *Things* aren't evil. Only *people* can be evil. And that evil is revealed by their actions. The Autarch uses magic in an evil fashion, but it's not the magic that is evil—it's *him*." She smiled at Mara. "When you contained the explosion at the mining camp, you saved scores of lives. How could that be evil?"

"It hurt Keltan," Mara said. "It may have hurt others. There were many who were weak and sick in the camp. I've feared . . . I may have killed others . . ."

The Lady shook her head. "Unlikely," she said. "You would have felt it."

"But still—"

"You weren't doing anything wrong, Mara," the Lady said forcefully. "You acted as you had to. Taking their magic hurt those people because you took it clumsily from at best unwitting, and at worst unwilling, donors. The magic I take—*skillfully*—from my followers is given *willingly*. They do not fight me, and so I can draw from them painlessly and at will. The wolves, too, are devoted to me . . . and this one, now, to you." She reached down and scratched Whiteblaze behind his ears.

Mara looked down at the animal. "He is?"

"I have given him to you," the Lady said. "I felt your distress last night as the nightmares took hold. I took a little magic from you—just a little— and linked it to Whiteblaze. Then I severed my own link with him. He is yours now as completely as the others are mine. One day you will be able to look through his eyes as I do through the eyes of his fellows."

Mara blinked. "Really?" Then she blinked again. "Wait. You took magic from me? But I didn't feel . . ."

"Only a little," the Lady said. "And let the fact you did not feel any distress from that reassure you as to how little distress I cause my followers." She rubbed Whiteblaze under his chin, and his tail thumped. "These wolves, which I have bred and magically modified for many of their generations, are . . . black lodestone with legs, if you like. Not only can you learn to draw magic from Whiteblaze, he can draw from you the magic that causes your nightmares, magic polluted with what I call the 'soulprint'— the imprint left by a living soul, like the imprint left in a blob of wax by a signet ring. When you kill with magic or are near someone who dies violently, that soulprint pours into you along with the magic they contain. It's as if the person has become a vengeful ghost haunting your mind. But Whiteblaze takes those ghosts into himself."

"Whiteblaze will dream my nightmares every night?" Mara said. She glanced down at him. "Sorry, boy."

The Lady laughed. "They are meaningless to him. And over time, they fade, until even without Whiteblaze, they would not return. Though, of course, without him you would be subject to new ones if you were once again exposed to violent death. And note that although he can help prevent the nightmares, he does not prevent the soulprint from making its mark on your mind."

Mara nodded, fascinated. "What about the potion Grelda showed me how to brew? How does it help?"

"The wolves drain away the nightmares. The potion only blocks them," the Lady said. "It contains, among various other substances, black lodestone dust. You are fortunate anyone at the Secret City had the recipe . . . and the ingredients. But as you know, once your body has eliminated it, the nightmares return, unless you continue to dose yourself with it." She shook her head. "Not a good idea. It contains substances that I think would gradually poison you if you used it for an extended period of time." A flicker of a smile crossed her lips. "There's a reason it smells so awful to the unGifted." She glanced at Whiteblaze again. "Your friend here will keep you free of nightmares whenever he is with you. And since I have turned his mind so that he is now devoted to you, as well as magically linked, that will be all the time, unless you send him elsewhere."

"Turned his mind?" Mara dropped her hand onto the wolf's head protectively. "You can do that?"

"A wolf's mind is a simple thing," the Lady said.

"What about a man's?" The question emerged from Mara's mouth before she'd fully thought it through. The Lady's eyes narrowed.

"A much more difficult undertaking," she said. "But, yes, it is possible. The soulprint . . . the essence of a person . . . is inextricably bound up in the magic which all living things produce. Modify the magic, and you can modify the soulprint: modify the *person*."

"If you can do that," Mara said, "then . . . can the Autarch? Can he also influence others? Make them do things they wouldn't otherwise do?"

"Probably," the Lady said. "Though his ability depends always on the Masks."

"Everyone wearing Masks?" Mara said. "He can control them all?"

The Lady shook his head. "Not the original Masks. At least, I don't think so. But the Child Guard . . . probably."

"And those wearing the new Masks?"

The Lady nodded. "So I believe. Indeed, I think that was partly the intent of changing the way the Masks were made, aside from providing him with a new source of magic: to provide him with new followers who will be absolutely loyal and obey him without question should he have need of them. Over the past couple of years that the new Masks have been in play, some four or five hundred young people will have become unknowingly linked to him, much like my wolves are linked to me . . . and Whiteblaze to you."

Mara shuddered. Sala. Mayson. Tamed to the Autarch's will . . . like Whiteblaze was tamed to hers. She dropped her eyes to the wolf, and felt hatred burn through her, hatred for the Autarch, brighter and hotter than ever before. Whiteblaze whined.

"I felt that," the Lady said. "You truly do have great power."

"So what?" Mara said. The anger faded as quickly as it had come, leaving behind gray sadness. "What good is it? The Autarch still reigns. My father is dead. Katia is dead. Ethelda is dead." Tears started to her eyes. "Everyone is dead."

"Not everyone." The Lady pulled Mara closer, her white fur cloak warming Mara's cold neck. The heat of the Lady's body was nothing compared to the blazing fire inside that slight frame, a power that both frightened and attracted Mara, like a candle flame attracted a moth.

Just remember what usually happens to the moth, Mara thought, but thoughts of caution seemed insubstantial compared to the indubitable power of the old woman at her side. She nestled closer.

The Lady said nothing more: just held her. And in the warmth of her embrace and the glow of her powerful magical Gift, Mara's eyes closed, and sleep washed all her concerns away.

THREE

Climbing to a Decision

THE FOLLOWING MORNING MARA, alone except for White-blaze, trudged through the snow several strides behind the Lady, who was in deep conversation with one of her villagers.

The Lady had a black wooden staff in one hand and two wolves with her, while the others continued to range ahead and behind. *Is she scouting along the trail even as she walks here, watching through the eyes of the wolves for any other hazards that might threaten us?*

Probably not, she decided after a moment's reflection. *She must have to close her own eyes to make sense of what a wolf's show her.* Nor did she think it likely the Lady could look through more than one wolf's eyes at a time. The confusion would be too great.

But still, to be able to do such a thing at all . . . ! The Lady's Gift . . . the power she had sensed within that small, old body, the power that had warmed her to sleep the night before . . . how great was it? *Greater than the Autarch's? Greater than mine?*

And if so . . . how does she control it?

The Lady glanced behind her and motioned Mara forward. Mara hurried to catch up. "Mara," the Lady said as she joined the other two, "I don't believe I've introduced you to Hamil yet. He's the headman of my village. Hamil, Mara is my new . . ." she paused, as if searching for just the right word, "protégée."

Hamil, a broad-shouldered man with a bushy gray beard and eyebrows to match, gave Mara a sharp look, but said nothing. He turned his attention back to the trail ahead. The slope went up and up ahead of them, the trail switchbacking through thick stands of dark trees and outcroppings of gray rock. "We'll be climbing for the rest of the day at this rate," he growled. "We'll have to camp at the top."

"The weather seems good," the Lady said.

"Let's hope it stays that way." He looked at her. "If I may be excused, My Lady, I will join the forward scouts to discuss possible campsites."

"Of course, Hamil. Thank you."

"My Lady." Hamil briefly turned his eyes to Mara, his gaze impassive. "Mara." He strode forward, his long legs bearing him quickly away.

Mara watched him go. "You took magic from him yesterday, to stop the avalanche."

"I took magic from all of those who came with me," the Lady said. "As they expected. As I said, they have all volunteered. In the village, it is considered a great honor to be selected to be part of the Lady's Cadre." She smiled. "That's the formal name. I believe informally they're called my 'human wolfpack.' In any event, as you can see, he was unharmed by my drawdown of magic from the Cadre yesterday to stave off the avalanche."

Mara said nothing. She watched Hamil climbing toward those toiling through the snow at the head of the column. "But when you stopped the avalanche," she said slowly, trying to think straight, trying not to be drawn in by the Lady's reasonable words and tone—she had been drawn in far too often, with disastrous results, by reasonable words spoken by reasonable-sounding people—"the members of your . . . Cadre . . . fell to their knees. As if they'd been stunned."

"A momentary weakness, that's all," the Lady said.

"But what if one of them had been doing something dangerous—swinging an ax, maybe, or lighting a fire. They could have been injured, even killed—"

"It was an emergency," the Lady said, with a flash of irritation. "I thought the risk of minor injury was worth the reward of saving all our lives. Didn't you?"

Mara said nothing. She *wanted* to believe the Lady: wanted so much to believe her. From Shelra, the Autarch's Mistress of Magic, she had learned to fine-tune her use of magic, to make it do precisely what she willed: but that was magic drawn from black lodestone, blended and smoothed by the strange rock. She had not dared speak to Shelra about her other means of getting magic. The fact remained that every time she had pulled magic from others it had hurt her . . . but it had also thrilled her, in a way she had no words to express. And every time Ethelda's words had echoed in her mind, warning that she might grow to like the taste of that raw magic so much that despite the pain she would become a soul-sucking, pain-loving creature of destruction like . . .

. . . well, the example she had always used was walking next to her right now.

Or like the Autarch, pulling magic from the enslaved children of his Child Guard, stunting their development, causing some to sicken and die, and now also drawing from the youngest of his subjects, those most recently Masked, sapping their will, altering their personalities.

Whom do I believe? Mara thought. Once, she would have asked her father: but he was dead, and even now her mind shivered away from the image of his death and what she had done afterward, brutally slaughtering Guardian Stanik, blasting a hole in the city wall, causing the ground to swallow a mounted patrol of Watchers, horses and all, blowing a boatful of Watchers out of the water, slaying more Watchers on the beach . . .

She might have asked her mother, but she, too, was lost to her, hiding somewhere in the far south.

She might have asked Ethelda, but Ethelda had died on the beach. Catilla would have no wisdom to impart, nor, she suspected, any inclination to share it if she did. Nor would Edrik, or Hyram. All three of them hated her, blaming her—with reason—for the destruction of the Secret City.

Prince Chell, she was convinced, was concerned only with his own kingdom across the sea, everything that had happened here only of interest if he could somehow turn Aygrima's magic against his realm's foes. He had hardly spoken to her since the events on the beach.

Not, she thought, trying to be fair, *that I have given him any opportunity*.

That left Keltan, and seeking wisdom from a fifteen-year-old unGifted boy who had kissed her and no doubt wanted to keep doing so but otherwise understood nothing about what she had gone through seemed the height of folly.

The thought of Keltan made her feel guilty. She had promised to go down to the camp and talk to him the previous evening, but once she had fallen asleep in the Lady's embrace, she had gone nowhere but to her own bed after a brief supper taken in the tent. This morning she had seen him at a distance but, not knowing what to say, hadn't sought him out. And he had so far made no effort to catch up with her.

In any event, she didn't want the advice of another youth. What she wanted was a grown-up to turn to, one she could trust, one who would understand, one who would tell her what to do and make everything all right.

The Lady of Pain and Fire was offering to be that grown-up. *Too bad*, Mara thought, *that she's the one I most want to talk to someone about*.

"Mara, don't shut me out," the Lady said softly. "There's no one else you can turn to who understands the Gift you have, and the burden it imposes."

Again, the Lady seemed to have read her heart. *Is my face that transparent?*

"I understand why you are hesitant," the Lady continued. She turned her eyes forward, as if to give Mara space alone with her thoughts. "Like Ethelda, you are a prisoner of your misconceptions. You have been told I am a monster, that I destroyed whole villages, that only the Autarch kept me from ravaging all of the Autarchy. It's hard to put aside what your tutors and parents and others you trust have told you, especially when you are young . . . and, Mara, you are very, very young." The Lady's voice broke a little on that, and Mara shot her a startled look. "As young as I was when my father died, and I discovered my power, and lashed out at the Autarch . . . just as you have."

Mara stared at her. That was new. "You were . . . my age?"

"Close enough," the Lady said. "Sixteen. There were no Masks in those days. My father arranged for me to be Tested for the Gift when I turned thirteen. What he learned puzzled and frightened him. He himself had the Gift, very strongly, but only one color: red. He was a talented Engineer." She smiled faintly. "If you have ever crossed one of the bridges over the river in Tamita, you have walked on his work."

Mara, who had not only walked on those bridges but hidden under one of them, nodded.

"My father had never heard of anyone who could see all colors of magic at thirteen. Nor had the Tester. He was duty-bound to report his findings to the Master of Magic at the Palace, but my father bribed the Master to keep the results to himself. Then my father went into the Library of the Palace . . . a place open to all scholars in those days, not kept under lock and key like today . . . and dug deep among the books and scrolls to find what they had to say about those with my—our—Gift. What he learned there led him to make arrangements for us to leave the capital quietly, for when he truly understood how powerful my Gift was, he knew it was only a matter of time before the Autarch would want to harness it—harness *me*—for his own purposes. We were going to move to Red-water, a farming village far south of Tamita, a tiny place where we could disappear.

"But before my father's plans came to fruition, a man came to him . . . *Catilla's* father." She jerked her head toward the back of the column; somewhere back there, Catilla rode on a toboggan pulled by the villagers' wolflike dogs. "He sounded out my father's feelings toward the Autarch, discovered they were aligned with his own. Gradually, my father was drawn into the incipient Rebellion.

"I knew nothing of that at the time, of course. I was only grateful that the plans for us to move to Redwater seemed to have been forgotten." She shook her head. "I was so blind," she said softly. "Sixteen. All I was interested in was boys. And there were several who were interested in me. I was going to dances, riding out through the Market Gate to picnic in the woods, joining carriage excursions to the old ruins in the Rose Hills. I noticed nothing . . . until the morning the Rebellion erupted into the open, the morning the old Autarch died horribly, poisoned, and the new Autarch sent his guards into the streets.

"They had a list of people. We never knew how they got it: someone within the ranks of the Rebellion must have been a spy. As fighting erupted, we fled the city, just ahead of the guards, who burned our home behind us. We escaped with our lives, a few clothes . . . and the precious books and scrolls my father had stolen from the Library, detailing everything the ancients knew about my special Gift. We fled into the Wilderness, seeking the Rebel army we'd heard was forming.

"We found them, joined them. For months the Rebellion spat and sputtered, ambushing caravans, killing guards, assassinating loyalist officials. But the people were never really on our side. Outside of Tamita, in those days before the Masks, the heavy hand of the Autarch's father had rarely been felt and they knew little of the new Autarch. They wanted only to be left alone. We could never rest in a village: someone was sure to inform on us. The Autarch offered hefty rewards to anyone who could report on our whereabouts, and there were many willing to take his gold. Eventually the Autarch assembled an army and sent it into the field, and it hounded us, driving us north, until we were trapped between the mountains and the sea. And there, in a series of bloody battles, the Rebellion, and most of its adherents, died." She was staring straight ahead now, as if she'd forgotten Mara even existed. "On a day like today, a day buried in a fresh white blanket of snow, my father's story came to an end. We had chanced upon a small store of magic, and my father was sent out with it to destroy a bridge the Autarch's army would have to cross to reach our last desperate redoubt. But some of the Autarch's scouts found us. They attacked from hiding. My father had magic, but the urn was on his back. He had no chance to open it, no chance to fight back. Five crossbow bolts struck him where he stood. Heart. Stomach. Leg. Left eye. Groin. Blood gushed everywhere . . . he fell, dead before he hit the ground.

"And that's when I felt it for the first time: the power of raw magic, the magic contained within a human being. It struck me with as much force as the crossbow bolts had struck my father.

"The guards, laughing, had ridden in close. They must have seen me as easy prey, thought to have sport of me before taking me back to be thrown among the camp followers. But I was full of the magic of my father, and I killed them all. Blew them apart into shards of flesh and bone. Their blood painted the trees and the ground . . . and me. And when they died, I felt *their* magic slam into me.

"I thought I would die. The pain . . . the horror . . ." Her voice trailed off.

"I know," Mara whispered. "I know."

The Lady turned to her then, almost fiercely. "But I did *not* die. I shaped that power with my hatred. I held it inside me like a weapon. I marched across the bridge we were to have destroyed, strode to the verge of their camp.

"The sentries grinned at me as I approached, a mere slip of a girl. They didn't seem to notice that I was covered in their fellows' blood. Perhaps they would have, had I come close enough. But I did not need to get close to do what I needed to do.

"I obliterated the camp. I killed them all, every last one of them, every horse, every dog, every man . . . every woman." Her voice shook. "I regret the last, but in my rage, I made no distinction. And when *that* magic rushed into me, I embraced the pain, hardly felt it as pain any longer. On the contrary, it felt good. It felt *right*."

Mara stared at her. "How did you . . . the nightmares . . ."

"The nightmares were just nightmares," the Lady said. "Better than the real world in some ways." She shook her head. "Having mastered the pain of using raw magic, I thought I could do anything. I thought my power would always prevail. I thought I could walk, alone and unaided, south to Tamita and bring the towers of the Palace crashing down upon the head of the Autarch.

"But I soon learned differently. The camp I had destroyed was not the main camp at all. *That* still lay some distance to the south, and the guards within it numbered more than I could count. I could not kill them all, and they had their own Gifted among them. When I came close, those Gifted sensed me, and struck out at me. Direct magical attack I could absorb, but I was—I *am*—as vulnerable as anyone else to arrow or bolt or mace or sword. Their Gifted warriors soon abandoned direct magical attacks in favor of trying to drop a boulder on my head or impale me with a tree, while their ordinary warriors were everywhere, seeking to take me by surprise." She brushed back her gray hair, which had escaped from her hood into her eyes. "I had several narrow escapes before I learned the limitations of my power. And as the Rebellion was whittled down to nothing, I soon realized that I was on my own. The guards left in the field were pursuing only me, and I could never win.

"So I fled north, deeper into the Wilderness, toward the mountains. I would pass through villages with the guards in pursuit, and knowing from bitter experience that I could not trust the villagers not to reveal my whereabouts, I instead used them as I needed, taking from them magic I hurled against the guards. I could fling trees a mile, bring down landslides from solid slopes, draw lightning from the sky. I left entire villages unconscious, but I killed none of them, despite the anger and contempt I felt for their cowardly residents. My hatred was reserved entirely for the guards."

Her lips tightened. "The guards had no such compunction. Or, rather, the Autarch did not. Eventually, he rode north and took personal command of the army, determined to crush me, the last remaining obstacle to his undisputed reign.

"My use of the villagers as a source of magic produced an unexpected benefit. The people who inhabited the tiny hamlets of the region became so terrified of me that none of them would any longer betray me willingly, no matter how large the proffered reward. The story had gone around that I was able to pull the living souls out of people, that those I attacked were left as empty shells, their spirits utterly destroyed. For believers in the Old Religion that still lingered in those days, before the Autarch eradicated its followers and its holy places, that meant they could never experience the afterlife. It was literally a fate worse than death.

"The Autarch put entire villages to the sword and torch trying to get someone, anyone, to point him to me. And eventually, inevitably, someone broke. The Autarch cornered me in my final hiding place, a secluded, wooded ravine on the side of the mountains.

"I killed his bodyguards, but I could not touch him. And that was when I learned the truth of him, as he no doubt had already guessed the truth about me: that in some measure, we shared the same gift.

"I killed his horse . . ." She snorted. "Keltan, first of that name. But I utterly failed to harm him. And the counterblow . . .

"I saw it coming. I could not stop it. I had no magic left, no one and nothing to draw on for more. So instead I retreated, deep into the cave in which I had taken shelter, deeper within it than I had ever gone before. I heard the ravine hurled to destruction behind and above me, tons of rock and ice and shattered trees choking the secluded glade where I had stood just moments before.

"I had no choice but to plunge even deeper into the darkness of that cave. I found a little black lodestone there, and enough magic that I could illuminate my way, but not enough to do anything else.

"I wandered for hours, and for a time I thought I was lost forever. But then I realized I was seeing things around me as deep black on lighter black, and then as shades of gray, and at last I emerged into sunlight . . . to find myself in another ravine, one that seemed to continue indefinitely through the range.

"The 'impassable' mountains were not impassible at all. I had found a way through . . . and a new lease on life."

Mara looked toward the head of the column, where Hamil and the Lady's other followers continued to break a trail through the deepening snow. "But if the cave was blocked behind you, and you had to go through it to find the pass . . . how did the villagers follow you?"

The Lady laughed. "They didn't. There was a village I had come across during my travels that had clearly been abandoned. I couldn't figure out where the people had gone. But I found out when I reached the end of the pass . . . which those villagers had discovered long before me, and used to make good their escape from Aygrima." Her laughter ended, and the accompanying smile faded. "I was half-dead," she said. "*More* than half-dead. The top of the pass was far below the peaks, but high enough. The air was thin and cold, the snowdrifts higher than my head. I had no magic to protect me. I came close to death; would have died, if a hunting party had not found me." She nodded toward the men and women struggling through the snow ahead of them. "Hamil's grandfather, a young man then, was the one who spotted me, half-buried, unconscious, slipping past shivering to the deadly stillness of freeze-to-death. He warmed me, bore me back to their village.

"I still might have died had I not, though barely conscious of it, sensed the magic all around me and tapped into it. I Healed myself."

"You took magic from them?" Mara said. "Without pain? Without harming them? And they were all right with that? What about the Old Religion? Everything that had terrified the villagers south of the mountains?"

The Lady made a dismissive gesture. "Of course it frightened them. But my youth protected me: they were not the sort of people who would kill a young girl just because she had done something alarming. And once I was Healed, I showed them just how useful my Gift could be. I helped them build stronger, warmer houses; helped them find food; helped them grow their crops. I even created for them a grand grotto in which they could practice their religion, though I have never been an adherent. It was a mutually beneficial arrangement. And so it has been ever since."

"But the pain," Mara said. "The nightmares . . .".

"As I already told you, they were bearable," the Lady said. "And soon enough a thing of the past, as I continued my study of the precious books and scrolls my father had obtained." She touched the amulet around her neck, and then turned toward Mara. "It is something you can learn, too, Mara. Something I can teach you." She placed her gloved hand on Mara's forehead. "I can sense the strength of your Gift. What can we not do, together? The Autarch cannot stand against us. No one can."

Mara didn't know how to respond. After everything that had happened, everything her unwanted "Gift" had stolen from her, all the pain and misery it had visited upon her, the possibility that it didn't have to be like that, that she could satisfy the constant aching desire to draw magic from others without harming herself or them, seemed too much to hope for—too good to be true.

The Lady withdrew her hand. "Thank about it," she said. "Walk by yourself for a time, or talk to your friends." She smiled. "Or to Whiteblaze."

Mara looked down at Whiteblaze and the two wolves with the Lady. "And where did *they* come from?" she asked.

The Lady shrugged. "I drew a half-dozen mated pairs from the wild with magic: the fact they responded to that magical call told me they had at least the beginning of the traits I desired. After that, it was a simple matter of selective breeding . . . and the judicious application of more magic at crucial times in their development."

Mara scratched Whiteblaze behind the ears, and his tail wagged. "Thank you for him," she said softly. "You may have found the nightmares bearable when you were my age, but I do not."

The Lady smiled again. "Go on," she said gently. "I will see you to-night, in my . . . our . . . tent."

Mara nodded mutely and slowed her pace to allow the Lady to draw ahead. For a time she toiled along in silence, her mind whirling, but her circling thoughts brought her no closer to deciding whether or not she could trust the Lady. She *wanted* to—oh, how she wanted to. But the guilt and pain and nightmares that had resulted every time *she* had drawn magic from living people, and even, in a strange way, the fact she so much *wanted* to believe there was a way to do so without suffering any of that, spoke against it.

About an hour after she had dropped back from the Lady, Keltan caught up with her. "You didn't come down last night," he said, panting a little. "You promised."

"I . . . fell asleep," Mara said. "I'm sorry."

"You could have joined us at breakfast."

Mara glanced at him. "I was talking to the Lady."

"And how'd that go?"

She frowned. She'd thought his flushed face was due to the climb. But there was also something odd about his voice. "Are you *angry* with me?"

"Me? No. Why should I be angry?" Keltan carried a roughly trimmed wooden walking stick. He stabbed it into the snow as if thrusting a spear into the Autarch.

"I don't know," Mara said, a little heat rising to her own face. "Why should you?"

"Maybe because I thought we were . . ." He paused. "Together. After the ship. After everything . . ."

"And because I chose not to come down to the camp for supper last night, you think that's changed?" Mara said. She heard the ice in her voice, but she didn't try to soften it. "I like you a lot, Keltan. And I know you like me. But that doesn't make me your property."

His face turned redder. "I never—" He bit off whatever he'd intended to say. "Never mind." He jerked his head at the Lady. "So what did the Mysterious Mistress have to say?"

"Don't call her that." Mara pulled her cloak closer around her. "She's earned her name."

"Lady of Pain and Fire? Who would want to earn *that*?"

Mara jerked her head toward him. "You know nothing about it!"

"And you do?"

Mara stopped. He took two more steps before he realized it, and turned back to face her. "What part of what's happened in the past few months have you missed, Keltan?" she demanded. "You were at the camp. You were in Tamita. You were on the beach. Don't you think maybe I know a little bit more about what the Lady of Pain and Fire—who shares my gift and earned her title *when she was the same age I am now*—has experienced, the burden she carries, than *you* do?"

Keltan's eyes widened. "Mara, I didn't—"

"You belong with the unMasked Army," Mara snapped. She knew she was hurting Keltan, but she couldn't seem to stop it. "I don't. I never did. I never can. Go back and walk with your kind. And I'll walk with mine."

She brushed past him and strode after the Lady as quickly as she could, closing the distance between them, Whiteblaze trotting, tongue lolling, at her side.

Keltan didn't follow her. *Good*, she thought. But already she felt guilty. She didn't want to hurt Keltan. She didn't want to ruin whatever had been between them. *But he shouldn't have said what he said.*

She sighed. It wasn't just in the heavy snow of the trail that she felt she was floundering.

The Lady glanced at her as she caught up. "Mara, what is it?"

"I don't want to walk by myself anymore," she said.

The Lady looked behind them. Presumably Keltan was still back there, but Mara didn't turn. "You are welcome, of course." She did not ask Mara to tell her in more detail what had happened. She did not ask her if she had yet made a decision. She simply let Mara walk with her, in companionable silence.

It was, Mara thought, exactly the right thing to do.

But the walking itself was beginning to wear on her. The slope was unrelenting. The snow, even beaten down by Hamil and the other members of the Lady's Cadre—the "human wolfpack"—up ahead, dragged at her feet with every step. "How much farther?" she asked after a while, panting along with the wolves, breath forming white clouds in the chill air. "To your home, I mean?"

The Lady, despite her age, seemed unaffected. "We will see it from the top of this ridge," she said. "Not from where we will camp tonight, I think, but in the morning, when we start down the other side. We will not reach it tomorrow. But the day after that . . ." She gave Mara a smile. "The night after next, you will sleep in a real bed, under a real roof."

Mara nodded. As they continued to climb, the Lady began to talk again, of inconsequential things: her own childhood, pleasant memories of growing up in Tamita . . . it all sounded exotic to Mara, for the Lady had been born under the reign of the Autarch's father, and there had been no Masks then. The idea of adults freely mingling in the streets of Tamita with faces uncovered seemed unutterably strange, even after months with the unMasked Army and days with Chell's sailors. She no longer blushed at the sight of an adult's uncovered face, but it still seemed somehow . . . immoral.

And yet, that was the future they were all working toward: the Lady, the unMasked Army, and Mara.

But not Chell, she reminded herself. For the first time in hours she glanced back. She saw Keltan, walking with Hyram and Alita, the latter two holding hands. She looked past those three to where Prella walked several ranks back, likewise holding hands with Kirika. She was glad they had found each other, too, even though . . . or maybe because . . . Kirika had almost killed Prella once. Right behind Prella and Kirika she saw Chell, walking with Captain March, who no longer had a ship to command, though at least he still lived, unlike his counterpart, Captain Gramm, who had died in the battle on the beach. On the other side of Chell walked a young man she didn't recognize, though she had seen him

on board *Protector* and knew he was an officer of some kind . . . a lieutenant, she thought they called it. A different pang touched her heart: not
of jealousy this time, but anger. Chell had helped her escape from Tamita.
Only his nautical knowledge had enabled them to sail north along the
coast, eventually delivering them to the shore where the refugees of the
unMasked Army straggled northward.

Her cheeks burned as she remembered a hut, the half-naked prince
asleep, kneeling beside him, her hand reaching out . . . *What was I thinking?*
she thought. But the truth was, she *hadn't* been thinking. Only feeling:
feeling desperate to be just a girl, not a magically Gifted freak.

He had stopped her. He was married, he had said. And years older,
despite his youthful appearance. In retrospect, she was glad nothing had
happened between them. He had treated her no differently after that.
She'd thought he'd remained her friend.

But now she wondered if he had only pretended to be her friend because he had needed her, needed her to sail to his own land, needed her to
use her Gift to help him fight his own enemies. Because when he had seen
the Lady of Pain and Fire, in an instant he had turned all his attention to
her. *I'm just a silly girl to him*, she thought sourly. *A silly young girl blinded by
her own infatuation and desires, desires he could manipulate when he thought
I could be of use to him, but which he could laugh off once he thought he had a
better source of the magical power that is all he's truly interested in.*

As though he felt her gaze upon him, the prince raised his head. Their
eyes met. Mara stared at him for a moment, cheeks burning, and then
jerked her head around, remembering his words on the beach before the
Lady put him in his place by destroying his ships. *I seek power to overthrow
our enemies*, he'd said. He'd looked first at Mara. *I thought I had found it*, he'd
continued—but then he'd turned back to the Lady and finished, *but now
I think I beheld only a reflection of the true power in this land.*

I'm nothing to him, Mara thought now, anger swelling within her.
*Nothing but a tool, a weapon, a poorly made dagger he could toss aside the
moment he found a fine-forged sword to replace it—the Lady of Pain and Fire.*

It made the memory of that awkward moment in the hut all the more embarrassing.

But if I'm nothing to him, why didn't he take advantage of me when I offered him the opportunity?

She shoved that thought aside. She didn't want to make excuses for Chell's behavior. *Let him try his wiles on the Lady of Pain and Fire,* she though, glancing at the old woman walking at her side, without any sign of distress despite the steepness of the trail. One corner of her mouth turned up. *Somehow, I doubt he'll find it as easy to talk his way around her as he did me.*

After her cold exchange with Keltan, she had no more desire to join the others down in the main camp that night than she had the one before. When they reached the top of the slope, the Lady's tent was the first pitched. Although the Lady and her wolves were elsewhere, Mara and Whiteblaze entered it the moment it was erected. A sizable fire already burned in the central pit, and had warmed the tent considerably. Mara removed her coat and sat by the blaze, holding out her hands to the blessed heat of the flames.

A blast of cold air caused those flames to dance, and she turned her head, expecting to see the Lady. Instead, Chell stood in the tent's entrance. Whiteblaze's head came up from where it had been resting on his front paws, but he made no sound, though he watched the prince intently.

"May I come in, Mara?" Chell said. His voice was soft. His eyes gleamed in the firelight, which lit his finely chiseled features with a flattering warm glow. But she couldn't feel about him the way she had when he had been her sole companion on the long sail up the coast of Aygrima.

She heard ice in her voice as she said, "I'm not stopping you," and didn't regret it.

The prince nodded. He glanced over his shoulder, and Mara glimpsed the young lieutenant she had seen with him and the captains earlier. "Wait outside, Antril," he said. The young man, dark-haired and dark-eyed, nodded and moved out of her view.

"A guard?" Mara said. "Do you fear me now, Chell?"

The prince entered, letting the tent flap close behind him. "No," he said. "But I'd like some warning before the Lady or one of her wolves arrive. *Her*, I fear." He looked around the tent's warm interior. His gaze followed the smoke of the fire for a moment as it poured up to and through the hole in the roof. "It's very pleasant in here." He lowered his eyes to her face, and smiled. "How have you been? I haven't spoken to you since we began this mad trek."

Every word he spoke scraped against Mara's nerves like a whetstone on a dagger blade, sharpening her response. "Mad trek?" she said. "To the one place where I might learn how to live with the magic that has almost destroyed me?" She glared at him. "And why *should* I have spoken to you? You made it clear enough on the beach that you only aided my escape from Tamita because you want to use me in your far-off war."

Chell shook his head. "No, Mara. Yes, I have my mission—but I would have aided you regardless. I care about you."

His words washed over her like water over stone, leaving no impression behind. "And what do you want now?"

"I told you . . . to see how you've been."

Mara stared at him. "And . . . ?"

"And to ask your help."

I knew it, Mara thought. "Let me guess. You want me to talk to the Lady for you, try to convince her to help you return to your kingdom, promise to help you in your war. Am I right?"

"Yes," he said simply. "Mara, I've told you how deadly the threat is facing Korellia. Magic may offer our only hope of survival. And the Lady—"

"The Lady will not help you until the Autarch is overthrown," Mara said. "And it will still be her choice whether or not to help you once that is done. There's nothing I can say that will change her mind." She kept her eyes locked on Chell's. "Nor will I try."

Chell stared at her another long moment. When he spoke, he sounded sad. *He should be on the stage*, she thought savagely. "I see," he said. He inclined his head formally. "Then I will leave you to your comforts." But he studied her a moment longer. "There was a time," he said, "when you were frightened of becoming like the Lady of Pain and Fire. Has that changed?"

Whiteblaze growled at him. Chell's eyes slipped to the wolf's for a moment, then back to Mara's; then he turned, cloak swirling, and swept back out through the tent flap in another blast of cold air. "With me, Antril," she heard him say, followed by their footsteps crunching away through the snow.

Mara stared at the sparks dancing up through the smoke hole in the wake of that wintry gust. Chell had clearly meant to hurt her with that last comment, but to her surprise—and fierce delight—she found it had not hurt her in the slightest.

Because, she thought, *I know the truth at last.*

The Lady is my future—but she's not a monster.

And neither am I.

When the Lady herself entered the tent a short time later, six of her wolves flowing around her feet, Mara stood and faced her. The Lady stopped. "You look like you have something to say to me."

"I want to learn what you can teach me," Mara said, through a throat almost closed with emotion, so that every word came out both soft and intense. "I want to know how to use my Gift. And I want to join you in destroying the Autarch . . . and every Mask in Aygrima."

The Lady let the tent flap close behind her, shutting out the camp, the unMasked Army, Keltan, Chell, Catilla, Edrik, Hyram, and all the others. "And so you shall," she said softly. "And so you shall."

FOUR

The White Fortress

THE NEXT MORNING, Mara saw the Lady's fortress for the first
time. Side by side, she and the Lady crested the ridge they had been
climbing so laboriously the day before, and looked down into the valley
below, vast and wide, blue and hazy. The rising sun lit from behind the
curling tendrils of smoke rising from a distant village, and silhouetted the
stone redoubt set high above it on the cliffs that marked the valley's eastern end. A wide white streak on those cliffs spoke of a waterfall, whether
frozen or liquid Mara couldn't see at that distance and in that light. It fell
to the river that wound along the valley floor, snow-covered fields and snug
farmhouses stretching out from it on either side. "My home," the Lady said
simply. "What do you think?"

"It's beautiful," Mara said. She lowered her eyes from the distant battlemented castle to the river. "Does that river flow to the sea?"

"All rivers flow to the sea," the Lady said. "But in this case, alas, not in any fashion that would have offered us an easier approach, if that is what you were wondering."

It was, of course, and yet again Mara wondered if the Lady could somehow read her thoughts.

"At the western end of the valley, below us and out of sight, the river plunges into a canyon and gallops through it all the way to the coast. The walls are sheer and the current fierce. Nothing can approach the valley via that route."

Mara nodded. "How many people live down there?"

The Lady cocked her head as if mentally counting. "Currently, two thousand, four hundred and fifty-six people make the valley their home," she said.

Mara shot her a startled look. "That many? But you said they were dwindling."

"They are," the Lady said. "Not enough children are being born. The population is aging. We need fresh blood." She looked right, to the south. "We need to regain our long-lost connection to the people of Aygrima. And so we shall. Now that I have you." She stared south for another long moment, then shook her head. "Well. That is a discussion for a later time. For now, we must concentrate on the descent into the valley. The path is steep and slippery. We may be able to see my home from here, but we will spend one more night on the trail, tonight at the base of the slope, before pushing on tomorrow. You and I will go ahead in the morning and leave the sluggards behind. We will reach my fortress by midday. The others may not arrive until almost sunset tomorrow."

Mara wanted to protest the use of the word "sluggards" to describe the struggling band of refugees in their wake, but her momentary outrage vanished beneath the exciting prospect of reaching the Lady's fortress and finally—finally!—beginning to truly learn how to use her Gift without hurting herself or others or engendering the mind-shattering nightmares that had troubled her for so long (she dropped a grateful hand to the mane of Whiteblaze, a gesture that had already become second nature).

The descent into the valley proved every bit as slippery and treacherous as the Lady had warned. No lives were lost during the long hours of cautious descent that followed, but the Lady was several times called to Heal sprains and broken bones from those who had slipped on the ice and, in one instance, tumbled twenty feet from one switchback of the trail to the next. Mara longed to help, but without any urns of magic at hand her only option would have been to draw magic from Whiteblaze or the Lady's wolves, or members of the Lady's Cadre, and neither of them thought that a good idea until she had been trained.

It was while the Lady was Healing the broken leg of the man who had tumbled down the slope that Mara found herself standing next to Hamil, leader of the Cadre. *Or top male of the human wolfpack*, she thought irreverently. He glanced sideways at her as she watched the Lady hurry down the trail to the fallen villager. "Is it true?" he said. "Do you have the same Gift as the Lady?"

Mara looked at him, surprised. "Yes," she said. "Did she tell you that?"

"No," Hamil said. "But I was talking to Prince Chell about other matters, and that is what he said." He turned his head to watch the Lady. "The Lady has made our lives better. Her magic has kept our village from starving, helped us build sturdier homes and buildings, given us a sacred space to practice our worship of the Great Ones. She moderates the weather and Heals our children and elderly. She helped us build the road you will travel tomorrow and the buildings of the town. We have much to thank her for."

"You saved her when she found her way through the mountains," Mara said. "She is only returning the favor."

"Yes, of course," Hamil said. "And she asks little enough in return." For a moment he was silent. "I . . ." he began abruptly, then stopped. He took a deep breath. "I have things to attend to," he said, and left her.

Mara stared after him. What had he been about to say before he thought better of it?

When she rejoined the Lady half an hour later, she thought about asking her more about her relationship with the villagers, and especially her Cadre, but she saw Hamil looking back at her, and something about his expression stopped her. He looked . . . apprehensive.

She tucked the question away for later. There would be time to figure out the ins and outs of the village's working once they'd actually reached it.

For the rest of the descent, Mara stayed at the Lady's side. She saw Keltan only once, as they made their way back into the column for the Lady to tend to yet another injury. He stood to the side and watched her pass, his gaze following her, but he made no move to join her or speak to her, and she pressed her lips together and kept her own eyes resolutely forward. When they returned to the front of the column, she didn't see him at all.

She did see Chell, staring at her and the Lady from a distance. He looked unhappy. She almost regretted her sharp words in the tent the night before. He really had been a friend to her on the terrible journey north after the death of her father. She could never have made that trip on her own. Yes, he had wanted her help . . . but he had helped her without any guarantee that it would be forthcoming.

She hardened her heart and turned her head away. Whatever his motivations, that journey, and their companionship, lay in the past. She intended to focus on the future.

The sun that had been before them when they looked down into the valley swung overhead and then, early in the afternoon, slipped behind the massive ridge they had climbed the day before and were now descending, plunging them into twilight that made the descent slower and more treacherous still. But it was over at last, and a pleasant surprise awaited at the bottom of the hill: warm longhouses like those they had enjoyed on their first night inland. They glowed with light, and the smell of smoke and roasting meat made Mara almost weep with relief and happiness after the long descent—and she knew full well she had been one of those who had suffered least.

The food would be most welcome. All of them had been on short rations, little more than bread and water, hard cheese, and nuts and dried fruit: good trail rations, but not very filling. Mara heard her stomach growl and blushed, hoping the Lady hadn't noticed. But the Lady clearly had other things on her mind, though exactly what, Mara couldn't tell. She had stopped and spread out her hands toward the huts below, her eyes closed. Her nostrils flared in her thin, white face, warmed by the glow of the fires they were approaching, but Mara didn't think it was the smoke or smell of meat she was sensing.

Abruptly she opened her eyes, lowered her arms, and smiled at Mara. "A good night's sleep," she said. "And then we will make haste toward my home at first light."

Mara nodded. She followed the Lady to the tent that was already being erected for them. Before she pushed through the flap, she looked over her shoulder, but if Keltan were watching her or hoping she would join him for supper at the communal fires, he made no appearance. She turned her back on the unGifted still struggling into the camp, put her hand on Whiteblaze's mane, earning a soft whoosh of happy breath, and stepped into the familiar confines of the tent she shared with the Lady.

She and the Lady ate together, roast venison, fresh bread with rich gravy to dip it in, stewed turnips slathered with butter, cold water to wash it down, and hot mint tea to follow it. The Lady did the talking for them both, though Mara was so tired her words might as well have been the drumming of rain on a windowpane for all the sense she took from them. ". . . much more comfortable than when I arrived . . . chambers already prepared . . . training as soon as we can . . . must work quickly, spring is coming . . . plan of attack . . ." Mara couldn't concentrate, and what little focus she had slipped even more as the warmth and food took hold of her tired body. Pleasantly stuffed for the first time since she could remember, Mara stumbled to her bed and fell instantly and wonderfully asleep, Whiteblaze at her side.

The Lady was true to her word: in the early morning twilight, while the rest of the camp was just beginning to stir, she and Mara mounted horses and rode toward the white fortress that rose in the east, the wolves ranging easily alongside them, six of the Lady's and Whiteblaze. Mara was glad for all the practice she had had riding over the past few months, for the pace the Lady set belied her advanced years. The road, which mostly followed the winding course of the frozen river, was wide and level—Mara remembered Hamil saying the Lady's magic had helped build it. The horses were able to keep up a steady trot—a gait she'd never experienced for such long distances before, since most of her riding had been through broken terrain that would not permit it. She kept falling out of rhythm with the horse, taking teeth-clattering jolts until she could find it again, and as a result she was feeling desperately sore and bruised by the time the Lady called a halt for a brief rest some two hours after they had set out. Climbing back into the saddle again she thought was about the bravest thing she'd ever done, and what followed hurt almost as much as using magic she had ripped from other people.

Not really, she told herself as the thought occurred to her. *Not even close.*

On the other hand, the pain of misusing magic was only a memory. *This* pain was current and extremely localized.

The ride ended at last, as they rode through the open gates of the village whose smoke she had first seen from the ridge the day before. A wall surrounded the community, less than a third as tall as the one surrounding Tamita on which she used to like to sit and watch the Outside Market—a lifetime ago, it seemed now, a distant time when the Lady of Pain and Fire was only a dusty historical oddity, not a living, breathing person who apparently could ride circles around Mara, based on the ease with which *she* sat her horse even after five hours in the saddle. The wolves milling around them looked similarly unfazed by the day's hard travel.

The houses beyond the wall appeared ordinary enough, if a bit thicker-walled and lower-roofed than the ones in the capital, as though they had been designed to hunker down in the face of vicious winter storms—as, no doubt, they had been. But Mara barely gave them a glance. Her gaze was drawn upward, as it had been throughout the ride, to the fortress that clung to the top of the cliff that towered above the village.

It looked to be made of ice, but she knew that had to be an illusion birthed from white stone and the season's snow. The cliff face merged seamlessly into its outside wall, which rose up to battlements and guard towers. Beyond that wall rose the fortress itself, half-hidden by the curtain wall and the rising steam and smoke of the village below. It looked smaller than the Palace in Tamita, but not by much, and it clung to the rocks more as if it had grown there than been built. "Magic?" Mara breathed, staring up at the impossible structure.

"Of course," the Lady said. "Although the method by which we will ascend to it is considerably more prosaic." She urged her horse followed. They crossed a bridge over the river, which flowed through the middle of the village, its winding path straightened and constrained by brick walls, and through the winding, cobblestoned streets. Snow lay in piles along every wall but had been shoveled from the middle of the road, allowing easy travel. There were many people about, all of whom moved aside to let them pass. There was something odd about the way they did it, though, and after a moment, Mara realized what it was: they didn't look up, as though they were avoiding the Lady's gaze. Mara resolved to ask the Lady about it later, but then promptly forgot about it altogether as their "prosaic" means of ascending to the fortress came into sight.

She realized as she saw it that she'd been subliminally aware of the sound it made for some time: a low rumbling, more felt than heard. When she saw the device itself, she was surprised it had taken her so long to re- alize what she was hearing, after the time she had spent in the mining camp, for this rumbling had the same source as that one: a giant water- wheel, this one driven by the cascade she had spotted from the western end of the valley and wondered if it were frozen or flowing. It was definitely flowing, falling for hundreds of feet, the rock to either side of its narrow ribbon coated with ice but the stream itself defiantly liquid. At the bottom of its long fall, down a cliff so sheer that it hardly splashed at all for much of the distance, the stream dropped into a kind of funnel and then rushed out again onto the paddles of the waterwheel.

The waterwheel in the mining camp had driven the man-engine, a terrifying device for moving workers up and down within the mine. This one, too, drove a device for lifting people, but of a quite different kind. The ever-rotating shaft of the waterwheel disappeared into a wooden tower attached to the side of the cliff. At the top, where the shaft entered, it was fully enclosed. Below that enclosure, the tower was more open, though its structure of exposed wooden beams was split down the middle by a wooden wall. At the very bottom of the tower was a matching enclosure to the one at the top. And constantly rising up the tower, emerging from the lower enclosure and disappearing into the top one, was a series of platforms, attached to each other by thick ropes at all four corners. No doubt on the other side of the wooden wall the platforms descended, flipping over out of their sight at the top tower. It seemed clear enough what they had to do: step onto one of those moving platforms and somehow not fall off until they stepped off it again in the structure that protruded from the fortress wall like a carbuncle.

"Couldn't we just fly?" Mara asked weakly. She remembered the man-engine with something akin to horror, although this at least had the advantage of being aboveground. She looked up the cliff face and gulped, wondering if that was really an advantage. The platforms looked neither very large nor very stable.

"Waste of magic," the Lady said shortly. "And dangerous. A moment's loss of concentration . . ."

"Never mind," Mara mumbled, while a part of her gaped in the shocking knowledge the Lady did not consider flying impossible, unlike the Mistress of Magic in far-off Tamita.

The Lady dismounted. Mara did the same and, seemingly from nowhere, two men arrived to take the horses, leading them to a stable that was one of a number of workshops and other outbuildings at the base of the cliff but obviously associated with the fortress. The Lady, in her turn, led Mara to the lift.

The platforms really didn't move all that fast, so stepping onto one was easier than catching the alternating platforms of the man-engine. In a moment both of them, each with a grip on one of the ropes (white-knuckled in Mara's case) rose into the air. "What about the wolves?" Mara said, looking down at the pack staring up at them, tongues lolling.

"There's a footpath, as well," the Lady said. "Hidden, narrow, and steep. They'll climb up on their own." And sure enough, even as they ascended, the pack dissolved, the wolves, including Whiteblaze, loping away to her right and out of sight.

Mara watched the snow-covered roofs appear and then dwindle beneath them; after a hard swallow, she raised her head to look down the length of the valley. She saw the column of refugees and sailors at once, still distant, trudging along the road she and the Lady had already ridden. "Still two or three hours away, I judge," the Lady said above the grinding of the lift mechanism and the rush of the cold wind around their ears.

Mara nodded. She tried to look up at the fortress, but she could see nothing but the underside of the platform above them. She looked down again and felt her knees grow alarmingly weak. "Are we almost there?"

"Almost," said the Lady. "Be ready to step off."

Mara nodded, not trusting herself to speak.

Two minutes later, they suddenly went from light to darkness as they entered the structure at the top of the tower, wooden walls sliding past, dimly lit from below by the opening through which they had just entered and from above by a yellow glimmer, a warm glow that waxed quickly until, suddenly, the wall in front of them slid away entirely and Mara found herself looking at a torch-lit chamber, its wooden floor giving way after a few yards to a stone corridor. At the end of that corridor, two figures descended a long, wide flight of stairs. "Now," said the Lady. As the platform came even with the floor of the chamber, she stepped off. Mara hastily copied her, stumbling a little on what had already become a longish step down. She straightened and turned to look up as the platforms disappeared into darkness. On the other side of the wall that divided the split tower, a platform passed heading the other way, descending to the level of the village. *Well,* she thought, *I guess it's better than the mine's man-engine.*

Of course, that wasn't really saying much.

The two people Mara had glimpsed coming down the stairs, a man and a woman dressed in white leather and fur, had reached the chamber entrance just as she and the Lady had stepped off the platform. "Lady," said the man, who was slight, bald, and smooth-shaven. He inclined his head. "All is prepared."

"Thank you, Galiot," the Lady said. She turned her head toward Mara. "Galiot is the head of the house," she said. "And Valia is my lady-in-waiting." She smiled suddenly. "Which makes me sound like a queen. I assure you I am not. Not yet, at any rate. But the term fits the duties, so I don't know what else to call her."

"I don't mind, Lady," said Valia. Round instead of slim, with a mass of curly dark hair, and at least a head taller than Galiot, she might have been designed to be his opposite. She gave Mara a friendly smile and a sly wink, and Mara found herself smiling back. "There's a hot bath waiting for you, young lady. And a hot lunch after that."

"And then," the Lady said, "we will begin your training in earnest."

Mara blinked at that. "That soon? But the unMasked Army will be arriving—won't you be going down to meet it?"

The Lady made a dismissive gesture. "I have arranged for them to be met, assisted in setting up camp, and fed," she said. "There is no need for me to descend."

Mara imagine Catilla arriving . . . and being ignored. She would be furious. So would Edrik and Chell. They'd demand to see the Lady. Keltan would probably demand to see Mara. She didn't think any of them would have any success.

But she had no desire to make her own way to the village to greet the others, even if it were permitted. The unMasked Army, after all, blamed her for what had happened. Chell, she was convinced, saw her as nothing but a tool that could be discarded and picked up at will. Keltan seemed to think he owned her, just because she had allowed him to kiss her. Only the Lady understood her, understood what she had suffered. Only the Lady had the knowledge to end that suffering.

She smiled at the thought, and at Valia. "A hot bath and hot food both sound wonderful." She turned that smile on the Lady. "And so does the rest."

The Lady returned the smile. "Excellent," she said. "Then let's go up." She offered her arm, and Mara took it. "Welcome to my home." Her smile widened. "*Our* home."

Feeling warmer than she had for a very long time, Mara climbed the stairs into the fortress of the Lady of Pain and Fire.

FIVE

Freeze and Thaw

MARA STOOD ON the ramparts of the Lady's fortress, staring down at the village wreathed in smoke and steam far below, and, half-masked by that fog, the tent city of the unMasked Army beyond the walls. A month had passed since she had ascended to the Lady's stronghold. She had yet to pay a visit to her old compatriots.

Winter had at last begun to yield reluctantly to spring: though it had snowed twice since their arrival, water now ran in the streets, the river had thawed and was beginning to swell, and the trees had long since shaken themselves free of their thick white burdens.

For the first couple of weeks in the fortress, she'd hardly given a thought to the unMasked Army, the Secret City, Catilla and Hyram and Chell and all the rest of them. They seemed to belong to a past life, a life that had nothing to do with either her present or her future.

Even Keltan had rarely surfaced in her thoughts. He *had* shown up in her dreams—which, thanks to Whiteblaze's presence, were now only dreams, and not nightmares—and she did miss him when she thought of him, but in some ways she'd been grateful to be cut off from him. His presence would have been a distraction—a pleasant distraction, but a distraction nonetheless—from what was most important to her, more important than anything else could be: learning what the Lady could teach her.

And she had already taught Mara so much.

She lifted the amulet that hung around her neck and held it up, admiring anew the way the light caught on the tube of clear glass, capped with gold on both ends, and the highly polished multifaceted piece of black lodestone it held, shaped something like a crystal of quartz, but manmade.

The very afternoon she had arrived at the fortress, after the promised hot bath and hot lunch, Valia had led her through the fortress' maze of corridors to the Lady's private quarters, in the central tower of the keep. "Welcome," Lady Arilla—as Mara now knew she was called—had said as Valia closed the door.

Mara had looked around with interest. The Lady, like Catilla in the Secret City, had made herself very comfortable: finely carved chairs and table, dresser and wardrobe, tapestries on the walls (featuring bucolic landscapes from around Tamita, whose unmistakable tiered shape rose somewhere in the background of all of them), a thick rug woven of blue and gold, a canopied bed likewise hung with rich blue fabric and covered with a gold bedspread. But Arilla had hardly given her time to take all that in before opening one of the two inner doors of the chamber. The room beyond was far less grand. Small and windowless, it contained a round wooden table with a simple chair shoved beneath it, a much more comfortable-looking armchair, a small cabinet of dark wood, and no fewer than four lanterns, each fitted with a mirrored reflector, together providing brilliant illumination. A thick, circular red rug covered the floor.

Arilla indicated Mara should sit at the table. Then she knelt, folded back the rug, and with a practiced tug lifted a loose stone from the floor beneath. From the dark space it revealed she drew out a small wooden chest. "I keep it here in case of fire," she said. "And thieves, I suppose, though no one from the village would ever steal from me." *She sounds remarkably sure of that*, Mara thought.

The Lady placed the chest on the table, then pulled a tiny key on a silver chain from beneath her white robe and inserted it into the chest's lock. "As I told you on the road," she said, "when my father fled Tamita, he did not go empty-handed. Aware of my unusual Gift, he helped himself to certain ancient items from the Palace Library." The key clicked in the lock. "If you were to go there now, you would find next to nothing that references the Gift you and I . . . and to a lesser degree, the Autarch . . . share."

She opened the chest's lid, revealing two tattered leather-bound books and three wooden scroll-cases. Mara stared at them. *Father*, she thought, feeling sick. Her father had gone to the Palace Library to try to find out more about her Gift . . . and had been arrested for it, the arrest that had revealed how he had modified his Mask, and had ultimately led to his execution. And all for nothing. Here were the very items he had been searching for. *They were never there at all.*

Her heart ached, but she could hardly blame the Lady, who had known nothing of her father's search and could have done nothing about it if she had. She schooled her face to be as impassive as possible and simply nodded.

"Even in these," the Lady said, "there is little enough. Our Gift arises once or twice a generation and is not always identified when it does. And many of those with our Gift prove . . . unstable."

That's putting it mildly, Mara thought. Several of their predecessors had become the great villains of their ages. In Tamita, children were taught the Lady of Pain and Fire was one of them. And then, of course, there was the Autarch . . .

"However, there have been one or two opportunities for scholars to work with our kind, and a few things were discovered. Some of these you already know, by virtue of having this Gift. But there are many things in these scrolls that have proved immensely valuable to me. Especially this one." She pulled out the ancient book, undid the tarnished silver clasp that held it closed, and carefully opened it to a place marked with a bookmark of red cloth. She put the open book on the table in front of Mara.

Mara blinked at it. "I can't read it," she said. "I don't even recognize the letters."

"I'm not surprised," Arilla said. "It's in a language no longer used in Aygrima. But my father was a great scholar, and he had learned it so he could read the ancient texts. He taught me, during our long flight."

"Will you teach me?" Mara said.

Arilla smiled. "Someday," she said, "you will read these texts with your own eyes, I promise."

What an odd way of putting it, Mara thought. But only in passing: her gaze had been drawn from the indecipherable words to a small drawing inserted into the text, showing a complex shape, accompanied by many arrows and symbols. She pointed at it. "What's that?"

"That," said the Lady, "is *this*." She held up the amulet Mara had noted many times before: a crystal cylinder, capped with gold at both ends, containing a black stone about the size of the Lady's thumb . . . carved, Mara saw now, in the exact shape of the drawing in the book.

"It's beautiful," Mara said.

"It is," the Lady said. "Black lodestone, carved in accordance with the instructions in this book, by a talented artisan in the village." She held it up and turned it this way and that, the light reflecting from its polished facets. "When I draw magic to myself from living things, I draw it through this carved stone. And the stone smooths and blends it, so that it does not hurt me."

Mara's mouth opened in surprise. "Oh," she said. It made perfect sense. The magic drawn from living people hurt because, Ethelda had explained (she still felt a pang when she thought of the old Healer, slain on the beach during the battle with the Autarch's Watchers), it was not filtered through black lodestone like the magic used by ordinary Gifted. "Do you use it when you draw magic from the wolves?"

"Usually," the Lady said. "Although the magic from the wolves does not hurt like the magic from humans. The breeding of them was something else I was inspired to attempt by reading these texts." Her hand touched one of the scroll cases. "A predecessor with our Gift had some success with dogs. I extrapolated his work to wolves. It was also from his notes I learned to see through their eyes, no matter how far away from me they are."

Mara nodded. "When . . ." She hesitated, uncertain if she should even ask the question. "When will I learn to draw magic from Whiteblaze?"

The Lady smiled. "Very soon now. I warn you, though, you will find it . . . 'tastes,' I suppose is the word . . . quite different from that of humans, or magic stored in black lodestone. Also—and here is your first lesson— you must be careful not to draw magic from Whiteblaze too fast."

"Why?" Mara said. "Will it hurt?"

"Yes," the Lady said. "But not you. It will hurt *him*. It could even kill him."

"But how can I control it?" Mara said anxiously. "Whenever I've had to take magic from people, it comes in a rush . . . all at once." Remembering that rush, she suddenly longed to experience it again, and found herself licking her lips. She pulled in her tongue in a hurry.

The Lady touched her amulet again. "This helps with that, as well. It's like . . . a tap. It helps you control how much or how little magic you take from living things."

Mara thought of all the times she had lashed out with magic, the uncontrolled fury that had destroyed the city wall, killed Watchers, almost killed the unMasked in the mining camp even as she saved them from the rockbreaker explosion. "Oh!"

"You begin to understand." The Lady smiled. "So now . . ." She turned to the cabinet and opened its hinged door, revealing a decanter of wine and a single glass and, resting next to them, a box of black wood, much smaller than the chest she had pulled from the hole in the floor. She took it from the shelf, turned, and held it out to Mara. "Open it."

Guessing what it must hold, Mara took it with a suddenly trembling hand. She opened the hinged lid. In a bed of red velvet lay an amulet, twin to the Lady's. Mara lifted it out. "It's beautiful!"

"Put it on," the Lady said, and Mara unclasped the chain and put it around her neck. Her shaking fingers couldn't manage to fasten it again. The Lady smiled at her fumbles. "Let me help," she said, and came around to Mara's back. Her cool fingers touched the nape of Mara's neck, raising goose bumps, as she deftly fastened the clasp. Mara looked down at the amulet nestled between her breasts and lifted it to get a better work. "When . . . when can I learn to use it?"

"Soon," the Lady said. "Soon."

"Soon" had seemed "long" to Mara. But a few days after that she had drawn magic from Whiteblaze for the first time (though the attempt to look through his eyes had been a failure, resulting in a killer headache for her and a lot of whimpering from him; the Lady had frowned and said they'd put that lesson aside for the time being), and today, at last, she would truly put the amulet to the test, drawing magic from some volunteers from the village the Lady had assembled for the purpose.

She desperately hoped she wouldn't hurt them. The day she had taken magic from Whiteblaze he had whined unhappily, earning her a rebuke from the Lady for drawing too fast, though she had soon gotten the knack of it. His magic hadn't *hurt*, exactly, but it had felt very odd, even after passing through the amulet.

But drawing magic from people . . . what if something went wrong?

You can learn this, she told herself. After all, she had learned the fine control of magic taken from black lodestone from Shelra, the Mistress of Magic in Tamita. But still . . . whenever she had drawn magic from other people, using her special Gift, it had come in a terrifying rush, and it had taken Keltan days to recover after he had been one of her unwitting sources in the mining camp.

Of course, typically when she had drawn that power, she had been in imminent danger of death or facing some horror like her father's execution.

The amulet was supposed to keep her from feeling the searing pain of unfiltered magic, and that was wonderful, because she never wanted to feel that pain again.

Except . . . the scary thing was that the memory of the pain *did* fade. Once it was gone—leaving only a faint shadow of its true horror—the memory of the power, the heady rush of raw magic, lingered. And *that* she wanted very much. In fact, the longer she went without tasting it, the more she wanted it.

If what the Lady told her was true, and she could draw on that power *without* pain . . . just how was that different from telling a drunk he could drink all he wanted without vomiting, blackouts, or hangovers? Freed from all consequences, such a man would happily drown himself in wine. Some did so even *despite* the consequences.

Mara's hand closed tightly around the crystal cylinder. *I can control it,* she thought fiercely. *I have to. The Lady needs my power. Even the unMasked Army needs it, however much they hate me right now. I need to control it so that we can destroy the Autarch and his evil Masks once and for all. For everyone.*

For Daddy.

A bell rang in a tower high above, marking the quarter hour, and she turned away from her view of the village and the unMasked Army. *I'll visit Keltan soon,* she promised herself, pushing aside her niggling guilt yet again. But now it was time to go to the Lady.

She made her way to a large, comfortable room on the second floor of the same square tower from which the bell had rung. The room was warmed by a massive fireplace in the outside wall, and lit by large arched, glassed windows on two sides. Today the fire burned low and the windows had been pushed wide open to let in the mild spring air. Drops of water from melting snow on the roof fell past outside, sparkling as they caught the sun, a constant stream of diamonds.

The Lady sat in a plush red armchair by the fire. An identical chair, empty, stood to her left. The only other furnishings in the room were a round table of polished wood and the six matching chairs ranged around it. Three young women and three young men sat there, silent and still, hands folded in their laps. In the center of the table rested a large gray stone.

Mara stopped as she entered the room. "Um, hi," she said to the unexpected sextet.

They looked at her unsmiling.

"These are people from my village," the Lady said, "who have volunteered to help you with your education."

"Thank you," Mara said, but still got no response. She looked at the Lady. "Are you going to introduce us?"

The Lady made a dismissive gesture. "Their names do not matter; they will only clutter your mind."

"I'd really like to—"

"Not now, Mara," the Lady said, with finality. "You must keep a clear head." She got up from her chair. "The stone," she said, pointing at it, "will be the target of your magic today. I would like you to lift it from the table."

Mara nodded. "I understand."

"Good." The Lady looked at her. "As you did with Whiteblaze, reach out for their magic. Remember, focus it on the amulet you wear, not on yourself. Draw it into the black lodestone crystal, and only then let it flow to you. Can you do that?"

"I . . . think so," Mara said. She closed her eyes. There was no real reason to do so, but it helped her focus. She reached out, feeling the magic in the bodies of the young people around the table. To her Gifted senses, the amulet she wore seemed heavy and solid as lead. She tugged tentatively at the magic within the volunteers. It flowed out easily, far more easily than she had expected, and rushed toward her. She gasped, and barely managed to direct it away from her and into the black lodestone amulet.

She sensed the magic pouring into the crystal, far more than an ordinary urn of black lodestone could hold. But the feel was the same: and magic collected in black lodestone she knew well how to control.

She reached into the crystal and cautiously drew some out.

The power *tasted* like the raw magic she had drawn on so many times before, fresh and powerful and alive, but it flowed into her smoothly and, above all, *painlessly*. It filled a void inside her, the vacuum that could only be filled by the life-magic she had never before tasted without searing agony. Now it was just *there*, inside her, making her tingle from toe to crown. She heard a slight moan of pleasure and knew it had issued from her own mouth, but she was beyond feeling any embarrassment. Breath coming in short pants, she opened her eyes. The people around the table sat with heads bowed, as though half-asleep. She no longer cared what their names were.

"The stone," the Lady said. "Can you lift it?"

Lift it? Mara thought contemptuously. *I can do more than that.*

She reached out with her magic, a lash of red fire that seized the stone and not only lifted it from the table but hurled it out the open window, driving it in a straight line unaffected by gravity until it vanished from her sight and she felt her connection to it vanish.

She turned to the Lady. "How was that?" she said, ready to be praised.

But the Lady glared at her through narrowed eyes. "Foolish," she said coldly. "I hope there was no one under that rock where you lost control of it and it crashed down."

Mara blinked. She hadn't thought of that.

The Lady's expression softened. "But as far as control of the power goes . . . that was excellent," she said. "Excellent, and very encouraging." She looked away from Mara to the six volunteers. "They will need time to regain their strength. Let us leave them to it. Walk with me."

They went out from the chamber and back onto the battlements where Mara had stood earlier. "How did that feel?" the Lady asked.

"It's hard to put into words," Mara said. "But it was . . . good. No pain. And so much power . . ." She glanced at the Lady. "Would the amulet . . . could the amulet . . . also protect me from the . . . the 'soulprints' of those who die in my presence?" *Or those I kill?* she thought, but didn't say out loud.

The Lady smiled. "Yes," she said. "The potion blocks the nightmares. Whiteblaze can take them away. And the amulet keeps them from happening at all. If you are alert, and direct the magic from the dying person into the black lodestone crystal, it will have no impact on you at all."

"Beyond the ordinary impact of a person's death," Mara said.

The Lady inclined her head. "Of course. I am not suggesting it prevents any *emotional* impact. But there is a difference between that and endless nightmares of the dead returning."

Mara nodded. "Thank you again for this, then," she said, touching the amulet. And then a new thought occurred to her. "These soulprints . . . the fact that magic is so intimately bound with a person's thoughts and feelings . . . that's how the Masks work, isn't it? There's a link between the Mask and the person's mind, and the Watchers know how to read it."

"Exactly," the Lady said. "Which brings us to the subject of tomorrow's lesson, since you passed today's with such ease." She smiled a little. "I'm going to show you how to make Masks—real Masks that will cling to and take the shape of their wearer's face and not fall apart, but also Masks that tell the Watchers nothing. I will also teach you how to take an *existing* Mask and alter its magic so that it can no longer betray its wearer. If all goes as I hope when we move against Aygrima, you will not need that skill. But if things go awry . . . then you may. I have plans for more than one contingency."

"Catilla's dream come true," Mara said. *A Maskmaker at last. Daddy would be so proud . . .*

She blinked away sudden tears. Then she frowned. "If you know how to make Masks . . . could you also make Masks that do what the Autarch's newest ones do: drain a little magic all the time, and feed it to you constantly?"

The Lady's smile vanished. "I could," she said.

"And Masks that put some of your magic into those who wear them, so that you can control their thoughts and actions?"

"I could," the Lady said. "But why would I? Those with sufficient command of the Gift can manipulate the magic that fills every living thing in endless ways . . . *without* Masks. I have that ability. I suspect you do, too." Her smile returned. "But that is a concern for another day." She looked down into the village. "No more lessons today. There is work in the village that requires my assistance. Every year when the ground thaws there are buildings that need repair. The villagers do most of the work themselves, of course, but in an emergency—if a building appears in imminent danger of collapse—I lend a touch of magic. Hamil has identified several structures he would like me to help with."

"Can I come with you?" Mara said.

The Lady glanced at her. "I don't think that's a good idea."

"Why?"

"You just used your amulet for the first time to draw magic from humans," the Lady said. "You should rest."

"I feel fine."

"I'm sure you do. But I am your teacher and your guardian." She put a hand on Mara's, to emphasize her statement. "Trust that I know best, Mara. Stay in the fortress."

Mara said nothing.

"I will be back in time for our evening meal together," the Lady said. She turned and walked back into the tower, leaving Mara alone.

Mara stared out at the unMasked Army's tents, fuming. "I feel fine," she muttered again. In fact, she felt better than fine. She felt elated, thrilled, excited. She was gaining control of her Gift/curse at last. She wanted to tell someone about it, someone who would understand what that meant to her.

She wanted to tell Keltan.

The Lady would be using the waterwheel-driven lift to descend to the village. But Mara, true to her promise when she'd first arrived on that infernal device, had long since discovered the narrow trail that the wolves used. Filled with snow and ice, it had looked terribly steep and dangerous. But the snow and ice were mostly gone. And if the wolves could do it . . .

She glanced at Whiteblaze. *But not him*, she thought. *Not this time*. It would be hard to sneak through the village with one of the Lady's wolves at her side.

She went into the tower and back to her room, Whiteblaze trotting happily at her side. She took her warmest cloak, which had the added benefit of having a large hood useful for hiding her face, and then went back to the door. "Stay," she told Whiteblaze. Obediently, he lay down, tail thumping. But he whined as she closed the door on him.

Alone, Mara hurried through the fortress' labyrinth of corridors until she emerged into a courtyard on the west end of the fortress, where it overlooked a narrow ravine that opened between the spur of the mountain on which the castle stood and the vastly larger bulk of the mountain proper beyond. An opening at the base of the wall, too low for a human to pass through without crawling but just right for a wolf, gave access to the wolves' trail, which zigzagged down the side of the ravine. Not *all* the ice had melted from it, and halfway down Mara slipped and fell painfully onto her rear, sliding a few heart-stopping feet before catching herself by jamming her boots against a boulder with a bone-jarring impact. Sore and shaken, she clambered to her feet again and made the rest of the descent at a snail's pace.

At the bottom she followed the ravine downhill to the right, emerging onto a stone-paved road that snaked up the mountain in one direction and led to a small side gate of the village in the other. The camp of the unMasked Army was on the other side of the river. To get to it, she'd have to enter the village and cross one of its three bridges, unless she wanted to travel miles down the valley, and she didn't have time for that. The danger, of course, was that the Lady, who had forbidden her to come, was somewhere in the village, and Mara had no way of knowing where.

She also had no way of knowing just how angry the Lady would be at her for disobeying her and sneaking out to see Keltan. She didn't particularly want to find out. *Well*, she thought, *at least I've had lots of practice sneaking through streets without being seen, dodging Watchers after curfew in Tamita!*

Although to be sure that had been at night, not broad daylight . . .

Steeling herself, she pulled the hood of her cloak up over her head, though it was really too warm for it, and slipped through the gate.

She wondered where the road she had followed led, up the mountain—a mine, perhaps? She had seen no one on it, and the street on the other side of the gate from it was likewise empty. She slipped along that street, splashing through puddles and dodging the drifts that still clogged the shadows. The stone buildings, sturdy and warm and well-built, would not have looked out of place in the better-off sections of Tamita. *Well, the Lady's father was a builder,* Mara reminded herself. She wondered what the village had looked like when the Lady had arrived there as a teenager. *Surely not like this. She really has made a difference in their lives . . .*

Even as she thought it, she rounded the corner of a tall stone house and found herself no more than twenty feet from the Lady herself. Mara gasped and ducked back behind the corner, heart pounding. Fortunately, the Lady had had her back to her. After she'd caught her breath, Mara peered around the corner again to see what the Lady was doing.

Arilla stood in the middle of a small courtyard, peering up, hands outstretched, at the house directly opposite Mara. Hamil stood beside her, along with others she recognized as belonging to the Lady's Cadre.

A flare of red light made Mara flinch before she realized she was seeing magic, not fire. The red glow encased the building opposite for an instant. The grinding sound of stone on stone filled the air. Then, both the glow and the sound abruptly ceased.

Around the Lady, three of the villagers sank to their knees, heads bowed, just as she had seen all of them do when the Lady had stopped the avalanche from destroying the camp. *She took magic from them,* Mara thought. *Why them, and not the wolves?*

Then she realized that, for maybe the first time since she'd met her, the Lady had no wolves with her. *Where has she sent them?* Mara looked around uneasily. She still didn't know exactly how the Lady used the wolves' eyes. *What if they're hiding all around the village as spies? What if one of them is watching me now?*

And then she got a shock as she realized she *was* being watched—but not by a wolf. Hamil, who had not been affected by the Lady's draw of magic, had turned his head and was looking straight at her.

She jerked back behind the house, heart pounding again. She waited for a shout, for the Lady to come around the corner of the house, for something to happen . . . but nothing happened at all except that she heard voices going away from her. She peered around the corner again as carefully as she could.

The courtyard was empty.

Mara took a deep breath, and hurried on.

She managed to avoid being seen again until she reached the eastern-most bridge. The village streets didn't exactly bustle anywhere, compared to Tamita, but there were still a score or more villagers out and about, because shops stood at both ends of the bridge: baker, shoemaker, candlemaker, tailor. But at least the Lady wasn't in sight. *There's no reason the villagers should be surprised to see me,* she told herself. They *don't know the Lady told me not to come down here.*

It still took her a minute or two to work up the nerve to step into the open, from the narrow space between the tailor's and the baker's, and walk toward the bridge, an elegant stone arch erected, no doubt, by magic. The village seemed too small to need three bridges: Mara suspected the Lady had built them in tribute to her father, and the thought made her feel closer to the Gifted young girl the Lady had once been. *If I'd known her then, we might have been friends,* she thought. *With the same Gift in common, the same fears . . .*

. . . the same enemy . . .

The villagers turned to look at her as she strode toward the bridge. She slipped the hood back from her face and gave them bright smiles. No one smiled back. She couldn't tell what they were thinking, but they didn't look afraid. In fact, they looked . . .

Hopeful?

Now why would she think that?

As she crossed the bridge, she met a woman coming the other way. The woman stopped dead, mouth open. "Hello," Mara said.

The woman's mouth clicked closed. "Hello," she said. "I . . . you're . . ."

"Mara Holdfast," Mara said.

The woman stepped closer. "Is it true?" she whispered. "You have the same Gift as the Lady? You're as powerful as she is?"

"I don't know," Mara said. "My gift is similar, but of course she's far more experienced . . ."

"Help us," the woman said, so softly Mara could barely hear her. "Help . . ." And then she looked past Mara and, sudden terror on her face, slipped by and hurried away.

Mara glanced back . . . and saw one of the Lady's wolves trotting across the courtyard behind her, seemingly unconcerned with her presence or the presence of the villagers, though they all drew back from it.

The wolf disappeared between two buildings. *Did it see me? Has the Lady seen me?*

Those uneasy possibilities propelled her on across the bridge and into the streets beyond. A few minutes later she hurried out through the village's main gate, hood once more drawn up over her head, and, two minutes after that, into the camp of the unMasked Army.

There was no point hiding her face *there*. They all knew who she was. And even though she knew many of them blamed her for what had happened to the Secret City, she would not slink among them. She pulled back her hood and strode boldly into the camp.

There weren't very many people in among the tents: presumably many were in the village, doing . . . whatever it was Catilla and Arilla had arranged for them to do. Chopping wood? Carrying water? Digging holes? Mara was uneasily aware she didn't have a clue how the affairs of the camp had been ordered.

Which meant there was no guarantee Keltan was even *in* the camp—a little flaw in her scheme she rather wished she'd thought of before she was actually walking toward his tent . . . assuming he was still using the same tent he had shared with Hyram during the journey to the village, recognizable by a distinctive black patch sewn into the white canvas.

He wasn't there . . . but Hyram was.

The great-grandson of the leader of the unMasked Army emerged from the tent as Mara approached. For a moment he looked blankly at her as if he didn't recognize her; then he straightened abruptly. "What are *you* doing down here? Shouldn't you be with your precious Lady?"

Mara felt a surge of anger, but pushed it down. Hyram had plenty of reason to dislike her, but he *had* saved her from falling overboard from Chell's flagship, *Protector*, during the storm that had driven them ashore. He might no longer be a friend, and the infatuation he had shown with her when she had first arrived at the Secret City was gone without a trace, but he wasn't her enemy.

"I'm looking for Keltan," she said levelly. "Do you know where he is?"

"He's with my great-grandmother," Hyram said. "Talking about you, I suspect."

He's trying to hurt you, Mara told herself, still holding her anger in check. "And where is *she?*"

"Arilla has provided her with a house in the village," Hyram said. "Just inside the gate. You must have walked right by it. You didn't need to come out here at all."

"If I hadn't, we wouldn't have had this lovely conversation," Mara said. She tried again to force down her anger. "Hyram, I'm sorry for what happened. How long are you going to hold it against me?"

"I don't know," Hyram said. "How long will my friends who died defending the Secret City stay dead?"

Mara's anger ran away from her, then, slipped through her fingers like water, even as she tried to hold onto it to shield herself from the dagger-thrust of his words. Her eyes blurred with tears. "I'm sorry, Hyram," she whispered. "I knew them, too. I'm so, so sorry."

"You already said that." Hyram's voice did not thaw at all. "Better go find your friend. He's the only one you've got down here."

Blindly, Mara turned and stumbled away from the tent and back through the camp, back toward the village. *So many mistakes*, she thought. *So many wrong decisions. So many people hurt and killed because of me . . . by me.*

But all of that pain and suffering, she reminded herself, as she slunk out of the camp she had promised herself only a few minutes before she wouldn't slink into, could be laid ultimately at the feet of the Autarch. The Masks were *his* creation. The mine of magic operated by the slave labor of the brutalized unMasked served *him*. The Watchers who manned it, the Watchers who had attacked the Secret City, were *his* warriors. The magic that had driven Chell's ships ashore after they had rescued the unMasked Army had been triggered at *his* command.

Everything came back to the Autarch. And only one person had the power, and a plan, to defeat him: the Lady of Pain and Fire.

Despite all her mistakes, Mara was convinced that following the Lady was absolutely the right thing to do now. She offered the only hope any of them had for the overthrow of the Autarch, and a future for Aygrima free of Masks and tyranny. Without her magic . . . *and mine*, Mara thought . . . the pitiful forces the Lady had assembled—eighty un-Masked Army fighters, fifty sailors, and about two hundred villagers—would be crushed the instant the Autarch turned his full attention to the task. With the Lady's magic, they just might stand a chance. Without it, they stood none at all.

And so Mara stiffened her spine again and put Hyram's words behind her . . . though she did not forget them, or the pain they had caused. Not because she hated Hyram for uttering them, but because they were true. The pain was her well-deserved punishment for past mistakes . . . and a spur to drive her to atone for them in the future.

She recognized Catilla's house, a modest two-story structure just to the left of the village gate, by the burly black-bearded man standing guard at the door: Captain Stamas, one of the unMasked Army's leaders. She had first met him at a meeting of the captains she had been summoned to in the Secret City months ago. She wondered how many of the other captains who had been at that meeting still lived.

His eyes narrowed. "You," he almost spat. "What do *you* want?"

"I'm here to see Keltan," Mara said. "Hyram said he was meeting with Catilla."

"So he is. But *you* are not invited."

"I think he'd want to see me."

"He might. But would Catilla?"

Mara glared at Stamas. Stamas stared back. *Impasse*, Mara thought, but even as she debated rushing the front door and seeing how far Stamas would go to stop her, it opened to reveal Keltan.

His eyes widened. "Mara?"

She nodded, her throat suddenly closed tight. *I should have come to see him before now*, she thought miserably. *He probably hates me.*

She heard a voice from inside the house, an old woman's voice. *Catilla.* Keltan turned. "Yes, she's here," he said. Another murmur. "I will." Keltan turned back toward Mara, stepped onto the porch beside Stamas, and closed the door firmly behind him.

"She doesn't want to see me, I'm guessing," Mara said.

"Not right now," Keltan said.

"What did she ask you to do?"

Keltan glanced at Stamas, then came down the steps to Mara. "It's good to see you," he said. He hesitated. She felt frozen in place. Then finally, tentatively, he reached out and pulled her to him. He felt warm and solid and she suddenly found herself returning the hug, tears in her eyes.

"I'm sorry I didn't come sooner," Mara said, her voice muffled by the shoulder of his leather coat. "I don't know why I didn't."

"I do," Keltan said softly. "It's what you said. You've been with your own kind."

She stiffened, pulled away. "Keltan, I never should have—"

"It's all right," Keltan said. He held her at arm's length, and smiled a little. "I was hurt when you said it, but I understand. At least I think so." The smile faded. "You have a Gift I can barely imagine, Mara. And it's dangerous. I've seen what it can do. I've *felt* what it can do. The most important thing *you* can do is learn to control it. I do understand. Really, I do." He glanced over his shoulder at Stamas again. "Let's take a walk," he said. "We need to talk."

Mara remembered that low murmur from Catilla, and realized Keltan had never answered her question. "What does Catilla want you to do?" she said.

"Walk with me," Keltan said firmly, and took her arm. He turned toward the village, but Mara resisted.

"Not there," she said. "Outside the walls. The Lady is in the village. She told me not to come down here. I disobeyed."

Keltan's left eyebrow lifted. "Really? That's good."

Mara's own eyes narrowed. "Why?"

Keltan said nothing, but led her out through the gate again. He didn't head toward the tents of the unMasked Army, though, instead taking her right, along the base of the wall, where snow drifts still lingered. They crunched along for a moment before he said, "I've missed you."

"I've missed you, too," Mara said. "But, Keltan, the Lady has taught me so much . . . I can control my magic so much better now." She told him about her success with the trial the Lady had set her earlier that day, when she had lifted the stone from the table and hurled it out through the window. "Ethelda was wrong, Keltan. I can use my Gift safely. Thanks to this," she touched the amulet at her neck, "I can use it without turning into a monster. I can—"

"Are you sure about that?" Keltan said softly.

"What? Of course I am. Arilla is proof that it's possible."

"Is she?" Keltan stopped, pulled her closer to the stones of the wall. "Mara, you haven't been in the village this past month," he said in a low voice. "I have. There's something *wrong* with these people. Not all the time. But every now and then, some of them, at least, are like . . . like

Axell, my best friend who was Masked before me. Like your friend . . . what was her name?"

"Sala?" Mara said.

Keltan nodded. "Sala. Remember how you told me she'd changed? There's something not quite right with the villagers. Some . . . spark . . . missing. Stolen from them."

"But there are no Masks here," Mara said. "I don't—"

"You told me," Keltan said, "that the Autarch has the same Gift as the Lady. As you. He can see, and use, all kinds of magic. He can draw magic to him. But he's not as strong as the Lady. As strong as *you*. He needs the Masks in order to pull magic from those around him—the ones on his Child Guard, and the new Masks, the ones made in the past couple of years, the ones that started failing more often, especially on the Gifted. But the Lady . . . the Lady doesn't need Masks in order to draw magic from people. What if this 'Cadre' of hers is the equivalent of the Autarch's Child Guard, the ones she draws a lot of magic from when she needs it in a hurry . . . but the rest of the villagers are like the kids wearing the new Masks, the ones the Autarch draws a little bit of magic from all the time, to keep him strong, keep him healthy, keep him young? What if the Lady is doing exactly same thing the Autarch is doing, only without any Masks at all?"

Mara stared at him. "That's crazy."

"Is it?" Keltan said. "Why? Because you don't want to believe it? Because you don't want to believe *me*?"

Mara felt anger building in her. "That's what this is all about, isn't it?" she said. "You're jealous of the time I've spent with the Lady. You want to turn me against her so I'll turn to you, like I was some . . . some princess from an old storybook that has to be rescued by the brave prince."

"You're being silly," Keltan snapped. "Mara, listen to me—"

"Silly?" The anger reached the surface. "Is that how you see me? *Silly?* A silly girl? Too stupid to understand anything? To make her own decisions?"

Keltan took a step back. "Mara, please," he said. "I didn't mean—"

"Yes, you did," Mara said. She heard again in her mind the murmur of Catilla's voice from the house by the gate. "That's what Catilla asked you to do, isn't it? To try to plant a seed of doubt in me, so I'll turn to her instead of the Lady." She pointed back the way they had come, at the gate. "So maybe you should go back and tell her your attempt to drive a wedge between me and the Lady has failed."

"Mara, I'm not trying to turn you to or away from anyone," Keltan said urgently. "I'm trying to warn you. To be careful. The Lady isn't—"

"You're following Catilla's orders," Mara said. "I heard her telling you something. I heard you say, 'I will.' She's using you, Keltan. Using you to get to me, because I'm the one she really wants to use. She wants my power under her command." Mara poked him in the chest. "But I'm not going to be used anymore by anyone, Keltan. I'm my own mistress. And I have decided—*of my own free will*—to help the Lady. Together we're going to destroy the Autarch. We're going to make him pay for all the deaths. For my father. For Tishka. For Ethelda. For Simona. For all those unMasked children sentenced to the mines. And you can either help us, or you can stay out of my sight." She poked him again, harder. "Or both."

She could feel his own anger now, feel it in the magic within him. "You're wrong, Mara," he said. "Yes, Catilla asked me to warn you about Arilla. But I would have done it anyway. Because I love you." His voice turned bitter. "I thought the feeling was mutual." He pushed past her and strode away toward the tents of the unMasked Army. Just for an instant she was so furious at him that she wanted to reach out and yank on the magic inside him, force him to come back and apologize.

But instead she let him go. *And that* proves *he's wrong,* she thought furiously. *I can* control *this. The Lady has taught me how.*

And then she realized what he'd said. *I love you.* Had he meant it?

She wanted to believe him. A part of her wanted to shout after him, "Of course I love you!" But she said nothing, instead watching him go without speaking, holding her fists clenched at her sides. Because she couldn't be sure. And the reason she couldn't be sure was the memory of that murmur from Catilla, telling him to do *something* . . . something he had agreed to do. Did he really love her, or was he just doing what Catilla had told him to do, trying to turn her from the Lady, trying to return her to Catilla's control?

Keltan still wants to portray the Lady as a monster—because that's what Catilla wants. She's jockeying for power, hoping to seize control of Aygrima herself once Arilla has destroyed the Autarch. She's hoping to turn me against the Lady. She probably thinks she can outmaneuver me more easily than she can Arilla.

But she's wrong. She turned and looked south along the village wall, toward the towering peaks of the mountains, still capped with deep snow, which separated them from the Autarchy. Keltan had accomplished the exact opposite of what Catilla wanted. She had her own doubts about the Lady's methods, but none whatsoever about Arilla's burning desire to destroy the Autarch: a desire Mara shared with every fiber of her being.

She headed toward the gate. She would return to the palace, and resume her training, and when the time came, she would do what the Lady needed done to allow them to enter Aygrima and throw down its ruler.

Nobody is ever manipulating me again, she thought. *I make my own choice.*

And I choose the side of the Lady.

SIX

Decision Point

A WEEK LATER Mara and the Lady stood together in a workshop achingly like her father's, looking down at the plain white Mask Mara had just crafted. It was the fifth in a row she had made successfully. She already knew the skills of decorating the Masks—she had learned that from her father before her failed Masking—and so knew she could make a Mask *visually* indistinguishable from those made by true Maskmakers. But although the Lady said these would also stand up to the scrutiny of a Watcher, it would be terrifying to trust someone's life—or her own—to that untested ability. She hoped the Lady's plan would not require it . . . not that the Lady had told her what her plan was. "Well done," the Lady said now. "You have made great progress in the few weeks you have been here, Mara. I think we can move as soon as we want."

"Move?" Mara said.

"Into Aygrima," the Lady said. "As soon as the passes are cleared, we march south. I will invite Catilla and Chell to dinner this very evening."

She smiled. "Tonight, at long last . . . we make plans to destroy the Autarch."

Now it was Mara's turn to smile. "I can't wait."

But of course she still had to. Messages needed to be sent to Catilla and Chell, and it was hours until suppertime. Mara spent the time practicing with ordinary magic and with Whiteblaze.

The sun touched the horizon at last, and Mara, accompanied by Whiteblaze, went down to the lift chamber to welcome the arrivals. The Lady would not be there. She had tasked Mara with the chore because, she said, they would be anxious to see her and far less anxious to see the Lady. "I have it on good authority," Arilla had said, "that I can be intimidating."

Mara had laughed. "Just a little."

But the truth was, Mara was the one feeling a little intimidated as she stood by the creaking lift, awaiting the imminent arrival of the delegation from below. She took a deep breath. She wasn't the frightened and confused girl who had arrived at the Secret City half a year before. She had seen and done terrible things. She had grown in power and, more importantly, in control of that power. She no longer feared she was a monster. She was strong. She was brave. She was . . .

She was breathing way too fast and her heart was racing. Whiteblaze looked up at her and whined, and she put her left hand on his furry head. He made a soft "woof" of contentment, and her heart slowed. She could do this.

With her right hand she pushed aside a strand of hair that had escaped the rather elaborate bun Valia had created that was held in place with jeweled pins. Then she smoothed the front of her blue-gray dress, bound round with a belt of broad silver links, likewise smoothed her expression, and, left hand on Whiteblaze's head, waited.

Heads appeared. For the first time in weeks, Mara saw the people who had once seemed so central to her life. Accompanied by a guard, they stepped off the still-moving platform into the fortress, just as Mara had weeks earlier.

Catilla, who wore a black cape over a black dress and carried a cane of pale blond wood, saw Mara at once. Her eyes blazed as brightly as ever. She looked far stronger than the last time Mara had seen her, when her body had still been recovering from the ravages of the cancer that Ethelda had Healed. What she didn't look was any friendlier. Her brows knit together in a ferocious frown.

With her was Edrik, wearing simple brown pants and a red-brown deerskin jacket showing the rabbit fur that lined it at throat and cuff. His face was unreadable as he looked at Mara, though he inclined his head slightly in greeting, after a momentary pause when he first spotted Whiteblaze.

The third individual was Captain March, commander of the two-ship flotilla that had brought Chell and his countrymen to Aygrima. He wore his Korellian naval uniform, though it now had patches on the elbows. He did not acknowledge Mara at all.

Finally, there was Prince Chell, dressed in similar fashion to Edrik. Like Edrik, his eyes widened at the sight of the wolf. They narrowed again as he looked to Mara.

She clasped the black-lodestone amulet at her breast without thinking about it, realized what she had done, and released it again. "Catilla. Edrik. Captain March. Prince Chell."

"It's good to see you, Mara," Chell said. "You look . . . different." *Better,* his voice implied. She remembered again what a good companion he had been on the journey north, how gentle he had been when she had . . .

Don't think about that, she ordered herself.

"You look the same," she said, doing her best to squeeze all emotion from her voice. "Please follow me. The Lady is waiting in the Great Hall."

She led them, Whiteblaze at her side, to the stairs, moving slowly to allow Catilla to keep up. The old woman toiled up the steps one at a time, face set, but made no complaint.

The Great Hall nestled at the very center of the fortress. They entered it by way of a passage at one end separated from the hall itself by an intricately carved wooden screen. Arched over with dark beams carved in the shapes of bears and snow leopards and eagles and wolves, warmed by a central hearth where a giant fire blazed, the smoke rising through a vent high overhead, the hall could not have been more different from the refined rooms of the Autarch's Palace in Tamita. Even by the standards of the Secret City it looked rather barbaric, an impression heightened by the imposing presence of the Lady. Seated on a high-backed golden chair on the dais at the far end of the hall, wrapped in wolf fur, her hair a silver cloud around her head, tinged blood-red by the light of the fire and the torches lining the walls, she did not look like a great lady of Tamita. Not at all.

And that was even before you took in the five wolves around her feet this evening.

A small table with six chairs, one at each end and two on each side, had been erected at the bottom of the dais. Off to the right, where a door led to the kitchens, servants waited.

Whiteblaze trotted ahead to greet his fellows. Mara followed him. "Lady Arilla," she said as she reached the dais. "Our guests have arrived."

"They are welcome," Arilla said. She got up from the throne-like chair and descended the dais. "Please, be seated and we will dine together." She indicated the chairs around the table, took her own place at the head, and one by one they all sat down.

Catilla very deliberately took the chair at the far end of the table from the Lady. Mara sat at the Lady's right hand. Chell sat next to her. Edrik took his place at the right hand of his grandmother, and Captain March sat down opposite Mara.

She didn't look at Chell, keeping all her attention on the Lady.

"We have much to discuss," Arilla said. "But we will not discuss it until we have dined."

"Arilla—" Catilla began icily.

"Not yet, Catilla," the Lady said firmly. "Dine. Enjoy. And *then* we will make our plans."

"Our plans for what, Lady?" said Chell.

"All in good time, Your Highness," the Lady said. She clapped her hands, and the servants sprang to life, bringing silver plates and goblets and utensils, plates of warm bread and bowls of butter, and flagons of wine. There were no fresh vegetables—even the Lady's magic couldn't conjure up *those* this far north at the tail end of winter—but the roast tubers in cheese sauce, the beef, freshly killed so no spices were needed beyond salt and pepper to make it delectable, and the rich dessert of candied blueberries and nuts, baked in pastry and drenched in cream, were as delicious as Mara had become accustomed to finding her meals over the past two weeks—and as the others evidently had not, since after the first bite or two they mostly ate in silence broken only by sounds of contentment.

Had the food not been as good as it was, the silence would soon have seemed oppressive. The Lady did not speak again until the last plate had been whisked away by the attentive servants. Then she folded her hands on her laps and said to Catilla, "I trust everything is well in your camp? The villagers have helped you settle?"

"Well enough," Catilla said. "No one is starving, and if we aren't as warm as we were accustomed to in the Secret City, I cannot fault you for that." She did not look at Mara, but Mara thought she could hear an unspoken, "But I can fault *you*," directed at her. "But the tents will not take us through the full brunt of another winter."

"Nor will they need to," Arilla said. "We will build new houses through the summer. By winter's descent, everyone should be under a proper roof and warmed by a proper hearth, just as I have made sure you are already."

Catilla inclined her head stiffly, as if her neck hurt. "I thank you for that."

The Lady glanced at Chell and Captain March. "And your men? How do they fare?"

"They are healthy enough," Chell said. "But they chafe against their confinement. They want to return to the ships and commence repairs."

"Repairs?" Arilla looked amused. "You really think you can repair those broken hulks?"

"We have excellent shipwrights among our crew," Captain March growled. "It would take many weeks of work, but from the wreckage of both ships I believe we could craft one that could be ready to sail by fall . . . *if* we were allowed to work on it."

Arilla shook her head. "I'm afraid my answer is still no," she said. "As I told you, I may need your men to overthrow the Autarch."

"This is not our fight," Captain March said. "You have no right—"

"You invaded my territory," the Lady said softly. "I have every right."

"I don't—"

"Quiet, Captain March," Chell ordered. His voice was soft, but carried a tone of command Mara had only heard once or twice, and which never failed to get results.

Captain March pressed his lips closed and jerked a nod.

"Then tell me, Lady," Chell said, smoothly picking up the thread of conversation, "how do you plan to achieve this overthrow? And if my men fight for you, will you assure me of your help in my own conflict? You know what I seek: magic and the Gifted to wield it in battle against Stonefell." He glanced at Mara. She saw it out of the corner of her eye but didn't turn her head an iota.

"Your men *will* fight," the Lady said. "Whether I agree to aid you or not. They have no choice." But then she softened the harsh words with a small smile. "But I promise you, Prince Chell, that once the Autarch is overthrown and I rule Aygrima, I will look favorably upon your request and will provide what aid I can."

For some reason Chell glanced at Mara again before saying, "I take you at your word."

"As you should."

"*You* will rule, Arilla?" said Catilla.

"Benevolently," said Arilla.

"As you do here."

"Indeed."

Catilla pressed her lips together, but she said nothing more.

"Then perhaps," Edrik said, "you will tell us exactly how you plan to achieve this miraculous outcome. That *is* presumably why you called us here, rather than just to show off the skill of your cooks."

"Quite right," the Lady said. "It is time. So . . ."

She raised her hands. Mara, alone among those in the room, saw the magic sheathing them, white light streaming to her from the wolves. Arilla flicked one finger, and the torches went out, doused by flecks of magic that darted to each like an arrow from a bow. She flicked another, and a splash of magic dimmed the fire to glowing coals.

Then she folded her hands together for a moment, concentrated, and spread them wide.

The air above the table shivered and glowed, and from the gasps of the others at the table Mara knew that they, too, could see *this* manifestation of magic: a representation of the mountains that formed Aygrima's northern border, in brilliant color and detail. "When I fled the Autarch's attack as a girl little older than Mara here, it was through a pass whose existence had been previously unexpected, because it can only be accessed by a network of caverns which—to my great good fortune—emptied into the very ravine where I made my final stand." She flicked a finger, and a winding trail of green appeared among the miniature mountains, leading to a not-to-scale representation of the redoubt in which they were even then seated. "Those caverns are now sealed, of course, collapsed by the Autarch's final attack, but shifting a few tons of stone is a trivial problem. Either I or Mara could easily reopen the path."

Out of the corner of her eye Mara saw the others glance at her, but she kept her own focus squarely and resolutely on the Lady.

"However, it is there, I am certain, and along the shore, that the Autarch will concentrate his forces against our potential return to Aygrima—because he does not believe there are any other routes through the mountains. Which is just what I want." Arilla smiled. "For while examining the mountains from *this* side, I discovered . . . this." Another flick of magic from her finger, and a blue trail appeared, far to the east of the green one, emerging right where the northern mountain range blended into the eastern one that likewise formed one of Aygrima's borders. "A *second* pass . . . well, a *potential* pass . . . far from the path along which I fled, and one that leads into Aygrima in a place where there will be no defenses. It's completely uninhabited. Our forces can move freely in Aygrima for days before the Autarch is even aware of our presence."

Catilla sat up straighter. "That," she said, "is excellent and unexpected news." Then her eyes narrowed. "*Potential* pass?"

The Lady shrugged. "The borders of Aygrima are currently closed to me. The Autarch has access to the magic the ancient rulers of Aygrima crafted to seal off the then-kingdom from the plague ravaging the world, the same magic, I believe, that forced your ships aground. That magic prevents me from reentering Aygrima. The Autarch, uncertain if I were truly dead, put that protection in place within days of our final confrontation, before he even returned to Tamita.

"But it does not prevent ordinary people from entering. And it will not be activated by Mara here." She nodded in Mara's direction again. "With my instruction, she can break that protection . . . only in the small area of the pass, but that is all I need to allow me to return to Aygrima."

"How can you be certain she will not likewise be attacked by this magic?" Catilla said. "Why would he not set protections against her return just as he did against yours?"

Arilla snorted. "Because he can only set those protections in *person*. Do you really think there is the slightest chance that the Autarch would risk his august personage on a journey to the northern mountains knowing that a new rebellion is afoot?"

Catilla inclined her head. "Fair enough." She studied the map. "So. We get our small force into Aygrima without being detected. We have some time to maneuver. Where do we maneuver to, and to what end?"

"There are two places in the north we must take before we even attempt to move south," Arilla said. "They are relatively close to each other." She flicked magic, and two red dots appeared, both close to the mountains, one slightly north of the other.

"The mines," Edrik said.

"The mines," Arilla agreed. "The new one to the north, identified with Mara's unwilling help, has barely begun to be developed, but already magic is being shipped from it—and a lot of that magic is going to the force of Watchers the Autarch has positioned near the ravine, and the garrison at the Secret City which guards the shore."

"Why hasn't the Autarch sent a force after us?" Chell said. "Why won't they simply come into this valley from the west as we did, following our trail?"

"I cannot match the magic of the Gifted who crafted the barriers around all of Aygrima," the Lady said tartly, "but I *can* manage a barrier to prevent *that*. They cannot pursue us. All they can do is what they are doing, and try to defend their own borders."

She turned her attention back to the two red dots. "So. First we take these two mines, to cut off the Autarch's supply of magic. He has substantial stores in the Palace, of course, but they are far from inexhaustible . . . and without that magic, his Gifted fighters are just ordinary men. Whereas Mara and I . . ." She smiled a cold smile. "We do not need the magic mined from black lodestone. We have other sources."

Catilla gave Arilla, and then Mara, long, level looks. Her expression betrayed nothing of what she was thinking. Then she turned her attention back to the map. "And then what?"

Arilla shrugged. "We march south. We attack Tamita. We take the city."

"With our tiny force?"

"The size of the force is sufficient to achieve its sole purpose: to allow Mara and me to reach Tamita."

"To do what?"

Arilla smiled. "Allow me *some* secrets, Catilla. I will make that part of the plan known to you in good time. Its success depends entirely upon secrecy."

"You ask us to take a lot on faith," Catilla said.

"Faith?" Arilla said softly. "Have you not seen enough by now, Catilla, to *know* the power both Mara and I command?"

Is that true? Mara thought suddenly. *Am I really capable of everything the Lady of Pain and Fire is?*

That was the fate she'd tried hard to avoid. And now she welcomed it?

She felt a sudden surge of doubt. Again she wished she could talk to Ethelda about it. But Ethelda was dead. The Lady of Pain and Fire herself had taken Ethelda's place . . . had taken everyone's place . . . in Mara's life.

Do I really want to become like Arilla?

Have I already?

The discussion of how best to organize their forces for the march into Aygrima began, but Mara had suddenly lost interest. She stood up. "Excuse me," she said. "I . . ."

Arilla waved a hand in her direction. "Go," she said. "No need for you to worry about all this. We'll talk later."

Gratefully, Mara turned and went out through the screened passage. But she did not return to her room as she had planned. Instead she made her way once more onto the battlements, and stared down again at the village and the tents of the unMasked Army. Keltan was there, presumably, eating the rougher food of the camp instead of the rich meal provided by the Lady.

She'd thought a lot about what he had said in the days since she had met him surreptitiously, a meeting the Lady had never found out about . . . *or at least*, Mara told herself honestly, *never saw reason to mention.*

He'd said he loved her. She'd thought about *that* quite a lot. But she'd also thought about what else he'd said, trying to make her doubt the goodwill of the Lady, trying to turn her toward Catilla. Now she knew why the Lady needed her. She, and she alone, could break the wardstone keeping the Lady from entering Aygrima. The power to either take the first step toward toppling the Autarch or halt the Lady's plans for revolution forever both lay within her—a different kind of power from the power of her magical Gift, but in some ways even greater.

The fate of Aygrima rests in my hands, she thought. It sounded absurdly pompous when baldly stated like that, but it was undeniably true.

She walked to the corner of the fortress wall, and this time looked south at the mountains that lay between them and Aygrima, their snow-covered peaks painted silvery blue by the moon.

The truth was, without meaning to, Keltan had accomplished the exact opposite of what Catilla wanted. She would do what the Lady wanted her to do. She would use her power as required. And together, she and the Lady would overthrow the Autarch.

Turning her back on the spectacular view, she headed back to the Great Hall. The Lady had given her permission to sit out the discussion of the march into Aygrima, but she no longer wanted to do so. *Nobody will ever manipulate me again*, she thought as she had before. *I choose my own path.*

And I choose to follow the Lady of Pain and Fire.

When at last the delegation had departed, the Lady took Mara once more to her private chambers, where hot herbal tea and sweet nutty pastries waited. They settled in what had become their usual places. The Lady filled their cups. "And what did Keltan want to talk to you about, when you saw him last week?" the Lady said, just as Mara lifted hers.

Her hand jerked, almost spilling her tea.

The Lady laughed. "Did you really think you could walk around the village without word getting back to me? I heard how you were skulking around." She shook her head. "I told you not to go down there, and I am not happy you disobeyed . . . but, I suppose, no harm done, and young love . . ."

"Young what?" Mara said.

"Your young man . . . the one named after the Autarch's horse . . . fancies himself in love with you, I'd wager. No doubt he hoped for a kiss or two. No doubt you hoped for the same. Did either of you get what you wanted?"

"That's not why I went down there." Mara's face felt hot. She told herself it was from the tea. Even though she hadn't touched it yet. She raised her cup, sipped from it, and carefully set it down again. "I just wanted to tell him how well my training was going. I wanted him to know he had nothing to fear—none of them have. I wanted him to know I wasn't going to become . . ." She let the final words trail off.

"A monster?" the Lady said softly.

Mara sipped more tea to avoid answering.

"And was he impressed?"

Mara sighed. "No. He told me . . . he tried to warn me about you."

"About me?"

"Tried to make me think that . . . that you're as bad as the Autarch. I think Catilla put him up to it. He was talking to her just before I arrived."

The Lady nodded. "Most likely," she said. "So he was trying to drive a wedge between me and you?"

"Yes," Mara said.

"What did he say, exactly?"

Feeling uncomfortable, Mara told her. "He said you are stealing magic from all the villagers all the time, making them docile—stealing their humanity, just like the Autarch is doing with his new Masks. He said your Cadre is no different from the Autarch's Child Guard."

The Lady's eyes narrowed. "And did you believe him?"

"No," Mara said. "You'd never do what the Autarch does. You hate him too much."

"Yes, I hate him," the Lady said. "And how did his accusation make you feel, Mara? Angry? Betrayed?"

Mara nodded miserably.

"That's good."

"Why?" Mara said. "I don't like feeling that way."

"Of course not," the Lady said. "But you can use it." She leaned forward. "You have done some amazing things with your magic, Mara. Stopping the explosion in the mining camp. Blowing down the city wall. Killing multiple Watchers at once. And every time, it was because of some powerful emotion: fear, rage . . . hate." She leaned back. "I learned very early on, Mara, that magic responds to emotion. Yes, you can use it with fine control and accomplish many things. But the truly astonishing achievements come only with deep emotion. When I fought the Autarch, I drew on hatred and anger in every encounter . . . and if I'd also had this," she touched the amulet, "I would have destroyed him then and there."

"But you can't control emotion," Mara said. "You either have it or you don't."

"You can generate it, Mara," the Lady said softly. "You have so many memories to draw on that will help you. So many injustices you have witnessed. And, most powerful of all, your father's death. Your anger and hatred is always there, even if you don't think you're feeling it. You're controlling it without even knowing you are. Reach down inside yourself and find your rage and hate, Mara. Don't fear letting it out. Learn to use it to power your magic. Do that, and there is almost nothing you cannot achieve." She reached out and took Mara's hand. "There are those who will tell you that love is the most powerful emotion," she said in a soft, savage whisper. "Perhaps Keltan is one of them. But he is wrong. Hate is more powerful than love. Grief is more powerful than joy. And both can feed anger, the most powerful of all. You cannot let them consume you. But you *can* use them. And I will teach you how."

Unbidden, the memory of her father's death, the sound of his neck breaking as his naked body fell from the gallows, rushed into her mind. "I'd like that," she said, her voice thick. "I'd like that very much."

SEVEN
Return to Aygrima

SIX WEEKS LATER, Mara stood staring up at a notch in the mountain skyline, trying to see the spire of rock she had to destroy. "I dare go no closer," the Lady had said when they had emerged from her pavilion into the early morning light. "You must approach it alone."

"Are you sure I can do this?" Mara had asked.

"I am sure, or I would not ask it of you," the Lady had replied.

Am I sure I can do this? Mara now asked herself, and her own answer was nowhere near as reassuring.

But she had no choice. She turned and looked behind her. She stood on an outcropping a quarter of a way up the slope from the camp of fighters, just over three hundred in all, assembled from villagers, the unMasked Army, and Chell's men; mostly men and older boys, with a sprinkling of the strongest single women. She knew well it was not a formidable force, though even now she could hear the shouts of captains putting squads through training exercises with sword and pike and bow. It was certainly not enough to take on the Autarch's Watcher Army in open combat. Their only hope was stealth: and the only way they could stealthily enter Aygrima was through the pass blocked by the obelisk of black lodestone preventing the Lady from passing the borders.

"Clearly, the great mages of old knew of this pass, though memory of it has been lost," she had told Mara, "or they would not have placed one of the black lodestone border guardians at its apex. The Autarch had only to trigger one of those stones to activate them all, and he would have used the one closest to the place where he last saw me, so I am certain he never came here himself and is unaware of both the pass and the stone.

"I cannot destroy it myself," she had continued. "The border guardians are tuned to my magic, and this one would rip my own Gift from me and tear me apart in the process were I to come anywhere near it. But if you do what I tell you, the magic will be rendered inactive in this one spot, at least for a time—long enough for us to pass through."

She had explained to Mara that the black spire, and the others like it every few miles along the border, drew magic from the very spine of the mountains, the vast deposits of the strange mineral tapped by both the old and new mines of the Autarch. "You cannot destroy the border guardian directly," the Lady had said. "Instead . . ."

And then she had explained.

And that was when Mara had started to worry.

She looked down from the rocky outcropping. For the first time, the Lady had sent all thirteen wolves with her, though Whiteblaze stayed the closest. She could feel the magic they held, ready to be drawn into herself, ready to be hurled at her target. It was the most magic that had ever been hers to control—perhaps not more magic than she had tapped at the mine, but then, that hadn't really been controlled, had it? And she hadn't had the amulet to focus and filter it.

She sighed and clambered down from the outcropping, then resumed toiling up the slope. All she was doing was stalling, and she knew it.

The Lady had pointed out a copse of pine trees some three hundred yards down the slope from the spire of rock. "That should be both close enough to the spire for you to accomplish your task, and far enough away to keep you safe."

Should, Mara thought. *If. Rather a lot of qualifiers, if you ask me.*

There was one good thing about all the walking she'd done in the last while: she had toughened. She did not believe the Mara who had gone to her Masking could have climbed as steadily as she did now, breathing hard, yes, but never needing to stop. It took her almost an hour to reach the trees. Then she did pause, to regain her breath and gather her wits. Whiteblaze bumped his nose into her hand and she scratched his head absentmindedly, while the other wolves clustered around her, tongues lolling, and waited to see what would happen next.

Despite the wolves, she felt very alone. She looked back downslope at the camp. Tents remained in place, horses continued to graze, smoke rose from cooking fires. The army would not break camp until *she* had broken the magic keeping the Lady north of the mountains. If she could not accomplish her task, the assault on Aygrima would fail before it ever began. She wondered how many of those distant figures were looking up at her now, wondering, like the wolves, what would happen next.

She turned away from them. *Well,* she thought, *let's find out.*

The problem, the Lady had told her, was that no magic they could bring to bear could destroy the obelisk. It would rebound any direct magical attack onto the one who sent it. Nor could it be destroyed by nonmagical means. A would-be demolitionist slamming a sledgehammer against it wouldn't live long enough to wonder why it wouldn't break, having been reduced to a drifting red mist on the wind.

But it *could* be attacked indirectly, and that was Mara's task.

She looked from the stone itself to the ice-shrouded peak of the mountain, still four or five thousand feet above them. She reached out to the wolves.

She drew on their magic.

It flowed into her through the amulet, filling her, overfilling her, swelling her until she felt enormous, powerful . . . and on the verge of exploding. She could only hold that much magic for a moment. It had to be released.

And so she let it go, a flash of pure red fire, the color of magic used to manipulate physical objects, a blast that hurtled the distance between her and the peak in an instant.

High above, mingled dust and smoke and steam puffed from the mountainside. It looked like nothing much, and for a moment Mara stood there, panting a little, horribly afraid she had failed, feeling suddenly weak now that she was empty of the magic she had pulled from the wolves, who had all, as one animal, dropped whining onto their bellies.

And then she realized the mountainside was moving.

It dropped away, obscured an instant later by a growing new cloud of dust. And then the sound arrived, a distant roar, a terrifying thunder of stone on stone on stone that waxed and waxed and waxed, until Mara suddenly thought maybe she was a little too close to the rock spire after all. She turned and dashed down the slope, pursued by the roar, until the thunder grew so loud she had to stop and look back up again, panting.

With terrifying speed, a wall of jumbled stone and ice thundered down on top of the standing spire of black lodestone—and obliterated it. One moment it was there, the next there was only the roar of the landslide, a cacaphony that stopped only as the mass of rock piled up against the slope on the opposite side of the pass.

Of course, not all of the rocks stopped: some of them, ranging from house-size to merely horse-sized, bounded down the slope toward Mara. Gasping, she pulled more magic to her from the wolves and struck out with it, shattering the four or five that seemed certain to crush her into pink paste, each blast accompanied by the whining of the wolves, until they had no more to give and Mara herself was on her knees, sobbing with weakness.

But the deadly stampede of boulders had stopped.

The noise of the landslide had stopped.

It was over.

Mara let herself fall forward and dug her fingers into the soil, grateful for its stolid permanence. She breathed deeply of the smell of damp dirt and crushed grass, then raised herself up again. Whiteblaze lay on his side beside her. He looked at her, and his tail flicked feebly. "Sorry, boy," she whispered. "I'm so sorry."

He whined and licked her hand.

She knew she should return to the camp, but she couldn't bring herself to move. Instead she lay down again, Whiteblaze warm against her side, and stared up at the sky, as empty of thoughts as she was of magic. She was still lying there when the Lady's Cadre arrived, led by Hamil. He knelt beside her. "The Lady comes," he said. "Can you stand?"

"I think so," Mara said. With Hamil's help, she climbed unsteadily to her feet. She looked around. The dozen burly men had formed a circle around her, as though shielding her from something. The wolves formed a closer circle inside that. Both circles opened as the Lady approached.

She strode toward Mara with her arms outstretched, and clasped Mara's hands warmly. "Well done, child," she breathed. "Well done." She put her arm around Mara's shoulder and gazed up at the tumbled mess of stone and ice and twisted, broken trees. "The way is open. I can feel it."

"I can't feel much of anything," Mara mumbled. "Drained."

The Lady nodded sympathetically. "There is a cost to such magic," she said. "But I can help." She released Mara's shoulder, took her hands again, and gazed into her face. Her eyes glowed white with magic. Mara couldn't have looked or pulled away even if she had wanted to. Peripherally she glimpsed the men around her dropping to their knees, but the strangeness of that seemed far off and unimportant. The light from the Lady's eyes waxed, spilling out over her face, spilling out over the whole world, blotting out everything else . . .

And then magic and life flowed into Mara, and she gasped as if awaking from a deep sleep, and jerked her hands free at last.

She looked around. The villagers' faces had gone slack, but they, too, were beginning to stir. Breathing deeply, one by one they climbed to their feet. Hamil nodded at the Lady, face grim, then turned and started up the slope with the others, presumably to try to find a way over the mess left by the landslide.

"You revived me with magic you drew from *them*," Mara said. She wasn't sure how she felt about that.

"I've told you," the Lady said. "They expect it. They trust me. They would follow me anywhere."

Mara licked her lips. "I'm thirsty," she said. "And *hungry*."

"I have brought both food and drink," the Lady said. "Sit."

They sat side by side on a flat boulder in an open space, watching the men of the Lady's Cadre toil up the slope. "Can they really find a way through that mess?" Mara asked. She gulped another handful of dried apricots, and washed it down with a swig of cold spring water from a metal flask.

"They will go as far as they can," the Lady said. "If there are places too blocked for them to proceed, they will wait for you or me to clear the path with magic."

"Where is everyone else?" Mara asked. She twisted around, but trees blocked her view downslope.

"I forbade anyone else to leave camp," the Lady said. "They will not advance until the path is clear. Ah, I see our four-legged friends are also recovering."

Mara took another drink of water, wiped her mouth, and looked at the wolves, yawning and sitting up and generally looking a bit more alive, much like herself. "I *emptied* them," she said. "How do they survive that?"

"Their life force is very, very strong," the Lady said. "And though you drew much, you remembered your lessons and did not draw enough to permanently harm them. However, I will not draw on them again for a week. I will not even use one for my eyes over the pass until tomorrow."

She held out her hand and three of the wolves trotted over, crowding to get their heads scratched. Whiteblaze sat up, looked around, saw Mara, and came to join her, giving her hand a quick lick before sitting on his haunches beside her.

Hamil reappeared, picking his way down the slope. He came over to the Lady and Mara, panting a little. "The going is very difficult," he said, "but we have a path as far as the crest. I do not think we will need any magic."

"Excellent," the Lady said. "Go down and tell the others to break camp." Her eyes flashed, though whether with magic or just a reflection of the bright morning sun Mara couldn't tell. "Tonight we make camp in Aygrima."

The journey through the tumbled remnants of the slide was long and difficult, and the campsite on the other side of the pass was not ideal, with neither particularly flat land nor any source of fresh water, but it was definitely inside Aygrima, and that alone felt like a triumph. As the sun set off to her right, Mara sat on a rock staring down the mountain into the rolling foothills beyond. No smoke spoke of hunters or loggers or villages or even bandits. The northeast corner of Aygrima, Mara had always heard, was the wildest part of the Wild. The nearest villages would be many miles south.

From here they would descend, then turn west, following the base of the mountains until, in some four days' time, if all went well, they would reach the new mining camp, built on the site of the fantastical cave of magic she herself had proved out.

They did not expect there to be a very large garrison at the mine, since the Lady was certain the Watcher Army, believing the borders secured by magic, had headquartered at the Secret City to watch the shoreline and the ravine where the Lady had made her last stand in Aygrima as a young girl. But they would not know whether their assumption was correct until they got closer.

Mara glanced back up at the landslide-choked pass. *I did that,* she thought again, as she had thought many times during the day, as though to convince herself to believe something clearly impossible through force of repetition. *I really did that.*

Someone cleared his throat off to her right, and she jerked her head around.

Keltan stood silhouetted against the setting sun. He wore mail and the blue-and-white tunic of the Lady's forces. "We are not bandits," she had said. "We are an army, and we will look like one."

Mara was suddenly struck by how much taller and . . . solid . . . Keltan looked than when she had first seen him in the basement in Tamita, just before her fifteenth birthday and just after his, more than half a year ago.

He's grown, she thought. *Well, so have I. In more ways than one.*

"Hello," she said, keenly aware of his parting words when they had met in the village, the last time she had spoken to him. *"I love you. I thought the feeling was mutual."*

It is, she wanted to tell him, but a proclamation of love seemed an awkward way to begin a conversation, and in any event, she wasn't certain he still felt the same way.

"Hi," Keltan said. "May I join you?"

She moved over on the rock. "If you like."

Keltan came and sat beside her. The wind brought her his scent, dusty and sweaty but strangely pleasant. "I saw you in the camp before we left," he said. "Saying good-bye to Prella and Kirika and Alita. That was nice of you."

Mara sighed. "Alita wouldn't talk to me. And Prella and Kirika were . . . cool." She glanced at him. "When did that happen, by the way? Prella and Kirika?"

"While we were away from the Secret City," Keltan said. "When I got back there, they were together."

"I'm glad," Mara said. "Prella needs love, and Kirika needs to give it. I'm glad they found each other."

"So am I," Keltan said. "As Alita found Hyram. As I . . ." His voice trailed off. He bent down and picked up a twig from the forest clutter surrounding the base of the boulder, turning it over and over in his fingers. "Mara, I'm sorry," he said, without looking up. "When I spoke to you outside the village . . . I wasn't trying to drive a wedge between you and the Lady. I wasn't acting on Catilla's behalf. I wanted you to know I was concerned . . . about you, and about what I'd seen in the village. I didn't think how it would seem to you."

"I was too harsh in my response," Mara said in a low voice, while her heart leaped in relief that his feelings toward her hadn't changed. "But, Keltan, you have to understand what working with the Lady has meant to me." She gestured behind them. "What I did . . . up there . . . I was in *control* of it. I did it without pain. I . . . I feel like maybe, just maybe, this Gift of mine really is a Gift, and not a curse, for the first time in . . ." Her throat closed. "For the first time since my father died, I think."

"I understand that," Keltan said. "Really, I do. But, Mara . . ." He turned fully toward her for the first time since he'd sat down beside her. "Please, don't be angry. But . . . you drew magic from the wolves, not from the villagers. Not from humans. The Lady . . . yes, she's using the wolves as a source of magic, but she uses the villagers, too, all the time. And I know you don't want to hear it, but it *is* changing them. Just like the Masks are changing people in Tamita. I'm not telling you not to trust her. All I'm asking is . . . be careful."

Mara, who had been somewhat distracted by the way the orange glow of the setting sun was backlighting Keltan's hair, stiffened as he spoke. "You're sorry for what you said before, but you're going to say it *again*?" she said. All her warm feelings evaporated like sweat in a cooling breeze. She felt herself growing angry. She seemed powerless to stop it, or the words she threw at him like stones. "Who sent you? Edrik? Hyram? Or did Catilla give you more instructions before we left?"

"What? No! Mara—"

"Save it." She turned away. "And leave me alone." She walked away. *What are you doing? Stay with him! Talk to him!* a part of her begged her, but the stronger part, the colder part, the angry part the Lady had been teaching her to draw on for power, kept her feet moving away from him, and kept her from looking back.

She didn't wipe the tears from her cheeks until she was out of Keltan's sight.

◆ ◆ ◆

Over the next four days they moved cautiously through the Wild. For the first two days, they saw no humans.

On the third, they came across a small stone building on a low, barren hill. "Magic collection hut," Mara told the Lady as they looked up at it from half a mile away. "We're getting closer to the mine."

The Lady nodded. She closed her eyes for a moment, and Mara knew she was looking through the eyes of one of the wolves. Which one became immediately obvious, as a big gray male trotted away from his fellows, slipping in and out of the trees, and in and out of sight. He finally disappeared completely for several minutes, only to emerge right by the hut. He trotted around it, sniffing, then looked back at them.

The Lady opened her eyes. "No one there," she said. She turned to her left, where Hamil stood quietly with the rest of the Lady's Cadre. She understood why they were nicknamed the "human wolfpack." The twelve men spoke little more than the wolves, and sometimes seemed to move at the will of the Lady without her speaking to them.

As if she has altered *them to serve her,* she thought, and shoved the thought away angrily, cursing Keltan for putting it there. *So they're loyal. Why wouldn't they be? Their village was barely surviving until she used her magic to carve something approaching civilization out of that frozen valley. Without her help, they couldn't grow crops or keep livestock alive.* Of course *they're loyal.*

"Hamil," the Lady said. "Take Mara to the hut." She glanced at Mara. "See if there is magic there we could use."

Mara nodded at her, then at Hamil. He led her into the woods, while behind them the entire column, which had been resting while the hut was investigated, swung into motion, curving off to the right on a path that would take them around the base of the hill Mara would have to climb.

The hut, when she and Hamil reached it, proved to be all but identical to the one, months before, where she had killed her would-be rapist, Grute, and discovered just how deadly her Gift could be. But it held no magic. "Recently harvested," she told the Lady when they reunited. "That could mean there's a Watcher not far ahead."

"There is," the Lady said. "Graymane picked up his scent at the hut and has been tracking him since." She closed her eyes and stopped walking. "He is almost on him . . ." She stood frozen for a minute . . . two . . . then opened her eyes. "He is down," she said simply. "Graymane is holding him for us." She pointed ahead and to the left. "That way." She turned to Hamil again. "We will interrogate this man. Tell Edrik and Chell to make camp." She glanced at the sky. "The camp needs to be under canvas in short order."

Hamil nodded and slipped away. The Lady set out into the woods without waiting for him to return. Mara, caught by surprise, had to run a few steps to catch up. She glanced uneasily at the sky, which had been clouding over all day. The Lady obviously expected rain, and soon. It was already late in the afternoon, and between that and the clouds, the forest had a dark and unfriendly look. "Shouldn't we have brought a few men with us?" she said tentatively.

The Lady glanced her. "Really, child? What do we have to fear in the woods?"

Mara opened her mouth to answer, and then closed it again. "I . . . suppose you're right." The wolves surrounded them, and with their magic, she had brought down a mountain. Whatever the wolves themselves did not frighten away—or could not bring down—she and the Lady certainly could.

I'm powerful, she thought. For some reason it hadn't really struck home until that moment, despite all that had happened. She had never thought of herself as powerful before; dangerous, unstable, a threat to herself and others, yes, but not *powerful*—able to *choose* to use her Gift, to control it, to bend it to her will.

Now all she had to do was choose to use it wisely.

Well, no pressure there.

They reached the Watcher after about twenty minutes' walk. He lay in a clearing in the woods, flat on his back, Graymane standing over him, growling whenever he moved. The Watcher's right leg, twisted beneath him at an unnatural angle, was clearly broken. The Lady bent over him. "You are in pain," she said. "I can help."

"Who . . . ?" the Watcher gasped out. "You wear no Mask." His eyes, behind the eyeholes of the black Mask, flicked to Mara. "Either of you."

"My name is Arilla," the Lady said. "But you would know me better as the Lady of Pain and Fire."

The eyes widened, jerked back to her. "The Lady . . . ?"

"I can ease your pain," the Lady said again. "But you must help me. I need to know how many Watchers there are at the new mine . . . and how many workers, both Masked and unMasked."

The Watcher stared at her. "You're planning to attack!"

"How many?" the Lady said.

"I will not tell you," the Watcher said.

The Lady sighed. "You will," she said. "But I would prefer not to expend magic on you." Mara shot her a startled glance. The Lady didn't appear to notice. "Well?"

"I will not tell you," the Watcher said. "No matter what you do."

"I do not think," the Lady said, "that you have the slightest understanding of what I can do." With her right hand she touched Graymane, who whined a little but never took his gaze from the Watcher, and with her left reached out and touched the Watcher's chest. Mara glimpsed a flash of magic—and with a sharp crack, the Watcher's Mask split down the middle and fell from his face, collapsing into shards of clay as it hit the ground.

The revealed face was young, only a few years older than Mara, and frightened. But even as she watched, the fear melted away, replaced by a look of peace—incongruous, considering his circumstance. "How many Watchers at the new mine?" the Lady asked again, in a light conversational tone, as though commenting on the weather at a dinner party.

"Depends," the young man said without a trace of reticence. "Full garrison is sixty, but of course there are always some out harvesting from the magic huts, and some on patrol, keeping an eye out for bandits. Generally more like forty of us actually on hand."

"And how many unMasked?"

"Must be close to a hundred up there already," the Watcher said. "Most of 'em are still at the old mine, but not for much longer. The ones at the new mine are busy building new longhouses and other buildings and some are already working underground, starting the new shafts and levels. There were *more* than a hundred," he went on, "but the roof fell in on a couple of dozen last week. Mostly strong ones, too—almost all men, only a couple of women and maybe three young 'uns. Nasty waste. Kind of putting a crimp in the work until we can get more sent up from the old mine. Not to mention making a hell of a mess."

Mara stared at the young man in horror, memories of her own mercifully brief time in the mine flashing back with almost as much force as the magic-driven nightmares she thankfully seldom had now, thanks to Whiteblaze. She touched his head and his tail wagged briefly, although he kept his eyes fixed on the supine Watcher.

"More Watchers at the new mine than the old right now, then?" the Lady said.

The young man pursed his lips. "No, still more at the old mine, I'd say. Maybe seventy or eighty. Probably five hundred unMasked. Should be more Watchers than that, of course—but a bunch of Watchers were sent out west. Heard that was in case you showed up, ma'am," he said respectfully to the Lady, "but I didn't really credit it. No offense, but I thought you were a myth."

"None taken," the Lady said. "Now tell me about the new mine. What does it look like inside?"

"Well, it all started with this huge natural cavern, right?" the Watcher said.

The Lady looked at Mara. "The one you found, presumably."

She nodded, remembering how beautiful it had been, the walls glistening with more magic than she had ever seen in one place before or since.

"Big underground lake in the cavern, water pouring out into the ravine," the Watcher went on. "But when they went in farther, they found that the water pouring into the lake comes down a long passage from high up the mountain. An underground cascade. They've harnessed that, of course."

"A waterwheel?" Mara said.

The Watcher nodded and flashed her a grin. "Got it in one, miss! They've just started sinking shafts—been busy mining out the big cavern—but eventually they'll put in a man-engine like they got in the other mine. Right now they're just using it to run a rock-crusher—helps them extract the magic."

The Lady looked at him thoughtfully. "Is this underground cascade natural?"

"Funny you should ask, ma'am," the Watcher said. "It ain't. That chute it comes down is smoothed the whole way. And there are stairs and passageways climbing up the mountain alongside it. Someone carved them all out. Must be centuries ago now. Probably the same folks who carved that Secret City we cleared the rebels out of."

"Fascinating," the Lady said. "And where do those stairs and passageways lead?"

"Right up to where the water pours underground. It starts way up near the peaks, see, in a glacier-fed lake. You look close from down in the valley, you can see it cascading down the side of the mountain. Where it goes underground there's a second entrance to the cave system—and more magic, too: there's a small crew of unMasked up there already, opening things up for mining."

"And is this second entrance guarded?"

"'Course it is," the Watcher said. "We're not idiots. Got a permanent garrison up there, watching the entrance, riding herd on the diggers. Poor bastards." Mara could tell he wasn't referring to the unMasked. "Kind of a punishment duty. Nobody's ever going to find that hole without knowing it's there." A slightly confused look crossed his face. "Not supposed to say anything about it," he added. "You won't tell anyone, will you?"

The Lady smiled at the Watcher, but there was no warmth in it. "No one who doesn't need to know."

His face cleared. "Well, that's all right, then."

"You've been very helpful," the Lady said softly. "Thank you."

"Fix my leg now, then, will you, ma'am?" the Watcher said. "Whatever you done made it stop hurting, but I'd like to get up. If your pet will let me, of course."

"Fix your leg?" the Lady said. "No, that won't be happening. But I can guarantee it will never hurt you again."

Before Mara could quite grasp what she meant by that, she reached out her hand again and touched the Watcher's chest once more. She saw a flicker of blue, the color of Healing, but no Healing took place.

Instead, the Watcher gasped slightly. His strangely trusting eyes, staring up at the Lady, widened, and glazed over.

He was dead.

Mara *saw* the magic rush out of him, the rush of magic that had so often before poured into her, causing pain and nightmares. But none of the magic streamed to her: instead, all of it went to the Lady, pouring into her black lodestone amulet.

The Lady stood up. Another flick of her hand, a flash, and the Watcher's body was gone, leaving behind only white dust . . . the same dust that had been all that had been left of Grute when she had burned away his naked, headless body from the magic-collection hut where he had attacked her. Her stomach twisted. He had been the first person she had killed with magic. He hadn't been the last. She didn't want to kill any more. But the Lady had just slain the young man she had been talking to an instant before as casually as swatting a fly. "You killed him!" she choked out. "*Why?*"

The Lady shrugged. "He could not be set free, to warn the mining camps, and we cannot spare a man to watch him day and night. Easier and cleaner this way. And he told us what we need to know."

"And that made it all right to kill him? You used him and discarded him like . . . like a dust rag. As though he were nothing to you!"

A flicker of irritation crossed the Lady's face. "What do you think we mean to do to the Watchers at the mine, Mara? Sit them down and explain to them the error of their ways? This is war, or soon will be. We will kill many Watchers at both mines, just as I killed this one . . . and at that, he is more fortunate than most. A simple death at my touch is far preferable to bleeding out from a sword blow to the thigh or dying in agony from a spear through the gut. His fate would have been the same no matter what. I hastened and eased his passage. I showed him *mercy*."

Mara looked down at the ground where the Watcher had lain, at the white dust still being scattered by the breeze. "He was only a little older than me."

"And already a cold-blooded little bastard," the Lady snapped. "With callous disregard for the suffering of the unMasked. He was an extension of the will of the Autarch, Mara. And if we are to bring the Autarch down, we must sever from him his only means of extending that will beyond the walls of the Palace: the Watchers, and magic." She turned away from Mara and strode back toward the camp. "Come," she said. "I must tell Edrik and Chell what we have learned. We have plans to prepare."

As they turned away, the rain began, washing the dust from the weeds of the clearing, all that remained of the first casualty of the Lady's invasion of Aygrima.

The first, but certainly not the last.

EIGHT

Through the Back Door

"THIS ISN'T GOING TO BE EASY," Chell muttered, late the next morning. The rain had poured down for hours, but cleared sometime after midnight, and now the sky was bright blue. Chell rolled over on his back and slid down the damp grass a little bit to get below the ridgeline from which he and Edrik had been studying the split in the mountainside hiding the magic-filled cavern Mara had found, and from which the unMasked Army had rescued her.

That had been in late autumn. Now it was mid-spring, and the Autarch had clearly not wasted the intervening months. The opening into the narrow ravine, clearly visible more than a mile away across a broad, barren, river-carved valley, had been blocked by a high wall of stone, penetrated by a single iron-bound wooden gate. Watchers patrolled the battlemented top of the wall. Beyond that wall smoke rose into the sky from the ravine itself.

"When we rescued Mara," Edrik said, "we climbed the mountain over there," he pointed right, toward a shoulder of the peak, "and came down on them from above."

"Clearly they remembered," Chell said. "Since they've also built a wall around the *top* of the ravine."

The Lady stood a few feet away, eyes closed. She hadn't bothered to climb to the ridgeline. Mara knew she was studying the situation through the eyes of her wolves, ranging somewhere in the valley or up on the mountain above the ravine.

Now her eyes opened, and she looked at Chell. "You still do not understand," she said. "This war against the Autarch will not be decided by force of arms, but by force of magic."

"Good thing, considering the size of our force," Chell muttered.

"If you can take the mine using magic, why do you need our people?" Edrik demanded, turning like Chell before him and sliding below the ridgeline. He stood and brushed uselessly at the mud on the seat of his pants. "Why should we risk our lives? Blast the Watchers and be done with it."

"Both Mara and I have drawn magic heavily from the wolves the past few days, so they are not at full strength," the Lady said. "My Cadre is likewise weakened, and with possible combat imminent, I do not want to risk drawing from the other villagers, partially incapacitating them just when they must fight. I do not think either your people, Edrik, or yours, Chell, want me taking magic from *them*. I could, of course, take magic from the Watchers themselves . . . but not from this distance, and not without putting myself at more risk than I think is wise."

"So what is your plan?" Chell demanded. "I presume you have one."

"My plan," the Lady said, "depends on Mara."

Chell and Edrik looked at her. Mara remembered when Chell's first reaction on seeing her had been to smile, when his expression had always been one of open friendliness. That had changed after their frosty encounter in the Lady's tent en route to the fortress. Now it was . . . carefully blank. Whatever he thought of her, he showed nothing of it. Nor did Edrik. Considering her actions had brought the Watchers down on the Secret City, she suspected that was for the best.

She shoved the old guilt aside and schooled her own face to stoicism. Guilt and doubt belonged to the old, powerless Mara. Not to the right hand of the Lady of Pain and Fire. *I am powerful*, she reminded herself. *And in control. And if my opening of the pass did not demonstrate that to my old allies, perhaps this will.*

"The heart of this mine of magic is—or was, they've probably destroyed it by now—" (she felt a pang for lost beauty) "a natural cavern with an underground lake, smaller than the one in the Secret City, but large enough. We learned from the Watcher we questioned that the lake is fed by an underground stream that pours down from the glaciers at the top of the mountain; that there is a second entrance to the caves far up the slope; and that it is possible to reach the main mine from that entrance, along stairways carved in the rock, like those in the Secret City." She pointed toward the glimmer of ice high overhead. "There is a garrison of about a dozen Watchers at that 'back door' . . . but it is still the weakest point in their defense. And there is magic to be found at that end of the cavern, as well.

"So," she continued, carefully enunciating the plan the Lady had spelled out to her, though the military terms didn't exactly come naturally to her, "rather than mount a frontal assault, we will take a small force to this alternate entrance, overpower the garrison, and descend from there. While our main force keeps the Watchers' attention focused outward, we will surprise them from behind. I will use magic to blow open the gate. Caught between my magic and our small force inside the wall, and the Lady's magic and the larger force outside it, the Watchers will quickly be overpowered." She glanced at the Lady, hoping she'd gotten the details right.

The Lady nodded approvingly.

"And *you're* going to lead this force?" Chell said. "Mara, I know you have magic, but—"

Mara felt her face heat. "Do you doubt my power?" she said, and though she recognized the echo of the Lady's words, it did not concern her. The Lady was no longer what she *feared* she would become, but what she *wanted* to become. "It's true I will not be swinging a sword. *But I don't need to.*"

"I don't doubt your power," Chell said evenly. "I was in Tamita when your father died. I was with you every step of the way north to the Secret City. I saw what you did to the Watchers in the boat from the Secret City, and on the beach. I saw what you did in the pass. But you didn't let me finish. It is not your power I doubt. It is your ability to lead: to lead my men, and Edrik's."

"My people will not follow you," Edrik said flatly. "You cost too many of them too dearly."

"They will follow her if I say they will follow her," the Lady said. "Or they will pay the price."

"They have already paid the price," Edrik snapped. "Will you kill them? Torture them? Force them to your will with magic? You said yourself your power is not unlimited. And every time you hurt one of the un-Masked Army, or one of Chell's men, or kill one of them, or force them to do something against their will, you are laying a trap for yourself. Because eventually you will be in a position of vulnerability, and one of them will seize the opportunity to take revenge."

The Lady trembled with anger. Mara could see, though she knew both Chell and Edrik were oblivious to it, magic, bright as the sun, shining in Arilla's eyes. She stepped forward hastily, interposing herself between the Lady and the two men. "Lady," she said softly. "Please."

The light faded. The Lady closed her eyes for a long moment. When she opened them again, the irises were their ordinary extraordinary ice-blue. "Sort this out, Mara," she said. "For their sake."

"I can," Mara said. "I will."

The Lady nodded and, without another word, turned and strode away toward the camp. Wolves slipped out of the trees, wolves Mara hadn't even been aware were there, and followed her. Whiteblaze watched them go, but stayed at her side.

She wondered how close those wolves had been to tearing out Chell's and Edrik's throats.

She turned toward them. "That was foolish," she said coldly. "Antagonizing the Lady will accomplish nothing but get the people you claim to care about hurt."

"*That* is the person you've chosen to emulate?" Chell said. "Mara, you're not her. You're—"

"Don't tell me who I am," Mara said. "I know who I am. I am Mara Holdfast, and I have power—power that will enable us to take this mine and free the unMasked slaves within it, and strike the first of many blows against the Autarch that you, Edrik, claim to hate so much." Edrik's stony expression darkened, and Chell's eyebrows drew together. But then Mara raised her hands in a conciliatory gesture. "But," she said, "I also know my limitations. As the Lady likes to say, 'My power is not unlimited.'" She smiled. It wasn't a real smile, because inside she shook with anger that echoed the Lady's, but apparently it was convincing enough, because Chell's frown eased, even if Edrik's did not. "I don't need to be in command," she said. "Order your forces as you see fit. When you are ready, we will climb to the garrison, and I will get us into the cavern . . . under your direction." She looked from one to the other. "One question, though. Which of *you* will command?"

Chell and Edrik exchanged startled glances, and Mara took that moment to turn and make her own grand exit, following in the footsteps of the Lady back down to the main camp.

◆ ◆ ◆

Mara had no idea how they had decided, but when the small strike force assembled early the next morning and began its long roundabout climb to the upper garrison, clearly Chell commanded. Indeed, the entire force was made up of men from the Korellian ships.

They began the climb by winding their way up a dry streambed. Chell fell in beside Mara and Whiteblaze, halfway back in the group of twenty.

"Shouldn't you be leading us, if you're in command?" Mara said to him. She was dressed in deerskin trousers, a blue blouse and, over that, a deerskin vest and then a snug sheepskin jacket. The air was still cool, cool enough she could see the breath she was puffing out, but she was already beginning to think she'd overdressed. She carried a stout black staff in her left hand, but with her right, she began unbuttoning the jacket.

Chell, like his men, wore the Lady's uniform: blue-and-white tunics over mail shirts. He had already shed his gray cloak—she could see the sleeves of it poking out of the top of his backpack. He bore a sword on his left hip and a dagger on his right. "Lieutenant Antril is up there," Chell said. "He's a fine officer, so I'm letting him . . . um, office."

"He's very young," Mara said.

"Look who's talking," Chell said.

"How did he get that scar on his cheek?"

"Cutlass wound," Chell said. "Just after we left Korellia, we were attacked by pirates. We weren't flying the royal banner—trying to slip away incognito—or they never would have dared. Their idiot captain must have mistaken us for merchants. They grappled and boarded us in the night. During the battle Antril—just a midshipman, then—killed three of the scoundrels even though blood was pouring down his face from a head wound, a sword cut that came within inches of splitting his skull. He made sure the more seriously wounded were seen to before he allowed the surgeon to do more than give him a cloth to staunch his bleeding. Captain March promoted him on the spot. He may be young, but he's seen and done his share."

I've seen and done my share, too, Mara thought. *I, of all people, shouldn't be surprised by anyone's youth.*

For a few minutes after Chell concluded his story neither of them spoke. A turn in the riverbed had brought them to a field of rounded rocks that rolled beneath their feet in a fashion all-too-conducive to turned ankles and required concentration to navigate safely. When they were through it, though, she glanced at Chell again. "Well?" she said.

"Well what?"

"Why are you walking with me? You obviously have something to say."

"I do?"

Mara snorted. "Of course you do. Just like Keltan. He's talked to me exactly once since we entered Aygrima, and he tried to drive a wedge between me and the Lady. Again."

"Why would he want to do that?" Chell said.

"For Catilla, of course." Mara shook her head. "That stubborn old woman has it in her head that she should rule in the Autarch's place. As if that could happen now that the Lady is back in Aygrima—and she's cooling her heels back in the village."

"The Lady will rule, then?" Chell said.

Mara shot him a look. "Who else?"

Chell shrugged. "I don't know. Not my land. Not my concern, except that I hope whomever is finally in control remembers what I and my men have done to assist in the Autarch's overthrow."

"Don't worry. I'm sure you will receive your reward."

She didn't realize how much bitterness she had let seep into her words until Chell said softly, "Why are you angry with me? You were angry when I visited you in the Lady's tent. You're still angry. And I don't believe I've done anything to deserve it."

"I'm not angry," Mara said, and winced. She'd barked her response like an angry dog.

"Uh-huh," Chell said.

Mara concentrated on climbing for a minute, marshaling her words. Finally she said, "Prince Chell. You assisted me in escaping from Tamita, and helped me travel north. But it became clear, when you met the Lady, that you had done so only because you had thought my Gift might be of use to you in your own country's war. You switched your attention to the Lady because she demonstrated the kind of power you need when she destroyed your ships. You came to me in the Lady's tent to try to get me to intercede on your behalf with the Lady. Now you seem to be trying to cultivate my friendship again. I presume this is because you now know I, too, have that kind of power. You are being friendly because you hope to take me back to your father and offer him my help in your war with . . . whatever the name of the kingdom was."

"Stonefell," Chell said. He shook his head. "Mara, that's . . . remarkably cold. I've never stopped being your friend."

"Perhaps that's because you were never my friend to begin with."

That statement fell between them like one of the rocks littering the streambed. Mara heard Chell's sharp intake of breath. She didn't look at him. If she'd hurt him, it was no more than he deserved. He'd hurt *her*, after all.

The *old* her. The one that had made that embarrassing attempt to initiate something physical between them in the magic hut down the coast. Not the new her, growing these past few weeks in the company of the Lady.

She no longer craved the friendship or attention of someone like Chell.

Or Keltan?

She pushed that voice of doubt aside. *I am powerful*, she reminded herself yet again. *I don't need any of them. I am* powerful.

"Mara," Chell said softly. "Do you really believe that I have only ever been interested in using you, that I never cared for you as *you*, with or without your Gift?"

"That's what it looked like to me," Mara said.

Another silence. "Do you know what it looked like to me, Mara?" the prince said at last. "I saw a girl who had saved my life. A girl who bravely reentered the most dangerous place in the world because she thought it had to be done to help her people. A girl with a terrifying ability that was almost undone by the most horrible event any young person could ever witness—the brutal murder of a parent—and yet was *not* undone, who gathered herself together and did her best to save her friends and community."

And failed, Mara thought, but she said nothing out loud and once again pushed the guilt down as a waste of emotion. *He's trying to soften you up. Stay focused. Stay centered. Stay powerful.*

"By that time, I no longer saw a girl," Chell went on. "I saw a brave young woman. A young woman I respected, and admired, and liked . . . and, yes, occasionally feared . . . but never, *never* saw as someone I could merely *use.* I hoped she would choose to help me, that she would decide that was something she could do and remain true to herself . . . but I always knew that decision would have to be her own to make.

"When I saw the Lady, and approached her in the hope she might help my cause, it was not because I had decided you would *not,* but because I thought there was an opportunity to remove you from the equation, free you from having to make a decision. My mission remains what it has always been, Mara. If we survive this . . . a rather large 'if,' I admit . . . then I hope to return to Korellia with magic to aid us in our desperate struggle against Stonefell. I still hope the Lady will provide that magic. If not, then yes, I hope you will see fit to do so. But all of that has nothing—*nothing*—to do with how I see you. You are still the girl who saved my life, who became my friend, and whom I have watched grow into a remarkable young woman." Now a trace of bitterness crept into his own voice. "I hope you can eventually find a way to look at me and see whatever it was you once saw. Because I have not changed, Mara. I am your friend. I will always be your friend. Whether you are mine or not."

And with that, he lengthened his stride and moved up the slope ahead of her, to rejoin Antril at the lead of the column of armed men, leaving Mara alone with her thoughts.

She tried to push his words away as she had pushed them away before. She didn't *want* to be the girl she had been, stumbling from disaster to disaster, every wrong choice leading to pain and suffering for others, unable to control her Gift, hurting, frightened, confused, plagued by night terrors. She wanted to be whom the Lady had tried to make her: Mara Holdfast, powerful sorceress, possessed of the rarest of all magical Gifts, sure of herself, sure of her goals, sure of her prowess. Confident. Calm. Self-assured. *Powerful.*

I'll show him, she thought. *I'll show him I'm not the girl he remembers. I'll show him who I am now.*

But even as she made the vow, a small voice deep inside her, a voice that sounded an awful lot like Mara Holdfast the Maskmaker's daughter rather than Mara Holdfast the mighty sorceress, whispered, *Are you sure you're not really trying to show yourself?*

NINE

Cavern of Blood

THEY HAD BEGUN climbing the mountain at dawn, but by the time they were in position to spy on the garrison, the sun had long since swung overhead and begun its descent into the west. They had left the streambed when it curved off in the wrong direction, and had spent the last several hours picking their way through a sparse pine forest, littered with boulders: boulders of black lodestone, though they seemed to have attracted little magic—none Mara could see, at least. For some reason magic tended to seep down into the ground, vanishing like the water from the rain two nights before. Today the sky was mostly clear, streaked by only a few feathery wisps.

Still, the fact that black lodestone could be seen on the surface this far up the slope made her wonder just how much black lodestone the mountain as a whole contained . . . and how much magic.

She remembered what the Lady had said about how the spire in the pass, the "border guardian," had a connection to the vast masses of black lodestone in the mountain range's spine. If every mountain contained black lodestone, and all of it had been collecting magic from the countless living creatures that had died on the slopes over millennia . . .

The thought was mind-boggling.

Now at last they were peering over a ridge through a thin screen of scraggly evergreens toward the mine's "back door." Three stone huts clustered around one side of a gaping hole into which poured a stream that splashed and tumbled down from a white wall of ice and snow another quarter of a mile up the mountainside. Mara shot that overhanging glacier an uneasy look and hoped it stayed exactly where it was. From the fact that the forest they had climbed through didn't really exist beyond the ridge, where everything had a distinctly scoured look, she suspected it occasionally . . . shed.

Four Watchers lounged by the huts. Others might be in the huts, asleep; more likely they were down in the cave with the unMasked workers, whom Mara assumed were housed in the largest of the three huts—the one that could be bolted from the outside and had only slits for windows. *A pen for animals*, she thought angrily.

Possibly some of the Watchers were patrolling, but they'd seen no sign of scouts during the climb and clearly the Watchers below had no clue they were themselves being watched. One looked sound asleep, two were playing some kind of board game, and one was whittling a piece of wood.

Chell snorted. "I think we can take them," he said dryly to Lieutenant Antril, on his other side. Then he glanced at Mara. "I don't think we'll need your special talents this time."

Mara nodded. She ruffled Whiteblaze's mane, and his tail thumped the ground in response. "Then I'll leave it up to you."

Each of Chell's men carried a bow. Below the ridgeline, they strung them, then nocked arrows. There was a brief murmur of conversation as they sorted out targets. Then, at Chell's signal, they rose up and fired as one.

The four Watchers died an instant later.

Even at that distance, Mara felt their deaths, but the magic did not rush to her as she expected. Instead, she felt it pulled away from her, down into the depths of the mountain . . . down to where the vast mass of black lodestone waited.

She felt a surge of annoyance. She didn't *need* their magic, certainly didn't need whatever seeds of horror their soulprints might plant in her mind if she failed to draw that magic through her amulet . . . but she had come to expect it, unless the Lady were around.

And if she really allowed herself to think the truth, she craved it.

Chell's men swarmed over the ridge, dropping their bows and drawing their swords as they rushed the huts. They kicked in the doors, and Mara felt two more Watchers die. Once again their magic plunged downward, into the mountain.

She got up then, and strode toward the huts, trying to project an air of perfect calm like the Lady's. Chell emerged from one, wiping blood from his blade on a towel he must have found inside. "All dead," he said. "But we're still short a half-dozen."

"They must be underground," she said. She glanced briefly, because she didn't want to look closely, at the Watchers dead on the ground outside the huts, their Masks already crumbled into dust and shards. "Will you hide the bodies?"

He shook his head. "Not seeing any Watchers would arouse suspicion if any patrols do come this way. We'll prop these," he nudged the nearest corpse with his foot, "up against the walls, so they look like they're snoozing, put their hoods up so anyone will have to get close to even see they're not wearing Masks. Might buy us some time."

Mara nodded. "I'll examine the cave entrance."

Chell turned to call out orders. Mara walked away from the dead Watchers to the thing they had been guarding so poorly.

From a distance it had been little more than a shadow in the ground. Now that she was next to it, she could see it was a perfect circle, clearly artificial, the sun penetrating only a short distance into it and showing nothing but black rock, wet on the uphill side where the stream poured over the edge and cascaded down, sparkling until it vanished into the depths. The water reappeared a hundred feet below, splashing into a torch-lit pool only visible to Mara after she shielded her eyes against the afternoon sun. She couldn't see anyone moving down there, or hear anything, but all six of the missing Watchers could be standing just outside her field of vision, and she wouldn't know.

She stood up and brushed dirt from her hands. "Well?" Chell said from behind her.

She glanced over her shoulder. "Hundred feet. Torches at the bottom. Nobody in sight, but I can't really see very well."

Chell nodded, and looked into the depths. "Your wolf won't be able to get down there."

Mara hadn't thought of that, and felt a moment of anxiety at the thought of losing her canine companion . . . and emergency source of magic. She kept it from her face and turned to Whiteblaze. Touching his head again, she projected an image of the Lady. "Go to her," she said. He yelped, turned, and loped away.

Chell stared after him. "I'll never get used to those things."

"Whiteblaze is a sweetheart," Mara told him. "He won't eat you unless I tell him to."

He gave her a raised eyebrow, and she returned an innocent smile. Then she let it slip away. "If there are Watchers at the bottom," she said, "this is a death trap."

Chell grunted. "Maybe we can fix that," he said. He turned toward Lieutenant Antril, who had followed him to the pit edge. Mara caught Antril's gaze over Chell's shoulder. The young man smiled at her and she found herself smiling back. Then his smile disappeared into a look of concentration as Chell spoke to him.

"Change of plan," the prince told the lieutenant. "Take the Watchers into the hut and strip them. Choose four of our men and have them put on the Watchers' uniforms. They'll go down the ladder first."

"Yes, Your Highness." Antril turned and started shouting orders.

Twenty minutes later, the four men Antril had chosen stood in *almost-fitting* Watcher's uniforms, still glistening with blood, at the head of the shaft, exchanging uneasy glances.

"Anyone down there may be surprised the ones up here are coming down, but they won't suspect an attack until they see you don't have Masks," Antril told them. "So keep your head down and your hoods up and strike without warning. If we can get a Watcher alive to question, wonderful, but it's more important none of them gets down to the main compound to sound the alarm. Understand?"

"Aye, aye, sir," each man said in turn.

Antril glanced at Chell, who nodded. The lieutenant turned back to the men. "Go," he said. "We'll be right behind you. Groll, you're first."

A bearded giant roughly twice Mara's size nodded, swung his feet over the side, and descended into the darkness.

The other faux Watchers followed, then Antril himself, then the rest of Chell's men, until only Chell and Mara were left. Mara leaned over and peered down. The first man was just reaching the bottom. She thought she heard shouts, a brief clang of metal, then silence, until Antril's voice called up, "All clear!"

Chell nodded his satisfaction, and indicated the ladder. "After you, milady."

"Thank you, Your Highness," Mara said. They hadn't talked much since their early conversation on the mountainside, but the tension Mara had felt before around Chell had eased. *I'm your friend. I'll always be your friend.* She'd told herself she didn't care about that, that she wanted only to be powerful, a sorceress, feared rather than liked . . .

. . . but wouldn't it be better to be powerful *and* liked? Maybe the two weren't mutually exclusive.

Getting onto the ladder was scarier than she'd thought it would be, but within a few minutes she was descending after the others, spray from the cascade dampening her hair and chilling her and making the wooden rungs more slippery than she'd expected. There was one bad moment when her foot slipped, but after a moment's hard breathing and a shouted, "Are you all right?" from Chell above her, she was able to shout back, "Fine," and resume her descent.

When at last she reached the bottom, stepping from the ladder onto a narrow ledge above the deep pool into which the water fell, then picking her way along that ledge to a broad flat space, she saw Chell's men forming a semicircle around the body of a single Watcher, blood a darker pool amid the glistening puddles left by the constant spray. The sailors had their backs toward the ladder, intently watching the multiple exits from the chamber. Mara counted three . . . no, four: not just the big ones, tall enough to stand up in, that first caught her eye, but another one, an opening near the cascade that looked just about big enough to crawl into and get stuck forever.

Mara really, *really* hoped that wasn't the one they'd have to take. Among her many nightmares were several involving crawling through the depths of the old magic mine, past the collapsed tunnel that held the never-recovered remains of a previous girl who had worked that level.

"Only one Watcher in here," Antril said softly, "but listen!"

Mara listened, and heard a sound she knew all too well: the ring of hammer and chisel on stone.

"Which one is it coming from?" Chell said.

"That one, I think." Antril pointed toward the middle of the three openings.

Chell nodded. "Then let's proceed as before."

Antril turned to the men in the Watcher uniforms. "Groll, Pech, Shreff, Corsan. You're up. Corsan, you take a torch."

He sorted out the rest of his men along similar lines, with every third man taking one of the torches lighting the entry chamber. Then they set off into the tunnel.

This time Chell walked with Mara in the middle of the column, ten men ahead of them and ten behind. The tunnel was broad and level for the first hundred feet or so, and Mara could see that quite a bit of recent work had been done to make it so—more proof they were in the right tunnel, even without the sounds coming from in front of them. Other tunnels opened at haphazard intervals to their left and right. Corsan thrust his torch into each one as they reached it, taking a good look around before motioning for the rest of them to proceed.

The half-dozen torches they carried made it too bright for her to see if any of the stones around them bore traces of magic, but if they did, there couldn't have been much: she didn't feel it calling to her, not nearly as strongly as she felt the magic in the men surrounding her—

Magic slammed into her, with a force she recognized at once. Someone had just died. Behind her.

Another blow. Another death.

She had been prepared for nearby death since entering the cavern, and despite the suddenness, the magic flowed into the amulet. She gasped with pleasure at the rush of it even as she spun to see what had happened.

Two of Chell's men lay on the ground, arrow shafts protruding from them. One had been shot through the throat, the other through the side. Their fellows were spinning and drawing their swords, but the arrows had obviously come through an opening in the rock, a mere slit. As one of the men near the rear reached out for his fallen comrade, another arrow whizzed through the opening, pinging off his helmet. He fell back, cursing.

Chell swore. "We can't even get at the bastard."

"Yes, we can," Mara said. She had magic in her. It needed to be used. She reached out her hand. No one but her saw the red light she hurled at the narrow opening in the rock—but they all saw that rock crack and then explode inward with the sound of a thunderclap, overlaid by a hoarse scream suddenly cut short.

Chell's men raced toward the opening, but Mara was already turning away. She had felt the archer die when the stone had blasted inward. She didn't think they'd find much of him intact.

His magic hadn't come to her like that from Chell's men, though. Once again, it had flowed into the rock.

Chell had started toward the opening, now he turned came back to her. "Are you all right?"

"Why wouldn't I be?" she said.

"The deaths . . . before . . ."

"Things are different now," Mara said. "Because of the Lady." She touched the black lodestone crystal. "We should hurry. I think we've lost the element of surprise."

"You think?" Chell said dryly. He shouted forward, "Antril! No more stealth! Find the Watchers." He turned back. "Leave the bodies. We'll take care of our shipmates after we've eliminated their killers." One of his men was just emerging from the now much-larger opening in the stone. "Drexel, is there a way through?"

"Not anymore," the man said. "Might have been a tunnel, but she collapsed it." His eyes slid from Chell to Mara and quickly away again. He looked frightened.

Chell nodded. "Then we keep moving forward. But I want every side opening thoroughly checked . . . and watched."

"Aye, sir."

The column moved faster now. The tunnel took on a downward slope, until it gave way to a staircase, smooth and even, carved into the stone. "The same rock-dwellers as the Secret City?" Chell said.

"I guess so," Mara said.

"I wonder why they were so fond of caves?" Chell said. "What threat were they hiding from?" He shrugged. "At least it makes our descent much—now what?"

The column had come to a halt at the bottom of the stairs. The sailors had their bows out, arrows nocked, and were peering over the edge of an abyss. "Foot and handholds cut into the rock, Your Highness," Antril said, as the back of the column bunched up with the front. "But if there are Watchers waiting down there, we'll be sitting ducks as we descend."

"I think we can safely assume there *are* Watchers waiting down there, Lieutenant." Chell peered cautiously over the edge. "No lights."

Mara suddenly realized that the sound of steel on stone had stopped, though she couldn't have said how long ago. "Unless they're just running ahead of us," she said. "Trying to get down to the mine and warn them."

Chell nodded. "Or both. Leave someone with a bow down there and the rest go ahead."

"And every minute we delay here they get farther ahead," Antril said. "So enough dithering." He paused. "Uh . . . Your Highness."

Chell raised an eyebrow. "You have a plan, Lieutenant?"

"We were told there were twelve Watchers," Antril said. "Four died up above, two in the entrance cavern, one behind us. That leaves five. They will send at least two to give warning. That leaves three. And there is no reason to leave more than one here. The others, if there are others, will lie in wait farther down the trail.

"The one below is waiting for us to use this stone . . . ladder, I guess you'd call it. So we don't use the ladder." He pointed up. "See that?"

Mara squinted into the dimness. Directly above the shaft, someone had driven a metal ring into the stone . . . no, more than one. Remnants of some long-gone version of the Lady's lift or the mine's man-engine, she guessed: some way to move people and supplies up and down the shaft more easily than via ladder or rope.

"Ah," Chell said. "Good thinking, Lieutenant . . . and good eyes to see that."

"Thank you, sir," Antril said. He turned toward a young sailor. "Staffel, you're our best archer. We're going to lower you into the cavern. Shoot whatever you find there."

Staffel turned a little pale, but nodded. "Just don't let me spin, sir," he said. "Weak stomach. All right on a ship, up and down don't bother me, but get me going in circles . . ."

"We'll do our best," Antril said. He glanced at one of the four sailors disguised as Watchers. "Groll, you're carrying rope. Haul it out. You four will handle this end." He pointed at an upthrust spire of rock attached to the stairs a few feet back. "Use that stalagmite to take some of the strain." Finally he turned to Mara. "We need light for this to work. Can your Gift help?"

"Of course." She could still feel magic inside her, thrumming in her veins, tingling along every nerve, warming her blood, making her feel . . . *alive*, she thought. *Very, very alive.* "I can light the cavern: very, very bright for a second, then more dimly for several minutes. If Staffel keeps his eyes closed, the first flash should blind anyone who is down there, then leave them lit up for him to see."

"Good." Antril looked at Staffel. "Got that, Staffel? Keep your eyes closed until you see light through your eyelids. When it fades, open them and loose at will."

"Yes, sir."

First, though, Staffel's archery skills were put to less bloody use: a thin bit of cord was attached to the end of one of his arrows, and the other to the end of the climbing rope Groll had produced from his pack. Staffel shot the arrow through the metal ring, nailing it on the first try. The arrow hit the roof and then dropped, swinging close enough on the end of the string for one of Chell's men to grab it. He pulled on it, tugging the rope in its turn through the metal ring.

Again Mara wondered about the ancient race that had built the Secret City and this place. They had left no records that anyone had ever been able to decipher—just stone ruins and a few very odd cave paintings that showed creatures that certainly did not exist in Aygrima now.

Had they had magic? No one knew.

Maybe they had it, and it destroyed them, Mara thought. *Maybe the threat they were hiding from in their stone cities was someone like the Lady of Pain and Fire. Someone like me.*

She put that unsettling thought out of her mind. *Ancient history,* she told herself firmly.

In a few minutes everything was set. Staffel tied one end of the rope into a kind of complicated sling that looped around his chest, his stomach, and between his legs. The rope ran through the metal ring in the ceiling back to Groll and the other three sailors wearing Watcher garb. It looped around the stalagmite. Groll and his fellows all had a firm grip on it; the slack lay in coils behind them.

"Haul away," Antril said. The sailors backed up, the rope sliding easily around the stalagmite's smooth, wet stone surface, and Staffel gasped a little as the rope pulled him off the ledge until he hung in space.

"Lower away," Antril said, and Staffel, bow in hand, sank silently into the depths as the four sailors let out more rope, hand over hand.

Mara reached inside for her remaining magic. The Lady had taught her this use of it and for just this purpose: she had told Mara it might prove useful in the battles they could have to fight. She had to be looking at the spot where she would conjure it, though, so she stretched out full-length on the stone and stuck her head over the edge, waiting for the signal.

It came: a brief whistle. Mara hurled the last of the magic she had absorbed from the dead Watchers down into the cavern below. Light exploded, blinding her—why hadn't she thought to close her own eyes?—then dimmed to a more tolerable glow and began to slowly fade away.

She could see Staffel now, a spider-like black blot at the end of the rope, and strangely glistening rock at the bottom of the cliff. *Must be water down there,* she thought. Staffel loosed a single arrow that flashed through the waning magical light and disappeared beneath the bottom of the opposite wall of the chasm. A moment later Groll shouted from behind her, "He's on the bottom!"

Chell looked over the edge. "Staffel?" he called. "Staffel, report!"

A long moment's silence, then, "Here, Your Highness. All clear. But there's . . . something you should see."

"The light will fade in a moment," Mara warned.

"Are there torches?" Antril shouted.

"Yes, sir," Staffel shouted back. His voice sounded oddly strained.

"Light them. We'll be down in minutes." Antril glanced at Chell, who nodded at him. He turned to the others. "Same order as before. Groll, let the rope go over the edge—we'll coil it up when we get down. Let's move!"

In a few minutes they were heading down, using the handholds cut in the stone, Mara once more second-last in front of Chell. She kept expecting to hear the chatter of conversation down below as the men reached the bottom, but it stayed strangely silent.

And then she reached the bottom herself and saw why the rock had glistened so strangely in her conjured light: not from water, but from blood.

Gore covered the floor of the chamber into which they had descended, high and vaulted like the Great Chamber, a lake of blood that had poured from the bodies that lay everywhere: unMasked men and women and boys and girls barely past their Masking age, beheaded, gutted, split from crown to crotch. The room stank of voided bowels, mingled with the coppery scent of blood and the reek of vomit. Mara fought hard not to add her own stomach's contents to the noxious mix, and though she'd always had a weak stomach, succeeded—because the white-hot rage choking her left no space for anything to rise through her throat.

Rage. The perfect fuel for her magical Gift, the Lady had taught her. She made no effort to control it, because she knew exactly how she would use it. "They slaughtered them," she growled. "Like animals."

"So they wouldn't slow them down," Chell said. "And to bring us to a halt." He glanced at her. "You didn't feel their deaths?"

"There's too much black lodestone around," Mara said. "It sucks away the magic unless I'm right on top of it like the men killed up above."

Antril stood wide-eyed and white-faced, staring around him with face slackened in shock. Chell strode over to him. "Get a grip, Lieutenant," he said in a low voice. "Give your orders."

Antril's gaze shot to him. "Yes, Your Highness," he said. He took a deep breath and turned to the others. "You see what . . ." His voice broke, making him sound, for a moment, even younger than he was, but when he spoke again, he had regained control of it. "You see what we're fighting against. And the ones who did this are getting away. All except that one." He pointed at a Watcher flat on his back in the gore, an arrow protruding from his left eye, his Mask in shards, his face wearing a look of blank surprise, bow still clutched in his lifeless hand. "Staffel did for that one. Could be four left. We need to get them all before they get to the main garrison down below. We need them to pay for this." His savage gesture took in the whole room. "So let's move out. Groll, leave the rope. We've got more." He pointed at the only exit from the room. "That way. Move!"

With a growl of assent, the men moved forward. Mara fell into her accustomed place in the line, fury seething inside her. She grabbed onto it as the Lady had taught her, shaped it into a white-hot flame at the core of her being.

The Watchers would pay for what they had done. All of them.

Leaving a trail of bloody footprints on the smooth black stone, the strike force hurried after the Watchers.

◆ ◆ ◆

"Will we be able to catch them?" Mara asked Chell privately as they descended yet another long flight of stairs carved by the ancients. The anger still burned in her, like a fire banked overnight, ready to break out the moment she needed it.

"Probably not," Chell said in a low voice, the sound of booted feet on stone masking his words from the sailors around them. "The best we can hope for is to be so close that whatever warning they give has little time to be effective." He glanced at her. "You'll have to be ready to open the gate as soon as we reach the bottom of the mountain."

"I'll be ready."

"You'll have enough magic?"

Mara, remembering the cavern she had discovered, the rainbow glow of pure magic painting its walls in ever-shifting colors, simply nodded.

"It looks like the ancients have provided us with a path all the way to the bottom," Chell said. "Did you see any sign of their work down below?"

Mara thought back to that terrifying journey into the heart of the mountain, rope tied around her waist, Watchers at the other end. She frowned. "I didn't think about it at the time," she said, "what with being terrified out of my wits and all, but . . . the passage the stream poured out of was very straight. It could have been shaped. The cavern I found looked natural . . . but I didn't explore it. I didn't have time before they were pulling me back out into the open."

Chell nodded thoughtfully. He looked to the right, where the stream ran in a clearly artificial channel, its constant rushing noise masking any sound of the Watchers they were pursuing, but hopefully also masking their own.

They had seen no light ahead of them, but the tunnels changed direction frequently, zigzagging in switchbacks to minimize the downward slope, the switchbacks alternating with stairs like the ones they descended now. Their own torches showed no decoration on any of the walls, but there were side tunnels and chambers carved in the rock, dark, gaping mouths that hinted of mysterious secrets, though many had collapsed, the torchlight giving glimpses of tumbled tons of stone.

If the Autarch is overthrown, Mara thought, *someone really has to come back here and explore all of this.*

But exploration would have to wait. They hurried on in the wake of the fleeing Watchers. And all the time, Mara kept her anger alive, deep down inside, a spark she could turn into a conflagration the instant she needed it—the instant she had magic to fuel it.

Some three hours after they entered the cavern, they descended a final flight of stairs and found themselves in a long corridor, gently sloping downward. The stream flowed alongside it down its artificial channel.

Mara caught a glimpse of torchlight far ahead of them. "There!" she cried, pointing.

"I saw it," Chell said. "Farther ahead than I'd hoped, but not as far as I feared." He looked at Antril. "Double-time," he said. "Let's see if we can't catch those bastards."

"Aye, Your Highness," said the young lieutenant. "You heard him, lads!"

And with that, the men started running. Mara would have dashed off with them, but Chell held her back with a hand on her arm for a moment. "I should be there if they catch them," she protested.

"There are eighteen of them and only a couple of Watchers," Chell said. "What would they need you for?" He frowned a little. "Unless it's to suck down the Watchers' magic?"

"You make it sound . . . disgusting," Mara said.

"Sorry," Chell said. "It's just not something I can quite get my head around."

But you're more than willing to use the magic I "suck down," aren't you? she thought angrily. "We've waited long enough." She charged after Antril and the others, Chell easily keeping pace with her.

Ahead, the light grew. There was too much now to be just from the Watchers' torches. *The cavern,* Mara thought. The light wasn't the multi-colored glow of magic, however, but the familiar yellow of open flames. *What have they done to that beautiful chamber?*

She couldn't see any details, just the glow of light, and the silhouettes of Chell's men against it. Swords glinted and flashed, there were shouts and curses. She gasped as someone died and she was brushed by his escaping magic, though it didn't reach her full-force because it was once more pulled into the black lodestone all around her.

She needed magic. She'd thought to use the magic filling the cavern, but she couldn't feel it, couldn't reach it. *I need to get closer.* Without even realizing it, she lengthened her stride, filled with new energy. The end of the tunnel swelled in her vision. She could see wooden platforms now, the lake, Chell's men battling Watchers, unMasked cowering in the dark. What she couldn't see, as she glimpsed the far wall of the cavern, was any sign of the vast storehouse of untouched magic the cavern had once represented, the magic she had counted on. *They've already ruined it*, she thought. *They've already stripped the walls, crushed the stone, sent the magic to the Autarch.* There had to be magic all around her, but buried deep in such an enormous mass of black lodestone, it would not let her draw it out in the amount, or as fast as, she needed.

But there was still magic to be had. So much magic, filling the unMasked. Magic she needed, magic she could ignite with the spark of rage inside her to do what needed to be done.

So she took it.

As she burst out into the cavern, the dozen or so unMasked closest to the tunnel fell to their knees, dropped their tools, and collapsed unconscious, the living magic they contained ripped from them like unripe fruit from a tree. The remaining unMasked screamed. But she knew she had killed none of those who had collapsed; she knew within the breadth of a hair how much she could safely take. The fallen unMasked would live. And so she did not spare them another thought, not with the power pouring into her. Filtered through the amulet at her breast, it did not hurt at all. Instead, it filled her, satiated her, satisfied the need that lurked always beneath the surface of her skin, like an itch that wouldn't go away.

She could control that need when she had to—but now she didn't have to. Now she could give into it, and give into it she did.

Half a dozen Watchers battled Chell's men. Chell was right, they didn't need her: one Watcher was already down and the others beset. But she didn't care. She saw the Watchers, and seeing them she saw all the Watchers: the ones she had known in the old mine, the ones who had stood by while her father was executed, and the ones who had attacked the Secret City and chased the unMasked Army along the shoreline. Most of all, she saw the cavern of blood where the Watchers they had followed here had slaughtered the unMasked workers rather than let them be rescued.

Rage-fueled magic leaped from her outstretched hands. She could have blasted the Watchers before her into white dust. But that was too clean a death. Instead, they exploded in a red rain of flesh and entrails, bone and blood. Their bodies' released magic tried to pour into the rock, but she greedily seized it instead, "sucking it down" as Chell would have it, once more filtering it through the black lodestone crystal so it did not burn, so their death-twisted soulprints would not haunt her dreams. Her nightmares were a thing of the past: more largesse of the Lady, the Lady to whom she owed so much.

Ignoring the horrified stares of Chell's men, ignoring Prince Chell himself, single-minded with focused fury, she stalked across the wooden walkway that had been built over the lake. The narrow passage she had crawled through alongside the stream had been shaped into a proper tunnel wide enough for two men to walk abreast. She strode out through it. No warning had made it out into the ravine beyond. The only Watchers she could see were standing atop the wall across the ravine's mouth.

Her instructions were to open the gate: a trivial use of the power filling her. Instead, she raised her hands and, with the magic from the unMasked workers and the dead Watchers, sent a blast of red light the length of the ravine. Wall and gate alike blew outward in a thunderous rain of stones, timber and iron, mingled with red blood and white bone. She felt a dozen Watchers die . . . but not all of them. Some still lived in the ruin of the wall.

She strode through the ravine, sensed a Watcher cowering behind a boulder, flicked a hand, and sent the boulder crashing back against the ravine wall. Blood sprayed the rocks.

Out in the valley beyond the gates the unMasked Army, the Lady, and her followers rushed forward. Mara held herself still, rage still boiling beneath her skin. She saw the Lady hold up her hand, saw the villagers stop in their tracks. Behind them, the unMasked Army and remaining sailors likewise waited. She picked out Hyram, grim-faced, sword in hand, Keltan beside him.

She'd left them nothing to do. She smiled at that, a death's head grin.

The Lady came on alone. "Well done," she said when she reached Mara.

Mara inclined her head.

"Let the magic go," the Lady said softly. "Give it to me."

Mara narrowed her eyes. Who was this old woman to take what was rightfully hers?

The thought shocked her. She didn't understand where it had come from. "Of course," she said. She reached out her hands. The Lady took them. Mara released the magic she still held within her, gasping a little as she did so. Suddenly drained, she swayed. The Lady caught her arm.

"Now let me see what is what," the Lady said. "Come." She took Mara's arm and led her back toward the cavern. Together they walked down the tunnel alongside the stream, emerging into the mine a few moments later. The unMasked workers were clustered together against the far wall. The ones Mara had taken magic from were groaning and beginning to stir. Chell and his men stood guard. "We were uncertain what to do with them," Chell said. "Do we release them?"

"Of course you release them!" Mara exclaimed.

"Quiet, child." The Lady let go of her arm. "Stay here."

She strode the remaining length of the wooden walkway spanning the lake, whose water, already sadly churned with mud, was now tinged with red from the slain Watchers. Mara gripped the amulet at her neck. She remembered killing those Watchers. She remembered *how* she had killed them. In her rage it hadn't seemed to matter. In her rage, it hadn't seemed to matter that she had torn magic from some of these unMasked without permission, without even considering what it might do to them. The fact that the amulet had kept both actions from hurting her as they always had before, that she had not felt the impact of the dying Watchers' magic, that she had not burned in agony with the influx of raw magic from living humans, did not change what she had done.

Reach down inside yourself and find your rage and hate, the Lady had told her. *Don't fear letting it out. Learn to use it to power your magic. Do that, and there is almost nothing you cannot achieve.*

The Lady had clearly been right.

She should have been happier about it. *This is a war,* she told herself. *The Watchers serve the Autarch. To destroy the Autarch, we must defeat the Watchers. And look at what they have done to the unMasked . . .*

But then, look what *she* had done to the unMasked.

Confused, troubled, she had been staring at the rough wooden planks of the walkway. Now she raised her head, and saw that the Lady had reached the unMasked.

She couldn't hear what Arilla was saying, if anything. But she saw what she did.

She waved a hand casually, and Chell and his men sank unconscious to the wooden planking. Then the Lady reached out and touched the forehead of a young unMasked woman only a couple of years older than Mara, though with the pinched, hard look to her scarred face Mara remembered all too well from her time in the labor camp. The girl's face went slack.

And then she collapsed, bonelessly, falling to the planks with the thud, like a sack of meal thrown from a wagon.

And Arilla stepped to the right, and touched the forehead of a burly, bearded man with a permanent sneer . . . and he dropped the same way.

The other unMasked trembled, faces pale, eyes wide, but they couldn't seem to move. Her feet, too, seemed to have grown roots. With great effort she stumbled forward. "Arilla, stop!" she cried. She found it hard to speak, and suddenly realized why: there was magic flowing from the Lady, subtle magic, so that even with her Gifted sight Mara had not recognized it, had only thought it brighter in the cavern than the flickering torches could account for. "Arilla, what . . . ?"

"They are all broken," the Lady said without turning around. Another touch, and a boy dropped lifeless. "The Masks rejected these for a reason. We cannot take them with us. We cannot leave them behind us. They are good for only one thing." Another touch. This time it was a skinny dark-skinned man who rolled off the planking as he fell, falling into the muddy water with a splash and floating facedown. "I am taking their magic to make myself stronger. I am storing it up in my amulet. And I will use it against the Autarch who has made such evil use of them. In this way their miserable lives will have had some meaning." A woman fell. A girl. A boy. "You left some magic in those you drew from. I will take it all."

Mara felt sick, felt betrayed, felt . . . anger. Rage. The same kind of rage she had felt against the Watchers just minutes before. It roared up in her like a bonfire of dry wood. The Lady had drained her, but there was still a little magic to be had in the walls of the cavern, if she pulled hard enough. She struggled to reach it, felt some of it flow to her, but sluggishly, like syrup on a winter's day. "Arilla, stop! You're *murdering* them!"

The Lady rounded on her, and Mara saw that her eyes blazed once more with magic, as bright and white as the sun. "You can't murder cattle," Arilla snarled. She glanced at Chell and his sleeping men. Then, face twisted with fury, she turned back to Mara, who had slowed again as she approached the Lady, unable to penetrate the magic permeating the very air around her. "How *dare* you! How dare you question *me!* I have been working toward the overthrow of the Autarch since before your father was born. No one else can destroy him. Certainly not *you*." Her voice dripped with contempt. "You will never be what I am. You will never even be what I was when I fought the Autarch as a young girl. You are a tool, nothing more. I needed you to breach the borders. You were of some use to me here, and will be useful again at the mining camp. After that, I have one final—one *very* final—use for you. Until then, you will remember your place, and keep to it. I will make sure of it. You will not challenge me again." She paused. "And I think . . . yes. I think it is time to prepare you for your final fate."

What fate? Mara burned with rage, but she had managed to gather only a flicker of magic to herself, and the Lady brimmed with power. She could do nothing against such a force.

The Lady strode toward Mara. She reached out her hand. She touched Mara's forehead.

In a soundless explosion of white light, the world went away.

TEN

Sequestered

MARA WOKE IN the Lady's pavilion, wearing only her under-clothes, wrapped in her blankets atop her usual bed of fragrant pine boughs. She stared up at the sloping white canvas, her mind a blank. What day was it? Where were they? What had happened?

Nothing came to her. She heard a whine from her right and turned her head to see Whiteblaze looking at her alertly. He gave a short yip and licked her left hand, which lay outside the blanket. She didn't remember entering the tent or lying down. In fact, the last thing she remembered was the discussion with Edrik and Chell of who would lead the strike force up the mountain to the new magic mine's "back door." Then she'd . . . gone back to the camp?

Gone to the Lady's pavilion?

Gone to *bed*?

That didn't seem likely.

What's wrong with me? she thought with a touch of panic. *What's happened to my memory?*

Whiteblaze yelped again, then turned and trotted out through the tent flap. Mara turned her head to watch him go, but she didn't try to sit up. She felt weak, drained. Her black lodestone amulet still rested on her chest, a reassuring weight, but she could sense no magic anywhere. It was almost like . . .

She blinked. It wasn't *almost* like, it was *exactly* like wearing the iron Mask placed on her when she had been taken prisoner in Tamita. Someone had blocked her Gift. And the only person with the power to do that, at least here, was the Lady.

But why would the Lady have done so? And had she also blocked Mara's memories in the process?

Could she *do* that?

Mara was uneasily certain she could. Hadn't she talked about how the way magic was bound up with a person's soulprint made it possible to manipulate people with magic? The Autarch did it through Masks. The Lady didn't need Masks.

Had Arilla removed her memories? And if so . . . what else had she done to Mara's mind?

She tried to raise her head, to get up and go in search of the Lady. But weariness held her down like a lead weight, and she slumped back again, breathing hard.

Fortunately, she didn't have to find the Lady. The Lady entered the tent a moment later, following Whiteblaze, three of her own wolves with her. She came over to Mara's side and looked down at her, unsmiling. "How do you feel?" she said.

"Like a lump of wet clay," Mara said. "What happened? Why can't I remember anything? We were planning to go up the mountain . . ."

"You did go up the mountain," the Lady said. "And successfully opened the gate to the mine. We have taken it. The Watchers who guarded it are dead."

Mara blinked. "I opened the gate?" She closed her eyes, tried to find the memories. But there was nothing. She opened her eyes again. "Why can't I remember it?"

"You were careless," the Lady said. "There was considerable death around you during the attack, and you let some of the released magic slip around the amulet. The soulprints tore through your mind."

"And destroyed my memories?" Mara said. "That's never happened before."

"No," the Lady said. "*I* have blocked your memories. I was afraid that if I did not, you might not wake at all."

Mara frowned. It made *some* sense. When she'd killed the Watcher outside the very cavern they'd been trying to find a way into, she'd awakened days later in the Secret City, in the chamber where Grelda placed those she expected to die. That had been when Grelda had introduced her to the noxious potion she had relied on many times since to block the nightmares. Grelda, though not Gifted herself, had said she had been suffering from "a surfeit of magic." But the circumstances had been quite different. She had killed the Watcher, and certainly his soulprint must have slammed into her with great force, but the real problem had seemed to be that she had drawn too much magic to her too quickly, the incredible store of it in the cavern tearing through her like a hurricane. She'd had no control at all of her Gift then. Now, she had, thanks to hours of practice with both Arilla and, before her, Shelra, the Autarch's Mistress of Magic. A mere "surfeit of magic" would not affect her now the way it had then. But why would the impact of multiple soulprints? She'd experienced that before, too, and though she'd paid the price in nightmares, she'd never been close to death herself as a result. What was different this time?

"You said the Watchers are all dead," she said. "What about the un-Masked workers?"

"I took care of them," the Lady said. "You need not worry."

Mara nodded. They were already fading from her thoughts. "Are we still at the mine?"

"Not far away."

"And when did all this happen?"

"Two days ago," the Lady said.

Two days! Mara shook her head. "It's hard to believe. It's so weird to have no memories."

The Lady smiled slightly. "They're still there. Just inaccessible. Perhaps someday it will be safe to return them to you."

"You've also blocked my Gift," Mara said. "Why?"

"For your own good. You will heal much faster this way."

"But why do I *need* healing?" Mara said, frustrated. "I've experienced this sort of thing before and survived without anyone blocking my memories or my Gift. What happened this time that made it so much worse?"

"You must trust me," the Lady said. She reached out and brushed the hair off of Mara's forehead with a gentle hand, and Mara felt a hint of magic in that touch. She suddenly felt both stronger and calmer. "Are you hungry?"

"Starving," Mara said. "And in rather desperate need of . . . um, relief."

"There is a chamber pot at the foot of your bed," the Lady said. "I will leave you for a short time, if you think you can manage on your own."

"I think so," Mara said. "I don't feel as weak as I did when I woke."

"I just removed a light muscle block I had placed on you," the Lady said. "You should be able to move around normally now. Just be careful getting out of bed—you may still be light-headed." She nodded at Whiteblaze. "If you have any difficulty, he will come get me. Otherwise I will send you food in, say, fifteen minutes."

Mara nodded. "Thank you," she said.

"You're welcome, Mara." The Lady touched her forehead again. "I am glad you are recovering. I have great things planned for you." She turned and went out.

With only a little shakiness, Mara used the chamber pot. She found her clothes in their usual chest, and dressed. She was sitting on the Lady's stool at the far end of the pavilion from the entrance when the flap opened and a villager came in whom she knew by sight but not by name, one of the Lady's Cadre. He crossed to her, carrying a tray bearing bread and stew and hard cheese and cold water. "Thank you," Mara said as she took it.

The man nodded and turned to go.

"Wait!" Mara said. "I wanted to ask you—"

But the villager left without even looking around.

Ordered not to tell me anything, she thought. *What's going on?*

She didn't find out that day. The Lady would tell her nothing more. "It's for your own good," she said. Mara wasn't allowed to leave the tent, and a guard at the door, another of the Lady's elite corps of villagers, made sure she obeyed. Whiteblaze stayed by her side. No one except the Lady and the villager who brought her meals entered the tent. Neither he nor the guard would speak to her, and the Lady would only say that they would be breaking camp the next day, and moving on to their next target: the old magic mine, the slave labor camp where so many unMasked had been used and abused over the decades.

"Will you unblock my Gift for that?" Mara asked the Lady that evening as they ate supper together. "Please. I want . . . I *need* to help you destroy it."

"Of course," the Lady said. "I need your help to do so. But not until we reach it. For your own good."

Mara tried to push away her mounting frustration with that answer. "Why aren't you allowing anyone to come see me? I've been alone all day."

The Lady reached for another piece of bread and dipped it in the mixture of oil and salt on her plate. "Mara, no one has even *tried* to see you."

"No one?" Mara said blankly.

"I'm sorry, Mara," the Lady said. She reached out and touched Mara's hand. "I was afraid it would come to this."

"To what?" Mara stared at her. "What are you talking about?"

"Your . . . 'friends.' I suspect they have not tried to see you because . . . they are afraid of you."

"Afraid . . . ?"

"Your clearing of the pass was impressive, and inspired awe. But in the ravine . . ." She shook her head. "I know you do not remember, but you were like a force of nature. You killed almost all the Watchers single-handed. Chell and his men were with you, but had they not been, it would not have changed a thing. Men like Chell, and those of the unMasked Army . . . yes, even Keltan . . . they do not like to be shown to be useless. Especially by a girl. They don't know how to deal with your power."

Mara looked down at the Lady's hand touching hers. There was some-thing about that touch that made her feel uneasy, though she couldn't understand why. She drew her hand back. "But I'd never hurt them," she said.

"And I'm sure they understand that . . . intellectually. But having seen what you did in the ravine. . . ." The Lady drew her own hand back and took another piece of bread. "Frankly, I was a little frightened of you myself."

"But I can't even remember it!" Mara cried.

"I know it's difficult," the Lady said. "But try not to fret. In time I hope it will be safe to return those memories to you. And in the meantime . . . the labor camp awaits."

"What if the same thing happens there? What if . . . whatever I do . . . ends up hurting me again? What if you have to take my memories of that battle, too?"

"I think it unlikely," said the Lady, "from what you have told me, that you could feel any ambiguity about whatever actions may be required to destroy the mine. Wouldn't you agree?"

Mara thought about the mine, about everything she had done there, about everything she had seen. Those memories were all-too-intact. "Yes," she said. "I would."

"Good," said the Lady. "Because I will need your help once again. You have shown a skill at destroying walls and gates. Would you like to destroy some more?"

This time she didn't hesitate at all. "Yes," she said fervently. "Oh, yes."

They moved out the next morning. The routine of the Lady's Cadre packing up the pavilion and loading it on the packhorses was familiar, but when Mara attempted to move away from the small circle of the members of the "human wolfpack" and their horses, Hamil stopped her at once. "No," he said. "The Lady forbids it."

He had put his hand on her upper arm. Whiteblaze growled at him, and anger, sudden and fierce, flashed into fire inside her. If she had had her magic, she would have made him regret that touch . . .

But her magic was still blocked, even if her anger was not. She jerked free. "Why?"

"She said to tell you, if you asked," Hamil said, lowering his hand, "that it would be unwise to expose yourself to the others' accounts of the events at the cavern: that to do so could damage you further. She said that she—and you—cannot afford to risk that when we are so close to the attack on the labor camp."

Mara stood still. "And what if I just walk past you?"

"Then I am ordered to stop you."

"You'd hurt me?"

"I am twice your size," Hamil said, spreading his hands. "I do not think I would need to."

Mara glared at him, then looked past him at the main part of the camp. The last of the tents and supplies were being loaded onto the horses. She could see Edrik and Hyram in conversation with Keltan, but no sign of Chell. *What are they talking about?*

She turned her gaze back to Hamil. "What did *you* see at the cavern?" she demanded. "What did *you* see me do?"

"You must know I cannot tell you that."

"Because the Lady told you not to."

"The Lady commands." Hamil blinked hard and his mouth twitched, as though some strong emotion had poured through him. "The Lady commands," he repeated. "Please do not make me use physical force, Mara. The Lady commands, and I will obey, but I would . . . prefer not to."

"Very well," Mara said. Her anger had subsided. Hamil had no more choice than she. *The Lady commands*, she thought. "I'll be good."

"Thank you," Hamil said. But he watched her closely as she turned and went back to stand with the packhorses. Whiteblaze growled at him one more time before following her. She put her hand on his head as he sat on his haunches close by her feet, and waited for the Lady.

But the Lady did not join her Cadre. Mara saw her, as they set out down the valley in which they had been camped, walking at the head of the column with Edrik and Chell. Hyram and Keltan walked together some distance behind. None of them looked back as though trying to locate *her*, and her anger flashed through her again, so strong and sudden it startled her. *You never used to get angry this quickly*, she thought.

Well, she answered herself, *if anger is a tool, the more you use it, the better you get at using it. And when we reach the mine, and the block is lifted from my Gift, I want to be very good at using it indeed.*

With anger warming her soul, she strode toward the one place in Aygrima she had once thought she never wanted to see again . . . and now wanted to see very much, one last—one very, *very* final—time.

ELEVEN
The Return

THE EXTENT OF Mara's isolation became clear as the trek continued. No one but the members of the Lady's Cadre came near her, but they were with her constantly, ready, like Hamil, to stop her if she tried to wander from their midst.

That night, the villagers set up the pavilion, lit the fire at its center, and brought her food. She ate sitting cross-legged on her bedroll with Whiteblaze curled nose to tail at her side. She felt cozy and comfortable . . . and yet very, very far from *relaxed*.

The journey from the old mine to the cavern had taken only a day and a half. They could potentially reach the mine on the morrow. She wanted—*needed*—to know what would happen then.

Whiteblaze's head came up and he barked once, then the tent flap swirled open and Arilla entered, accompanied by four of her wolves, the rest presumably serving as scouts and guards as they came ever nearer to the mine and its Watchers. "Mara," said the Lady. "How are you feeling?"

"How do you think?" Mara demanded. "I'm missing my memories *and* my magic, and I've also discovered I can neither talk to nor be approached by any of my friends. I'm a prisoner."

The Lady sighed. "I know it is difficult," she said. "And I know I've said this overmuch, but . . . it's for your own good. And as for your 'friends' . . ." She shook her head. "As I told you earlier, I do not think they are as anxious to see you as you might think." She went to her bench, opposite the fire from the tent's entrance, and sat down on it. The wolves settled around her feet. "They are ordinary people. Not even Gifted. You know how frightening our abilities can seem to those who have no grasp of the world of magic."

"But Chell and Keltan have seen me use magic before," Mara protested. "They have seen me *kill* before, in horrible ways." She remembered Watchers and their horses entombed in earth suddenly become liquid, then solid again, crushed to death in an instant, as Chell looked on. "What could I have possibly done at the ravine that would have been worse?" She let some of her so-ready-to-hand anger into her voice. "You're keeping them away from me on purpose. Your human wolfpack won't let them near."

"It's true I *told* my Cadre to do so," the Lady said, "but in fact they have had to do nothing. Neither Chell nor Keltan nor Hyram nor Edrik nor any other member of the unMasked Army or Chell's crews have asked, or tried, to see you." She spread her hands. "I'm sorry, Mara, but that is the truth."

The tent flap swished aside and Mara turned, heart leaping, thinking one of her friends was about to prove the Lady wrong: but it was only one of the villagers with the Lady's supper.

Mara watched the Lady eat with her long, thin fingers, her teeth, strong and straight despite her age, delicately tearing the pale flesh from the bones of a roast fowl of some sort, hunted from the forests through which they traveled. *How does she do it?* Mara wondered. *She's of an age with Catilla, but while Catilla is spry enough, she could never have made this journey. And yet the Lady seems sometimes to find the going less strenuous than I.*

Only one answer made sense. *She must be using magic to keep herself strong.* And the source of that magic had to be the villagers. As the Autarch did through Masks, the Lady did without them.

Before the journey had begun, she had tried to deny Keltan's claim that there was something odd about the way the Lady interacted with her followers. But now, since the Lady had blocked both her Gift and her memories of the events in the ravine, she was no longer certain she could trust the Lady as much as she'd once thought. Even though the Lady told her everything that had been done to her had been to keep her from harm, how could she be certain of that when she couldn't remember what had happened?

How could she be certain of anything?

The Lady set aside her plate and wiped her fingers and mouth delicately on a white cloth napkin. "Now," she said, laying the napkin over the polished bones of her meal, "let us discuss our plans for tomorrow. Come, sit beside me."

Mara moved to the Lady's side as the Lady moved over to make room on the red-cushioned bench. The Lady gestured, and an image of the mine appeared in thin air in front of them, perfect in every detail. Mara gasped. "How could you know what it looks like?"

"My wolves have scouted it for me many times," the Lady said. She smiled. "I could also project what it smells like to a wolf, but I don't think you would enjoy it."

Mara shook her head. "I didn't enjoy smelling it as a human."

"My plan is simple," said the Lady. "There are two gates into the mine. The main gate in the south wall," she pointed to it, "and the smaller gate at the northern end of the east wall through which the wagons loaded with magic depart for Tamita." She indicated that one. "We have two tasks: to destroy the Watchers, and to make sure the mine can no longer function."

"And to free the unMasked," Mara said.

"I have not forgotten the unMasked," the Lady said. "But I do not think they will be fighting in defense of the mine."

"Some might," Mara said. "Some of the trustees—the ones who lord it over the others."

"If they fight with the Watchers, they will die with the Watchers," said the Lady. She indicated the main gate again. "You will use your Gift to open the front gate. The Watchers will swarm there, where our main force will be arrayed. Between your Gift and the skill of our fighters—who greatly outnumber the Watchers—the battle should be over in short order."

"What if they have Gifted fighters among them?" Mara said. "I was outmatched when we encountered them during the battle on the beach."

"I think it unlikely," the Lady said. "Remember that the Autarch's forces are massed at the ravine where I was last seen, and north of the Secret City. The mines are guarded, certainly, but the Watchers are far more focused on keeping the unMasked *in* than repelling attack from *without*. Those with enough of the Gift to use magic in combat are too valuable to waste on mere prison duty."

"And while *we* are storming the gate," Mara said, "what will *you* be doing?" She heard the note of accusation in her voice, kin to the anger and suspicion she felt, and wondered again where both had come from.

The Lady, if she even noted it, did not take offense. "I and my Cadre—my 'human wolfpack'—will be waiting for your attack. Once it is underway, we will simply and quietly open the corner gate . . . and I will see to it that this mine never again produces magic to serve the Autarch."

"There'll be unMasked workers in the mine," Mara said.

"I am aware of it," the Lady said. "I assure you, I will take proper care of them, just as I did at the ravine."

Mara stared at the camp and felt butterflies in her stomach—but countering the trepidation was a feeling of fierce joy. *At last*, she thought. *At last.*

For Katia.

She had failed to save the only friend she had made in the mining camp . . . but maybe she could avenge her.

They reached the vicinity of the camp at noon the next day. Scouts reported that it seemed to be operating normally. The Watchers in the guard towers were, as usual, focused far more on the prisoners in the camp than the surrounding forest. The unMasked Army and Chell's men prepared for combat quietly out of sight and sound of the camp, checking armor and weapons, talking in low voices. Mara saw Chell and Keltan from a distance, talking to each other. *About what?* she wondered.

The Lady also spoke to Chell and to Edrik during those hours of waiting, before going off with her Cadre. They were getting into position for their portion of the attack, which was to commence the moment the sun dipped behind the foothills to the west.

The very last thing the Lady did before slipping away through the woods was to come to where Mara sat with her back against a tree trunk, her knees drawn up, Whiteblaze stretched out at her side, waiting for the interminable time until sunset to drag by. Mara looked up as the Lady approached, accompanied by four wolves. The rest were keeping watch all around the camp to ensure no hunter or magic-gatherer or wagonful of unMasked came near enough to spot the Lady's army and give the alarm. "It's almost time," the Lady said. "Stand up."

Mara clambered to her feet.

"Stand still," the Lady commanded, and reached out her hand and touched Mara's forehead.

Instantly she felt her Gift flood back, so suddenly she gasped and staggered back against the tree trunk.

The Lady withdrew her hand. "We brought several urns of magic from the ravine," she said. "I am leaving Hamil with you, and he will make those available for the attack. You may also draw on Whiteblaze, of course . . . and the Watchers, if you get close enough." She shrugged. "Or, in extremity, draw from any of our fighters. It is more important that you can use your Gift than whether or not one of them can lift a sword."

"Unless he's in combat at the time," Mara said sharply. "Drawing on magic at the wrong moment could get someone killed."

"Not drawing on magic at the wrong moment could get a lot of some-ones killed," the Lady replied acerbically. "Including you. Do not let your overdeveloped sense of ethics interfere with the greater need of destroying the mine . . . and, ultimately, the Autarch."

Mara pressed her lips together. "I still don't remember what happened at the ravine," she said.

"Because I have not returned those memories to you," the Lady re-plied. "They would be a distraction. Once the mine is secured . . . then, possibly."

"Or possibly you will strip my memories of this battle, too?"

Now the Lady's mouth thinned in turn. "I will do what I think best," she said, her voice cold. "I command. And one day soon I will rule . . . you, and all the rest of Aygrima. Remember *that.*" She turned and stalked away.

Mara stayed where she was, breathing hard, feeling her Gift coursing through her again. It felt like . . . hunger. She felt empty. She wanted—needed—to be filled. She needed magic.

And she needed, above all else, to destroy that cursed mining camp.

She could argue with the Lady about restoring her memory when they had successfully done what they had come here to do.

It is my duty to open the gates of the mining camp.

She smiled.

No. It is my pleasure.

◆ ◆ ◆

As the lengthening shadow of the western hills finally finished crawling up the stockade wall of massive, unpeeled logs, Mara stepped into the clearing surrounding the mining camp. She studied the wall. No Watcher had yet seen her. A constant low rumble filled the air, grating on her ears and her nerves, the sound of the waterwheel that drove the man-engine, the terrifying arrangement of reciprocating platforms by which workers moved up and down the levels of the underground mine. In that deep growl Mara heard death, degradation, and debasement. She couldn't wait to silence it.

Just a few yards behind her were ten black lodestone urns, each filled with magic, waiting in the shadows of the trees. Beside her stood White-blaze, filled with his own wild magic. She had more than enough magic to do what had to be done. All she needed was the will to power it . . . and that, too, she had.

Rage. Fury. Hatred. With those emotions to drive her magic, the Lady had said, she could accomplish great things. And here was the perfect focus: the camp to which she and so many others had been exiled when their Masks failed, some of them, yes, people like Grute, the would-be rapist whom she had slain with magic, but some of them, maybe *most* in the last three years, no different than she had been: happy, excited, celebrating their fifteenth birthday and their Masking alike, looking forward to the party afterward and beginning life as an adult. Then, in a horrifying moment of pain and blood, all of that had been torn away from them. Their faces scarred, their childhoods destroyed, they had been sent on a one-way trip in a stinking wagon to a short, miserable life of exploitation *here*.

She remembered her friend Katia, for whom she had risked so much in a rescue attempt, only to fail. She remembered the nightmare nights in the longhouse, the brutal labor in the mine. She had only tasted it, had avoided the fate of so many girls taken as playthings by the Watchers, because of her Gift. She felt guilty about that now, guilty to have avoided the worst of the horrors the camp had visited upon so many other girls over the decades. *But I'm through with guilt*, she thought. *Thanks to the Lady, I am powerful. Now comes revenge.*

Off to her left, Keltan and Chell appeared in the blue-and-white uniforms and silver mail shirts of the Lady's Army. Steel helmets capped their heads. Keltan, she saw, had a crossbow slung over his back. That was new, but they had been separated for weeks both before the sacking of the Secret City and since reaching the Lady's fortress, and much of that time must have been spent in training. No doubt he had learned several fighting skills she had yet to see him demonstrate. "Keltan," she called, and saw his head jerk around.

"My lady," growled Hamil. "You are not to speak to—"

"The longhouses," she shouted, ignoring him. "Open them. Free the unMasked as soon as you can."

"You will do nothing of the kind!" Hamil shouted, taking a step toward Keltan and Chell, hand on his sword hilt. "The Lady has expressly ordered that the unMasked are to remain in their longhouses until the camp is secure. We cannot be certain some of them will not fight with the Watchers." Then he spun on Mara. "The Lady commands. *Not you.*"

Mara said nothing for a moment. She didn't need to, for when she looked past Hamil, she saw Keltan nod his head ever so slightly in her direction.

Perhaps Hamil was right, and some of the unMasked laborers in the camp, most likely the trustees who had gained their own paltry measure of lordship over their fellows, would choose to fight with the Watchers. But far fewer had prospered than had suffered. *The ones who might fight with the Watchers will be too busy trying to keep from being torn limb from limb by those whom they have abused to cause us any trouble,* she thought. *And the others will be free to fight with us, or simply to save themselves.*

"Very well," she said at last to Hamil, though he had no way of knowing it was not strictly in response to his last comment. "Then with your permission . . . ?" She indicated the wall.

Hamil glanced at the setting sun. "Yes," he said. "It is time."

Mara nodded, closed her eyes, and summoned anger.

The fury came easily, more easily than ever before. *I did this at the ravine,* she thought, *used rage-fueled magic to attack,* but she had no memory of it.

The Lady's doing. She stole those memories. She stole my magic.

She used that as additional fuel for the pyre of her anger. She could feel herself breathing harder. Her heart pounded. She knew she had be-

come flushed. Her fists clenched. The abomination before her had terror-
ized, brutalized, *murdered* generations of unMasked. Today it would end.
Today . . . it would fall!

With her rage at its peak, she strode into the open, calling magic to
her from the open urns in the forest. It poured into her like hot oil and
ignited in the flame of her anger. No one behind her had the Gift to see
the white-hot magical radiance pouring through her eyes, glowing through
her skin, but she knew there were those among the Watchers on the pali-
sade wall with sufficient Gift to see it, and sudden, urgent shouts confirmed
the truth of that.

Watchers. The Watchers who had abused Katia and so many others.
The Watchers who kept the Autarch's grim grip tight on Aygrima. The
Watchers who had hauled her father and so many others to the gallows of
Traitors' Gate. *Let them die*, she thought savagely. *Let them all die!*

She raised her hands. She could have blasted the entire southern
stockade wall back into the camp, every pointed stake smashing through
the buildings beyond like bolts from a giant ballista—but that would certainly have killed many of the unMasked they were trying to free. And so
instead she clenched her hands into fists, poured magic into the gate and
wall . . . and pulled it *toward* her.

The wall creaked, cracked, trembled—and then slammed to the
ground, hurling the Watchers atop it away like stones from a catapult.
Their bodies thudded into the clearing, some in a spray of blood, some
with the sound of breaking bones. She felt deaths and took the magic she
could to replenish what she had expended on the wall, careful to pull it
through the amulet around her neck. Of those Watchers who survived the
fall of the wall, few could rise. Those who did slumped instantly, pin-
cushioned by the arrows of the unMasked Army.

But only a score of Watchers had been on the wall. Dozens more were
running from their guard posts or the barracks at the far end of the camp,
swords gleaming in the light of the torches that had been lit in preparation
for the coming night. Not all had armor. Some were half-dressed, some

even unMasked. They closed ground in a hurry. The archers managed two more flights of arrows, bringing down another dozen of the Watchers, before they had to drop their bows and grab their swords. With a clash of steel, the two forces met.

Hamil had hurried her to the back of their lines as the Watchers rushed to defend the camp. Now he drew his sword and joined the fray. More Watchers died, and Mara took still more magic into herself. Still, she dared not hurl magic willy-nilly into the seething mass of fighters. The light was uncertain and the deadly dance of swordplay too complex: she could easily kill some of their own.

But she had another purpose in mind anyway, a private purpose of which the Lady, who had told her to stay well clear of the battle once the wall was down, only assisting if she could do so safely, knew nothing. She set off to the left, Whiteblaze at her heels, to skirt the battle and find her way into the compound beyond, staying within the shadows of the trees as much as she could. It would not do for some Watcher archer to glimpse movement and put an arrow into her on general principles.

Far from the fracas, she stepped out of the forest into the dimming twilight. The fighting had begun to subside as the outnumbered Watchers fell one by one. She and Whiteblaze darted across open ground and reached the scattered logs of the stockade undetected.

But she was not the only one hard to see in the failing light. As she slipped into the camp, a Watcher hiding from the battle lunged at her from the darkness of the doorway leading to the still-standing guard tower. His blade missed her side by a span, but not through any failure of aim: rather, he discovered in that instant just how hard it was to wield a sword with a hundred and fifty pounds of angry wolf clamped to your wrist.

A moment after that the Watcher no longer had a sword hand, and a moment after *that* he no longer had a throat.

His magic slammed into Mara so suddenly she barely managed to filter it through the amulet. She seized the fresh power eagerly, and let the near-miss feed her fury. "Enough of this," she snarled. "Let them all die."

She strode into the camp. She ignored the longhouses—Keltan and Chell would open those soon enough. At first she kept close to the stockade wall, trusting to the shadows to keep her hidden and Whiteblaze to warn her of any other lurking cowards, but that could only take her to the stream that split the compound down the middle. A walkway around the inside of the stockade allowed Watchers to cross it high above, but at ground level the only way across was the bridge in the center of the camp. If it were held by Watchers . . .

She felt the magic boiling inside her with the heat of her anger, and smiled. *I hope it is.*

It wasn't. But it *was* held by armed men: two of the Lady's Cadre stood guard on its short span. She strode boldly out into the light of the torches burning at each end of the bridge. One of the men raised a crossbow in a startled reflex, but lowered it again immediately as he recognized her. "Where is the Lady?" she demanded.

"In the mine," said the other man. "As planned."

"Then I will join her." Mara had no intention of joining the Lady immediately, but it seemed the best way of convincing the villagers to let her cross the bridge.

Instead, to her surprise, the question prompted the man with the crossbow to raise it again and the other to lift his sword. "No," the swordsman said. "She forbids it."

Mara's anger swelled. "*Forbids* it?"

"She does not want you to join her in the mine. She gave us strict orders."

"The Lady commands," the crossbowman said.

"And do you really think you can stop me?" Mara said. Her hands clenched. She could wipe them from the bridge with a single blast of magic. Behind her, Whiteblaze growled his own warning.

The swordsman looked pale. "Please. I have my orders. The Lady commands."

Mara shoved down the murderous rage threatening to choke her.

What's wrong with me? I can't kill these men. The Lady has her reasons. She'll explain it later.

She tore her eyes away from the bridge, breathing hard, and looked north. At the end of the road stood a two-story stone building: the Warden's mansion. At the sight of it, her anger rose again.

She glanced south. The fighting outside the wall seemed to be over, but she could still hear the ringing of blades and the cries of men from inside the camp. Soon Keltan and Chell would be releasing the prisoners in the longhouses.

She looked north again at the Warden's house. The Warden she had known was long-dead, slain by Katia on the night Mara had first discovered her ability to draw magic from living things—and just how powerful that magic could be. But there would be another Warden there, a man cut from the same cloth, willing to live in luxury while all around him men, women, boys, and girls struggled and sweated and suffered and died. *He* would not be fighting with his Watchers, of that she was certain. He would be cowering in fear, wondering what was happening.

He'd find out soon enough.

"Have you been ordered to stop me from crossing the bridge?" Mara asked the villagers.

"No, lass," said the man with the sword.

"Then let me pass," she said. "I will not trouble the Lady. But I will most certainly trouble someone else."

The swordsman glanced at the man with the crossbow, who nodded. They both lowered their weapons and stood aside, pressing their backs against the bridge railing as Mara crossed. Neither met her eyes. Both drew back even more as Whiteblaze passed, growling at them one more time for good measure.

She dismissed them from her mind the moment she and Whiteblaze were across the bridge. Now she could let her rage blossom inside her again, hone it into a weapon. It spilled over into Whiteblaze, so that his growling became almost constant, a counterpoint to the rumble of the waterwheel. Together they strode up the path, past the baths and the dining hall, past the empty guardhouses. There were corpses there, Watchers slain by the Lady's Cadre, no doubt, after they had entered the compound through the small corner gate and were en route to the mine-head. Mara paid them no mind. She mounted the steps of the house, Whiteblaze trotting at her side. She raised her hand, magic flashed red, and the heavy door smashed open with a scream of tortured metal as the bolt sheared away.

"Stay," she commanded Whiteblaze. He growled again, but settled onto his haunches.

She walked into the foyer.

It had changed little since she had last been there, although the amateurish paintings that had been the work of the previous Warden had been replaced with art of considerably higher quality. She took that in with a glance, then turned to her right to face the Warden's office.

Two Watchers stood guard, swords gripped tight. She could sense the magic inside them . . . and the magic, tinged with terror, of the man inside the office.

The Warden.

The Watcher to the left of the door stepped forward, sword raised, but the one to the right grabbed his arm. His eyes were wide behind his Mask. She had no idea why he had stopped the other one, but it didn't matter. Even as she saw it, she unleashed her attack.

The Warden thought himself safe behind his locked doors. But she knew that office well. She knew there was a large hearth opposite the door. And it was there that she directed her fury-fed magic.

The fire in the hearth expanded a thousand times. A wall of flame roared through the office, incinerating the Warden where he stood—she felt him die and ripped his magic into herself through the amulet. The blast blew the office door outward, smashing aside the two Watchers. Mara had been prepared for it, and neither the searing heat she had unleashed nor the burning fragments of the door touched her or Whiteblaze. She caught more magic: one of the Watchers had died in the blast. That meant the other still lived.

She exerted her will, and the flames vanished as though they had never been. She strode forward. The Watcher who had stood to the left of the door was the one she had felt die. His throat had been torn open by a dagger-like shard of wood still lodged in the wound, one end burning, the blood on it sizzling and popping. His Mask had fallen away into dust and shards, revealing a grizzled veteran of perhaps fifty years, gray-stubbled chin stained with blood from his mouth, brown eyes blank and bulging.

She turned the other way. Though the second Watcher still lived, she thought his back was broken. His breath came in shallow, agony-filled gasps. She stood over him, looked down. His blue eyes widened behind the mask. "Mmm—"

He got no farther. With a contemptuous flick of magic, she twisted his head. His neck broke with the same sound her father's had made when he died on the gallows. His Mask fell away . . .

. . . and Mara found herself looking down at the blank dead face of Mayson, once one of her best friends, her schoolmate, her beloved companion in childhood adventures, the boy who even as a Watcher had been kind and helpful when she had been held prisoner in the Palace.

She had just used her Gift to murder him in cold blood.

Rage vanished. Horror rushed in. Her control evaporated. And because of that, the magic pouring from Mayson slammed into her full-force, without any filtering from the amulet around her neck. The pain of the raw magic was nothing compared to the pain of what she had just done. She heard screaming and only dimly knew it was coming from her.

When she had witnessed her father's hanging, the combination of her grief and the impact of his magic had shattered the iron Mask that kept her magic bound. This time, the howling wind of horror at what she had done, melded with Mayson's magic and soulprint, tore apart the barriers the Lady had placed around her memories as if they were made of paper. In one terrible instant she remembered all she had done at the new mine, how she had casually torn magic from the unMasked to feed her anger-driven need, how she had blown one Watcher to bloody scraps, crushed another against the ravine wall like a bug, destroyed the wall and the Watchers atop it . . .

. . . and she *also* remembered what the Lady had done to the un-Masked mine workers—and what she had said to Mara afterward.

And *that* memory, and the fury and fear it engendered, gave her back control of herself. She had fallen to the tiled floor of the foyer, curled into a ball, shaking and weeping. Whiteblaze stood over her, eyes wide, whining and trying to lick her face. She pushed him away, then forced herself to get to all fours, then to her knees, one thought repeating and repeating in her head. *I have to stop the Lady. I have to stop the Lady.*

She was just struggling to her feet when Keltan burst in through the magic-shattered front door.

TWELVE

Desperate Measures

"**M**ARA! Are you all right?" Keltan reached her in an instant. His arms encircled her. He smelled of smoke and sweat. Blood smeared his face, but she didn't think it was his.

"No," she gasped, clinging to him as her knees threatened to give way. "I didn't know . . . she blocked my memories . . ."

"Didn't know what?"

"The Lady. She's not rescuing the unMasked. She's killing them. Draining them of magic. Storing it up for her assault on the Autarch."

Keltan stared at her. "*What?*"

"At the ravine . . . what did she say? What did she tell you had happened to the unMasked?"

"She told us you killed them," Keltan said.

"*What?*"

"Unintentionally, by failing to control your magic. She told us she had blocked your memories to keep the horror from you, and we could not say anything to you about what had really happened for fear of what the knowledge might do to you. Chell and Antril remembered entering the cavern . . . and that was all, until they woke to find both the Watchers and the unMasked dead."

Mara shook her head miserably. "She lied. *She* killed the unMasked. And she's going to kill all the unMasked in this camp, too, unless we stop her." The room swayed and she gripped his arm. "Have you opened the longhouses?"

"No," Keltan said. "The villagers won't let us. They're standing guard. 'The Lady commands,' is all we can get out of them. They seem . . . bewitched. In thrall. Short of killing them . . ."

"They *are* bewitched." She took a deep breath. "The Lady is in the mine. We have to get there." *And do what?* a part of her wondered. *"You will never be what I am,"* the Lady had told her in the ravine. How well she remembered it now, remembered the contempt in Arilla's voice. *"You will never even be what I was, when I fought the Autarch as a young girl. . . ."*

How many unMasked had Arilla already slain, in the depths of the mine? How much magic had she absorbed?

And what would she do with it?

She's making herself so powerful she can destroy the camp, the unMasked Army, Chell's men . . . all of them. She will descend on Tamita like a hurricane and suck its inhabitants dry to defeat the Autarch . . . and when he is defeated, she will set herself up as a tyrant a thousand times worse. She won't need the Masks. She can do what the Autarch does without them. She already is, with her villagers.

But she still needs me. She remembered the Lady's strange words about Mara's "final fate," and something about "preparing the way" just before she obliterated Mara's memories. *Does that mean she won't kill me? At least, not right away?*

A slender thread on which to hang the hope of survival, but it was all she had. Perhaps it would at least give her time to mount some kind of attack before Arilla crushed her.

Even Mara's youth would give her no advantage in a direct confrontation, since the Lady had counteracted the effects of the passing years by drawing magic from her villagers. And Arilla had decades' more knowledge and experience than Mara . . . and quite possibly a stronger measure of the Gift. *I can't hope to defeat her.*

But she still had to try.

"We have to get to the mine," she said. "*I* have to get to the mine. Get underground. Try to stop her . . . save as many as I can."

"The mine is guarded by both of her wolfpacks," Keltan said. "Human *and* canine."

"You have to clear me a path," Mara said. "You and Edrik and Chell. I have to get down there."

Keltan looked at her, nodded. "All right," he said. "Wait here."

Mara shook her head sharply, feeling the dead, accusing eyes of Mayson staring at her even though she wasn't looking in his direction. "Not here," she said. "I'll wait on the porch."

Keltan hesitated. "There could be more—"

"The house is empty of Watchers," Mara said. "I can feel it." She could sense people cowering in rooms at the back of the house, but none were Gifted. They were almost certainly servants.

Keltan nodded again. He dashed off. She walked outside and sat on the steps of the Warden's house. Whiteblaze plopped himself down beside her. She put her arm around his warm furry shoulders and pressed her cheek against him. The only magic she had left was what she could draw from him . . . and what she had taken from Mayson and the other dead Watcher.

It wouldn't be enough. It couldn't possibly be enough.

Her breath caught. And she wouldn't even have Whiteblaze if she descended into the mine. He couldn't possibly negotiate the man-engine.

Well, neither can the Lady's bloody wolves, she thought savagely, but it was cold comfort. The Lady was stripping magic from unMasked. Arilla would have all she could possibly need.

And yet, Mara had to try. There was no one else who could even hope to stand up to the Lady.

How could I have been so blind? How could I have trusted her?

There had been hints from the beginning, more hints along the way, outright warnings from Keltan and Chell. But Mara had ignored all of them, pushed aside her own doubts, because she had been so thrilled to find someone in whom she could confide, someone who fully understood the nightmarish Gift with which she had been cursed, who knew what it was to draw magic directly from the living . . . someone who had also struggled with its addictive power.

The Lady had told Mara she could control that deep, soul-devouring need to draw more and more magic. She had told her the amulet she had crafted for Mara could help. But now Mara knew her initial doubts about the amulet had been well-founded, if only she had listened to them. The amulet did nothing to control the *need* for living magic—it only made it easier to *feed* that need by removing the agonizing effects of drawing raw magic directly into herself.

The magic from Mayson had bypassed the amulet. The pain of that impact still echoed through her body, as though tiny creatures were clawing her nerves. But the worst of it was she could feel Mayson's presence, as if he were sitting beside her on the steps, as he had once sat beside her on the walls of Tamita, gazing down at the Outside Market.

I killed him, she thought again, the agony of that thought worse than the agony of the unfiltered magic she had taken in from him. *As surely as if I had pushed him to his death from the wall when we sat there together as children.* She pressed herself so hard against Whiteblaze that the wolf whined. *Ethelda, you warned me. I have become a monster.*

Though not as much of a monster as the Lady.

Yet.

Clash of steel, cries of pain. She looked up to see, by torchlight, the villagers guarding the bridge fighting with Chell's men. One crumpled. The other, closest to her, dashed away into the darkness, heading toward the towering bulk of the waterwheel—and beyond it, the minehead.

A few minutes later Keltan, Chell, Hyram, Edrik, and a dozen fighters, some Chell's men, some she recognized from the unMasked Army, arrived at the Warden's house. She stood up, trying to hold on to her dignity, trying not to openly weep. They watched her warily, all except Keltan, who came forward to offer his arm. She brushed it away. She didn't want to show weakness.

"What's going on?" Edrik demanded. "The villagers who were fighting with us against the Watchers have suddenly started fighting *against* us. They killed several of our men before we could strike back. They're still fighting outside the walls." He grimaced. "And because of that, several Watchers have escaped. They'll bring the main force down on us from the Secret City. We're going to be pursued all the way to Tamita."

"The Lady is controlling the villagers with magic," Mara said. "All of them, now, not just her Cadre. She has been drawing magic from them to keep herself strong and to keep them docile—just as the Autarch has been doing in Tamita. She killed the unMasked laborers at the ravine and drew on their magic to strengthen herself even more. Now she is killing the unMasked in the mine. When she emerges, she won't need the villagers or the unMasked Army or Chell's men any longer. No Watchers will be able to threaten her. Nothing will be able to stand against her."

Edrik's face glistened with sweat or blood: in the red light of the torches lighting the porch, it was hard to be certain. "Can *you* stop her?"

No, Mara thought, but, "Yes," she said aloud. "Maybe. If I can trap her in the mine. But I have to reach her while she's still underground. And the mine is guarded by members of her Cadre, just like the bridge was." She looked from Edrik to Chell. "I need you to help me get into the minehead."

Edrik's eyes narrowed, but then he nodded, once. "How do we get there?"

"Over the bridge. South side of the stream. There's a door into the minehead close to the south wall. You can approach it directly along the wall, or along a boardwalk along the south side of the trench containing the waterwheel."

"A single door," Edrik said. "Easy to defend. We'll never get you through there in time."

"Are you sure that's the only way in?" Chell said.

Mara started to nod . . . and then stopped. "Maybe not," she said. She was remembering the first time she had gone underground, walking along the boardwalk, looking down at the massive reciprocating beams, driven by the waterwheel, which in turn powered the man-engine that took workers up and down the main shaft. "There are beams," she said. "Stretching from the waterwheel into the minehead. They pass through an opening in the wall at the bottom of the trench. It might be possible to get in that way."

"So we need to get you to the bottom of the trench without you being seen," Chell said. He glanced at Edrik. "We'll need a direct attack as a diversion."

Edrik nodded.

"Do you know how to get into the trench?" Chell asked Mara.

She shook her head. "Not exactly. But there must be a ladder near the waterwheel. They'd have to have some way to get down there for repairs and maintenance. But I can't go that way. I have to have Whiteblaze with me. I need his magic."

"He can't possibly descend into the mine with you," Chell protested.

"I know that. But I may need him in the minehead just to get to the man-engine . . . or after I emerge." *If* I emerge.

"I've got rope," Hyram said. "We can lower the wolf . . ." He glanced at Mara. "If he'll let us."

"To stay with me, he'll let you," Mara said.

Edrik nodded. "Hyram and Keltan will go with Mara," he said. "The rest of us will mount a diversionary attack. Circle around and come along the wall."

"Not everyone," Chell said. "There could be archers on this side of the trench." He looked around. "Antril?"

The young lieutenant stepped forward. "Sir?"

"Pick four men. Clear out any villagers you find on the north side of the trench. Be as noisy as possible. We want to draw attention."

"Sir!" Antril turned and pointed. "You, you, you, and you." Four of Chell's sailors stepped forward.

"The rest of you," Chell said, "are under Edrik's command."

"What about you?" Edrik said.

"I'm going with Mara," Chell said.

Edrik hesitated, then nodded. "All right," he said. "With me, you lot."

He moved off into the night. Chell nodded to Antril. "Off you go," he said. "No need to wait. Make some noise. Draw their attention. Kill any you can. That'll help Edrik surprise them from the other direction. And meanwhile we'll be taking the back door."

If it exists, Mara thought. She *thought* there was room to get past those beams. But she couldn't be sure until they got there . . . and first they had to get there.

Antril headed toward the waterwheel. They gave him a couple of minutes, then moved toward the bridge. "If there's a ladder, most likely it comes down from the boardwalk on the south side of the trench," Mara said.

Chell grunted. "And most likely there are at least a couple of the Lady's Cadre on that boardwalk."

They reached the bridge. The torches had been extinguished when the villagers guarding it had been killed. The only illumination now came from the stars, and the stray light from a handful of torches burning here and there around the compound. From the south came shouts and the clash of steel, as villagers continued to fight the unMasked Army and Chell's remaining men.

The boardwalk began at the bridge and stretched to the east, past the giant rumbling waterwheel. Two torches burned far down along it, their circles of light showing only bare wood. "Any guards will be hiding in the shadows," Chell said. "The torches are only to confuse the eye. But it works both ways: they can't see us, either."

"This way," Mara said, and led them to the steps that went down to the boardwalk. Chell and Keltan walked in front, Chell with his sword drawn, Keltan with his crossbow at the ready. Hyram served as rear guard.

Off to their left, shouting and the clash of steel shattered the night. A man screamed hoarsely. "Antril has attacked," Chell murmured.

Mara, trying desperately to pierce the darkness ahead, said nothing. They had almost reached the waterwheel. Its rumble shook the boardwalk, and the white splash of the water pouring over it gleamed like a pale ghost in the starlight.

Ahead, a figure appeared, silhouetted just for an instant against the nearest torch. Keltan's crossbow sang, and the man tumbled over the edge of the boardwalk, the sound of his fall lost in the rumble of the waterwheel. Mara pulled his magic into her amulet as he dropped out of sight. *Every little bit helps.*

"I've found a ladder," Chell said. Mara could just make him out, crouched by the side of the boardwalk. Keltan stood a little farther along the walk, silhouetted against the torches, reloading his crossbow. More shouts echoed from the far side of the stream. Something moved on the fringe of the pool of light ahead of them. Keltan fired again, and the dim shape jerked and vanished. No magic rushed to Mara; the man still lived. Keltan reloaded.

And then more shouting erupted, this time coming from the direction of the minehead. Swords clashed. Footsteps pounded along the boardwalk, heading away from them. "Edrik's attacking," Chell said. "Quickly! Mara, help Hyram sling the rope on Whiteblaze. Keltan goes down first. Then Mara. We lower Whiteblaze and come after you."

Hyram was already pulling a coil of rope from his pack. Mara, fumbling in the dark, helped him tie it around the wolf, who stood quietly, trusting her. "You follow," she whispered to Whiteblaze. "I need you."

His tail wagged and he licked her face. Grimacing, she wiped her cheek. Wolf breath was no better than dog breath. She turned toward the ladder, where Keltan already waited to descend. "Go," she said, and he disappeared down into the trench.

Mara followed, on rungs made slippery by the cold spray from the turning waterwheel so close at hand. At the bottom she found herself on another boardwalk, running alongside the pool into which the water tumbled. The stream flowed out of the pool along a channel dug into the north side of the trench, which took it around the minehead at the far end and out of the compound. The center of the trench was taken up, she knew, by a series of upright posts, each of which had a giant bolt driven sideways through it at the top. Centered on each bolt was a shorter upright beam, able to swing freely, which in turn was attached at both ends to the massive beams, each longer and thicker than the masts on Chell's lost ships, which rocked back and forth with the turning of the wheel.

The noise was deafening this close to the waterwheel and the reciprocating beams. Mara turned and stared up the ladder. The earlier cloud cover was beginning to clear, patches of stars showing through, and against that starlight she saw the shaggy silhouette of Whiteblaze as he was lowered to her. She untied him the moment his paws touched the planks, and gave him a quick hug—and got a lick in return—before moving aside.

Chell and Keltan joined them a moment later. "Fighting still going on at the entrance to the mine," Chell said. "And up there." He gestured, barely visible, at the other side of the trench. "Everyone's busy. They won't be looking down here."

"I hope so," Mara said. "Let's go."

They trotted along the boardwalk. As the noise of the waterwheel fell behind them, they could hear the sounds of battle above and to their right. To their left, Mara heard nothing. She hoped that meant Antril and his men had cleared away all the villagers from that side. Antril had impressed her in the short time she'd known him. Despite his youth, he did what he had to, time and time again. Like her, she supposed, except unlike her, he tended to succeed, whereas she always seemed to fail.

Not this time, she swore to herself. Neither Antril nor anyone else would be "all right" if she couldn't somehow stop the Lady.

They were almost to the minehead. Torches inside the building cast a dim yellow glow through the opening through which the massive beams slid back and forth. It was nothing more than a slit, framed with large timbers. The bottom of the opening was a good six feet above the board-walk, which formed an L-shape at its end to run along the base of the minehead. Within the opening, it looked like there might be four feet of clearance beneath the lowermost of the restless timbers.

"We'll have to crawl in there under the beams," Chell said. "Sitting ducks if we're seen."

"Headless ones if we rise up and that beam catches us," Hyram muttered.

"We have to try," Mara said. "*I* have to try." Somewhere beneath their feet, the Lady was systematically cleansing the mine of an entire shift's worth of unMasked laborers. How many dozens had she slain already? How much magic could she absorb?

"Too high to scramble up on your own," Chell said. "And you can't go first."

"I'll go first," Keltan said. "You can lift me up far enough to see in, then push me up the rest of the way. Once I'm in, I can pull Mara and the rest of you up behind me."

"I'm bigger and stronger," Hyram said. "I should go first."

"No," Keltan said. "I—"

"Hyram is right," Chell said. "He goes first. I go second. Then Mara. Then you. You lift up the wolf and come in last to guard the rear."

Even in the dim light Mara could see Keltan's disapproving frown, but he nodded without further objection.

Together Chell and Keltan, with folded hands beneath his booted feet, boosted Hyram up far enough to peer inside. "No one in sight," he whispered back, "but I can't see much. Push me up the rest of the way."

With a mutual grunt, Chell and Keltan lifted him higher. He clambered over the edge and vanished, reappearing a moment later with his hands outstretched. "Prince Chell."

Chell grabbed the proffered hands and clambered up the wall. Mara followed, pushed up from behind by Keltan (who, she had the irrelevant thought, was certainly taking a hands-on approach to "guarding her rear"), and pulled up by Hyram from above. Inside, she glanced around. They crouched in deep shadow and not, as she had thought, at floor level: instead, they were on a raised platform with a railing around it and a short ladder reaching down to the floor, about the same distance below as the walkway inside the trench from which they had just climbed. The reciprocating beams so terrifyingly close above them stretched past the end of the platform, out over the floor, to the mechanism that transferred their horizontal movement into vertical movement: two more beams (really a series of beams cobbled together, probably by magic, since the mine was hundreds of feet deep) that moved up and down in tandem. Attached to them for their entire lengths were platforms which met at the end of each stroke. To descend into the depths, you stepped from platform to platform, taken lower with each transfer. To ascend, you reversed the process.

It was the most terrifying device Mara had ever been on. Fatal accidents, she'd been told, were not uncommon. And yet the Lady, well over eighty years old, had apparently negotiated it with no problem: another sign of how much stronger stolen magic had made her.

Whiteblaze, uncomplaining, was lifted up over the edge of the platform, scrabbled for purchase, and then trotted over and pushed his head against her leg. She rubbed his ears while Keltan was pulled up, mentally preparing herself for what she had to do next.

"I'll go down into the mine," she said when they were all together again. "I'll try to trap the Lady down there. But if she comes up, you must be prepared to kill her the moment you see her, before she can use her magic."

"If Whiteblaze cannot go with you," said Chell, "where will you find your own magic?"

"There may be some in the mine. And I'm still carrying some from . . . before." *Mayson's.* She wondered what nightmares lay in wait for her if she slept with Mayson's soulprint still inside her and without Whiteblaze at hand.

Whatever they are, I'll deserve them. Then she snorted. She was about to face the Lady of Pain and Fire in head-to-head conflict. It seemed unlikely she'd ever sleep, or dream, again.

"Let me come with you," Keltan said urgently. "You've drawn magic from me before. I'm not afraid—"

"No," Mara said, snapping the word so vehemently he drew back in startlement. "No," she repeated, more gently. "You'd be throwing your life away. I cannot overpower her with magic, no matter how much I take with me. My only hope is to take her unaware and bring the roof down on her. I have enough magic for that."

"And if you can't take her unaware?" Keltan said.

"Then I'll . . . talk to her."

"You will not challenge me again." She heard the Lady's voice in her head as if Arilla were standing right next to her.

Sure, talk to her. That'll *do the trick.*

"Aren't *you* throwing *your* life away?" Chell said.

"I hope not," Mara said. "But if I am, or if I fail . . . you must stand ready."

Someone shouted from above. Footsteps clattered down the stairs.

"Might be difficult," Chell said, unsheathing his sword. "I think they just spotted us."

THIRTEEN
The Depths of Magic

EVERYTHING SUDDENLY started happening very fast. Keltan leaped down to the floor of the minehead and raised his crossbow, but in the same instant cried out and twisted left, the crossbow flying from his hands. It skittered to the edge of the shaft, but didn't fall in. Keltan clutched his upper arm, blood welling between his fingers. The arrow that had clipped him quivered in the wooden floor. Then he released the wound, tore his sword from its scabbard, and leaped toward the stairs.

Mara, suddenly terrified she would lose either the opportunity or the nerve to do what had to be done, jumped down from the platform and dashed toward the man-engine.

A villager appeared as if from nowhere from behind the housing, sword drawn, his expression masklike—and for the same reason as those who wore actual Masks, Mara knew now, though this mask was flesh and blood. With senses heightened by the magic she held within her, she could see the glow of the magic ensorcelling him: the magic of the Lady, sewn into the very fiber of his mind, bending weft and warp to her will.

She stopped, gasping—and Whiteblaze went by her like a streak of furred light, leaping and tearing. Blood sprayed through the air as his teeth found the man's throat.

Steel flashed and rang as Hyram, Chell, and Keltan met the villagers who had just reached the bottom of the stairs. At the top of the stairs, the sound of battle between villagers and Edrik's men continued. More than just the Cadre were involved now: with the villagers having been turned against the unMasked Army and Chell's men, many more must be rushing to the minehead. Presumably, so were more of Edrik's and Chell's fighters. There would be running battles throughout the compound.

But here, around the man-engine, there was an oasis of calm. Mara took a deep breath and stepped onto the platform that had just reached the top.

It took her down several feet. She stepped onto the next one. Down farther. There were twelve levels in all. As she passed each level, she strained her senses for some sign of the Lady's presence, but all were quiet—deathly quiet. No chisels rang against stone, no overseers shouted, no one waited at the levels' entrances with baskets of ore to be sent up the shaft by the dangling ropes that hung from a crane high overhead. The mine had already shut down, and Mara could only think of one reason:

The Lady had already killed everyone within it.

But she hadn't come up. Mara was certain of that. Arilla was still down here somewhere, and though Mara had only a small reservoir of magic to draw on, her senses remained keen. She passed the tenth level. The eleventh.

And then she was at the very bottom of the mine, the level where she and Katia had worked, where she had had her arm broken, where Katia's previous partner, Shimma, still lay entombed beneath tons of rock.

And there, at last, she sensed the Lady.

She stepped off the man-engine onto the cold stone floor. As she did so, she heard a scream in the distance, echoing off the tunnel walls, and felt brushed by the edge of the magic from a dying . . . girl. She knew it had been a girl, though the power had just touched her.

She knew then that she had been far too slow. She could sense no other life on the level. She had sensed no life during the descent.

The Lady had done it. She had slain every unMasked laborer in the mine, taken as much of their magic into herself as she could. And Mara . . .

Mara had the remnants of Mayson's magic, and the Warden and Watcher who had died with him, and a little from the villager shot on the boardwalk above, and that was all.

She'll squash me like an insect.

Every instinct of self-preservation screamed at her to step back onto the man-engine, ride it to the top. But she stayed where she was.

And the Lady came to her, returning from the farthest regions of that lowest level of the mine. Mara saw the penumbra of her magic first, lighting the darkness for her Gifted sight, though had Keltan or Chell stood beside her, they would have seen nothing.

Then the Lady herself appeared, so full of magic that she blazed like a star fallen to Earth, the power pouring out of her skin, so bright it was as if she were naked, her clothes invisible to Mara's sight. The revealed body looked young, young as Mara herself: young as the Lady had been when her power had first manifested and she had fled with her father into the Wild to fight against the Autarch, all those decades ago.

The Lady smiled when she saw Mara. "You came," she said. "I thought you would, even though I forbade it. I did not really think you could resist the call."

"The call of what?" Mara said, barely able to speak through the terror choking her . . . terror, and a rising anger at this woman who had betrayed her and lied to her in so many ways.

"The call of power," the Lady said. "To feed the hunger." She took a deep breath. "I have taken all I could find. I could take even more. But I have enough to give you some. To satiate your need." Her eyes narrowed then. "Though you do have a little. I sense an active soulprint . . ."

"From a Watcher I killed," Mara said.

"And you failed to draw it through the amulet? Oh, Mara, you still have so much to learn." The Lady smiled as she spread her hands. "And I will gladly, gladly teach you. I forgive you for disobeying me. Shall we ascend? Now we are ready to march on Tamita. We no longer need anyone else. Together, we will free the land of the Autarch."

Mara licked her lips. "No," she said.

"No?" The Lady cocked her head. "I don't understand."

"Your block on my memories is gone," Mara said. She tried to speak calmly, steadily, but the fear and fury mingled inside her made her voice quaver. "I remember everything you said to me in the cavern of magic. I remember what you did there. I know what you've done here. You've been *using* me. You used me to get into Aygrima. You used me to help you capture the new mine and this one, so you could kill the unMasked and strip them of their magic. And you have something else planned for me—what, I don't know, but I know it will be evil."

"I see," the Lady said. She didn't seem particularly concerned. "Just out of curiosity, how did you regain your memories?"

"Because of the Watcher I killed. The one whose magic bypassed the amulet."

The Lady raised an eyebrow. "Really? What was so special about one Watcher?"

"His name was Mayson," Mara said. "He was my friend. Once one of my best friends."

"Ah." The Lady nodded. "Yes, a sudden emotional surge . . . I can understand why the memory block fell. Just as the iron Mask shattered when you witnessed your father's death." She gave Mara a curious look. "If your memories have returned, why are you down here with me? Why didn't you simply flee?"

"I came to stop you," Mara said.

The Lady laughed, the clear, delighted laughter of a young girl. "Oh, Mara. You jest, of course."

"I'm not joking," Mara said. "You've killed countless unMasked in this mine alone; more at the ravine. They're the people we're supposed to be rescuing. You see them as cattle. You see them as . . . food." The anger she had used to such deadly effect in the attack on the camp rose higher, swamping the fear. "You are everything I was warned I would become if I used my power. Everything you told me, trying to convince me I would *not* become those horrible things, was a lie. You are a monster. And if I continue to help you, to use my power as you want me to, I'll become a monster, too. *And I won't allow that to happen.*"

The Lady straightened her head. Her lip quirked into a smile. "You won't."

"No."

"But it's already begun," the Lady said. "You've tasted the power. You blasted a hole in the wall of Tamita itself, when your father died. You entombed a troop of Watchers and horses in the earth. You tore down the wall outside the ravine, using magic you took from the unMasked without a second thought. You ripped the stockade from the ground and opened this camp to attack. You may think you can turn your back on all that, but you're deluding yourself. The Gift you and I have . . . it's more powerful than you can imagine yet. Even if you could kill me now—which you can't, the very idea is preposterous—you would still become what I am." She spread her hands. "Not a monster, Mara. A goddess."

"Goddesses are immortal," Mara said. "You aren't. The Autarch is having to take more and more magic to stave off old age. So will you. Eventually there won't be enough magic in the whole world to keep you hale."

"But I have a solution to that, Mara," the Lady said. "A solution you are a part of." She spread her hands, indicating her glowing body, nude beneath the pale shadows of clothing to Mara's Gifted sight. "Even if I am not a goddess, I am as close to one as the world will ever know. The un-

Gifted, even those with the ordinary Gifts—they will obey me. They will bow down and worship me, if I demand it. With the power I will wield, I will hold their lives in my hand. I will reward those who serve me, and punish those who oppose me. I will make Aygrima the most powerful nation in the world. Chell's little kingdom will not be able to stand against us. This Stonefell he is so frightened of will fall as easily." She stepped forward then, reaching out to Mara as if to embrace her. "Don't fight me, Mara. Join me. I still need you. I do not want to destroy you." Something darker flashed through her expression. "But I will, if I have to."

Mara took a step back. "I will not join you," she said. "I will stop you." And with that, she released the magic she had been hoarding, driving it with the full force of her boiling fury.

She did not hurl it at the Lady. She knew that would be futile. Instead she aimed it at the rock above the Lady. Every time she had been forced to crawl through the tunnels to the rock face she and Katia had been working she had been horribly aware of the countless tons of stone over her head, aware that the slightest shrug of the earth could crush her like an insect. She hoped to bury the Lady before she could react.

Just as she had planned, her magic tore into the stone, cracking it with a noise of thunder . . .

. . . and it simply flowed back together again, re-formed as though it had never been broken, sun-bright magic blazing from the Lady to knit the rock together as fast as it broke apart.

Mara had no more magic. The Lady had brushed aside her attack as though it had been a gnat. Her anger evaporated. Fear flooded back to take its place.

"Mara," Arilla said. "Now do you see how futile your resistance is?" She strode forward, and flicked her hand. A flash of red light, and Mara felt a force like a giant wind pick her up and throw her across the floor, so that she tumbled like a windblown weed, fetching up against the wall with a thump that almost drove the breath from her body. Aching, she sat up. "I will see you on the surface," the Lady said, "and we will discuss what I have in mind for you next . . . after I have dealt with whomever I find there." She stepped onto the man-engine and was gone.

Keltan! Mara stumbled across the floor and leaped onto the next platform that presented itself. Platform by platform she ascended the shaft, dreading what she would find at the top. She and the Lady were locked into the same rate of ascent, and the Lady had been at least half a minute ahead of her.

Half a minute could be an eternity.

She looked into each dark level she passed, and still sensed nothing living: only the sun-like presence of the Lady, somewhere above her.

Three more platforms. Two. The final one. She rose above the floor of the minehead and leaped off.

The Lady, blazing with the light that only Mara could see, stood in the middle of the building, surveying the scene but taking no action. Glancing frantically around, Mara saw Chell fighting at the base of the stairs and Hyram slumped against the wall, clutching his side, blood pouring over his fingers. Three of the Lady's Cadre lay dead, one lying just at the edge of the pool of light from the torches atop the shaft. Whiteblaze lay against one wall, his sides heaving but his eyes closed.

But she didn't see Keltan.

Her heart pounded in her chest. *Where is he?*

"Can you feel it, Mara?" said the Lady, as though simply continuing a conversation. Even through the clash of blades and the shouting atop the stairs, her voice carried as clearly to Mara as though spoken directly into her ear. "Can you feel the magic in all those active, battling bodies, fighting each other so futilely? I can take it all: drain the magic, the very life, from your friends, my villagers, the unMasked dregs still cowering in their longhouses. And once I do, I will need no one's help to free Tamita from the bloated, poisonous spider spinning his flimsy webs at the city's heart."

"I will not become like you," Mara gasped out, her own voice, half-lost in the drumbeat of her pounding pulse, sounding weaker than the Lady's in her ears. "I'd rather die."

The Lady laughed. "As if you have a choice." She turned toward Mara and raised her hands toward her, palms out. "You're becoming a nuisance. I'll deal with you shortly. For now, stay still."

White light poured from the Lady's hand, surrounding Mara, pinning her in place, immobile as a statue. She tried to access her own Gift, tried to pull some of the Lady's magic into her as she had absorbed attacks from ordinary Gifted in the past, but she couldn't.

But in that moment, while all the Lady's attention was focused on Mara, Keltan staggered up from the shadows beyond the dead villager, where he had been lying unseen. A cut in his forehead had turned his face into a Mask of blood. He'd lost his helmet and his sword, but he drew his dagger, eyes fixed on the Lady.

Mara's glance might have betrayed him, but her eyes could not even flick in his direction.

Keltan lunged, plunging his knife into the Lady's back.

The magic holding Mara in place vanished. She dropped hard to the wooden floor, just at the edge of the shaft. She saw Arilla turn. The knife flew from the Lady's body, clattering against the wall. The wound it had left had already closed. Magic wrapped Keltan, held him as Mara had been held. "Watch, Mara," the Lady snarled. "Watch as I crush the life from your would-be lover and take his magic for my own. See the fate of all who oppose me."

But though Mara no longer had any magic left, she was no longer frozen in place. And there, right at the edge of the shaft, lay the crossbow Keltan had dropped earlier, cocked and loaded.

Mara grabbed it, raised it. The Lady must have seen the movement from the corner of her eye. Her head started to turn. Her eyes flared white—but Mara's finger had already tightened.

The bolt tore through the back of the Lady's neck, angled upward so sharply the point burst through the top of her skull in a spray of blood, bone, and brain. Keltan fell to the wooden floor, gasping. The villagers still fighting on the stairs dropped as if clubbed, two at the top thudding down the first flight like sacks of meal. The Lady's eyes blazed in Mara's Gifted sight like twin suns . . . and then went out. Arms still outstretched, the Lady toppled backward into the shaft, dropping out of sight into darkness.

And all her magic slammed, unfiltered, into Mara.

Two screams echoed in her head: hers, ripped from her throat by the agony of that impact, and the Lady's, a scream of fury and betrayal and denial that could not be coming from Arilla's plummeting body but Mara heard nonetheless. Her own blood turned to acid in her veins, invisible knives flayed her skin, her brain seemed to burn and boil in her skull. If she had had nowhere to send that magic, it would have slain her, for she was not the Lady, and had not the Lady's endless decades of study and practice and experience.

But she *did* have somewhere to send it. She lay at the very edge of the shaft, and though the mine was all but played out, there were still vast deposits of black lodestone below her, lodestone to help draw the magic out of her.

She hurled the Lady's magic after the Lady's corpse. She poured it into the mine, down to the very bottom, filling every shaft, releasing it with the force of tens of thousands of the rockbreakers that had almost destroyed the camp once before. The ground heaved and shook. The mechanism atop the man-engine twisted, and then broke. The vertical beams and their hated platforms collapsed into the shaft, and with that, the reciprocating beams, suddenly unsupported at their ends, slammed down, still moving, smashing the wooden flooring into splinters and continuing to grind away at it.

They came within a hairsbreadth of crushing Mara beneath them, but strong hands pulled her out of the way just in time: Chell. "We have to get out of here," he said.

Mara couldn't speak. She was seeing double, as though looking through two sets of eyes. Yet the world seemed strangely dark. Where had the bright light of magic gone? Limp, she let Chell pull her toward the stairs. Hyram, still clutching his bleeding flank, was already climbing them. Keltan staggered after them. Whiteblaze, whining, had clambered to his feet and pushed past Keltan to be closer to Mara. Mara could only think that the Lady had somehow immobilized him on first emerging from the mine. He seemed unharmed now, but she felt so emptied out inside she could barely muster relief at the fact.

"Out!" Chell shouted at Edrik, who had just appeared at the top of the stairs, bloody sword in hand. "Everyone out! Evacuate the camp! Everyone!"

The ground shook. The giant moving beams, splintering the wooden flooring, suddenly caught on some floor support they could not move. With a terrible cracking sound, they froze. More tearing and breaking noises came from outside, from the direction of the waterwheel.

Somehow they made it to the top of the stairs, which were bucking as though trying to throw them off. They emerged into the night air. "Out of the camp," Chell said to the men there. "Get everyone out—all the un-Masked, everyone!"

Mara turned her head as, with another enormous cracking sound, the waterwheel, caught between the force of the water and the jammed beams, tore free of its axle and fell over onto its side, smashing the boardwalk. The water poured over it and down the trench. In the silence following, with the rumble of the waterwheel finally stilled, Mara could hear a far deeper and more ominous rumbling coming from the shaking ground itself.

"Run!" Chell shouted.

But Mara couldn't run. She could barely move one foot in front of the other, and stumbled as she did so, uncoordinated, unable to control her own movements. Whiteblaze kept pressing against her leg as though to support her, but that only made her slower. Keltan and Hyram weren't in much better shape. All of them trailed the rest of the unMasked Army and Chell's men, who were spreading out through the camp, urging everyone to get out. A mob of people, workers freed from the longhouses, unMasked Army fighters, Chell's sailors, villagers no longer controlled by the Lady, even a few surviving Watchers, ran and scrambled and limped toward the fallen southern stockade wall through the flickering light of the torches still alight throughout the compound.

Mara and Whiteblaze and Chell and Hyram and Keltan brought up the rear. They weren't quite to the fallen wall when the ground shook so violently all of them but Whiteblaze were thrown from their feet. Mara hit hard, rolling over and over. Once again Chell helped her up. But now they were both facing into the camp, and they both froze, staring.

From the minehead out, the ground simply fell away.

The tower that had supported the waterwheel toppled into the trench and vanished into darkness. The minehead collapsed and disappeared, its dim light extinguished. The Warden's house shook and shattered into rubble and then sank into the rapidly widening hole that had already swallowed the mess hall and the baths. The first row of longhouses vanished. The second. The third.

The line of destruction and darkness raced toward them, swallowing the camp and the torches that lit it. Chell turned again, urging Mara to run. Whiteblaze, whining, stayed by her feet. Hyram and Keltan limped ahead of them. But they couldn't run as fast as the ground was collapsing. It would engulf them in seconds, entomb them in the ruin of the mine . . .

And then, just like that, the shaking stopped. The roar of falling earth and stone and timber faded away. Panting, Chell stopped and, with Mara, looked back again.

The mining camp had vanished, devoured by a round crater whose bottom, dozens of feet below, was a jumbled mass of broken buildings and broken stone, lit by flames now flickering in the wreckage, where oil lamps had ignited tumbled timbers. By that hellish light Mara could see that the stream now poured down the western edge of the crater, vanishing without a trace into the mess below.

The edge of the hole was just a dozen steps from where they stood, and Chell, after that one horrified look, urged Mara and Keltan and Hyram farther away from it.

They joined Edrik and Captain March outside the camp. Antril found his way over to them; Mara was pleased to see he'd survived. Hyram collapsed onto the ground, face white. Keltan sat down heavily, breathing hard. All of them stared at the destruction and said nothing.

Here lies the Lady of Pain and Fire, Mara thought. The circle of complete devastation seemed a fitting grave marker.

A wet nose nuzzled her hand, and she looked down at Whiteblaze, who gazed back at her with amber eyes and made a whuffling sound. She rubbed his head and wondered what had happened to the Lady's wolves. Had they died when the Lady's magical link was so violently severed? Or were they running free in the forest, nothing but ordinary animals once more?

And then Chell asked the question that Mara had been dreading.

"Now what?" he said.

FOURTEEN

"I Know the Lady's Plan"

"WE CANNOT CONTINUE," Edrik said. The sun had risen at last, but behind such a thick gray curtain of cloud that it cast only a wan gray light, and no warmth at all, across the overcrowded camp, where the refugees from the mine had spent an uncomfortable night cheek by jowl with their rescuers. All had shared alike in the shock of what had happened.

And then there were the villagers, those who remained, who had collapsed when the Lady had died but had been far enough outside the camp not to be swallowed by its destruction. They had regained consciousness perhaps half an hour after the ground had stilled and were now under guard in a segregated section of the camp: perhaps eighty men and youths in all.

Dawn had revealed the answer to the question of what had happened to the Lady's wolves. Five gray bodies had so far been found, all lying where they had fallen in the forest near the camp, scattered in a semicircle around it with their noses pointed at its heart, as though they had been rushing to the Lady's aid when Mara's bolt had taken her life. Mara could only think that once their magical links to the lady had been severed, the magic had rebounded, striking them down where they lay. That was why the villagers had collapsed, and the wolves had been more closely linked to the Lady than even the members of her Cadre . . . of whom only one remained: Hamil, who had been fighting outside the walls. It had taken him many hours more to recover from the shock of the Lady's death than the ordinary villagers.

Whiteblaze, at least, remained. For that she was grateful. She did not know what nightmares might have awaited her during her restless and abbreviated sleep if he had not been there. Even with his presence, her dreams had been troubled, confused, with snatches of strange images: un-Masked in the streets of Tamita, Watchers battling unMasked in the woods, the Lady's fortress oddly half-built, none of it familiar, bubbling up from who-knew-where in her magic-addled subconscious.

She shuddered and dug her fingers harder into Whiteblaze's fur. But she also spoke up, as calmly and forcefully as she could. "We must continue," she said. "We have begun this, we must finish it."

"How?" Edrik said. They sat in his tent, he and Chell, Mara and Hyram and Keltan, but with a gesture he took in the larger camp outside. "Some Watchers escaped. They fled the camp's destruction and kept running. My men chased down a few, but not all. Even now they're hurrying to the Secret City. Within four days, five at the outside, the Watcher Army will be on the move. The Watchers will come here first, and then they'll follow us. If we advance to Tamita, they will crush us against the walls, even if they don't catch us beforehand . . . which they almost certainly will. We cannot move quickly with so many people to shepherd, many of whom are barely able to walk."

"And, Mara, even if we reach Tamita," Chell said, "what good will it do? The Lady is dead. Can you destroy the Autarch single-handedly as she clearly believed she could?"

"No," Mara said. "Not in the same way. Nor would I want to. It's clear now she only needed us to get her this far. From here, charged with magic from the ravine and its unMasked and the unMasked here—and magic from you and all of your fighters, as well, had she lived to take it—she would have simply marched straight to Tamita, blasted open the gate, strode into the Palace, and killed the Autarch. That's what would have happened had we not stopped her." *Had I not killed her.* She swallowed, remembering the terrible sound of the crossbow bolt tearing through Arilla's skull, the spray of blood.

"But we did stop her," Edrik said. "And without her, we cannot defeat the Autarch."

"You're wrong," Mara said. "The Lady had another plan, if her first failed. I know what it is. And it can still work."

Edrik's eyes narrowed. "The Lady told you this plan?"

"Of course," Mara said. "How else would I know it?"

"When?"

Mara opened her mouth, closed it again. "I . . . can't remember," she admitted. *How odd. I know exactly what she planned if the attacks on the mines failed and she did not get the magic she was counting on from each. I know it in every detail.*

But I can't remember when she told it to me.

Clearly not all of her memories had returned when she'd killed Mayson. She wondered what else she had forgotten.

She wished she could forget killing Mayson.

"I can't remember," she repeated. "But what difference does that make? I *do* know her plan. And I can still make it work without her, with a few alterations."

"You trust the Lady's plan?" Edrik demanded. "Even after what happened yesterday?"

"Her first plan failed. That doesn't mean her second will."

"And you are strong enough to carry it out?"

"Yes, I am. With, as I said, a few alterations."

Edrik still looked skeptical.

"What do you have to do?" Chell interjected.

"I have to make Masks," Mara said. "Not inert ones, like Catilla wanted—but functioning ones, ones with magic inside them."

"Why would we want *those?*" Edrik demanded.

"Because they would not contain the Autarch's magic," Mara said. "They would contain the magic of the Lady." She frowned at her own turn of phrase. "Mine, I mean."

"To what end?" Edrik said.

"To allow us to infiltrate Tamita without being detected by the Watchers, of course."

"The whole army?" Chell said skeptically.

"No," Mara said. "I could not make that many Masks."

"How many *will* you make, then?"

"Three."

Edrik blinked, then laughed harshly. "Three? What good would that do us? Perhaps the Lady could do something with a 'force' that size, but she's dead. What could you possibly accomplish with only two companions, even if you got into the city?"

Anger surged in Mara. "I did enough when I was trapped there and escaped through the wall!"

"Not enough to overthrow the city," Edrik said.

Mara took a deep breath and forced the sudden fury down . . . instead of tearing magic from someone and strangling Edrik with it, as she wanted. She had to learn to put aside the anger that came so quickly now. Anger was the Lady's tool. For that reason alone it shouldn't be hers.

Anger drove me to pull magic from the unMasked at the ravine. Anger drove me to kill Mayson without a second thought. The Lady told me to release it, but instead I have to learn to control it. Otherwise I'm still becoming what the Lady wanted me to be.

"I don't have to overthrow the city," Mara said. "I just have to kill the Autarch."

"How?" Edrik demanded. "How will you even get close to him?"

Mara took a deep breath. "I will infiltrate the Child Guard."

They stared at her as if she were crazy. She wished she could be certain she wasn't.

Her memory of the Lady's backup plan had returned to her during the night, as she lay awake between snatches of troubled sleep. With the Lady dead, her first thought had been, like Edrik's, that the mission had failed, that the best they could hope for was to slink back to the Lady's village and permanent exile . . . though that would likely be short-lived, since it would not take long for the Autarch to discover the pass through which they had infiltrated Aygrima and send his Watchers north to root them out and destroy them.

She knew as well as Edrik that their small force could not take Tamita by force even with her magical help—not even if she were committed to pull power from the city's citizens as the Lady would have, because she could not hold as much magic as the Lady. Not yet, at least, and having seen in the Lady the end result of the unbridled use of her Gift, she did not want to. Despite all the horror of the day before she *still* felt the pull of the magic in the people around her . . . felt it, and *wanted* it. Even now, even here, the thought had crossed her mind that she need not convince Edrik and Chell that her plan had a chance of success, that all she had to do was reach out into their minds and twist them a little so they would agree . . .

She pushed that temptation aside. She could convince them. She had to.

She could not—no, *would* not—execute the Lady's backup plan as the Lady would have. The Lady had intended to don a fake Mask, enter the city, and then tear magic from the citizens of Tamita to give herself the power to enter the Palace and strike down the Autarch. But Mara had realized in the night, as she tossed and turned, that she didn't have to launch such a frontal attack, one the Lady might have pulled off but she knew she could not. Stealth would serve her far better. If she could get close to the Autarch without his being aware of her presence, she could strike at him with far less magic, or even without magic at all. He was as vulnerable to physical attacks as the Lady had proven to be.

Who was always close to the Autarch? The Child Guard.

She dug her fingers even harder into Whiteblaze's fur. "Listen," she said. "The Child Guard are not completely cut off from their old lives. They receive messages. I know one of the Guard, a boy named Greff. More importantly, I know his parents . . . they were the farmers who took me in the night the dog frightened my horse on our journey to Tamita, remember? With their help, I can make contact with Greff . . . and then take his place."

"You would kill him?" Edrik said.

"No!" Mara snapped. "Convince him. Offer him a chance to return to his parents. He will leap at it. Any of the Child Guard would."

"And you could disguise yourself as this boy?"

"The Child Guard wear loose robes," Mara said. "I was told I'm of a height with him . . . close enough, anyway." Although she was uneasily aware that boys had a nasty habit of gaining several inches over short periods of time . . . just how tall would Greff be now? "I can take a . . . soulprint . . . from him, and impose it on a Mask of my own making, so that any Watcher will see me as Greff."

"The Autarch, too?"

"The Lady assured me, when she taught me how to make Masks, that they would fool anyone. Including the Autarch."

"So once again we must rely on the goodwill and truthfulness of the Lady?" Edrik growled. "She had neither."

"Do you have a better idea?" Mara countered. "Besides retreat and eventual defeat, I mean?"

Edrik grimaced. "What is our role in all this?"

"You still need to march south," Mara said. "I will have better luck infiltrating the Palace if all eyes are focused outward. An attacking army should do it." She frowned. "And I'll need a small force inside the walls with me. Bodyguards. The most likely place for my confrontation with the

Autarch is within the Palace somewhere. His Sun Guards will move to protect him if he realizes he is under threat. I'll need my own guards to hold them off. I'll also need someone to accompany me, disguised as a Watcher in another Mask of my making. A girl traveling alone might attract unwanted attention. One escorted by a Watcher should not."

"This 'small force' you need," Edrik said. "How will you get *them* inside—inside the City *and* the Palace? More false Masks?"

"No," Mara said. "No time to make that many. But I know a way." *If it's still there, and if we can get to it.* "I know the walls of Tamita well, especially near the Market Gate. We can't open the Market Gate itself: it's too well guarded. But two towers over from it there is a door—what I think they call a sally port. Narrow, just big enough for one man to pass through at a time. It's tucked around the curve of the tower, completely hidden from the Market Gate. I've never seen a guard on it. I don't even know if the Watchers remember it's there. The city, after all, has never been threatened . . . until now. Locked and barred, of course, but magic should make short work of opening it."

"And once they're inside the city? How do you get into the Palace?"

"I know a back way," Mara said. "The path the unMasked follow as they start their exile. The path *I* followed."

Chell was giving her a faint smile. She almost thought it was of approval. But Edrik wasn't through with his objections. "So you want *us* to attack Tamita from the outside to buy *you* time inside," he said. "But why should the Autarch even react to us? Our force is tiny. He can simply sit behind his walls and wait for his Watcher Army to crush us."

"He could sit and wait if the walls were intact," Mara said. "But they aren't. Not since I blew down a large chunk of them. Strike there, where they are still rebuilding, and he will have to respond. Focused on that threat, he'll be less likely to spot the true danger inside his own Palace. Then, once he is . . . dead . . . you'll have to be ready to seize control of the city. Most of the Masked will turn against the Watchers. Even some of the

Watchers will side with the people . . . but there could be bloodshed and chaos if there's a complete power vacuum."

Edrik looked at her with narrowed eyes. "I was not aware you had thought so long and hard about this."

"The Lady and I talked about many possibilities," Mara said. *I guess. Because even though I can't remember it, I can't imagine where else this is all coming from. I sound like a military commander. Which I'm not.*

She blinked. *Or I guess maybe I am now.* After all, the part about letting a small force in through the sally port and sneaking into the Palace the back way, disguised as a Child Guard, had never been part of any of the Lady's plans.

It was an uncomfortable thought. She was asking other people to risk their lives for her again, to trust her judgment. How many had already died for her, or because of her . . . or her judgment?

Well, there's only one way to make their sacrifices count, she told herself fiercely. *Kill the Autarch. Free Aygrima.*

And then what?

She had no immediate answer: but then, killing the Autarch seemed to be more than enough to focus on to start with. What came after—if anything—would have to take care of itself.

"The plan seems sound," Chell said. "But we cannot march south with the refugees from the camp: they'll slow us down too much. And they can't stay here: they'll starve. I suggest we send them north, back to the Lady's village."

"Accompanied by whom?" Edrik demanded. "We have few enough fighters as it is."

"Accompanied by the villagers," Chell said.

"After what they did?"

"*Because* of what they did," Chell said. He nodded at Mara. "Mara says they were under the control of the Lady, and from the horror with which they have reacted to what they remember now she is gone, I do not think they are a threat. I agree, however, that our own men are unlikely to be particularly happy about being asked to fight alongside them again. So we send them back north, with the refugees, through the pass and beyond."

"Once the members of the Watcher Army arrive here and see what has happened, they may pursue them," Edrik said.

"I think that's unlikely when they see that our force has headed south," Chell said. "Their first concern will be the capital. I think we can be certain the Autarch's orders have made that clear."

"Our 'force' will be reduced to just over one hundred fighters," Edrik said.

"Still a threat. And the Autarch is sensitive to threats."

Edrik grunted but raised no more objections. "It will be a difficult journey back to the Lady's village," he said. "We can give them some supplies, but not enough. They will have to forage and hunt."

"The villagers are good at that," Chell said. "It's the best we can do. And it's still better than life in the mine."

"Send them back to the ravine, first," Mara suggested. "There should be some supplies there."

Chell nodded. "Good idea."

Edrik took a deep breath. "Very well," he said. "It seems we are still following the Lady's wishes, even after she betrayed us. Even after she is dead." He glanced at Mara. "If she really is." He stood and went out.

Mara sat there, stung by his words. *It's not true*, she protested to herself. *I'm not becoming the Lady.*

But she remembered the force with which the Lady's magic had torn into her, the way her eyes had blazed just before she died. Mara had poured most of that magic into the mine—she could no more have contained it than she could have drunk the ocean—but how much of a soulprint had the Lady left? Could it be influencing her somehow?

Whiteblaze whined and nuzzled her hand.

No, she thought fiercely. *No. I am using the knowledge she gave me, but I am not her. I will never be her.*

Chell had remained, watching her. She turned her head to him. "I am not the Lady," she said. She needed to say it out loud to *someone*, someone who might believe her. "I am not her, and I will not become her."

"You are not her," Chell said. "But you are not what you were, either." He stood. "I suppose none of us are." He, too, went out.

Mara took a deep breath, and followed.

◆ ◆ ◆

It took half the day to strike the camp and divide the supplies. Hamil, who seemed to have aged ten years overnight, his face haggard, his eyes shadowed, had taken charge of the mine refugees and his remaining men. "You cannot trust all of the unMasked from the mine," Mara told him privately. "Some are as bad as any Watcher." *And worse than some*, she thought silently, with another pang of grief and shame at her murder of Mayson. She could not imagine *he* had been turned into one of the monsters who abused the unMasked.

She wondered why he had even been stationed at the camp. Her horrible suspicion, though she would never know for sure, was that he had been punished for being kind to her when she was in the Palace. She had destroyed his life in more ways than one.

I'm good at destroying life, she thought. *It may be my one true Gift.*

"I know," Hamil said. "But under the conditions in which we will be traveling, I think the need for survival will exert its own discipline."

Mara nodded. "Good luck," she said. "Bear word to Catilla."

"I will." But Hamil did not turn away. "Before I go, Mara, there are two things I must say. First . . . thank you. For myself, and for all those who live in our village. When I first met you, knowing you had the power you have, I hoped that somehow you might be the one to free us from the Lady's reign. I could never tell you that . . . it wouldn't have been safe. But I am grateful."

"You're welcome," Mara said, though it felt wrong for someone to be grateful that she had killed another person. "And the second thing?"

"A warning. Beware, Mara. The Lady . . . Arilla . . . was only a little older than you are now when she first came to us. We took her in, and she used her magic to help us. But over the years, that changed. She never *decided* to become what she became. It just happened. Do not let it happen to you."

How do I stop it? Mara wondered. But she nodded without speaking.

Hamil left her. She watched as the camp refugees straggled away, back along the trail they had followed from the new mine to the old.

"Mara," said Keltan's voice behind her.

She stiffened. She had used a little magic from Whiteblaze to heal his and Hyram's wounds the night before, but she had not spoken to him since. She swallowed, and turned.

"Hello, Keltan."

She was struck again, in the gray light, by how much he had changed since she had first met him in the basement in Tamita. Much taller—he was one of those boys she had been thinking of earlier who shot up inches in just a few months—but also . . . harder. He no longer looked like a boy, but a man: a young man, but a man.

"Chell tells me you plan to infiltrate Tamita," he said. "And that you need someone to accompany you, disguised as a Watcher."

She nodded.

He spread his hands. "Take me."

The offer warmed her heart, but she shook her head. "No."

His face hardened. "I see." He turned to go.

"Keltan!"

He stopped.

"It's not that I don't want you with me," she said desperately. "It's not that I don't still care for you. It's *because* I care for you. It's just . . . I don't . . . I don't know if it's safe. If *I'm* safe."

He turned around then. "Safe?" he said, his tone incredulous. "Do you really think I care about 'safe'?" He took a step toward her. "I care about you, too," he said. "I care that you don't give in completely to this . . . this *thing* inside you. This damned *Gift*." He spat the last word. "The Lady was alone except for her wolves. She lived apart from her villagers. Eventually, she was *feeding* off of them. She forgot they were human, and as a result, *she* stopped being human." He took two more quick steps back to her and reached out and took her shoulders. "Don't make her mistake," he said, voice soft, intense, urgent. "Don't cut yourself off from the people who care about you. *Don't cut yourself off from me.*"

She swallowed, unshed tears stinging her eyes. "All right," she whispered. "All right. You can be my Watcher, if I can make it work. You can help me get into Tamita." *No!* a part of her protested. *If it doesn't work . . . they'll kill him.*

But she'd pushed him aside once before, only to regret it. She'd pushed aside too many people who wanted to help her, people who cared for her, people . . . who loved her. The Lady had died friendless and unloved—and that was another way she did not want to end up like the Lady.

Keltan's face split into a smile. "Thank you!" He slid his hands down her arms, took her hands. "Thank you, Mara."

They looked at each other from just a few inches away. Mara looked into Keltan's eyes. And then, since he was taking way too long, she kissed him. His arms went around her, and hers around him, and they kissed for a long time.

They might have kissed longer if not for the fact that, as the kiss went on, Mara felt the magic inside Keltan so strongly it was all she could do not to pull some of it from him and into herself . . .

. . . and so she broke away, gasping, and pushed him away. He stared at her. "Mara, what . . . ?"

"I can't," Mara mumbled. "I can't . . . you can come with me, but I can't . . ." In confusion and fear, she turned and stumbled away from him. She didn't look back.

◆ ◆ ◆

Though no longer sequestered from the rest of the army by the Lady's villagers, she chose to ride apart that day, accompanied only by Whiteblaze. They would spend one night more in the Wild before they reached their first destination. She and Edrik had talked about it early that morning, with Chell standing silently by, since he knew little of Aygrima's geography.

"We're going to a town called Silverthorne," Mara said. "The Lady and I discussed this." *When?* she asked herself again, but had no answer. She knew without a doubt where she needed to go, though, and how could she know that without the Lady having told her? . . . even if she couldn't exactly remember it. "It's remote, so no word can reach Tamita ahead of us. It has a population of four or five hundred, so it will have its own Maskmaker. And most importantly, it's a silver mining town. I must have silver to make a Child Guard Mask. You know the place?"

Edrik nodded. He drew his sword, used it to draw a rough map in the dirt at his feet. "We're here," he said. "The road to Tamita heads straight south," he drew it in, and marked the city on it. "Silverthorne is over here." He moved his sword to the east of his map. "There are quite a few towns in the east, and they each have a road that leads to the main road, but because they are located in folds of the eastern range, and the terrain is difficult, most do not have roads leading to each other. Silverthorne has only one road in or out."

"How do you know?" Chell asked. "Not that I'm doubting you, but surely that is far outside your usual patrol area from the Secret City."

"There are bandits in the Wild," Edrik said. "And hidden among them are members of the unMasked Army. Our eyes and ears." He glanced at Mara. "A town that size will also have a Watcher garrison."

Mara nodded. "Of course. But only a small one."

"Then it can certainly be taken," Chell said. "But not without cost."

"No," Mara said.

The men looked at her. "Then how—" Chell began.

"I need a Maskmaker. But I don't want another bloodbath," Mara said. "I'm already planning to sneak into Tamita. I should be able to sneak into Silverthorne."

"Without a Mask?" Edrik said.

Mara spread her hands. "I'm not yet sixteen," she said. "And my face is unscarred. I can still pass for a child."

The men considered her. "Barely," Edrik said at last. "You are taller and . . . rounder . . . than you were."

Mara blushed a little, and felt angry at herself for doing so. "Even so. There are fourteen-year-olds taller and 'rounder' than I am, are there not?"

Chell glanced at Edrik. "Yes," he said. He looked back at her. "But if this does not work . . . ? What if you are captured?"

"Then I will free myself," Mara said. "I am not the Lady of Pain and Fire. But I have enough power to handle small-town Watchers, wouldn't you say?" She glanced in the direction of the collapsed mine.

Though it was hidden from them by forest and hill, Chell clearly took her meaning. He smiled. "Fair enough."

"How long will this take?" Edrik said. "Remember there may be an army heading our way. If they catch us before we reach Tamita . . ."

"Two days," Mara said.

Edrik looked unhappy. "That's cutting it fine."

"I know," Mara said. "But I must make these Masks, or we have no chance at all."

Edrik sighed. "Very well." He looked at the map again. "There is a good place to camp about three hours' ride from the town—far enough out we are unlikely to be seen, and well off the road. Who will you take with you?"

"No one," Mara said. "Except Whiteblaze."

"You should have an escort, at least until you are closer to the town," Edrik argued.

"No," Mara said. "If I'm seen with armed men, my ruse won't work."

Edrik looked stubborn.

"You cannot force me to let anyone accompany me," Mara pointed out quietly. "You cannot force me to do anything I don't want to do. Not anymore."

Edrik met her eyes, then. And he looked away first.

Now, riding by herself, she wished she really felt the confidence she had tried so hard to project. Because once again lives relied on her good judgment—and all of her judgment for the past few months seemed to have been bad, leading only to death and destruction.

What if I'm wrong this time? she wondered.

Then more people will die. And I'll be one step closer to matching the Lady's tally of pain and fire.

She pulled her hood closer around her face against the chill of the air and her thoughts, and rode on, Whiteblaze trotting beside her horse.

FIFTEEN

The Maskmaker

L ATE THE NEXT MORNING, Mara left the camp and rode alone
to the town of Silverthorne.

She spotted the smoke from the town half an hour before she saw any
buildings. Knowing it was home to a mine, she had wondered if Silverthorne would look like the mining camp she had just destroyed with the
Lady's power, but in fact, she discovered when she rode over the low ridge
that had hidden the town from sight until she was almost upon it, it looked
nothing like it at all.

Silverthorne nestled up against a cliff face that was pierced with many
dark openings, giving it the look more of the Secret City than the labor
camp. As she watched, a cart laden with ore and pulled by a small donkey
emerged from one of those openings, and trundled along a road covered
with crushed stone to the building whose smoke she had been watching
rise into the sky for so long. Smaller buildings surrounded that big smoking
one, and a fence surrounded all of them.

Behind the big building, a waterfall poured down the cliff. Mara thought the big building must be the smelter, where the silver was extracted from its ore and shaped into ingots to be shipped south to Tamita. A strange deep-throated wheezing came from the building, as though it were alive and breathing through giant lungs, a sound as unnerving in its own way as the constant rumble of the now-destroyed waterwheel in the mining camp.

The town itself, however, appeared completely ordinary: a main street with a few larger buildings (presumably containing shops, stables, and the like), houses spreading out along side streets branching out from the main one, and at the head of that street, a large stone building which she thought must be the Watchers' barracks and town hall.

No cropland or rangeland surrounded Silverthorne. Although she could see some gardens and chicken coops, clearly the town couldn't feed itself. Which must mean regular shipments of food from farther south. Silverthorne existed solely for the production of silver.

The material used for the Masks of the Child Guard.

She rode into the town along the main road. Only a handful of people were about, but they all turned to look at her. She had done her best to look as young, and nondescript, as possible. She had her hair tied back in a ponytail, and had even gone so far as to uncomfortably bind her breasts to reduce her "roundness." The horse wore an old leather saddle that had seen hard use. She did carry a dagger in her boot and a bow slung over her back—no one would ride the Wild without *some* sort of protection—but again, both were as plain as could be.

Of course, Whiteblaze was rather . . . distinctive.

She smiled openly at the people who looked at her, getting an occasional tentative smile in return . . . a smile that often faded into alarm as they got a closer look at the wolf. But she let her smile fall away— because that was what people did—when she neared the center of town and a Watcher stepped off the boardwalk, hand raised. "Hold, girl," he said in a deep voice. His eyes behind the Mask were dark brown, but wrinkles at their corners, caught by the sun, indicated he was older rather than younger. Mara hoped he had a daughter and she reminded him of her.

"Yes, sir," she said, reining the horse to a halt.

The Watcher's eyes flicked to Whiteblaze, then back again. "Name and age?"

"Frina," she said. "Fourteen."

"You're tall for fourteen."

"Fifteen next month," Mara said. "That's why I'm here. To see the Maskmaker."

"Haven't seen you in Silverthorne before," the Watcher said.

"We've just taken up ranching . . . back there," Mara said, gesturing vaguely behind her. "We were all going to come in, but Mom took ill and Dad thought he should stay with her. So he said I had to come to town alone because we're getting too close to my Masking not to get the Maskmaker working."

The Watcher grunted. "Dangerous," he said. "Bandits in these woods."

Mara allowed herself to look alarmed. "Bandits? The man who sold my father the ranch didn't say anything about bandits."

"Probably why he sold it," the Watcher said. He stepped back. "Go on. Maskmaker's at the end of the road, just by the town hall, left side. Got a guest room or two for people like you who come in from out of town to arrange Maskings." He looked past her down the road. "When you go back, I'll send a couple of men with you. They can make sure you get home all right, and check on your parents."

Mara groaned inwardly. But out loud all she said was, "Thank you very much."

"Don't mention it. On your way." He watched her as she trotted the horse on up the street. She was glad he couldn't see the trickle of sweat making its way down her back beneath her clothes.

The Maskmaker's shop was clearly marked by a wooden sign carved in the shape of a Mask, painted white, with rather garish wide blue eyes looking out through the eyeholes and lips an unnatural shade of red behind the mouth opening. Mara tethered her horse to the rail in front of the building, and glanced back up the street. The Watcher, true to his calling, was still watching. She gave him what she hoped looked like a cheery wave, told Whiteblaze, "Stay," in a low voice, and then went through the door into the shop.

Her father, as Master Maskmaker, had never really had a shop. He hadn't needed one, because everyone Gifted *had* to come to him, even from out here: any child born in Silverthorne who proved to have the Gift would be sent to Tamita for Masking.

Though not by my father anymore, Mara thought bitterly. She realized she didn't even know who had taken her father's place as Master Maskmaker. Once, she had hoped it would be her. No longer. But if things went as she hoped, she might soon be making Masks after all . . . and Masks of a kind, and for a purpose, of which her father would surely have approved.

A half-dozen sample Masks were lined up on a ledge at the front of the counter. None were colored, of course, since only the Gifted wore Masks of color, but their white or beige or, in one case, rather daringly dark brown (a little too close to Watcher black, she would have thought, but since the Mask was on display, clearly it had triggered no concern from the Watchers themselves) were inset with decorations that made Mara's eyes widen. The delicate use of filigree and jewel was on a par with her father's, much as it pained her to think it. The Maskmaker in Silverthorne was clearly more talented than she'd had any reason to hope. *He's certain to have the tools I need*, she thought. Then she looked up and saw the woman standing in the curtained door behind the counter. *Or she.*

Wearing a simple gray dress and, despite the artistry of the Masks before Mara, a simple Mask of beaten copper marked only by a single red jewel—a far cry from the ornate Mask her father had made for her (and made to fail . . . she still ached for that beauty lost)—the Maskmaker stared at her. "Do I know you?" she said. Her voice was remarkably deep for a woman's. "You look familiar."

"No," Mara said hastily. "I'm . . . we . . . my family just arrived. We're ranchers. I'm fourteen. But I'll be fifteen soon. So I need a Mask."

You're babbling, she thought, but the woman's question had startled her . . . and worried her.

"No, that's not it." The woman came closer, stared into Mara's face from the other side of the counter. "It will come to me . . . *oh!*" The last word exploded out of her. She came around the end of the corner in a rush, closed the door, pulled the shade, and only then turned to Mara. "You're Mara Holdfast," she whispered. "Charlton Holdfast's daughter. *Why are you here?*"

Mara's heart had leaped into her throat. Her first instinct was to grab magic—she could feel it in the other room, in the workshop, no doubt waiting in an urn like her father's—and silence the woman, to strike her down before she gave the alarm. But she did not.

And when, she wondered, *did violence become my first instinct?*

"How do you know my father?" she asked instead.

"I trained with him," the Maskmaker said. "Four years ago. I met you. You were just a little girl." Mara saw the Maskmaker lick her lips behind the mouth opening of her copper Mask. "But your father is dead. And I heard you failed your Masking." Her eyes flicked to Mara's face. "Though I see no scars . . ."

"My Mask failed," Mara said. "My father made it fail. To protect me. To keep me from the clutches of the Autarch."

The Maskmaker took a step back. Her hands went to the unmarked cheeks of her Mask. "I can't listen to this."

"You have to," Mara said. "Because there is an army of the unMasked. We have destroyed the Autarch's mines of magic. And we're going to destroy the Autarch." *Or at least I am,* she thought. *If he doesn't destroy me first.*

"An army . . ." The Maskmaker's hands fell to her sides again. "The unMasked Army is *real?*"

"It's real," Mara said. "My father arranged for them to rescue me. They wanted me to make Masks for them. But I didn't know how." She spread her hands. "Now, I do."

"No . . ." The Maskmaker's gaze flicked over Mara's shoulder to glance at the door. "You can't make fake Masks. It can't be done."

"It can if you have the right Gift."

"You had the same Gift as your father. I was told that by—"

"That was a lie. A lie I told. I don't have the same Gift as Father." Mara took a deep breath. "I have the same Gift as the Autarch . . . the same Gift as the Lady of Pain and Fire. I can see and use all kinds of magic. The Lady taught me how to make Masks, Masks that aren't tied to the Autarch, so they won't break if you betray him. Masks the Watchers can't detect as fake. Masks that I can use to infiltrate the Palace and remove the Autarch from power once and for all." She regarded the Maskmaker steadily. "Don't you want that?"

"I—" The Maskmaker hesitated. And in the moment of that hesitation, her Mask, with a sound like a thunderclap, broke neatly down the middle and fell away from her face: a kind, middle-aged face that instantly turned white. The Maskmaker's hand flew to her mouth, and her dark brown eyes widened in terror. "What have you done to me?"

"I didn't do anything," Mara said. "Except force you to take a side."

The Maskmaker dropped to her knees behind the counter. Mara walked around the end of it to see her kneeling there, holding the two halves of her broken Mask together as if she could fix it just by wishing it whole. "You've murdered me!" she whispered. "When the Watchers find out . . ."

"They won't find out if you help me," Mara said. She knelt beside the woman and took the broken Mask away from her. "I can restore your Mask. I can make it so that it will never break or reveal your secrets to the Watchers, no matter what you think about them or the Autarch."

The woman stared at her. "If you're wrong . . ."

"I'm not," Mara said, with more confidence than she felt, but she let none of her own self-doubt show in her face. She wanted this woman's help—wanted it given voluntarily, so she did not have to do what she had been fully prepared to do when she rode into town, and use magic to coerce that help. If she had to do that, it would be one more step down the road followed by the Lady of Pain and Fire, and every time she could choose to not take another of those steps, she wanted to do so.

"You have left me with no choice," the Maskmaker said bitterly. She took back the pieces of her broken Mask, and stood. "My name is Herella. Tell me what you need." She swept open the curtain into her workroom, and went inside.

Mara got to her feet and followed her.

The workroom was very different from her father's cozy retreat in their house. Unlike the dark wooden paneling he favored, this room had brightly painted walls: blue and green and yellow and red. Instead of a long work counter along one wall, Herella had a round table in the middle of the room. And rather than standing alone, her basin of magic, shipped from Tamita, was built into that table, so that no matter where around its circumference she worked, she had only to reach out for the magic she needed.

Her tools hung on the red-painted wall. The green wall was centered by the archway that led into the front of the shop. Shelves on either side of that arch held the raw materials of the Maskmaker's trade. Large bins filled with clay lined the bottom shelves, while the higher ones held the components of various glazes and decoration. The blue wall, to Mara's left, was mostly taken up by large windows which Herella was hastily shuttering, though they opened into a walled courtyard and there was no one to see.

The back wall, painted yellow, held more shelves, with Masks in various stages of completion. A wooden door, standing open, showed a short cobblestoned path to a small stone building with a chimney from which smoke rose in a steady stream. *The kiln*, Mara thought. All of the Masks Herella normally made began as ordinary clay. Beyond the back wall of the courtyard, she could see far greater clouds of smoke rising from the silver smelter.

The rest of the courtyard was taken up by a vegetable garden, filled with the bright green growth of spring.

Herella closed the back door, cutting off Mara's view. "Well?" she said, turning around so that they stood on opposite sides of the round worktable, on which rested Herella's broken Mask.

"I need to make three Masks," Mara said. "And repair yours."

"What kind?"

"An ordinary white one such as any country girl might wear," Mara said. "A black one, for a Watcher. And a silver one, for a Child Guard."

"You're mad," Herella breathed. "I do not create Masks for Watchers or the Child Guard. I create no Masks for the Gifted. That is the sole responsibility of the Master Maskmaker . . . as you well know."

"You've made a dark-brown Mask," Mara said. "I saw it out front."

"We have workers from all over the Autarchy," Herella said. "Many of them are from the southern coast where dark skin is more common than light. Some prefer a Mask that reflects that. But brown is not black."

Mara made an impatient gesture. "It's not hard to blend pigments to create black."

Herella looked like she had a bad taste in her mouth. "All right. We might manage a black Mask. But I have only a little silver in stock. I use it only for decoration. We cannot possibly create a silver Mask."

"There's a silver mine practically in your backyard," Mara said.

Herella snorted. "You think I can just walk up there and ask for an ingot?" she said. "Especially *now*?" She gestured at her unMasked face. "If I set foot out of my door I'll be arrested and hanged, thanks to you."

"Then we start by repairing your Mask," Mara said with a touch of irritation. "And while we're doing that, we'll talk about how to get that ingot."

"You can't—" Herella began, but Mara cut her off.

"I can. Now give me your Mask."

Herella, expression skeptical, pushed the pieces across the table to her. Mara reached for the magic seething in the basin at the table's center, but then stopped. *No*, she thought. *Time to show her a hint of what I can really do.*

"One moment," she said, and went back into the shop. She opened the front door. Her horse flicked an ear. Whiteblaze, lying beside the horse with his head on his paws, raised his head and stared at her hopefully. "Come in," she told him, and he got up and trotted into the shop. She closed the door and led him into the workshop.

Herella backed up when she saw him, her face going pale again. "That's a—"

"Wolf," Mara said. "Yes. And full of magic I can use."

"That's impossible!"

"Watch." Mara touched Whiteblaze's head and drew out magic through the amulet. He wagged his tail. Then she reached out, took the two halves of the broken Mask, and pressed them together. She poured magic into the copper face. For a moment the crack in it glowed red, then white . . . then it darkened.

The Mask gleamed unbroken as before, without even a hint of a seam marking its smooth surface. Herella gasped. "How . . ."

"How do you think? Magic," Mara said, more of her irritation boiling to the surface. She was getting tired of the Maskmaker's skepticism. "But if you put it on now, it will only break again. So . . ."

She took more magic from Whiteblaze. The Lady had explained to her, while teaching her how to make a Mask, that the magic in the Masks reflected the individual's soulprint on the Mask's surface. The Watchers could see that soulprint, or at least some of them could. The Lady had agreed with Mara's father that likely only a very few Watchers could read the soulprint in detail, but she suspected many more could see a few broad strokes of it, enough to know whom they needed to keep a closer watch on, or question.

So to alter a Mask into one that would fool a Watcher, one needed to do two things: remove the enchantment that would make the Mask break if betrayal of the Autarch were detected in the soulprint of the person wearing it, and place on the surface of the Mask a *fake* soulprint, one showing only loyalty and faithfulness to the Autarch and his rule. The former was easy. The latter was much more difficult. "If you don't want this Mask to betray you to the Watchers," she said to Herella, "stay quiet until I am done. I have to concentrate."

She put her hands on the Mask.

When she had last attempted this, during her training with the Lady, she'd found it very difficult to call on the portion of her Gift that corresponded to the Watchers' sight. "Just because you can see and use all types of magic doesn't mean some forms will not be easier than others," the Lady had warned. "It's clear you have a knack for what they call in Tamita 'engineering,' the ability to manipulate matter and energy. You've shown proficiency in healing. You should be strong in enchantment, given your father's Gift. But I do not think you are as strong as I am in the ability to manipulate people's minds and read their souls . . . not yet." *If I were, perhaps I would have read hers and seen her for what she was.*

Then she sighed. She'd told Herella not to distract her, and here she was distracting herself. She concentrated again . . . and to her surprise, touched that aspect of her Gift easily. She could see the soulprint, like a ghostly copy of Herella's face laid over the copper skin. She could also see within it the discoloration, almost like a tumor, marking her betrayal. *So if I just remove that*, she thought, *and then smooth the rest . . . and freeze it in place . . .*

Her hands moved over the copper. Magic flowed out of her. More magic flowed into her from Whiteblaze. The work was delicate. If even a hint of betrayal remained visible . . .

Time passed. She had no notion of how much. And then, finally, it was done. She released the Mask and stepped back. She took a deep breath.

The room had gone dark, only gray twilight showing through the cracks in the shutters.

Herella was gone.

SIXTEEN

Black and Silver

MARA SPAT OUT a curse she'd learned from Chell's sailors and spun toward the archway into the shop. She stopped dead as she saw the Maskmaker standing there, a covered platter in one hand and a bottle of wine in the other. "I thought you might be hungry when you were finished," she said, and Mara swallowed her anger, again wondering why it had come so easily, and managed a small smile instead.

"Thank you," she said. "That's very considerate."

"Is it done?" Herella asked. She crossed to the table, put down the platter and the wine, and leaned over the Mask. "It's . . . perfect," she breathed. "You can't tell it's been broken."

"Wouldn't be much use if you could," Mara said. The smell of roast chicken from the platter was making her mouth water. "May I . . . ?"

"That's why I brought it," the Maskmaker said absently. She picked up the Mask. "And the magic . . . ?"

"Think what you want. Say what you will. The Mask won't care." Mara lifted the lid of the platter. The bird looked as wonderful as it smelled, and there were roast carrots and potatoes accompanying it, plus a small loaf of crusty bread with a pat of butter melting inside it. "You made this?"

Herella laughed. "Well, it's not as if I have servants. I cook for myself. And I'm pretty good, if I do say so myself."

"I'd say you're wonderful," Mara said, and sat down to eat. But she froze with a piece of bread halfway to her mouth as pounding erupted on the front door.

"Watcher!" Herella said, her hand flying to her throat.

"Put on your Mask," Mara said. "I'll answer it."

She got up and went out into the shop. The pounding came again. Mara reached up and undid her ponytail, letting her hair fall loose around her shoulders. She gave it a good mussing with both hands, rubbed her eyes, and then reached out to open the door, yawning as she did so, so the Watcher on the other side got a good look at her gullet before he saw anything else. "Oh!" she said, snapped her mouth shut, and then laughed. "I'm sorry, you woke me."

"I apologize." It was the same Watcher who had met her in the street. "The sun has set. You cannot leave your horse on the street. Have you even fed and watered him?" He peered past her into the dim interior of the shop. "Is the Maskmaker here?"

"I'm here, Tranik," Herella said from behind Mara. She glanced over her shoulder. The Maskmaker was wearing the renewed Mask, though there was a slight tremor to her voice that hinted to Mara that perhaps she was not entirely sanguine about its effectiveness.

Mara, holding her breath, looked back at the Watcher—Tranik. But if he noticed anything strange about her Mask, he didn't say anything— and he certainly would have, being a Watcher. "Hello, Herella," Tranik said. "The girl will stay with you tonight?"

"Yes," Herella said, and the tremor in her voice was gone. "We are still discussing her Mask, and I can hardly put her back on the road in the night with bandits about."

"Her horse must be stabled," Tranik said. "Curfew is already upon us."

"I'll see to it," Herella said.

Tranik nodded. He lowered his gaze to Mara. "Remember, when you go back, I will send two Watchers with you to talk to your parents."

"I remember," Mara said.

The Watcher grunted and stumped away.

"What will you do about *that*?" Herella whispered.

"I don't know yet," Mara said. "Where do I take the horse?"

"The stables are in the building in back," Herella said. "Bring the horse around the side of the house and I'll let you into the yard."

Mara stepped out into the deepening gloom. There were still a few people on the street, but all seemed in a hurry to get somewhere else. *Curfew,* she thought. *Just like Tamita.* She untethered the horse. "Sorry, boy," she said. "I should have looked after you the moment I arrived." He nuzzled her coat, looking for food, and she felt guilty. She turned to lead him to the stable, then paused. She had the feeling she was being watched, and unlike most people, it was just possible she really *could* sense that. She looked around. No one appeared to be paying her any mind, all focused on getting to wherever they needed to be rather than out on the street after curfew. She raised her eyes. There were hills to the south of the town, nothing but dark silhouettes in the fading light.

Edrik, she thought. *He couldn't leave well enough alone. He sent someone to watch me.* She felt the flare of anger that was becoming all too familiar, and tamped it down. Even if she were right, and Keltan or Hyram or someone else from the unMasked Army were in those woods overlooking the town, there was nothing she could do about it. She just hoped they didn't do anything foolish.

She led the horse around the side of the house as instructed. The Maskmaker was holding open a gate in the courtyard wall. Mara led the horse through, and then around to the back of the outbuilding she had thought held only the Maskmaker's kiln. There were only two stalls, neither occupied, but there was fresh hay and fresh water and the horse was pleased to see both. Leaving him happily munching, Mara followed Herella back into the workshop. Herella bustled around, lighting the oil lamps that punctuated the walls. In their yellow light, amplified by oval mirrors, she stepped to the round workshop table and reached up to remove her Mask once more. She held it out at arm's length, staring at its copper face. "You did it," she said in wonder. "You actually created a Mask that can fool a Watcher."

"Now do you believe I can do what I say I can do?" Mara said. "Now will you help me do it?"

"I'll help," Herella said. "If you can really overthrow the Autarch . . . I'll do anything." She gave her Mask a nervous glance, but it remained merrily intact.

"Then let's get started," Mara said. "After I finish eating." She sat down to conclude her interrupted repast.

"I still don't have enough silver to make a Child Guard Mask," Herella said as Mara munched.

"But can you get it?" Mara said. She regarded the bottle of wine, but decided not to have any. It didn't seem like a good idea before sculpting a Mask on which the overthrow of the Autarch might depend. She and wine had never really gotten along very well.

Herella chewed on her lower lip, a childlike sign of uncertainty that made her look younger. "Perhaps," she said. "But not until the morning shift at the mine. I know the morning foreman. Maybe I can sweet-talk him."

"Let's start with the Watcher Mask, then," Mara said. She pushed aside the now-empty plate, and turned to regard the pigments on the shelves. "As I remember my father's lessons, for black we need cobalt, manganese, and iron rust?"

Herella nodded. "Very good." She pointed to the green wall. "They're all on the top shelf, just to the left of the door. If you could fetch them down for me . . . ?"

They labored into the night by yellow lamplight. Mara found herself enjoying the work more than she expected. It brought back memories of . . . was it really just last year? . . . working with her father in his workshop during her pre-apprenticeship, learning the shaping and firing of clay even though she was prohibited from learning anything of how to infuse them with magic. That knowledge had come from the Lady. *If this all ends well*, she thought as she kneaded the clay, *I could become a potter. I'd like that. Nice and peaceful. Safe* . . .

When the clay was mixed with the elements that would turn it black when fired, Herella hesitated. "This is the point where I would normally infuse it with the 'recipe,'" she said. She went to the shelf and brought down a black lodestone urn. She opened it, and Mara looked inside. It contained black lodestone dust, pulsing in her Gifted vision with all the colors of magic . . . magic Mara knew she dare not touch, for it was linked to the Autarch.

"Leave it out," Mara said.

Herella nodded. She put the urn back on the shelf, then returned to the table. "Will you sculpt it, or shall I?" she asked.

"I will," Mara said. "I've seen more Watchers than you have." *That* was an understatement.

"Did your father craft Watcher Masks, too?" Herella asked as Mara took the clay and began to mold it onto one of the blank wooden face molds that formed the basis for all Masks.

"Only for high-ranking Watchers who wanted something special," Mara said. "The Watchers have their own Maskmaker, I was told, though I never knew who it was."

The Mask quickly took shape. Mara cut out the eyeholes and the mouth opening, the latter smaller than a normal Mask's. She had done this basic level of sculpting for her father many times during her pre-apprenticeship; she had done it for herself during all her failed attempts to make fake Masks for Catilla. She thought she could have done it in her sleep.

All Masks looked the same until they were placed on the face of the person being Masked: then, through the magic they contained, they shaped themselves . . . or failed, tearing apart the wearer's face in the process.

Pain . . . terror . . . the crunch of her nose breaking . . . blood on white stone . . . her mother's screams . . .

She shuddered, and deftly adjusted the brow; one side was slightly thicker than the other. Then she was done.

"That was good work," Herella said. "You would have made an excellent Maskmaker."

"No offense," Mara said, "but I'm hoping that soon there won't be any Maskmakers at all." She smiled a little. "I'm afraid that means you'll be out of a job."

Herella smiled back. "Nothing would make me happier." She regarded the blank Mask. "So will you add the final enchantment?"

Mara shook her head. "I know how to do it . . . now . . . but you have more practice. Please?"

"Of course." Herella reached into the basin of magic. Mara watched her. This was the step she had not been able to replicate when she was making fake Masks for Catilla, the reason her Masks had been nothing but heavy bits of pottery.

Herella deftly passed her hands over the Mask. Mara could see redgold magic flowing into the clay, which continued to glow in Mara's Gifted sight even after Herella withdrew her hands. "Done," she said. She looked at Mara. "It needs days of drying before you can fire it, you know. Can you wait that long?"

"No," Mara said. "I can't. But I don't need to." She dipped red from the basin of magic in the middle of the table and passed her hand over the Mask. It hissed and a cloud of steam rose into the air and vanished. "Bone dry," Mara said.

Herella touched the Mask. "Well!" she said. "I wish *I* had that trick." She glanced at the basin. "But I will run short of magic by month's end at this rate."

"If all goes well, that won't matter," Mara said. "Now for the plain white Mask."

"I'll do it," Herella said. "Second nature." And indeed, it took her less than an hour to produce it. Once again, Mara used magic to dry it. Herella put both of the new Masks on a tray, said, "I'll put them in the kiln," and went out the back door into the darkness.

This time, Mara started not with clay, but with wax. Casting a metal Mask was far different from carving one from clay. First the Mask had to be modeled in wax. The wax Mask would then be covered with a heavy coating of clay—leaving one strategically placed opening. The clay would be fired, melting the wax and hardening it. The melted wax would pour out through the open channel, and then, once the clay had cooled, the molten silver would be poured in through that same channel. One it had solidified, the clay covering could be broken, and the Mask polished.

Casting a metal object normally took a matter of days, but that was without magic involved. With what the Lady had taught her, Mara could do it in a day, cooling clay and silver far faster than normal: but it still started with the wax carving. She had barely begun when Herella returned. "Tomorrow night at the earliest before we can pull them out," she said. "Couldn't you fire the Masks with magic as well?"

"Maybe," Mara said, "but it would be delicate work, and if they cracked, we'd have to start over. No, we'll leave that part of it to the kiln."

She bent back to her task. Herella watched for a while, then disappeared. She came back in half an hour or so. "I've prepared your bed," she said.

Bed! The word sounded wonderful. Mara brushed her hair out of her eyes with the back of one hand. "Can't come until I've finished this."

"Top of the stairs, first door on the left," Herella said. She continued to watch Mara work. "You look a lot like your father," she said softly after a few moments. "I watched him work by gaslight one evening during my training . . . you stick the tip of your tongue out between your lips when you're working, just like he did."

Mara stopped working. She'd forgotten that. She pulled her tongue back into her mouth and blinked away sudden tears. Then she picked up her scraper and bent over her work again.

By the time she had finished the wax Mask, covered it with clay, and put the mold into the kiln, Herella had been long asleep. Mara straightened her aching back. She had no idea how late it was. She turned down the lamps, went out into the shop, found the stairs and the room at the top of them, undressed, and was asleep within seconds of laying her head on the pillow.

◆　◆　◆

The next day they went to get the silver.

"The foreman's name is Ginther," Herella said as they climbed the road to the mine, paved, like the road she had seen running along the cliff face, in crushed white stone. Mara had told Whiteblaze to stay put, and the last she'd seen of him, he was contentedly snoozing in a patch of sunlight in Herella's courtyard. "Ginther was sweet on me once, I think. Married now, and three near-grown children—all of whose Masks I have made—but I should be able to talk him into giving us what we need. Some of the other foremen, it might have been harder. There aren't a lot of Gifted in Silverthorne except for the Watchers, so there's a bit of superstitious wariness."

Mara remembered how even Keltan had reacted when she had first used magic in his presence to repair Kirika's torn cloak in the cavern they had passed through on the way to the Secret City. "I've encountered that myself."

"You," Herella went on, "just stick to the story you told Watcher Tranik. Same story, mind: last thing we need is Ginther and Tranik comparing notes and something not adding up. Tranik is sharper than you'd expect a Watcher in the back of nowhere to be. Maybe because what we mine is valuable to the Autarch. But don't speak at all unless Ginther asks you a direct question."

They were approaching the top of the road, and a kind of guardhouse, a little hut that stood outside the gate through the fence surrounding the mine buildings. One window in the hut faced their direction; the other was at right angles to them. Both were unshuttered, and inside the hut Mara could see the shadowed figure of a man, bent over.

The morning shift had entered an hour before and the night shift was long departed, so they had the road to themselves. They went up to the guardhouse. The man inside, who wore a plain gray mask marked on the cheeks with the crossed hammer and chisel of a miner inlaid in silver (naturally), looked up as they approached.

"Maskmaker," he said. "What brings you to the mine?"

"Hello, Shanks," Herella said briskly. "I need to see Foreman Ginther. Is he in his office?"

The miner nodded and got up. "I'll take you—"

"No need," Herella said. "I know the way."

The miner nodded again, and shifted his gaze to Mara. "And who's this?" he said. She couldn't see his expression, but she heard the leer in his voice.

"Ranch girl, in to make Masking plans," Herella said. "How's your wife, Shanks?"

Shanks looked away from Mara. "Fine," he mumbled. "She's fine." He sat down. "Go on in," he said without looking at them again.

"Thank you," Herella said. She led Mara through the gate in the fence, a simple wooden construction maybe six feet high—nothing on the scale of the stockade around the magic mine. *Well*, she thought, *they don't have to worry about their workers escaping.*

The smelter loomed ahead of them, smoke rising from it, and behind it, the waterfall cascaded down the cliff face. The wheezing sound grew louder. "What *is* that noise?" she said. "It sounds like the building is breathing."

Herella laughed. "Suppose it is, in a way. Although a human making that sound wouldn't be long for this world . . . it's bellows. They're driven by the waterfall back there. Keeping the fires hot enough to smelt the ore."

"Are we going in there?"

Herella shook her head. "Shanks said Ginther's in his office. It's in one of the outbuildings—that one, over there." "Over there" was a modest one-story structure made of stone, with a slate roof. Herella led the way to it and stuck her head in the open door. "Ginther?"

"Herella!" boomed a voice. Herella stepped back, and a giant of a man with lots of bushy white hair showing beneath his Mask and no hair at all on the brown leathery pate above it appeared in the doorway. "What an unexpected delight! What brings you to the mine?" He glanced at Mara. "And who's your young friend?" Unlike Shanks, there was nothing salacious in his tone.

"I'm short of silver, Ginther," Herella said. "I was hoping you could help." She indicated Mara. "This is Frina. She's from a new ranch family a few miles away. She's staying with me while we plan her Mask. Her folks want something a bit special for her."

"Hello, Frina," Ginther said. But she saw his lips curving into a frown behind the Mask and tensed for a moment, afraid he was going to challenge her story. Instead, though, he looked back at Herella. "Short? Did you not get your usual shipment just a couple of weeks ago? It's in the ledger—"

"I got it," Herella said. "But I need more."

Ginther scratched his chin beneath the beard. "Bit irregular," he said. "Can't you wait until your next shipment?"

Herella shook her head. "I'm afraid not." She lowered her voice. "Ginther, can I be honest? I've been experimenting with silver-copper alloys to get different colors for decoration, and I overdid it. I used up all my silver and some of the alloys are too dark to be good for anything. And now I've got an . . . important client who desperately wants silver—a lot of silver—for his daughter's Mask."

"Headman Larmic?"

"You know I can't tell you that," Herella said.

Ginther laughed. "I think you just did." He scratched his chin again. "How much do you need?"

"An ingot should do it," Herella said.

Ginther's eyes widened behind his Mask. Then he laughed. "You're joking."

"No," Herella said. "This . . . client . . . wants something really special."

Ginther shook his head. "Can't be done, Herella. You've got an allowance of silver. You've already had it for this month. I can advance you next month's, but then you'll have to wait until the regular shipment for the month after that. And you only get a quarter of an ingot per shipment anyway. You know every ounce is accounted for. Are you trying to get me in trouble with the Watchers?"

"Ginther," Herella said, a hint of pleading in her voice. "Please. For me?"

Ginther sighed. "Herella, you know I'd do anything for you if I could . . . but this is impossible. I'll give you next month's allotment, but no more."

That's not enough, Mara thought. Anger swelled in her. *And I have no time for this.*

And then, without even realizing she was about to do it, she found herself reaching inside Ginther, into his soulprint, the magic bound to his mind. She could see the flow of his thoughts. A touch of magic there, a touch there . . . she withdrew, and took a deep breath.

That had felt *good*.

Ginther had sucked in air as if startled. For a moment he stood still, then he let the breath out in a *whoosh* and said, "What am I thinking? Of course you can have an ingot, Herella. For you, anything." He jerked a thumb back toward the interior of his office. "There's a shipment waiting in the lockup. I'll just pull an ingot out of that. They won't even notice there's one missing until it gets to Tamita. Plenty of time for me to come up with a story to cover the oversight. You two just wait here." He disappeared inside.

Mara turned toward Herella . . . and reeled back as the Maskmaker's hand lashed out and slapped her face so hard it made her ears ring. She raised her own hand to her stinging cheek as anger roared up inside her again. She barely restrained herself from reaching inside the old woman as she had Ginther. *How dare she . . . !*

"What was that for?" she snarled.

"I saw what you did," Herella said in a furious whisper. "I don't know how you did it, but I could see it being done . . . the flash of magic, the way Ginther just froze for a minute . . . you manipulated him. You used magic on his mind."

"So what if I did?" Mara said. "Your womanly wiles clearly weren't up to the task."

Even as she said it, she recoiled in horror from what she was saying. And what she had just done. *This isn't me*, she wailed inwardly. *It doesn't even sound like me. It sounds like . . .*

No!

But she couldn't deny it.

She sounded like the Lady of Pain and Fire. And what she had just done, the way she had manipulated Ginther's mind . . . that was pure Lady.

Have I used so much magic I'm becoming like her? she thought. *Or . . . ?*

A nastier thought struck her.

Or when the Lady died, and all that magic poured out of her, poured through me, when her soulprint hit me like a hurricane . . . did it change me? Did it change me into someone more like her? The sudden anger . . . the rush to use magic even when it's not necessary, even when it's wrong . . . I wasn't like that . . . before.

Maybe every soulprint I've encountered has changed me a little. Maybe mostly it's too faint for me to notice. But the Lady was so powerful . . . and so full of magic when I killed her. . . .

"Herella," she gasped out, "I'm sorry. I'm so sorry. That wasn't . . . I'm not . . . that wasn't me."

"Then who was it?" Herella snarled.

Mara swallowed and looked down at the ground.

Ginther returned and handed Herella a leather satchel. "Brought my lunch in that," he said. "Bring it back sometime, will you? Can't have you walking out of the mine with a silver ingot in plain sight." He chuckled. "Even Shanks would notice something like that."

"Thank you," Herella said tightly.

"Any time, Herella, any time," Ginther said. He gave them both a friendly wave and went back into the office.

"Will he get in trouble?" Mara said in a small voice as she trailed Herella back to the mine gate.

"Stealing silver from a shipment for Tamita?" Herella said. "He could be executed. So could I." She shot Mara a still-angry look. "You'd better succeed, Mara Holdfast. Because if you fail, if you don't overthrow the Autarch, you won't be the only one who pays the price. And you'd better start thinking long and hard about when and where and how you use that cursed Gift of yours." She turned away and didn't speak to Mara again during the walk back to her workshop.

I've been thinking about nothing else, Mara thought, *and yet I keep finding ways to misuse it. No matter how hard I try, I end up hurting people.*

But then she hardened her resolve, pushing aside the guilt. Because Herella was right about one thing. The only way to redeem herself for past and future mistakes was to succeed: to cast down the Autarch and the entire evil system of Masks that he had created. If she could do that, then nothing else she had done or would do would matter in the slightest.

Yet even in those thoughts, she heard an echo of the Lady of Pain and Fire.

SEVENTEEN
Old Friends

TWO DAYS LATER, Mara carried her saddlebags containing the three new Masks out into the street and slung them over her horse's back. Whiteblaze sat watching her, tongue lolling.

The making of the silver Mask had gone smoothly enough, thanks to her magic allowing her to cool and polish the metal in far less time than it would have taken her father. The Mask looked exactly like the Child Guard Masks she had seen day in and day out at the Palace during her time there, minus the delicate carving, which she couldn't begin to recreate until she had Greff's Mask in front of her for comparison.

Despite the heat of the molten silver, the Maskmaking process had been a chilly one. Herella had become distant, doing what she had agreed to do but speaking little otherwise. Mara had tried to apologize again for what she had done to Ginther, had even tried to explain her fears about the Lady's influence on her, but Herella would not listen.

"I don't want to know anything more about it," she snapped. "If the Watchers come calling, it is better if I don't."

"At least your Mask won't give you away," Mara pointed out. "You have me to thank for that."

"I do," Herella said. "And I do thank you." She was unMasked in the privacy of her own home, and so Mara could clearly see the anger on the Maskmaker's face as she confronted her. "I thank you," she said, "but I will *never* trust you. Nor anyone else with your monstrous Gift. I accept that only someone with your power can hope to throw down the Autarch, but if not for that, I would say the Autarch was in the right when he exiled the Lady."

After that, Mara had given up trying to mend things with the Maskmaker. And now, with all three Masks finished, it was time to rejoin the unMasked Army.

The sun had barely risen high enough to lift the darkness, and still had not cleared the towering Eastern Range, and Mara's and Whiteblaze's and the horse's breath made white clouds in the chill air as she mounted. She had said farewell to Herella inside. Herella had not responded.

By starting so early, Mara had hoped to elude Watcher Tranik and his "kind" offer of an escort back to her ranch. But he must have expected her departure; as she reined the horse around, she heard the sound of other horses riding toward her, and she looked over her shoulder to see Tranik and two other mounted Watchers approaching from the barracks at the end of the street.

She resisted the urge to flee. There was no need to risk an alarm. She waited as Tranik and the other two rode up to her. "I told you, child," Tranik said reprovingly, "that I would send an escort with you. You know it is not safe. The supply wagon is overdue, and we fear it has fallen prey to bandits. We would not want the same to happen to someone as young and pretty as you. I thought you would be leaving this morning and have been waiting for you."

Silently, Mara swore. But out loud all she said was, "I didn't want to trouble you, Watcher Tranik. I really *can* look after myself. Especially with Whiteblaze, here." She indicated the wolf.

"I wouldn't feel right if anything untoward were to befall you," Tranik said. "Cornil and Morden will keep you safe. And make sure your family are safe, too."

"Thank you," Mara said, because what else could she say? Short of trying to use her magic again as she had on Ginther—and she wasn't at all sure she could do that to three men simultaneously, particularly Watchers who might have their own measure of the Gift, even if she weren't still horrified by the ease with which she had done it *once*—there was nothing she could do to stop the Watchers from accompanying her, whether she wanted them to or not.

Tranik nodded. "Have a safe journey, then," he said.

"Thank you," Mara said again, and rode toward the edge of town, the two Watchers trailing in her wake and Whiteblaze ranging ahead.

She expected the Watchers to keep grim silence behind her as they rode, but in fact the moment they were out of Silverthorne they began chatting with each other. From their voices they sounded quite young, and they clearly had known each other a long time. Neither of them was from Silverthorne—it would have surprised Mara if they had been. From what she knew of Watcher practice, only in Tamita were you likely to find Watchers native to the community they watched. Throughout the rest of the country, the standard procedure was to post Watchers who had grown up elsewhere.

As they continued talking, though, she realized that the young Watchers were both from the same part of Aygrima: the salt marshes of the south, as far from Tamita in that direction as the northern range of mountains was in the opposite one. And it was *that* which drew her into conversation with them, for her mother had grown up in the south, and had told stories of pushing a long shallow punt through the winding channels; of vast flocks of seabirds lifting as one from the water, the morning sun shining on their wings, the air filled with their plaintive calls; of wading bare-legged in the rice fields while fish nibbled her toes; of paddocks filled with water buffalo whose milk put that of northern cows to shame and whose meat had more flavor.

Mara's father had told her that her mother had gone south again after the failure of her Masking. She wondered if she were still there. She hoped so, because the farther she was from the Autarch the safer she would be.

But she had never met anyone else who had grown up in the south. Hearing the two young Watchers talk about it made her feel closer to her mother; and so, almost without realizing it, she began to chat with them, until they were riding three abreast and laughing like old friends.

Of course, Mara had to tell lie after lie, spinning a convoluted tale about her imaginary father and mother and brothers, how they had left Tamita after that frightening day when an enormous hole had been blown in the city wall by magic and several Watchers had died. "Father had a bakery near where it happened," Mara said. "He said there was trouble coming and we should be far away from Tamita when it arrived. And so he sold the bakery and used the money to buy the ranch. And here we are."

"I heard about that," Cornil said. "I thought it was mostly made up. Nobody could blow a hole in the Tamita wall by himself. It would take a dozen Gifted Engineers."

"Probably some Gifted criminal escaped through some old forgotten gate and the story's been growing ever since," Morden said. "Anyway, the Watchers will have him by now."

"It was real," Mara insisted. "I saw the hole myself. And it wasn't a 'him.' I heard it was a girl." She was beginning to enjoy this. "Daughter of the Master Maskmaker, if you can believe it. They say she blew the head right off of Stanik and killed a lot more Watchers as she escaped. And by the time we left, they hadn't brought her back. Or at least they hadn't hanged her yet. We lived not far from Traitors' Gate. I would have noticed." She didn't have to work hard to summon a shudder.

"Hmm," Morden said thoughtfully. "I *had* heard a lot of Watchers were sent up north somewhere, way over west by the coast," he gestured vaguely in that direction, "and I wondered why. Nobody was saying anything."

"I thought Watchers would always know what other Watchers were doing," Mara said, and that was almost truthful.

Cornil snorted. "Not bloody likely. The senior Watchers use the mushroom approach when it comes to us lowlifes."

"Mushroom approach?"

"They keep us in the dark and feed us bullshit," Morden said, then ducked his head. "Sorry, lass."

"I'm a farm girl," Mara said, laughing *and* lying. "I know all about bullshit."

The young Watchers laughed in turn. Then Cornil pointed ahead. "Crossroads in the trail," he said. "That's where we turn south, right? That other road just takes us into forest and rocks for miles and miles until you get to the Autarch's prison mine."

Mara felt her momentary good spirits drain away like water from a pricked bladder, because she could not turn south. The unMasked Army waited to the west.

I'll have to use magic on them, she thought. And wished she were more horrified than excited by the notion—but it wouldn't have been true to say so, because it had felt good to use her magic on Ginther, and she knew it would feel good to use it on these two, as well.

And what does that say about what I'm becoming? Or how strong the Lady's influence still is?

She pushed the thought away. *It's about time I stopped second-guessing myself*, she thought angrily. *It's time I pushed away the guilt. I don't care if that's the Lady's influence on me or not. It's me now. However I became what I am, I am what I am.*

She glanced at Whiteblaze, wondering if she needed his magic. *Probably not*, she thought. She hadn't needed it to influence Ginther. She turned her head to Cornil, reached out to feel the magic inside him—

And then he said, "What's with your wolf?" and she released her perception of him and turned her head toward Whiteblaze. He had stopped in the middle of the crossroad, and was staring into the thick trees into which the westward-bound branch of the road disappeared. He barked once.

Mara heard the whisper of steel on leather and turned to see Cornil drawing his blade. "He's seen some—" the Watcher began.

With a meaty "thunk" his chest sprouted a feathered shaft. He looked down at it, started to reach for it, then toppled sideways from the saddle, hitting the ground with a dull, crunching thud atop the sword that had dropped from his lifeless fingers.

"Bandits!" Morden shouted. "We have to—"

A second bolt took him in the throat, ending his words in a dying gurgle. In a spray of blood, he, too, thudded to the ground.

Despite the shock of sudden violence, Mara managed to take the magic released by the Watchers through her amulet, to avoid being slammed by their unfiltered soulprints. She readied herself to use it to defend herself against whomever came out of the woods . . . and then relaxed, though her body still thrummed with magic, as Keltan and Hyram appeared, each holding a crossbow. She felt a surge of anger at the brutal, unnecessary killing of the young men she had been joking with just moments before, but she forced it down. "Strip them," she said coldly to Keltan and Hyram "We need their uniforms."

Only when the two young Watchers lay pale and bloody on the road, naked but for their drawers, did she finally release the magic within her. The bodies vanished. White dust blew away in a gust of wind, spreading all that remained of the two young Watchers across the road they had ridden to their deaths.

And only *then* did she turn toward Keltan and Hyram and let her anger free. "You didn't have to kill them," she snarled. "I was about to use magic. They would have given me their uniforms and ridden away unharmed, with no memory of what happened."

"They were Watchers," Hyram said coldly.

She turned her glare on Keltan. He looked down at the ground, refusing to meet her eyes. "He's right," he said gruffly. "They were Watchers. Two fewer Watchers puts us that much closer to the day when there aren't any of them."

"They had names," Mara said. "Cornil. Morden. They grew up in the south, like my mother. They were sent out here to protect me."

"They were Watchers," Hyram repeated. Unlike Keltan, he had continued to glare at her. "I don't get you. I saw what you did on the beach. I saw what you did at the cave of magic. And I saw what you did at the magic mine. You've killed more Watchers than anyone else in the unMasked Army." His voice grew bitter. "And caused more deaths among the unMasked Army—many of them my friends—than the Watchers have. So why are you suddenly squeamish?"

"Because I have a heart," she snapped.

Hyram snorted. "You *pretend* to have one," he said. "Maybe you should stop pretending. Now that the Lady of Pain and Fire is dead, you're the biggest mass killer in Aygrima. So don't lecture me about not sparing the life of one stinking Watcher." He turned his back on her and strode away. "Father is waiting," he called without looking back. "Let's get moving."

Mara fought down the fury that wanted her to take magic from Whiteblaze and crush the insolent youth where he stood. White-faced and trembling, she turned to Keltan. "Do you feel the same?"

"About the Watchers, yes," Keltan said steadily. "But about you . . . no." His eyes met hers, and her anger melted in that gaze. "Your power is terrifying. But underneath it all is still the girl I fell in love with. Your heart is still where it always was, Mara." He suddenly licked his lips nervously and turned away. "Our horses are just inside the wood. If we get moving, we can make it back to the unMasked Army before dark." He walked off.

Mara stared after his retreating back for a long moment, the heart Hyram denied she had aching in her chest. She wanted to believe Keltan; wanted to live up to his unwavering love. But there was a dark worm of doubt within her. What if Hyram was right? What if she had already become the ruthless sorceress she'd sworn she'd never become, the Lady of Pain and Fire all over again, and she was just refusing to admit it?

She could not deny the facts. She had killed. She would kill again. She had, on more than one occasion, *enjoyed* killing. Did the fact she occasionally felt guilty about it absolve her of all the bloodshed she had caused?

Absolve me in whose eyes? she thought then, a cold thought that rose from some strange quarter of her mind to drive away her doubt. *Who can judge me? There are only two other people with my Gift. I killed one in the magic mine. And now I will kill the other.*

I *am the only one whose judgment matters. I am the only one who can make me feel guilty. I am the only one who can punish myself.*

Her lips thinned. *And I don't choose to. Not yet. Destroy the Autarch. Then feel guilty. But not until then.*

Who was she to upbraid Keltan and Hyram for shooting the Watchers? True, she wouldn't have killed them—probably—but she would have violated their minds, as she violated Ginther's, as the Lady had violated so many minds over the decades, as the Autarch did on a daily basis.

She had faced the threat of rape more than once in her young life. She had first discovered how deadly her Gift could be when she had slain Grute as he tried to assault her in the magic-collection hut where they had taken shelter en route from the Secret City to the mine of magic. Yet she had already raped one mind, and had been prepared to rape two more. Wasn't violating an individual's mind even worse than violating his or her body?

She thought it must be. But she resolved not to feel guilty about that, either.

No more guilt, she thought again. *No more guilt until the Autarch is overthrown. And then I can wallow in it.*

If I survive.

She dug her heels into her horse's flanks and trotted past the boys as they mounted. "Catch up," she snapped at them. "Time's wasting." Then, with Whiteblaze trotting ahead of her, she rode on into the forest without another glance at them. And she didn't feel guilty about it.

I don't, she assured herself. Several times.

Apparently abolishing guilt was harder than she thought.

All the same, she did her best to ride into camp with all the imperiousness of the Lady of Pain and Fire. Edrik waited outside her tent: she dismounted right in front of him with as much authority as she could, which wasn't all that much, because she was still only a mediocre rider at best. Still, at least she didn't catch her foot in the stirrup and sprawl at his feet.

"Done," she said, before he even spoke. "The Masks are in my saddlebags."

"Took you long enough," Edrik growled. "Considering that right about now an army of Watchers in the northwest is probably decamping to chase us down."

"It took as long as it had to take," Mara said. "We can move out at first light."

"We will," Edrik said. "But we'll be slower than our pursuers. We'll have to ride in the wilder valleys to the west of the Heartsblood to avoid detection. Though I think it's a fool's hope to believe the Autarch will not know we are coming long before we come anywhere within sight of Tamita."

"He sent the bulk of his forces north," Mara said. "There should not be a force strong enough to challenge us between here and Tamita, even if we *are* detected."

"He could send one out from the city," Edrik said.

"He could, but he won't," Mara said, wondering again as she did so where her sense of authority and knowledge on matters military came from, yet not doubting that what she said was true. The words spilled out of her as though she had been planning campaigns all her life. "The Autarch is cautious to a fault when it comes to his own safety. His walls have been breached recently—by me—and cannot yet have been repaired, because the massive stones required could neither be quarried in the mountains nor transported to the Heartsblood valley during the winter. He will keep his remaining forces within Tamita to defend it—and his own august personage—and simply wait for you to arrive, confident he can hold Tamita even with its damaged wall long enough for the returning army from the northwest to crush your tiny force."

"Which it assuredly will if you fail in your attempt to eliminate the Autarch," Edrik said.

"If I fail," Mara said, "the Autarch will rule in perpetuity—and tyranny—for another century. Better dead than that, don't you think?"

Edrik gave her an odd look. "Do *you*?" he said. "Are you done with life before you even turn sixteen?"

"No," Mara said. "But I hope the Autarch will be."

Edrik sighed. "Well, there's certainly no going back now. The Watchers would catch us before we could reach the pass. We might as well play this out to the end, and trust to this 'Gift' of yours." He smiled, surprising her. "And here I thought it might be useful mostly as a way of mending torn cloaks, when you first revealed you still had it. Remember?"

Mara couldn't help but smile back. "I remember."

Edrik glanced past her at Hyram. "All clear on her trail?"

"For now," Hyram said. "She was accompanied by two Watchers. We shot them."

Mara felt another surge of anger at his casual tone, but said nothing.

Edrik gave her a sharp look. "You didn't mention them."

"They're dead. They didn't seem important anymore." *No guilt*, she told herself fiercely. "The head Watcher in Silverthorne sent them to keep me safe from bandits as I rode back to my supposed ranch."

"Then the Head Watcher in Silverthorne will be coming to look for them," Edrik pointed out.

"He won't find a trace of them," Mara said. "I made sure of that."

"Maybe," Edrik said. He shrugged. "Well, I don't suppose it matters. A few small-town Watchers don't pose much of a threat. Very well. We'll head south in the morning. You're in command. It seems *you* are the Lady of Pain and Fire now."

Don't say that. "I suppose so."

"Her pavilion is yours," Edrik said. "If you want it."

"No," Mara said vehemently. "Tear it apart. I just want a regular tent."

Edrik's eyebrow raised. "Very well." He glanced at Keltan and Hyram. "Will you two find a spare for her and set it up?"

Hyram shot Keltan a glance. There had been a time when that had meant they were vying for her attention. Now she suspected Hyram was wondering how to get out of the task. He'd made it clear he hated and mistrusted her, and anyway, he and Alita had been inseparable during the trek to the Lady's fortress and after.

I don't care, she thought.

"There's space near ours," Keltan said.

Hyram opened his mouth in what Mara was sure would be a protest, but closed it again without speaking. He nodded.

"Go on, then," Edrik said.

With Whiteblaze trotting at her side, Mara followed Keltan and Hyram into the camp. The unMasked Army and Chell's men still segregated themselves, she saw: the sailors' camp was a little ways off among the trees, while the unMasked Army's tents were on a flat space next to the bubbling little stream she now knew reached all the way back to the waterfall that poured down the cliff above Silverthorne.

There were a lot of bundles of one sort or another piled up on a shelf of rock a good distance back from the stream, including a handful of the two-man tents the unMasked Army favored. Hyram and Keltan grabbed one of the long white bundles and, in silence, hauled it down to the far end of the camp. "Our tent," Keltan said, pointing to it. He and Hyram went to work erecting Mara's tent a few feet away from it. Mara sat down on a rock to watch. It took them no time at all; she would never have managed it. She'd never watched one of them being set up—hadn't even been inside one, spending all her time on the trek in the Lady's luxurious pavilion, easily five times the size.

By the time they were done, the sun, touching the western hills, had turned the thin clouds high above into long ranks of feathery gold. The smell of roasting venison drifted from the center of the camp. "Food," Keltan said. "Then you'd better grab some blankets from the pavilion . . . unless you change your mind about leaving it."

"I won't," Mara said. She trailed the boys to the fires.

The unMasked Army and Chell's men ate together, at least. Hunting parties had been at work and there was plenty of meat for everyone, plus some kind of savory vegetable stew and even flatbread, baked in pans over the fires. Nothing to drink but water, but the stream provided plenty of that.

Heads turned as she walked up to the fire, men and the handful of women among the unMasked Army nudging each other and pointing her out. A general silence fell. She forced herself to walk right up to the main fire and warm her hands, ignoring everyone. Gradually, ordinary conversation resumed, though in the murmurs she caught snatches of words that told her much of it concerned her.

Keltan brought her meat, stew, and two pieces of flatbread. "I'm glad you decided to join us," he said in a low voice. "The others have started to think of you as . . . not quite human."

Mara took the food and sat next to him on a log that had been pulled up close to the fire. Whiteblaze dropped down on the grass next to her. She gave him a piece of her meat and he wolfed it down. She'd see about feeding him more later.

She dipped a piece of flatbread into the stew. "And you haven't?" she said as she took a bite.

Keltan chewed his own food silently for a moment, swallowed, and said, "No. But I do think you've changed."

"Of course I've changed," Mara said. "So have you."

He shot her a startled look. She snorted. "You're about six inches taller than you were when I met you in the basement, you've got muscles on your muscles, and when did you become such a good shot with a crossbow?"

"Practice," he said. "All winter long."

"And killing people . . . doesn't bother you?"

"Of course it bothers me!" he snapped. "But it has to be done." His face hardened. "They're Watchers. What they did on the beach . . . at the Secret City . . ."

"See," Mara said softly. "You've changed."

"But not as much as you," Keltan said. "You were so concerned about your Gift turning you into a monster like the Lady of Pain and Fire. And what I've seen you do . . . the wall destroyed at the new mine, the collapse of the old one, the way you just . . . dissolved . . . those two Watchers . . . your power has grown so much, Mara, that it's frightening. And if it's frightening to *me*," he gestured at the others around the fire, some of whom continued to glance in their direction from time to time, "imagine how frightening it is to *them*."

Mara ate silently for a few minutes. "I know I've changed," she said at last. "Every time I've killed someone, or been around someone who is killed, and taken their magic unfiltered by this," she touched the amulet at her neck, "I've felt what the Lady called their 'soulprints' in my head. That's where my nightmares came from. Those are better now, thanks to this," she squeezed the amulet, "and Whiteblaze. I think . . . I *think*, I don't *know* . . . that the nightmares are my way of fighting off those 'soulprints' . . . like a fever fighting off infection. But all the same, I think every soulprint has changed me, just a little. And now . . ." She looked down at her bowl. "The Lady," she said softly. "She had so much power, and so much magic in her when she died, and it all roared through me. I had to get rid of it, so I cast it into the mine, but I still think she . . . left an imprint. In a way, she's still with us." Her voice dropped to a whisper. "With me."

"I don't think," Keltan said after a moment, "you should tell that to anyone else." He paused, then whispered, "But I'm glad you told it to me."

His hand slid over and covered hers, and she almost wept at the touch . . . and at the proof, from her reaction, that she was still human, still Mara, still fifteen, still capable of reacting to the touch of a boy who loved her . . . and whom she loved.

She wanted to hug Keltan, wanted even more to kiss him, but mindful of the eyes on her and uncertain how that would impact Keltan's standing among his fellows, contented herself with his hand on hers as she finished her meal.

Her bedroll on the ground that night was far harder and less comfortable than her bedroll on a bed of branches in the Lady's pavilion would have been, but with Whiteblaze stretched out beside her, and knowing Keltan was only a few feet away, she slept soundly and contentedly until the morning light glowed through the tent walls.

Through the next day, Keltan rode beside her, just behind Edrik, who led the column south down a long valley, parallel, Mara knew, to the Heartsblood River, somewhere off to their right, which wound down its own broad, fertile valley to Tamita. How far away the Heartsblood was she had no clue. One thing, at least, hadn't changed since her first journey led by Edrik, after he had rescued her from the wagon taking her to the mining camp; she still didn't understand how he managed to navigate the rough, wooded terrain without getting lost.

Their only hope was secrecy and subterfuge. She had to get to Tamita undetected and infiltrate the Palace. She and she alone could defeat the Autarch, now that the Lady was dead . . . *if not exactly gone*, she thought, rubbing her temple. She'd had no nightmares through the night, but as the day had passed she'd developed a slight headache. She didn't *think* that was a sign of the Lady's soulprint still clinging to the inside of her head, but she didn't know for a fact that it wasn't, either.

I wonder if there are answers in those scrolls the Lady guarded so jealously, she thought suddenly. *If we survive this, and I can get back north, I must have those.*

She put the thought aside. The possibility of it coming to pass seemed remote.

She and Keltan talked about inconsequential things, mostly, laughing about memories of the weeks they'd lived in the Secret City before Mara's ill-fated journey to meet her father, the journey that had ultimately led to his death and the Secret City's destruction. They wondered what Chell's homeland of Korellia was like and how it fared in its war against Stonefell. They wondered if the Lady's villagers had reached the pass . . . and what trouble some of the unMasked from the mine might be causing them. "They weren't all innocents like you and the other girls we rescued," Keltan said. "Some of them were as bad as Grute. Or worse."

"Believe me, I know," Mara said.

They camped that evening in a side fold of the valley they were following. "We're nearing more densely populated country," Edrik said that night, speaking to the whole camp. "Scouts, keep hidden and keep your eyes open. If you see anyone, report at once. If they see you first . . . we can't allow word of our presence to get to Tamita ahead of us."

Mara winced. It was too easy to imagine some innocent hunter in the wrong place at the wrong time paying the ultimate price. And what if they came across a farm?

She found out the next day. A scout galloped up to the column, horse lathered. "Farm ahead," he panted. "Just out of sight around the next bend."

Edrik swore. "I was afraid of that. More and more settlers have been spreading out from the Heartsblood in this direction. Anyone at home?"

"Woman hanging laundry in the yard," the scout said. "Two kids playing with a dog. Farmer and an older boy out seeding."

"We'll have to lock them up," Edrik said. "Means losing a couple of men to guard them."

"For how long?" Mara demanded.

"Until we succeed . . . or fail," Edrik said. "So that's up to you."

She sighed. "Right."

Edrik turned in his saddle, shouted commands. A dozen men galloped away. The rest of the army followed at its usual pace.

As they rode up to the farmyard, Mara heard children crying. She spotted them a moment later, sitting against the wall of the log-cabin farmhouse, a boy about four, a girl about six, their mother between them, comforting them. Mara could not see her expression behind her plain gray Mask, but her eyes were wide with fear and bright with tears.

And then she saw the farmer, kneeling, weeping, beside his son, who must have been younger than fifteen, since he was still unMasked. He lay on blood-soaked ground gasping for breath, left arm deformed: a sword-blow had gashed his shoulder and broken his collarbone. He stared up at her, eyes wide and terrified in his white, sweat-beaded face.

An unMasked soldier turned to Edrik. She recognized him—she recognized them all, having lived in the Secret City for weeks. "I'm sorry, sir," he said, looking stricken. "He came at me with a pitchfork, I just meant to knock it aside, I don't know how it—"

"It's all right, Pippik," Edrik said heavily. He looked down at the farmer. "My apologies," he said. "We didn't want to—"

"Out of my way," Mara said, pushing him aside. She dropped to her knees beside the wounded boy. "Whiteblaze!" she called. The wolf trotted to her side. She closed her eyes, and pulled magic from him. He whined a little. Then she turned the magic blue, and poured the healing power into the boy. The body knew how it was supposed to be constructed, and that knowledge was encoded in the magic every living thing generated. With encouragement, and the power she was providing, the body could put *itself* back together.

And so it did. Under her touch, the shattered bone knit, the flesh re-formed, the skin closed. In a moment only his torn, blood-soaked tunic showed the boy had been wounded at all.

He gasped, and blinked, and tried to lift his head to look, but then moaned and flopped back again. "Easy," Mara said. "You've lost a lot of blood. Your body needs time to replace it."

The father gaped at her, mouth and eyes wide behind his brown Mask.

"But . . . you're not a Healer. You're unMasked." He looked up at Edrik. "You're *all* unMasked. Who are you? What's going on?"

"We're the unMasked Army," Edrik said. "We are marching south to Tamita. We're going to overthrow the Autarch and put an end to Masks forever."

"You're mad!"

"Quite possibly," Edrik agreed. "I'm sorry, but I am going to have to leave you under guard to ensure you don't warn anyone. We may be deluding ourselves, but we'd like to think it's still a secret this far south." He smiled. "Clearly *you* weren't expecting us."

"You're not going to just . . . kill us?" the farmer's wife said. She hugged her smaller children closer. "Any of us?"

"We aren't killers," Edrik said. "Not unless it's necessary."

Disturbingly aware of just how often it *had* been necessary, and how much of the killing she herself had done, Mara said nothing. But as she looked down at the boy, just a little younger than herself, who was already starting to get more color in his face, she thought, *That felt good. Magic isn't all about death and destruction. I have to remember that.*

But she suspected death and destruction would still figure far more prominently in her future than Healing, at least anytime soon.

Dealing with the farm cost them more than an hour, but before noon they were on their way again. The farmer had told them he was the only settler he knew of who had yet come this far east. "Mostly the new settlers go west, toward the sea," he said. "Terrain is friendlier there and there are more roads and villages, so you can get supplies easier. It's a day's ride to the nearest village for me," he gestured at the western hills of the valley, "over that ridge and another three or four hours beyond that."

"What brought you out here?" Mara asked.

"Less crowded," the farmer said. "And fewer Watchers." He turned to Edrik. "If you can do what you say, you'll have my support. And many others'."

"We can do what we say," Mara said, and the farmer looked her way in surprise. She didn't blame him. Edrik had said she was in command, but it would be hard to convince anyone else of that.

When they made camp that night, Edrik called Mara to his tent. Chell was there, too. Mara hadn't seen much of him the last few days: he'd been sticking with the sailors. She suspected their morale wasn't the greatest—the only reason they were part of this force was because the Lady had coerced them. She was half-surprised some hadn't deserted, but then, where would they go? Without Masks, they could only live as bandits, and if they abandoned their fellows, they would also abandon all hope of ever returning home. "We're roughly east of where you spent the night in the farmhouse," Edrik said. "Half a day's journey, though. And you'll have to find it yourself. That means traveling by day, which is dangerous."

"I'm not the only one who might be able to pass as unMasked," Mara said. "Keltan is the same age I am. He's gotten rather annoyingly tall, but he might still pass as a fourteen-year-old. He can come with me to the farmhouse. They met him, too. And he probably has a better idea of how to find it than I do."

"My thought exactly," Edrik said. He hesitated. "You don't think it's time to try your fake Masks, yet? As you say, Keltan *might* pass as too young to be Masked . . . but he might not. If the local Watchers are at all suspicious. . . ."

Mara shook her head. "No," she said. "We can't use the Masks here. We'd have to disguise Keltan as a Watcher, and a lone Watcher leading a young girl would probably attract more attention from any Watchers we're unlucky enough to cross paths with than would two unMasked youngsters traveling from village to village. Watchers wouldn't have to question Keltan very long before they'd realized he's not really one of them."

Edrik still looked unconvinced, but he shrugged all the same. "Your call. First light, then?"

Mara nodded.

"I'll send scouts out behind you for as far as they can go safely. They'll watch for your return . . . or for the Watchers that will be heading our way if you're captured."

Mara nodded again.

"Be careful," Chell said, the first time he'd spoken. Mara gave him a brief smile of thanks, then pushed out through the tent flap.

She found Keltan waiting in front of her tent, sitting cross-legged, idly drawing in the dirt with a broken twig by the light of the nearby cooking fires. This night they were quite close to the center of the camp. He scrambled to his feet as she approached. "What did he want? Was it what you expected?"

She nodded. "We're a few hours' ride from the farm, he figures. I'm heading to it tomorrow, first light." She paused. He stood still, waiting, eyes fixed on her, and her mouth quirked. "And you can stop the puppy-dog eyes. Yes, you're coming with me." She grinned. "For one thing, I couldn't find the farm on my own if my life depended on it." Her smile faded. "Which, I guess, it does."

"Good," Keltan said. He held out his hand. "Then let's get something to eat."

She let him take her hand to lead her to the fire.

It astonished her just how good that felt.

EIGHTEEN

The Farm

FIRST LIGHT, Mara reflected as she heaved her sore, tired body into the saddle the next morning, sounded way more romantic in stories than it felt in real life. And of course "first light" was getting earlier and earlier as the days lengthened toward summer, though the solstice was still some weeks away. *Why couldn't we leave at second light? Or even third?*

Nobody answered her, since she was just talking to herself, so she straightened and sighed and glanced at Keltan who, like her, had just achieved upright status in his saddle. *Even the horses look sleepy and grumpy,* she thought.

"All right," he said. "Ready?"

"Ready," she said.

Edrik watched from nearby. "I'll give you today and tonight," he said. "Tomorrow morning, we move on. If you are not here, you will have to catch up to us. If you don't . . . we will assume the worst."

Mara nodded her understanding and agreement. Then she raised a hand in farewell and, with Keltan at her side and Whiteblaze ranging ahead of them, set off west.

They picked their way up the valley slope, winding through trees whose trunks had turned gold in the light of the rising sun behind them. At the top of the ridge Mara reined to a halt, then twisted in her saddle to look behind them. "Anyone could see that camp," she said. "Tamita may already have been warned."

"Then you'd better be right about the Autarch being too fearful to send his forces out of the city," Keltan said.

Mara pulled her horse around and sent him trotting downhill. "Well," she said, "It's not like there's anything we can do about it even if I'm wrong."

She'd been thinking that a lot recently. But it was true. There was very little she could do about any of the imponderables she and the Lady had set in motion. Events now had a momentum of their own, and even deflecting them from their course would be difficult. The Watchers' main force was in the northwest of Aygrima because she had clumsily betrayed the Secret City to Stanik, the late Guardian of Security. The remnants of the unMasked Army and Chell's crews were where they were because the Lady had found another pass into the Autarchy. The Autarch did not yet know his ancient adversary was dead . . . or that Mara, the girl who had caused him so much trouble, still lived. Even if he learned of the presence of the unMasked Army, heard of the destruction of his mine of magic, he would not know that Mara still lived or the Lady was dead. He would almost certainly still be focused on the Lady as the real threat.

Which was what Mara was counting on. If she could find her way into Tamita and infiltrate the Child Guard as she planned, the Autarch might be so focused on the army that had just appeared outside his walls, thinking the Lady must be with it, that he would be less likely to notice the snake in the grass at his feet.

She frowned. She'd just called herself a snake.

Well, she thought, *maybe it's not such a bad thing to be. Small, slithery, hard to see . . . and deadly.*

Not that she would be very deadly if things went awry at the farm. She'd just be dead.

They rode down the western side of the hills, crossed another valley, crested another ridge. By that time it was almost noon, and the sun, high overhead, flooded the broad valley in front of them with light. Winding back and forth in great shining loops, the Heartsblood River flowed south toward Tamita. Farms spread out on both shores and far up the valley slopes. Directly ahead of them, a village nestled on both sides of the riverbank. Keltan nodded with satisfaction. "We're in exactly the right place. That's the village closest to the farm. Which means the farm itself is on the other side of the river . . . probably the other side of those woods over there." He pointed. "We were riding through trees just before we happened upon it."

"Technically, I think it happened upon us," Mara said. "Or at least Stafin happened upon me."

"Stafin?"

"The dog. What was the village's name again?"

"Yellowgrass," Keltan said. "And we'll have to go through it."

"What?" Mara shot him a startled look. "Why?"

"The farm is on the other side of the river," Keltan said patiently. "The only bridge is in the village."

Mara felt stupid. "Oh."

"Kind of wish I hadn't grown so much recently," Keltan said. He looked at her. "Can I really pass for fourteen?"

"I've seen fourteen-year-olds as big as you," Mara said stoutly. *Just not very many,* she added silently.

"Well, I think *you're* still all right," Keltan said, looking her up and down. "But not for much longer." Mara raised an eyebrow, and Keltan suddenly raised his eyes and turned away. "Better keep moving," he said. The tips of his ears were red. Laughing a little to herself, she followed him.

But her amusement died as she thought about what he'd said. She had to pass, not just for a fourteen-year-old-girl, but eventually for a teenaged *boy*, for her plan to work.

How much has Greff grown since I saw him? she wondered.

Nothing I can do about it, she thought yet again, and sighed.

They reached Yellowgrass in midafternoon, earning a few curious looks from Masked passersby on its main street as they clip-clopped down it after crossing the bridge. Yellowgrass was about the size of Silverthorne, Mara judged, and so of course it had Watchers. Though their black-Masked faces also turned to watch as she and Keltan rode casually through, no one shouted at them or tried to stop them. In fact, the villagers seemed far more interested in Whiteblaze than in his human companions.

Still, she didn't breathe easily until they had left Yellowgrass behind and were riding south. "I don't think we should follow the road," Keltan said once a bend in it had put the village out of sight behind them. "We were riding closer to the river, in among the trees, when we found the farm . . . or it found you," he added with a quick grin.

Mara nodded her agreement. They rode off the road and toward the river, and then, leaving it to their left, continued their trek.

An hour later, Keltan suddenly halted as they entered a clearing. He rose in his stirrups and looked around. The river glinted silver through the branches of a thick hedge of willows to their left. "This is where we camped until we could come get you," he said. "I know exactly where we are now." He pointed ahead. "The farm is only a half a mile ahead, just over that low rise." He looked at Mara. "What are you going to say?"

"For once," Mara said, "I'm going to tell the truth . . . or at least part of it." She dug her heels into her horse's flanks and rode ahead, leaving Keltan to play catch-up. Which he did, of course, so that they were side-by-side as they rode into the farmyard.

Mara had fully expected Stafin, the big black dog, to rush out at them, and worried what that would mean with Whiteblaze at her side. But no barking greeted them. The little farmhouse looked unchanged, but for a horrible moment she thought it was deserted, that Filia and Jess, the couple who lived there, had abandoned it, or were away on some journey of their own. She hadn't even considered that possibility until this moment. What would she do if they weren't there?

But then the door opened, and the short round farmwoman she remembered, wearing a white Mask, stepped into the farmyard. She looked at Mara and Keltan, and her eyes widened. "Well, I never . . . ! Prella? Is that you?"

Right, Mara thought. *I'd almost forgotten I borrowed Prella's name last time.* "Hi, Filia. Yes, it's me."

"And your brother, too. My, how you've both grown."

Mara felt an unexpected lump in her throat. Nobody had measured her since the week before her Masking, when her mother had stood her against a whitewashed beam in the kitchen and marked her height with a stroke of charcoal from the fire. "Kids do that," she said.

Filia laughed. "They certainly do. Greff . . ." Her voice trailed off. "Well, anyway," she said. "What a pleasant surprise!" Then her face grew confused. "But . . . why aren't you Masked? You said you were only a couple of months away from your fifteenth birthday . . ."

"I lied," Mara said, telling the truth for just an instant before lying again. "I was afraid I'd get in trouble if you knew how young I really was. I'm sorry."

"Oh, pish-tush," Filia said. "Water under the bridge. Well, come in, come in. Jess is down by the river."

Mara slid from her saddle. There was a pile of hay and a water trough, and a handy hitching post, in one corner of the courtyard: she led the beast over there and looped the reins around the post, and he bent his head to eat. While Keltan followed suit, she returned to Filia. "Is Stafin with Jess?" she said. She dropped a hand to Whiteblaze's head. "I was worried about what would happen when he got a look at my Whiteblaze."

Filia's face fell. "Stafin died just before spring," she said sadly. "We need to get a new dog, but we haven't had the heart yet."

"Died how?" Mara said.

"I don't like to say . . ." Filia looked around, as if someone would over-hear, then said in a low voice, ". . . but if you must know . . . it was a Watcher."

"A Watcher?" Keltan had rejoined Mara.

"Came into the yard just like you did that winter morning. Bit later, though—the sun was almost up. Well, you know what Stafin was like. He came bounding out barking his fool head off. We thought it was a good thing to have a dog like that. Bandits don't come down here very often, but there was a farm burned out west of here just a year ago . . . well. The Watcher's horse reared, almost threw him. And the Watcher ordered us to tie Stafin up . . . and then he shot the poor dog with his crossbow." Though her Mask hid her expression, her voice was strained. "Nothing we could do, of course. You don't cross Watchers. 'Specially not that lot in Yellow-grass. They like to flex their muscle a bit too much, if you know what I mean."

"I know exactly what you mean," Mara said, and Keltan shot her a glance, as if he were wondering if she were talking about her own experi-ence with Watchers . . . or her own power. *Or maybe he's not thinking any-thing of the sort*, she chided herself. You're *the one that's thinking it.*

Sometimes she thought she did too much thinking.

"I'm so sorry," she added.

"Well," said Filia. "Nothing to be done about it." She stepped to one side. "Won't you come in?"

They followed her into the farm kitchen. Mara looked around, re-membering the night they had brought her into it to tend her wounds after she'd fallen from her horse. Filia took off her Mask and set it casually aside, then put a kettle on the fire. "I have some lovely herbal tea a lady in Yel-lowgrass blends for me . . . will you have a cup?"

While they waited for the water to boil, she brought out a plate of molasses cookies, and Keltan and Mara sat there and nibbled them (Mara thought they were excellent, though of course not as good as her mother used to make), and Mara very carefully did not say what she had come to say. Not yet.

"Now, then," Filia said. "How old are you really? Don't lie, this time." She smiled as she said it to take the sting from her words. "Masking must really be close, now, isn't it?"

I won't get a better opening than that, Mara thought. "Well, Filia," she said carefully, "despite what I said in the yard, the truth is we *aren't* younger than I claimed last time . . . we're actually older."

Filia blinked. "What? But that would mean you're . . ." Her voice trailed off.

"Exactly," Mara said. "We'll both be sixteen this fall. Keltan has never been Masked. And my Masking failed." She took another bite of the cookie. "These are really very good."

Filia stared at her, wide-eyed. Then she burst out laughing. "You're joking! I admit, you had me going for a minute."

"No," Mara said steadily. "I'm not joking. Nor am I lying. For once, I'm telling you the truth."

Filia's face turned white and she stumbled to her feet. "Get out," she whispered. "You have to get out!" She shot a horrified glance at her Mask. "It could shatter—"

"No," Mara said. "It won't." She'd been planning for this since the moment they'd sat down. She got up and went over to Filia's Mask. This time the work was easier than it had been with Herella's Mask. Drawing a modicum of magic from Whiteblaze, she had no trouble seeing Herella's soulprint glowing through the clay of the simple Mask. She froze it as it was. No matter what Herella thought or did now, that soulprint would not change. Her Mask could no longer betray her.

Mara straightened and took a deep breath. "It's done," she said.

"What is done?" Filia said. She hurried over and touched her Mask gingerly. "Child, if you—"

"I told you, I'm not a child," Mara said. "I'm unMasked. And I'm

Gifted, Filia. I have a Gift more powerful than anyone else in Aygrima . . . including the Autarch."

"You're insane," Filia snapped. She stepped back. "Get out! Get out of my house! If the Watchers—"

The door banged open. A bearded bald man filled the doorway, eyes wide behind his Mask. "Filia, there are Watchers riding toward the house. Whose horses are—oh!" He had suddenly seen Mara and Keltan. "You two? Are the Watchers after *you*?"

"Yellowgrass," Keltan said to Mara. "Guess we can't pass as children after all." He glanced at Whiteblaze, who stood staring at the door, ears pricked, clearly hearing the approaching horses though Mara couldn't, yet. "Or maybe it was the wolf."

Filia turned on Mara. "What have you done?" she cried. "You've destroyed us!"

Mara took a deep, shaking breath. "No," she said. "I'm going to save you. Whiteblaze, heel!"

The wolf gave her an interested glance, then followed her as she went to the door, pushing past Jess, who stepped back and out of her way. "Filia, Mask yourself," he snapped into the kitchen at his wife.

Once in the yard, Mara could hear the Watchers clearly enough. The jingle of harness rang out through the still air, and a moment later the Watchers themselves appeared: two of them. They reined to a halt, but didn't dismount. "You," said one imperiously. "Girl. What's your name?"

"Prella," Mara said.

"Where are you from?"

"Riverwash."

"And how old are you?"

"Fourteen."

The blank black Mask turned toward Keltan. "And you?"

"Hyram," Keltan said.

"Brother?"

"Boyfriend," Keltan said.

"Also fourteen?"

"Yes, sir," Keltan said. "You can see I have no Mask."

"Indeed I can. And I can also see you look awfully big for a fourteen-year-old. You know the penalty for being unMasked after your fifteenth birthday?"

"Everyone knows, sir," Keltan said.

The Watcher's gaze slid to Jess. "Do you know these two?"

"They came by a few months ago," Jess said. Mara could hear how carefully he was choosing his words, knew he was trying to ensure every word was true. "They said they were brother and sister then. The girl spent the night. Said she was lost. The boy came by the next morning, and then they rode off together."

"So you either lied then, or you're lying now," the Watcher said, turning back to Mara. "Which is it?"

"We were lying then," Mara said. "We went out at night to . . . be alone together." She let herself blush. It wasn't hard. "But . . . we had a fight, and I ran off, and got lost, and found the farm, and they put me up and then the next morning Hyram found me and we made up."

"How old did they say they were then?" the Watcher said to Jess.

"Fourteen," Jess said.

Don't ask the next question, Mara thought, but of course the Watcher did. "And when did they say their Masking would be?"

Jess hesitated, but he had no choice. "In a couple of months," he said.

"And this was how many months ago?"

Jess sighed. "Five."

The Watcher turned back to Mara. "Again I must ask, were you lying then, or are you lying now?"

"We were lying then, not now," Mara said desperately. "I wanted them to think I was older in case they found out what I was really doing out at night."

The Watcher looked at her for a long moment. "What's the name of the Maskmaker in Riverwash?" he asked softly.

And that was that. Mara had no idea. "I . . . I don't remember."

"You don't remember the Maskmaker in a village of two hundred people?" the Watcher said. "You are a liar, 'Prella of Riverwash.' And you are under arrest on suspicion of being abroad without a Mask." He turned to the other, hitherto silent, Watcher. "Take them, tie them. They can ride their own horses back to Yellowgrass. We'll lock them up and—"

"No," Mara said. "No, you won't." And just as she had with Ginther at the silver mine, she reached out to the magic inside them, disrupted the flow, adjusted their perception, changed their thoughts. *Lady of Pain and Fire*, she thought with a hint of self-loathing even as she did it, but that couldn't stop her. Nor did that touch of shame overpower the pleasure she took in her power, in the flow of magic, in the way the Watchers suddenly froze in mid-action, then started to climb back into the saddle . . .

And then the one who had been speaking to them suddenly began to jerk uncontrollably. Limbs flailing, head snapping back and forth, he dropped heavily to the ground. Mara stared as he spasmed two or three more times: then his back arched, his head twisted back, he uttered a single, strangled gasp . . . and went limp. His horse, startled, galloped away, but his magic slammed into Mara.

She had not been prepared for his death, had not expected it, and it bypassed the black lodestone amulet. His soulprint felt muddied, confused, distorted. She lost control of the other Watcher's magic, and he swore and drew his sword and drove his horse at Mara. The beast's broad shoulder bowled her over. The sword whistled over her head. Filia screamed and ran back into the house. Jess dashed across the yard. Mara tried to gather her wits and her magic, but the deformed soulprint of the fallen Watcher rang discordantly within her and she couldn't seem to grasp it . . .

Keltan grabbed the Watcher from the other side of his horse and tried to pull him down, but the Watcher's left elbow drove savagely back into his forehead and Keltan reeled away. The horse reared, and Mara rolled desperately out of the way to avoid being trampled. Whiteblaze was snapping at the horse's heels, forcing the Watcher to struggle to control it, and she took her chance and scrambled away, first on her hands and knees, then into a stumbling run. At the corner of the house she turned. She reached for magic again, but again it slipped away from her. The horse landed a solid blow that sent Whiteblaze rolling across the yard, howling. Keltan was getting to his feet, swaying, blood streaming down his face. The Watcher saw him, turned on him, raised his sword to split Keltan's skull like a melon. Mara screamed—

—and Jess drove the pitchfork into the Watcher's back so hard the prongs burst through his belly.

The Watcher dropped his sword, arched his back, tried to scrabble at the protruding handle as Jess let go of it convulsively, and then toppled sideways and landed in the dirt next to the body of his fellow.

This time Mara *was* prepared, and took the magic through the amulet. She immediately turned it around and let it blaze out across the farmyard. The fallen Watchers vanished. So did the rearing horse, screaming as it was flayed from the outside in, skin and muscle and organs and bones appearing and vanishing into white dust in the same instant.

She dropped to her hand and knees and retched into the dirt of the farmyard. The twisted magic of the Watcher she had failed so spectacularly to turn to her will had nauseated her as it flowed in and out of her again, and *hurt*.

Booted feet appeared in her vision. She spat and wiped the back of her mouth with her hand as she reared back on her knees. Jess stood over her. His Mask was gone. *It must have broken when he killed the Watcher*, she thought. She expected to see fury and hatred in his face, but instead all he saw was awe. "What are you, girl?" he whispered. "And why have you come to us?"

"My name is Mara Holdfast," Mara choked out. "And I'm here to ask your help in overthrowing the Autarch."

NINETEEN
Keltan's Masking

AFTER ALL THAT had happened in the farmyard, it seemed strange, ten minutes later, to sit once more sipping tea at the kitchen table. Mara had already mended and modified Jess' broken Mask. Now the farmer and his wife were sitting across the table from her and Keltan, although they both looked as though they would have preferred to be anywhere else.

"Your Masks will protect you now," she was explaining. "Those two Watchers must have told others they were following us, but you can say that you never saw them, or the boy and girl they were investigating, and your Masks will show that you are telling the truth. The Watchers will not question that. They can't even imagine that someone wearing a Mask could lie to them. They'll eventually find the horse that galloped away, and probably put the whole thing down to bandits."

"How can *you* imagine such a thing?" Jess said. "How can you *do* such a thing?"

"I have an . . . unusual Gift," Mara said.

Keltan snorted. "You could say that."

She shot him a look to tell him he was being less than helpful, then turned back to the farm couple. "I still don't know everything I can do with it . . . and can't do with it," she said. "I messed up out there. I thought I could easily influence both of them, get them to simply turn around and ride off and believe they talked to you and everything was all right. But something went wrong. The second Watcher . . . I couldn't manipulate him the way I thought. He . . . twisted. It was like . . ." Epiphany struck. "It was like when a Mask fails," she said, almost in a whisper, speaking more to herself. "The magics are related . . . Masks are failing more often, especially the ones for the Gifted, because the Autarch has changed the 'recipe' to allow him to better influence and draw on Mask wearers' magic than ever before. Maybe they're failing because some people, especially some Gifted, are simply harder to bend than others."

"Be that as it may," said Jess. "Do you really believe this unusual Gift of yours will allow you to overthrow the Autarch?"

"If it doesn't," Mara said, "then the Autarch will never be overthrown. And he may outlive this entire generation. He is using magic to prolong his life. He could live for decades more. If I fail, then there is no hope. And his tyranny will only grow. He needs more and more magic. The Masks will get stronger and stronger. If he is not stopped, eventually the people of Aygrima will be reduced to little more than cattle, milked for his needs, kept docile and obedient."

"And how can we possibly help you in this impossible task you have set for yourself?" Filia said.

Here it comes, Mara thought. "I've met your son, Greff," she said. "I met him when I was being held in the Palace. How would you like to have him back?"

Filia gasped.

"Impossible," Jess said flatly. "He's in the Child Guard."

"What if someone could take his place?" Mara said.

Jess' eyes narrowed. "You?"

"Keltan," Mara said, "would you be so kind as to go fetch my saddle-bags?"

Keltan nodded and went out without a word.

"Of course, me," Mara continued. "Can you think of a better way to get close to the Autarch than infiltrate the Child Guard?"

"By taking Greff's place?" Filia said. Her eyes still held doubt and fear, but also, just maybe, the beginning of hope. "But . . . how?"

Keltan came back in with the saddlebags from Mara's horse. He slung them over the chair in which he'd been seated. Mara got up, opened the one hanging over the chairback, and took out the cloth-wrapped bundle inside. She placed it on the table and unfolded the covering. Silver gleamed in the lamplight. Filia's breath caught in her throat. "A Child Guard's Mask?" she whispered. "But . . . how?"

"I am the daughter of the Master Maskmaker of Tamita," Mara said. "And as I've already proved," she nodded at Jess' miraculously intact Mask, "I have other skills with Masks beyond the sculpting of them." Honesty compelled her to add, "And I had help from a very talented Maskmaker in Silverthorne."

"A Maskmaker helped you . . . in your quest to overthrow the Autarch?" Jess said.

"Who knows the tyranny of the Masks better than a maker of them?" Mara said. "My father was the first to understand how the Masks had changed, and the first to act against the Autarch . . . and paid the price."

Filia nodded. "I heard about that," she said. "They hanged him, and in his death throes he still had power enough to tear down the city wall . . ." Her voice trailed off. "That wasn't him, though, was it?" she said with wonder in her voice. "That was you. You said you were held in the Palace . . ." And then her eyes widened. "Oh, child," she said, her voice suddenly full of pity, "did you witness your father's death?"

Her concern, so warm and unfeigned, brought a lump to Mara's throat. "Yes," she said. "Yes, that was me. And, yes, I . . . I saw my father hanged."

"You are very close to Greff in height," Jess said. "He is not a tall boy. And with careful clothing you might pass as a boy in other ways."

Thanks, Mara thought, but didn't say.

"But how do you plan to make this exchange? And what assurance can you give us that Greff will be in no danger if it goes ahead?"

"As to the latter . . . none," Mara said honestly. "Greff will be in danger. Terrible danger. As will I. But," she added quickly as Jess opened his mouth to protest, "Greff is in terrible danger *now*. The Autarch is feeding on the Child Guard every day, drawing more magic from them than from any other source. If he is called upon to defend himself, it is likely he will drain the Child Guard dry and discard the husks. And even if all goes on as it has, Greff will be lucky to grow to adulthood. Many of the Child Guard do not."

Filia's hand went to her mouth. Jess looked grim. "Even if what you say is true," he said, "I don't see how *you* can hope to take his place."

"I heard," Mara said, "when I lived in the city, that it is possible for the parents of a Child Guard to visit that child, if the need is great enough."

Jess nodded. "You can't simply drop in on them," he said, "but if it's really important, there is a way. They give you ten minutes. We were also told not to contact Greff for anything less than a death in the family, so we've never tried."

"What do you have to do?" Mara asked.

"You go to the Palace," Jess said. "Main gate. You don't go in, of course. There's a kind of guardhouse out in front, on the right side as you're looking at the gate."

"I know it," Mara said. "Petitioners go in there." *And some never come out again.*

"Well, they told us you go in there, ask for a man named Prilk. Tell him you need to see whichever Child Guard it is. He arranges it. Could be hours before you actually meet, in that same guardhouse. Like I said, you get ten minutes. Deliver your message, get out. The Child Guard goes back into the Palace. That's it."

"Do you get ten minutes in private?" Mara said.

"Don't know about that," Jess said. "Might be Prilk is right there listening."

"I can make it work," Mara said, "if Greff will cooperate. I can get myself into the Palace and Greff out of the city and back home to you."

"What good will that do?" Jess said. "We can't hide him here for long."

"Don't even try," Mara said. "Head northeast. There's a pass through the mountains where the northern range bends around into the eastern one. Get over that pass, there's a path. It will lead you to people who aren't under the Autarch's sway."

"A desperate journey," Jess growled.

"Less so in spring than winter," Mara said, "and less desperate than staying here. The Watchers already killed your dog. The Autarch is slowly killing your son. Is your own illusion of security so important to you you'd rather cling to it than try to do something about the forces that threaten it?" *That sounded like the Lady*, she thought uneasily.

"No," Filia said. The fact she answered, rather than Jess, surprised Mara for a moment, but only for a moment. From her first meeting with the couple she'd seen how Jess deferred to his wife. He did so again now, turning at once to look at her. "No," Filia said, "it is not. If you can do this, we will be forever grateful. Even if we must flee into the Wild."

"Thank you for your help," Mara said softly. "I promise you, whatever I can do to protect Greff, I will." She stood. "Until he returns to you . . . carry on as normal. Remember, your Masks can no longer betray you to the Watchers. For the moment, you are the freest people in Aygrima . . . but I hope everyone will soon enjoy the same freedom."

"So do I," Filia said. "So do I."

The couple watched Mara and Keltan exit. They offered no final farewells.

Keltan and Mara rode through the night to return to Edrik and Chell's forces, arriving at (Mara sighed) first light. The fighters had already struck the camp; another half hour, Mara judged, they would have moved on. She and Keltan galloped to where Edrik and Chell, also on horseback, were watching the forming column. Antril sat beside Chell. All of them turned as Keltan and Mara rode up. "I feared we'd have to leave you behind," Edrik said. "The scouts have reported in. The main force of Watchers is less than a day behind us."

"Then this is the final push," Mara said.

"Did you get what you went for?" Chell said.

"We did," Mara said. "I think I can get close to the Autarch. After that . . ." Her throat closed. "After that," she said, "I'll do my best." She thought for a minute, dread growing in her. "The Watchers . . . they'll send riders ahead to warn Tamita, won't they?"

"Yes," Edrik said.

"They could well get to Tamita before you can."

"They *will*, unless our own scouts are able to intercept them. But even if we get a few, I think it highly unlikely we can get them all."

"And once Tamita is warned, the gates will be sealed," Mara said. "They might not let me in."

Edrik nodded.

"Then Keltan and I must ride ahead."

Keltan sighed. "We've already ridden all night."

"Then you'd better ride all day," Edrik said. "The force we've assembled to join you in the city once you open the sally port will also set out at once—but separately, of course."

"I'll be commanding it myself," Chell said. "With the help of Lieutenant Antril."

Antril flashed Mara a brief smile.

Someone else willing to risk his life for me, Mara thought. "We'll just grab some fresh supplies and head out, then," Mara said. "But from here on . . ." She glanced at Keltan. "You heard what the Watchers at the farm said."

"Watchers?" Chell said sharply.

"Don't worry," Mara said. "They're not there anymore."

"Or anywhere else," Keltan added under his breath.

"They made it clear you, at least, can't pass for a fourteen-year-old anymore," Mara pressed on. "Or at least not one that a Watcher won't stop for questioning."

Keltan nodded.

"So it's time for you to become a Watcher."

"Already?"

"I'm afraid so." She smiled. "A little late, perhaps, but it's finally time for your Masking . . . and my second one."

The event—she wouldn't call it a ceremony, which implied a celebration, which this certainly was not—took place just half an hour later. They had replenished their food and water so they could set off the moment it was done. Keltan had changed into one of the uniforms, long since washed clean of blood, from the Silverthorne Watchers he and Hyram had killed . . . Cornil's, she thought it must be: he had been much of a size with Keltan. And only slightly older . . .

No guilt, she reminded herself.

From her saddlebag, she drew out the Watcher's Mask she had crafted with Herella for Keltan, and the plain one she had crafted for herself. The unMasked Army had already moved out. Edrik, along with Chell, Antril, and the rest of the small force that would infiltrate the city—assuming Mara succeeded in letting them in—remained. In addition to Antril, that force consisted of Hyram, three unMasked Army fighters (two men, Prescox and Danys, and a woman, Lilla) and four of Chell's sailors whose names Mara didn't know.

"I'm very interested in watching this 'Masking,'" Antril said to Mara. "The whole concept is fascinating." He grimaced. "Repellent, but fascinating."

"I hope it works," Mara said. She glanced at Keltan. "Ready?"

"I guess," he replied, voice tight.

She stepped forward and put the Mask on his face.

Even as she did so, she feared it would break and shatter as hers had, that in a moment she'd be trying frantically to heal Keltan's torn skin and broken nose. But though he gasped and staggered back a step or two as the magic-infused clay came to life and writhed into its new form as an exact copy of the face beneath it, the Mask did not shatter. "That . . . was unpleasant," he said, voice muffled by the Mask's small mouth opening. "Glad I skipped out on it the first time around."

"You think that was unpleasant, you should try donning one that fails," Mara told him. Then wished she hadn't, since that brought back memories of her first horrific Masking just as she reached for the white Mask to complete her second. She took a deep breath and placed the Mask on her face. It squirmed horribly, just as she remembered—but this time, it stayed intact, and so did her face.

It felt very strange to look out at the world from behind a Mask. Edrik, Chell, and Antril were staring at them both. She licked her lips, and her tongue jerked back in surprise as it encountered the slick ceramic surrounding her mouth. "I really hate this," she muttered.

"You and me both," Keltan said.

"And you're sure these Masks won't betray you?" Hyram demanded.

Mara turned her head toward him. "I'm sure. Mine reveals nothing except purity and innocence. His reveals only unwavering loyalty and obedience to the Autarch. No Watchers viewing either will have the slightest suspicion that whatever we tell them is anything but the truth."

"Which will come in very useful if you're stopped along the road," Edrik said. "Unless, of course, they decide to execute you on the spot. But at least you have a better chance of making it than I thought." He thumped his fist on his heart in salute. "Good luck, Mara Holdfast. Good luck, Keltan." He turned to the others. "Good luck, all of you. May we meet again in the courtyard of the burning Palace." He mounted and rode away without looking back.

"That's a rather grim version of 'see you later,'" Keltan commented.

"This is an enormous risk, Mara," Chell said. "Are you sure it's the only way?"

"I'm sure," Mara said.

"Well, if anyone can do it, you can," he said. "You saved my life the first time we met. Before I even knew the power you could wield, I thought you were an extraordinary girl. I haven't changed my mind." He looked at Keltan. "Do what you can to keep her safe."

"I intend to," Keltan said.

Chell copied the salute Edrik had used, though Mara had never seen any of the Korellian sailors make the gesture before. "Good fortune to you both," he said. "We'll be in position tomorrow night. See you at the wall."

Antril repeated the salute. "Good fortune," he said.

Chell gestured to the others in the small strike force and they rode away, following the departing army, though they would soon be far ahead of them. To Mara's surprise, Hyram hung back. "Good luck to both of you," he said. "I hope . . ." His voice trailed off, and without saying what he hoped, he turned his horse and galloped after the others.

"There's a friend I lost," Mara said sadly.

"Maybe not forever," Keltan said, gazing after Hyram thoughtfully. Then he shook his head and turned back to her. "We'd better get moving, too. We're in a race."

Mara nodded and climbed wearily back into the saddle of her horse, a roan mare this time. Knowing he would be traveling incognito as a Watcher, Keltan had chosen a black gelding to match his black uniform and Mask.

"I hate you," she said conversationally to her new mount, whose ear flicked back in her direction as she reached forward and patted the mare's neck. "I hate all horses. Nothing personal."

Keltan laughed. "At least you don't fall off of them every few minutes like those first few times you tried riding. Remember?"

"I remember. I've had a *little* practice since then." She sighed. "Well, then . . ." She dug her heels into the mare's flanks, Keltan followed suit, and they were off.

They needed to get to the main road that ran down the Heartsblood valley to make the best possible time, but cutting straight across it again would cost them more time than they'd save. Instead they angled, riding up the western slope of the valley and down the other side in a generally southwest direction. Mara's buttocks and thighs ached and burned from the all-night ride she'd already endured, but she held on grimly as they trotted when they could and walked when they couldn't. A gallop would have been smoother, but that was one gait they *didn't* use. They needed to make haste, but they also had to save the horses. If one went lame, all was lost. Whiteblaze trotted along happily, sometimes ahead of them, sometimes with them, sometimes off to the side.

They reached the road in midafternoon. After that, the going became easier for the horses, though not for Mara, who was beginning to seriously wonder if there were any way to use magic to add padding to her rear end.

Then, without warning, they rounded a corner . . . and confronted a Watcher heading the other way. Whiteblaze growled softly. "No, White-blaze," Mara murmured, and he subsided.

The Watcher stopped in the middle of the road. Keltan and Mara had little choice but to do likewise. Whiteblaze sat on his haunches a little ways off and watched, eyes narrowed.

"Where are you from, brother?" said the Watcher. "And who's your young friend?" He glanced at Whiteblaze. "Nice . . . dog?"

"Silverthorne," Keltan said. "Name's Cornil." He and Mara had talked about what he should say in just such an instance; now she was glad they had. He gestured at Mara. "This is Prella, daughter of the village headman. Got a fiancé in Tamita she's never met—arranged marriage." He pointed at Whiteblaze. "And that's no dog. It's a wolf. Raised as a pup by the Head-man to protect his daughter."

The Watcher laughed. "She'll have to pen it up for the wedding night if he's to get grandchildren. Wolf's likely to think she's being attacked."

Keltan laughed heartily, playing his role. Mara sat as still as possible, doing her best to project a vacant air. Apparently she was succeeding. After the initial glance, the Watcher hadn't looked at her again.

"Anything else new in Tamita I should know about?" Keltan continued.

"You'll find the barracks rather empty," the Watcher from Tamita said. "The Autarch ordered three-quarters of the force out a few months ago to squelch a bandit uprising, and they're still garrisoned up north along the coast somewhere. Keeps the rest of us hopping, I can tell you that. Double shifts. Triple, sometimes." He leaned forward, lowering his voice even though there was no one in sight but the three of them. "And you want to hear something even weirder? The Autarch has everyone aged fifteen to eighteen, boys and girls alike, doing weapons training. Started the same time he sent out so many Watchers. Almost like he thinks bandits might attack Tamita itself." He leaned back in his saddle again. "It's made the whole city jumpy. People getting into fights for no reason, that sort of thing. We've even had a spate of Mask shatterings. Followed by a spate of executions, of course."

"We had some trouble with bandits near Silverthorne," Keltan said. "People kind of jumpy up there, too. Haven't had any Masks shattering, though."

"Just a city thing, probably," the Watcher said. "It was a nasty winter. Maybe it's just spring fever." He touched his finger to his Masked forehead. "Ride safe. I'm off to Yellowgrass. Had a report a couple of Watchers have gone missing. Bandits again, I'm thinking. Keep your sword loose in its scabbard, lad."

"Thanks, I will," Keltan said, and the Watcher from Tamita rode past them. They both turned to watch him go, then looked at each other.

"Good job," Mara said. She felt immensely relieved. Her fake Watcher's Mask had worked perfectly. And that gave her reason to hope that her fake Child Guard one would as well.

Keltan touched his Mask. "You, too," he said. "And you have no idea how glad I am about that."

About an hour later they came to an inn. Mara wished they could have taken a room, but there was no time. At least they could water the horses and give them a rest, and while the horses were recovering, enjoy a hot meal. Mara found it awkward and uncomfortable to eat while wearing a Mask. Drinking was easier: public eating establishments served wine and beer and water in special cups with elongated spouts for slipping inside a Mask's mouth hole. Whiteblaze had a raw steak to eat and a bone to gnaw on. After an hour and a half they rode on into gathering twilight.

During most of their journey from the village the weather had been excellent. But that night a wind came up, and the stars vanished, and it was in a cold, driving rain that they finally crested a ridge and gazed at the city of Tamita. The lights of the houses and towers climbing Fortress Hill behind the wall looking warm and inviting . . . and a very long way away still.

"Can't get through the gate until—"

"First light," Mara said. She sighed. "Of course."

"We might as well camp."

They'd brought only one tent with them. They couldn't manage a fire in the driving rain, and so they climbed into the tent to eat cold bread and cheese by the light of a single candle lantern. Then they stretched out side by side to sleep, rolled in their blankets against the chill.

The rain thrummed on the canvas. Whiteblaze was off somewhere in the storm, hunting, Mara supposed. She hoped he didn't try to shoulder his way in later, sopping wet.

"Don't touch the sides of the tent," came Keltan's voice out of the darkness just inches from Mara's head. "It will let the water through."

"Thanks for the warning," Mara said.

She felt strangely tense, and sleep simply wouldn't come. Part of it was knowing that tomorrow she would try to infiltrate the Child Guard, and then to confront the Autarch, the terrifying goal she had been working toward for so long . . . but had never thought she would be attempting to achieve without the help of the Lady.

But part of it was the nearness of Keltan. She was acutely aware of his body so close to hers, and not *just* because of the magic she could sense in him. She found herself thinking of his kisses. Of the feel of his arms around her. She imagined him rolling over, whispering to her, "As long as we're alone . . ." She imagined warm kisses, hot hands on bare skin. But she also imagined tasting his magic, draining it from him. How could she ever give herself over to the former when she would always long for the latter?

She imagined all those things, and could not sleep.

Keltan apparently did not have the same problem. He was already snoring gently.

She sighed.

Some day, she thought. *If I live.*

If I'm still me.

It was a thought she had barely dared to express even to herself until that moment, but lying in the dark, listening to rain and wind and Keltan's deep breathing, she could not hide from her own mind. The impact of the Lady's magic, of her powerful soulprint, had changed her somehow, made her more like Arilla.

So what, she wondered, *will become of me when the* Autarch's *soulprint fills my mind?*

She fingered the black lodestone amulet. She did not think it would be much good in that tidal wave of magic.

Keltan rolled over, his back to her. Mara tried to put her fantasies and fears alike out of her mind, and fall into the sleep she desperately needed . . . but she had very little success.

TWENTY
The Walls of Tamita

THE NEXT MORNING, in broad daylight, they rode to the main gate of Tamita. The clouds had blown away overnight and the rising sun turned the dew-laden grass along the road into fields of diamonds. Mara felt horribly conspicuous, especially as they drew closer, passing among the tents of others who had camped outside the wall to be ready for the gate to open in the morning or to make their way around the city to the Outside Market. The feeling eased, though, as she noticed the people they were passing rather conspicuously *not* looking at her, their eyes sliding past her once they glimpsed Keltan's blank black Mask. Even the pair of Watchers they passed, mounted and stationary at the side of the road to keep an eye on the people heading into the city, looked first at Keltan, clearly saw nothing amiss, nodded, cast a cursory and incurious glance at Mara, and then turned their attention elsewhere. And thus it was without any fuss at all that they rode into the capital of the Autarch, whom they hoped very soon to assassinate. It was almost surreal.

All the same, Mara kept her head down and her hood up. There had been a lot of morbidly curious onlookers at Traitors' Gate the morning her father had been hanged and she had blown down a large chunk of the city wall, and she suspected they had vivid memories of that day—and therefore, potentially, of her. Even though she was Masked now, the Mask unavoidably looked like her, and gazing boldly out at the citizens of Tamita seemed an unnecessary risk.

She was also horribly aware that somewhere on the road behind them, and probably not very *far* behind them, riders were galloping toward Tamita to warn the Autarch of the approach of the unMasked Army. If they did not penetrate the Palace before that warning was given, they might lose their chance . . . and it seemed slim enough as it was, despite the confidence she had tried to display to Greff's parents and to Edrik.

They rode up Processional Boulevard from the gate, past high-class shops only the wealthiest of Tamita's citizens could afford to patronize. Well-dressed ladies with elaborate hairdos piled high above their ornate Masks chatted coolly with one another along the boardwalks bordering the boulevard, paved with massive blocks of white stone. Mara remembered sitting on the city wall with Mayson (she felt a pang and pushed it aside ruthlessly—*no guilt, not now*) and laughing at the countrywomen in the Outside Market who did nothing with their hair. She had not had her own hair done properly since her disastrous Masking. Now she was one of those country girls she had mocked. *Well*, she thought, *it's hardly the only change since then.*

The guardhouse was just where Jess had said, and just where Mara remembered it: to the right of the Palace Gate, which stood open, though of course it was heavily guarded by Watchers. "Here we go," she murmured to Keltan. "Ask for Prilk."

"I remember," he said. Together they rode up to the guardhouse, a stone building about half the size of Mara's old house, and dismounted. The only door, which faced Processional Boulevard, stood open. Keltan stuck his head inside. "I'm looking for Prilk," he said to someone Mara couldn't see.

"You found him," said a voice. Keltan stepped back, and a Watcher appeared in the doorway. He had a thick thatch of silver hair and brown eyes. His already thin lips thinned further in a moue of disapproval behind his Mask's mouth slit. "Who's this, then?"

"Her name is Prella," Keltan said. "She's from Yellowgrass."

"And why is she here?"

"She's a cousin of one of the Child Guard. Greff," Keltan said. "She has bad news about his parents."

"Greff." Prilk nodded. "I know him." He cocked his head to one side. "Why'd she rate a Watcher escort?"

"Coincidence," Keltan said with a shrug. "I was coming this way on my own business. Offered to ride with her."

Prilk's lips twitched. "Coincidence. Right." He looked at Mara. "How long since Masking, girl?"

"Couple of months," Mara said. She kept her head down and barely murmured her reply, hoping Prilk would think her shy rather than terrified of being identified.

"Have a good trip?" he said to her.

She nodded mutely.

He looked past her at Keltan. "Bet *you* did," he said, a leer in his voice, and sudden anger seized her. She could kill him where he stood—

She shoved the fury down, hard, and swallowed.

"Yes, I did," Keltan said, with a dirty chuckle. And that made the fury surge again, even though she knew he was only playing a role.

I've got to control this rush to anger, she thought. *I've got to. It'll get us both killed.*

It's the Lady. She's still in here with me.

She's also dead, she told herself firmly. *And you're not. You can control it. You have to.*

"Let me check the schedule," Prilk said. He disappeared inside, came back a minute later. "All right," he said. "Greff will be released from the Autarch's presence in two hours. I'll have him brought here. You can meet him in the back room, girl." He jerked a thumb over his shoulder. "Ten minutes. And I'll be in there with you." He glanced at Keltan. "No need for you to be there," he said.

"I'd like to be, if I can," Keltan said. "I knew Greff growing up."

Prilk shrugged. "Suit yourself. Two hours."

He went back inside.

Mara and Keltan walked away from the guardhouse, leaving their horses tethered outside it. "Two hours," she murmured to him. "And the riders from the Watcher Army could arrive any minute. Once the Autarch hears their warning, will he allow his Child Guard to leave his presence at all?"

"I don't know," Keltan said. They walked a few more minutes, ambling back down Processional Boulevard toward the main gate. "Mara, can this actually work?" He glanced at her. "I don't want you hurt."

"I won't be hurt if this fails," she said. "I'll be dead. So will you. So will everyone we know in the unMasked Army. So will Chell and all his men. But we will *also* be dead even if we *don't* try to overthrow the Autarch. Maybe not right away, but soon enough. So what choice do we have?"

Keltan sighed. "Perfectly true. Perfectly depressing." He looked up and down the boulevard. "So. Two hours. What's a good place to eat?"

"Do you have money?" Mara asked.

Keltan shook his head.

"Neither do I. And we might be just a little conspicuous in a restaurant anyway, don't you think?"

"But I'm hungry," Keltan said plaintively.

"There's still some sausage and hard cheese."

"Which we ate for the last three meals," Keltan grumbled, but in the end, they ate the last of their marching rations sitting on a low wall that bordered a fountain and watching the Masked denizens of Tamita go by. "I hate eating in a Mask," Keltan complained. "You have to cut everything up into small bits to fit through the opening. Which is extra-small in a

Watcher Mask." He tossed a piece of sausage to Whiteblaze: the wolf gobbled it up and looked up hopefully for more.

"It looks funny, too," Mara said absently. She wasn't really paying much attention to Keltan. She was feeling the ebb and flow of magic all around her as people passed by. A little from most, a lot from the occasional Gifted. So much magic. *And how much of it is the Autarch drawing on through the newest Masks?* she wondered.

She remembered what the Watcher on the road had told them about the Autarch forcing youngsters "fifteen to eighteen" into arms training. All of them would be wearing the new Masks. Could he control them, as the Lady had controlled her villagers in the mining camp?

She remembered thinking, when she was little, that the Autarch could see everything at once, that he was looking out through the eyes of the Masks. Her father had told her that was nonsense. But now she had met the Lady, who could look out through the eyes of her wolves . . . though Mara had never mastered the trick. Had the Lady also been able to look out through the eyes of the villagers in her Cadre, her "human wolfpack"? Did the Autarch have that knack, as well?

Could he be looking at them through someone's Mask even now?

She shuddered. Keltan noticed and scooted closer on the bench. "Cold?"

"It's not that," she said. Then she reconsidered. "Not *only* that. It *is* chilly. And I left my cloak in my saddlebags."

"Cold air must have moved in with that rain last night," Keltan said. "Here." He took off his Watcher's cape and passed it to her; she draped it around her shoulders, not so much because she was really cold as because Keltan had been so thoughtful. That alone warmed her. "This uniform is warm enough without it," he went on. "Warmer than ordinary clothes, anyway."

"Not really that ordinary," Mara said, and it was true: she'd felt horribly self-conscious since entering the city, dressed as she was in the usual unMasked Army garb of sturdy brown trousers, scuffed brown boots, a forest-green shirt, and a padded black vest. (The entire army had shed the blue-and-white uniforms of the Lady, for obvious reasons.) She remembered how, as her Masking had neared, she had hated wearing the modest long skirts and long-sleeved blouses her mother had insisted she wear instead of the short tunics she'd worn as a child, but she wished she had something like that now.

All around were Masked women, all of whom wore proper long dresses, not trousers, and in a riot of color: blues and reds and greens, white belted with gold, black studded with pearls harvested from the shallows of the southern sea. *Well, well-off women wear those things*, she amended herself, but they were pretty much the only women to be seen along Processional Boulevard. There were plenty more women in the city who made do with ordinary white blouses and staid blue or black skirts like her mother had made her wear. And a few, she knew, who wore a good deal less, but only at night and only in certain neighborhoods. The Masks and everything else came off once they were indoors with their male "friends."

She blinked. She didn't usually think about such things.

You were thinking about them in the tent last night with Keltan, she thought. *And in that hut with Chell a few months ago, when you tried to put your hand down his—*

"Pants," Keltan said.

She jumped like she'd been stuck. "What?"

"Pants," Keltan said. "That's what sets you apart right now. No women in Tamita seem to wear pants."

"Not on Processional Boulevard. It's a place to see and be seen."

"Yeah? Didn't spend much time in this part of town when I was growing up," Keltan said sourly. "Father wouldn't have liked it. And he'd have taken it out on Mother." He looked down. "I tried so hard to be good, so he wouldn't hurt Mother. And in the end . . ." He shook his head.

Mara glanced at him. He'd rarely talked about his family, but he'd told her that his father had killed his mother when he was ten, and had been hanged for it. He'd witnessed that, just as she had witnessed her father's hanging, but unlike her he'd been pleased to see his father die. "What did you do, after . . . that?" she said. "You've never told me. How did you survive?"

Keltan shrugged. "Apprenticed to a tanner."

Mara made a face. "Yuck."

"Important work," Keltan said. "Skilled work. I learned a trade."

"But the smell . . . !"

"You get used to it," Keltan said. Then he laughed. "Actually, no, you don't. And it kind of follows you around. Which is why, even after my parents were gone, I wasn't on Processional Boulevard very often. I was glad enough to leave the tannery when I decided to flee my Masking."

"Did you tell your Master what you intended?"

"How could I?" Keltan said. "His Mask would have cracked if he'd lied for me. Fact is, I've often wondered what he did after I left."

"Maybe you'll find out when this is all over."

"Maybe."

Shouts suddenly erupted at the main gate. A horse neighed. A moment later it came galloping up the boulevard, whipped to a frenzy by the Watcher on its back, who used the same lash on anyone who didn't get out of his way fast enough. Mara saw an elderly woman, struck across the back of the head, cry out and fall to her knees, and anger flared inside her. Whiteblaze stood up and growled. So much magic around her. She could—

No, she told herself. *You* can't.

"Rider from the Watcher army, I'll bet," Keltan said softly to her. "The Autarch is about to find out the unMasked Army is on the way."

"And he'll close the Palace," Mara said. She jumped up, pulling off Keltan's cloak and tossing it to him at the same time. He caught it deftly. "It's almost time to go back to meet Prilk, isn't it?"

"Close," Keltan said, glancing at the sundial that shared the small plaza with the fountain. He fastened the clasp of the cloak around his neck again. "Not quite time yet."

"Maybe Greff is early," Mara said. "Let's get back there."

They made their way back up the boulevard toward the walls of the

Palace. A general sense of agitation hung over the coiffed heads of the wealthy ladies in the wake of the Watcher's turbulent passing, heads which turned sharply as a trumpet blared from the far end of the boulevard. "They're closing the gates," Mara said.

They reached the guardhouse. Prilk stood in the doorway. "Oh, good, you're here," he said. "Greff is in the back room. Something happening up in the Palace, though, so I don't know if you'll have your full ten minutes . . ." He stepped aside to allow them to enter his office. He glanced at Whiteblaze. "Should . . . *that* . . . be in here?"

"Yes," Mara said. She gave the paper-strewn desk, wooden chairs, and round pot-bellied stove only a cursory glance. "Where . . . ?"

Prilk opened a door in the back of the office. "He's in here."

The three of them plus Whiteblaze crowded through the door into another room, half the size of the office. A slender youth dressed in white robes stood by the window that faced the Palace, staring at the Gate. He turned as they entered, light flashing off of his silver Mask. "They said you have a message for me," he said, voice trembling. "Is it . . . is it my parents?" His glance fell to Whiteblaze, and his eyes widened behind the Mask. "Is that a wolf?" Then his gaze rose to Mara again, and he frowned. "Who are you?"

"Prella," Mara said. "From Yellowgrass."

"Who? I don't know any Prella."

Prilk stepped forward. "What's going on?"

Keltan quietly closed the door to the office, positioning himself behind Prilk, hand on his dagger. They'd discussed this: if what Mara was about to attempt failed as it had with the Watcher in the farmyard, he'd be ready.

She felt the flow of Prilk's magic. She reached into his mind with her Gift, and bolstered by the magic she drew from Whiteblaze, altered it. *It seems so easy now*, she thought. *But is that because I'm getting better . . . or because of the Lady's soulprint?*

Keltan drew his dagger . . . but he didn't need it. Prilk drew a deep breath, and then simply turned without a word and went out, closing the door behind him.

"What . . . ?" Greff said. "What did you . . . ?"

"Simply convinced him he didn't need to be in here," Mara said. "He won't think anything more about it. Which means he won't remember this encounter if questions are asked later."

"Questions? What questions?"

"How a member of the Child Guard was replaced by an imposter," Mara said. She reached up and removed her fake Mask. "One with the power to bring down the Autarchy forever."

TWENTY ONE

The Worm in the Apple

"MARA?" Greff breathed. Then his hand flew to his Mask. "No! I can't—"

Mara stepped over to him. "It's all right," she said. She pulled his hands away, then touched his Mask herself, the silver cool beneath her fingers—and lifted it from his face. He gasped and stumbled back, but she ignored him, holding the Mask in both hands, eyes closed.

Thrice now she had modified Masks. She expected the Child Guard Mask to be harder to reach inside, but in fact it was easier, and she frowned as she realized why: it was designed to allow more magic to flow through it, so the Autarch could more easily draw the power he needed from the enslaved children with whom he had surrounded himself. She concentrated, closing off the pathway to the Autarch, then freezing the soulprint so that, as with the Masks of Herella and Filia and Jess, any Watcher would see only an obedient citizen.

She opened her eyes.

Greff stared at her, brown eyes wide in his pale face. Though he had to be older than Keltan, he looked younger. The hood of his white robe had fallen back, revealing smoothly oiled black hair. "What have you done?" he breathed.

"Freed you," she said. Now she examined his Mask with her eyes open. She had left hers smooth, but Greff's real Mask had decorative patterns etched into it. She turned and put it down on the table, unslung her backpack, and drew out the one she had made. Studying them carefully side-by-side, she drew magic from Whiteblaze. This was where the careful control she had practiced right here in the Palace with Shelra, the Mistress of Magic, came into its own. A red line of magic traced the pattern from Greff's Mask onto the plain silver of her own. When she was satisfied, she released it. The silver glowed white hot for a moment, there was an acrid smell, and then her Mask looked just like Greff's . . . almost.

Another moment of concentration, and she had copied Greff's soul-print, and his face, onto the new Mask. It twisted and bent, looked almost liquid for a moment, and then froze into its new shape.

Two identical silver Masks bearing Greff's face stared blankly up from the table.

She handed his original Mask back to him. "Now I need your clothes," she said. "Don't worry, you can have mine."

"You're going to get us all killed!" Greff said.

"I may get myself killed," Mara said, "but you should be all right. Ride my horse to the Gate. There's no way they'll stop a Child Guard who tells them he's under orders from the Autarch to head out on the road, not if your Mask doesn't belie it—which it won't."

"And go where?" Greff demanded.

"Home," Mara said simply. "Your parents are waiting for you."

Greff blinked. "Home? To my parents? You *talked* to them?" His face paled. "The Watchers will—"

"The Watchers *won't*," Mara corrected. "I've given them unbreakable Masks, like yours is now. The moment you rejoin them, you will all flee north. Whatever happens in Tamita, there is freedom beyond the mountains." *For now*, she thought. If she failed, the Autarch would crush the Lady's hidden hideaway as surely as he had crushed the Secret City.

And it will be my fault again.

No guilt!

It was getting harder and harder to uphold that mantra.

"And what are *you* going to do?" Greff demanded.

"Take your place," Mara said. "And kill the Autarch in his own throne room."

"You're mad," Greff breathed. "He'll know the moment you enter—"

"Not if I've made this Mask right." Mara touched the copy of Greff's Mask. "Not if you quit talking and take off your clothes."

"I hope you don't say that to a lot of boys," Keltan said dryly.

"You haven't left me any choice," Greff said. He pulled off his robe. Beneath it he wore a white tunic which he likewise stripped off, revealing a body thin to the point of emaciation, ribs standing out beneath pale skin, belly sunken. He kicked off his white boots and pulled down his white pants, then tugged them over his stockinged feet. His thighs and calves were every bit as scrawny-looking. He stripped off the socks and then, naked except for his drawers, wrapped his arms around himself. "Hurry up, it's freezing."

Mara pulled off her own clothes and passed them to Greff. It *was* cold, standing there in her under tunic and drawers, and she was glad to pull on Greff's pants and tunic and socks. Despite his thinness, they fit all right—a little tight in the hips and chest, but they had clearly been made for someone heavier than he was.

No, she thought harshly, *they were made for him before the Autarch started sucking the life out of him.*

Once she had donned the white robe over his clothes, she looked down and thought with satisfaction that there was no way anyone could tell she was a girl just by looking at her.

When they were both dressed, she handed Greff the plain white Mask she had worn as they rode through the streets. "My horse is the roan mare outside," she said. "You're me until you're out of sight of the guardhouse. Then find somewhere secret and put on your silver Mask and my cloak from the saddlebags. I know it's unusual, a Child Guard leaving the City on his own—"

"Unusual?" Greff said. "It's unheard of."

"—but the Watchers are completely dependent on the Masks. If you're wearing your Mask and you tell them the Autarch ordered you to ride north alone, they will believe you. They can't imagine a world in which Masks don't work."

"I can't either," Greff said. "But I hope you create one."

"There's one more thing I need from you," Mara said. She explained her plan for getting into the Palace, through the tunnel down which she had been taken when her Mask failed. "I know part of the Palace well enough, but not where the Child Guard are quartered. I'll need to get into your quarters, so I'll be found where they would expect to find you."

Greff shook his head. "I still think you're mad," he said, but he went ahead and provided detailed directions all the same. When he was done, he held out his hand. "Good-bye," he said. "I fully expect to meet you both again outside Traitors' Gate just before they strip and hang us. But good luck all the same."

"Thank you," Mara said seriously, shaking his hand. "Go home to your parents, Greff. They're good people, and they love you."

"I know," Greff said. He shook Keltan's hand, too. Then he put on the fake Mask Mara had created, cautiously, as if expecting it to squirm like a new Mask: but it just sat on his face, still looking like Mara. "Not very comfortable," he said. "It doesn't match my face." He took his hand away slowly. "At least it stays on."

"It's still magical," Mara said. "It's just a different . . . recipe."

"Maybe you *can* do this," Greff said. He hesitated, as though he were going to say something else; but in the end he turned without another word and went out. Mara caught a glimpse of Prilk sitting at his desk staring at nothing, and wondered if she had overdone it in trying to twist his perception. *What if I damaged him, like that Watcher in the farmyard?*

Remembering Greff's emaciated body, she couldn't work up much concern.

"Our turn," she said to Keltan. "Market Gate, then the warehouse."

Keltan nodded. "One other thing first."

She frowned. "What?"

Keltan took off the Watcher's Mask and set it aside. "This." He reached out and pulled her to him, and kissed her, long and lingeringly. At first she resisted a little—there was no time!—but somehow that thought vanished as the kiss continued. Her arms went around Keltan and she pulled him tight against her even as his arms tightened around her.

But she could not give herself completely to the kiss, as much as she longed to do so, both because they had no time—and because she could *still* feel the magic inside him, and *still* longed to draw it out. Afraid she wouldn't be able to resist that urge if the kiss continued, she pushed him away before she really wanted to. "We've got to go," she murmured.

Keltan nodded. He stepped back from her almost convulsively, as if breaking free from something. "We'll, uh . . . explore that further sometime soon. I hope."

"If we survive," Mara said. *And if I don't give in to the desire to suck you dry of magic before then.*

Keltan grimaced. "You sure know how to spoil the mood." But then he smiled. "We'll survive," he said softly. "We have reason to."

Mara nodded. But in her heart she knew that was no real assurance at all.

She put on her new silver Mask and pulled the hood of Greff's robe over her hair. "Let's go," she said.

Keltan had already put his Watcher's Mask back on. He nodded and opened the door.

Prilk still stared at nothing. Keltan went over to him and touched his shoulder. He jerked back to life as suddenly as if waking from a dream, turned to look at them. "Time's up!" he snapped, then blinked, confused. "Where's the girl?"

"She already left," Keltan said. "You must have been too busy to notice."

"Yes, I must have," Prilk said, but sounded more confused than ever. "She left?"

"Just a moment ago," Keltan said. He nodded at Mara, who didn't dare to speak lest her voice give her away. "Greff has had some very disturbing news and has asked if I will escort him as he takes a walk to clear his head. I have agreed to do so."

"Oh," Prilk said. He looked at Mara's Mask, and she held her breath, but he seemed to see nothing amiss. "Very well." He waved his hand. "Off you go, then. I have to get back to . . . work . . . ?" He stared at his desk. It was completely empty of papers.

"Thank you," Keltan said, and led Mara out.

They were both Tamita born-and-bred. Keltan knew the streets on this side of the city better than Mara, at least the streets away from Processional Boulevard, but she knew the streets on the far side of the Palace, along Maskmakers' Way. Between them they made good progress, choosing lesser-traveled paths where there were fewer people to react to the admittedly unusual sight of a single Child Guard, and the even more unusual sight of a tame wolf. Those who did see them—a baker, a blacksmith, a lamp maker, a handful of children, a few housewives en route to or returning from the market—quickly averted their eyes when their gazes slid from the glistening silver of Mara's Mask to the stern unmarked black of Keltan's. Mara got a perverse pleasure out of using the Watchers' reputation for brutality and infallibility against them.

About an hour after they left the Palace—long enough, Mara thought, that Greff should be safely through the Gate and away—they stood outside the stone fence that surrounded the warehouse that had once been her grandfather's, the warehouse where she had been dragged on the nightmarish day her Mask had failed. She wondered if the fat warden were still in there, the man who drew pictures of naked unMasked children for shadowy clients in the streets of Aygrima. She hoped so.

But the pleasure of seeing him again under far different circumstances would have to wait. For now, the wall of the warehouse only provided a conveniently shadowed lurking place as they waited for the sun to set. They settled themselves on the cobblestones and watched the traffic passing on the Great Circle Road. There was little of it; the alarm that had closed the main gate had closed the gate to the Outside Market as well. Mara could imagine the consternation that had caused. Mara gazed up at the wall. "I used to sit up there and watch people in the Outside Market." *With Mayson*, she thought with a pang of sorrow and . . .

No guilt. No guilt!

"How is the sally port sealed?" Keltan said.

"Barred and padlocked," Mara said. She patted Whiteblaze's head. "But I think we can handle it."

"All right," Keltan said. He glanced at the sun, which was sinking low in the west. "All we have to do is wait."

The hours dragged by. The sun set. The Great Circle Road, already unnaturally empty of traffic, cleared completely as the nightly curfew took hold. Masked citizens could use the Great Circle Road at night, but there was little reason for any of them to do so on this side of the city: only Processional Boulevard and a few other streets with various entertainment establishments were permissible destinations, and all the buildings close to the Market Gate were warehouses and other business-oriented structures.

As darkness closed in, the lamplighter came by, lighting the oil lamps hung on the tall posts at twenty-foot intervals around the Road. Mara's house had been lit by rockgas, but that was a rare and precious commodity that only the wealthy could afford, especially since the extraction and storage of it in special cisterns beneath the ground required the careful attention of Gifted Engineers.

On the heels of the lamplighter came a Watcher, who went into the tower Mara had pointed out to Keltan and filled and lit the lamps inside it. The top of the wall remained dark, of course, since the sentries patrolling it did not want their eyes dazzled . . . but just as in the mining camp, the sentries mostly turned their gaze inward; a fact of which she had apprised Chell. There had never been a threat to the city, and so the sentries' primary function was to watch for fires or curfew-breaking children— Mara suspected that was how she and Sala had been spotted swimming in the ornamental pool behind the Waterworkers' Hall (had that really just been last summer? it seemed a lifetime ago) and hauled home to their families in disgrace.

The lighting of the lamps began the countdown. Bells tolled every hour in Tamita to mark the passage of time, and when four hours had passed, Mara, Keltan, and Whiteblaze at last emerged from hiding. Mara looked both ways along the Great Circle Road to make sure no Watchers were in sight, took a careful look at the top of the wall for the same reason, and at last dashed across to the tower, its interior dimly lit by the flickering lamp just inside the open arch that gave access, but bright enough after their long hours in the dark.

The stairs Mara had so often trotted up as a child spiraled to their left. But the door they wanted was on ground level, in the deep shadow behind the stairs. Mara had discovered it one day when a group of Watchers had barged in just as she was coming down and she'd had to get out of their way. It was just as Mara remembered it: thick black timbers, strong iron bands, massive hinges. A steel bar held it closed, locked in place by a huge iron padlock, so rusted she doubted it could have been opened with the key even in the unlikely event someone in the city remembered where it was.

But she didn't need a key. She took magic from Whiteblaze, just a little. It sheathed her hand in glowing red. She touched the lock and released magic into it. The hasp simply broke apart, and the ancient lock dropped to the stone floor with a clatter.

With Keltan's help, she lifted the iron bar out of the brackets bolted to the door and set it to one side. "Here goes," Keltan said. He tugged on the door. It gave an alarming groan as it opened, and Mara shot a look over her shoulder at the archway and the Great Circle Road beyond, but heard no shouts or sound of running feet.

A dark figure appeared in the doorway, face hidden in the shadows of a deep hood, eyes red sparks in the lamplight. A hand swept up, pulled back the hood, revealing Chell. "No alarm," he said. "As you said, Mara. The sentries rarely look outside the city." He entered the tower, and after him came the rest of the small force Edrik had assigned: first Hyram, who nodded at Mara, unsmiling, then Prescox, Danys, and Lilla, the three unMasked Army fighters, followed by the four sailors. Antril brought up the rear. He alone flashed Mara a quick grin. She felt absurdly grateful for that.

"Edrik?" Mara said to Hyram.

"We haven't seen any sign of the unMasked Army," he said. "But my father will be where he is supposed to be, waiting out of sight of the walls. He'll attack the damaged portion of the wall at first light—just as you ordered." His tone made it clear he resented the fact she was able to order his father to do anything.

"The Watcher Army must be close as well," Keltan said. "Their messengers arrived yesterday."

"And our force will be caught like a nut in a nutcracker when they do arrive," Hyram growled. "Trapped between the Watchers and the city."

"Then we'd better do our part," Mara said. "Shut up, all of you, and follow me." *Huh*, she thought, surprised at her own forcefulness. *Maybe getting walloped with the Lady of Pain and Fire's soulprint has done me some good.* Whether that was where that tone of authority came from or not, it worked. The men (and one woman) fell in behind her as she looked both ways along the road again, then led the force at a run across it—but not into the alley where she and Keltan had lurked earlier. Instead, they entered the alley farther down the Great Circle Road from the Market Gate, on the opposite side of the warehouse from where they had waited. There was a side door in that alley. Mara had not seen it when she was inside the warehouse after her failed Masking, but she'd seen it often enough in her years running these streets as a child.

It was bolted from the inside, of course. Mara paused long enough to remove her silver Child Guard Mask, handing it to Chell, who slipped it inside his pack without a word, then called up red magic from Whiteblaze again, and eased the bolt open. Taking a step back, she nodded to Hyram, who slipped his sword from its sheath, a motion copied by the others in the small force, pressed quietly down on the latch—and then eased the door open.

The room beyond was dark, too dark to see anything. Deep, rumbling snores proved the chamber was not empty, however. Hyram stepped inside, and a moment later the snores choked off and then turned into moans of terror.

Everyone crammed through the door, Mara last. She closed it behind her. She called up a touch more magic from Whiteblaze, just enough to cover one finger with white light, illuminating the room for her alone. Seeing the oil lamp on the wooden table next to the cold fireplace, she reached out to it. The spark of magic from her finger leaped to its wick, and yellow light filled the room.

Wide white eyes stared at her from Chell's men and the unMasked Army fighters. She ignored them. She walked over to the bed where Hyram was holding a gloved hand over the mouth of the fat man, whose eyes widened as he saw her, and widened further when he saw the wolf at her feet. "Move your hand," she told Hyram. Then to the fat man she said, "If you shout, my wolf will tear your throat out." She touched Whiteblaze's head. "Won't you, boy?"

Whiteblaze, his eyes never leaving the man's face, growled even as his tail thumped.

Hyram lifted his gloved hand. Sweat beaded the fat man's face and there was a dark spreading stain on the blanket between his legs. Remembering her time in the warehouse, she couldn't summon much sympathy.

In fact, she couldn't summon any at all.

"You!" the fat man moaned. Whiteblaze growled, and his voice dropped to a strained whisper. "I remember you. The one with no scars . . . I sold your picture for a pretty penny . . . but you went to the mine!"

"I came back," Mara said. "This is the second time, actually. You may remember a large hole being blown in the wall of the city? The execution of Stanik? The slaying of several Watchers at Traitors' Gate?" She smiled. "That was me." She let the smile slip away. "Now where are your keys?"

"Mantelpiece," the fat man said. "Please, don't kill me!"

"Not entirely up to me," Mara said. She went over to the mantelpiece, found the keys. "Bring him."

Hyram hauled the fat man up. He clutched at his blanket, and Mara realized he was naked beneath it. It seemed fitting.

The inner door of the chamber opened into the warehouse proper. It was not entirely dark. As she had remembered, a couple of lamps were kept burning, presumably so the fat man could check on his charges if he needed to. Everything was as she remembered it: the two rows of cells down the sides of the warehouse, the chair where the fat man sat to draw his prisoners, the table and chests where prisoners took off their own clothes and put on the gray prison smocks.

There was stirring in the darkness as they entered the warehouse. A boy's voice cried out, "What's going on?"

Then a girl, voice shocked, said, "They're unMasked!"

"Is that a wolf?" said another girl.

All the children were locked up on the same side of the warehouse, Mara realized. She counted three girls and two boys.

More than anything else, she wanted to let them out of their cells. But if they went out into the street and the Night Watchers found them, their precious element of surprise would be squandered. Nor could they afford to leave a guard.

"Listen to me," she said, standing in front of the very cell in which she had once been imprisoned, now occupied by a slender boy with red hair, his freckled face crisscrossed by white scars from his failed Masking. "If we succeed in what we're trying to do, tomorrow you'll be freed to go back to your families, and you'll never have to worry about Watchers or Masks again."

"Then let us out!" cried the red-haired boy. "Let us out now."

"I can't," Mara said. "Not now. There's nowhere for you to go."

"Then we'll stay in the warehouse," the boy said. "Until things change."

"If they don't, you'll just be locked up again." And then a horrible thought struck her. They had destroyed the Autarch's mines of magic. There was nowhere for the unMasked to be sent where they could be useful. And before that labor camp had existed . . . those who failed their Masking had just been executed.

She *couldn't* leave them locked up. No matter what happened, they were better off trying to escape.

"Listen," she said. "There's an open door, in the tower across the street. If you can get into it, you can get out of the city, flee into the fields and woods."

"We'll starve out there," a girl cried.

"I'm not telling you what to do," Mara said. "I can't. But you're right," she said to the boy. "I can't leave you locked up, either."

"Mara," Chell warned. "If they tell the Watchers—"

"None of these will tell the Watchers," Mara said. "Of all the people in Tamita, they're the last ones who will tell the Watchers anything."

She unlocked her old cell, and then the others. The children in their prison smocks stumbled out into the dim light. "Bring the fat man," she told Hyram. "He can have my old cell."

Hyram, with Keltan's help, forced the fat man to the door of the cell. He resisted, and they shoved him through so hard he stumbled, the blanket falling away as he fell to his hands and knees, revealing massive white buttocks like pale hams. He scrabbled for the blanket and pulled it around him again, then stared up at them. Now that he was away from Hyram's knife, hatred filled his face. "You'll all pay for this! You'll hang outside

Traitors' Gate, every one of you, and I will draw your naked bodies and laugh while I do it."

Mara glanced at Hyram. "Gag him."

"With pleasure," Hyram said. He grabbed a filthy towel, lying on the floor next to the noisome bucket half-filled with excrement, and bound it around the fat man's head, forcing it between his teeth.

"Charming gentleman," Chell commented.

Mara turned to the red-haired boy. "Here is the key to his cell," she said. "We're four hours from first light. I leave him in your care."

The boy's eyes narrowed. "Oh, we'll take good care of him," he said softly, and the fat man's red face suddenly paled again. He got up and stumbled to the cot, where he huddled in his blanket, eyes wide and white with terror as the children from the cells gathered around his door and stared in at him.

Mara turned her back on him and on the children. "This way," she said to the others, and led them to the back of the warehouse, where it butted hard against the stone of the first tier of Fortress Hill. There was the door she remembered, rough black wood banded with rusty iron. Once again she pulled magic from Whiteblaze to unlock it, then pulled it wide.

No lamplight flickered in the tunnel beyond. She suspected it was only illuminated when there was to be a Masking ceremony, just in case it was needed in the aftermath. Chell sent two of his men back to the fat man's chamber; they returned with the lamp Mara had magically lit and two others they had found. Thus provided with illumination, they entered the tunnel, closing and locking the door behind them.

In silence they followed the tunnel up through Fortress Hill, climbing rough-hewn stairs, trudging along stone passageways, chill and damp. When gray stone gave way to polished white, Mara called a halt. "We're under the Maskery," she whispered. The stairs down which she had been dragged by the Watchers, bleeding and in shock, led up into darkness from which came the sound of rushing water. It took little imagination for her to also hear the sound of her mother's screams. "I know these tunnels connect to the Palace, but I don't know exactly how. We have to be even more cautious from here on."

"We weren't exactly planning to bang on the walls and sing marching songs," Hyram growled.

Chell shot Hyram a sharp, frowning glance. "Let's keep moving. First light won't wait."

The white hallway stretched ahead of them. Following it, where in the Palace would they emerge? Greff's instructions had been clear enough, but she had to get her bearings before she could make use of them.

At least the hallway remained deserted. There weren't even any doorways, which she took to mean they were still traversing the space between the Maskery and the Palace. They climbed another flight of stairs, and finally saw an end to the corridor: a brightly lit opening across which a figure suddenly passed right to left, an indistinct silhouette.

Mara held up a hand to stop the advance. "Just Keltan and I go ahead," she said. "Everyone else wait here."

Keltan had never removed his Watcher's Mask. Mara retrieved the Child Guard Mask from Chell and put it back on, knowing as she did so that she would not be removing it again until she had either succeeded or failed.

In which case . . . she wondered if the Masks she had made would likewise crumble and crack when their wearers died, or if that was only a characteristic of the Masks of the Autarch.

She turned to Whiteblaze, touched his head. "Stay," she whispered, and he sat down heavily, with a disgruntled sigh. She scratched him behind the ears, and set off toward the light, Keltan following her.

The tunnel ended in a large chamber lit by hissing gas lamps, with corridors extending left and right and ahead: an underground crossroads. The person they had seen pass in front of the light was disappearing down the corridor to the left. *Not a Watcher*, Mara thought, though from behind she could not tell what kind of Mask the person had been wearing.

But it didn't matter. She knew where they were now. She had passed through this chamber herself during her time in the Palace, though she had never realized the corridor from which they had just emerged joined up with the tunnel down which she had been taken to the warehouse and its loathsome warden. From here she knew exactly how to get to where she needed to be.

More importantly, she knew how to get the armed infiltrators she had left in the corridor where *they* needed to be. She turned and went back down the corridor. Whiteblaze scrambled to his feet, grinning at her. "I've got my bearings, so everything proceeds as we discussed," she said swiftly. "Keltan is a Watcher, so he can move freely. He will escort me to 'my'— Greff's—chambers. As we go, I'll show him the route to the throne room." She glanced at Keltan. "If we're stopped, you explain that you found me outside the Palace, distraught over my parents' death. No doubt there was consternation when Greff didn't return from his meeting in the guard-house. Say you've been ordered to stand watch outside my room. Your Mask will show anyone who questions it that you're telling the truth, so they'll have no choice but to believe you."

Keltan nodded.

"The rest of you," she said, turning back, "wait here. I doubt this tunnel is used except when there is a Masking, so it should remained deserted. If anyone does come down it, you'll have to quietly take care of whomever it is."

"No problem," Hyram said.

"When I'm summoned to go to the Autarch—and I suspect that will happen the moment Edrik makes his presence known, because the Autarch will want all his magical resources at hand the moment he feels even the slightest threat—Keltan will return and lead you to the throne room. Keep everyone else out while I deal with the Autarch."

"You're talking about the Sun Guards," Hyram said.

"Sun Guards?" Antril said.

"The Autarch's elite bodyguards," Hyram said.

"Oh," Antril said. "Good to know."

"Probably," Mara said. "But whatever I have to do to defeat the Autarch, I can't do it with a Watcher dagger in my back."

"I have seen the foyer to the throne room," Chell said, not to Mara, but to the rest of the force. "With ten fighters, we can defend it against an army . . . for a time."

"Whatever happens in the throne room," Mara said, "won't take long." *One way or another.* "Keltan, let's go."

"Good luck," said Chell.

Mara didn't expect Hyram to say anything. But as he had when she and Keltan had ridden away from the army after donning their false Masks, he surprised her. "Good fortune," he said gruffly. And then, as if to make certain she understood him, added, "To both of you."

"Thank you," Mara said, finding her own voice surprisingly rough. She knelt beside Whiteblaze. "Stay," she told him. "Follow Chell." She exerted a little magic to be sure he understood. He whined, but she knew he would do as she said.

She got back to her feet, and together she and Keltan walked into the Palace.

Murmuring instructions as necessary, Mara guided Keltan to the chambers of the Child Guard. They rounded a corner and saw the entry door Greff had described to them dead ahead—and on either side of it, the expected Watcher guards.

The two men stiffened as Mara and Keltan came into view. "Greff!" one of them snarled. "You bloody brat, where the hell have you—"

"He had some bad news from home," Keltan said. "He took it hard."

The man's gaze shifted to him. "Who are you?" he said suspiciously.

"Hyram," Keltan said. "New to the city. Was serving in Yellowgrass." He jerked his thumb at Mara. "Prilk down in the guardhouse grabbed me off my regular street patrol and told me to go after this one. Ran off after hearing from a girl from his village his parents had died. Led me on a merry chase, too. Lost him for a while, but finally picked him up down by the Market Gate. Prilk told me once I found him to bring him here—and stand guard over him until morning, make sure he doesn't try to run off again."

"He won't run off with *us* here," the Watcher growled.

"Don't I know it," Keltan said sourly. "But I have my orders, senseless though they seem. I've got to stand outside his room for the rest of the night."

The guards exchanged glances, then the one who had been doing all the talking shrugged. "No skin off our noses. Go tuck him in. Third room on the right."

The other guard opened the door, and Keltan shoved Mara through it. The third door on the right stood open. Mara stepped into the room beyond and looked around. There was a bed, a table, a chair, a lamp, and a chamber pot. That was it. Aside from the fact everything was clean, it wasn't much of an improvement over the cells down in the warehouse.

More like a stable for a prized milk cow, she thought.

"Mara . . ." Keltan whispered as he stood in the doorway, but she shook her head sharply and closed the door in his face. Good-byes were a risk they could not take. The die was cast, and they had to live with the roll.

She lay down on the bed. No doubt, Child Guard were able to remove their Masks while they slept, but she kept hers on, as she kept her borrowed clothes. She did not expect to sleep anyway.

As it happened, she was wrong about that. She dozed almost at once, her body more exhausted than she had guessed.

She woke to a sound she had never heard before: a deep, shuddering moan that made the hair stand up on the back of her neck even as she gasped her way out of sleep.

TWENTY-TWO

Face to Face

THE DOOR SWUNG OPEN, just a crack. "They're coming," Keltan whispered, and the door closed again. Mara swung her legs over the side of the bed and stood up. Her heart pounded in her chest as though trying to break free from the cage of her ribs. Despite all the planning and thought that had gone into this moment, despite all the fear and horror and heart-wrenching grief that had led her to this place—or maybe *because* of it—she felt woefully unprepared. *What have I done?* she thought in sudden terror. *I can't defeat the Autarch. It's ludicrous.*

But from somewhere deep inside her rose a bubble of calm, though it was the kind of surface calm that holds back fiery rage. *Yes, we can.*

We?

"What's going on?" she heard Keltan say. "What's that noise? I've never heard it before."

"No one has," said a gruff voice. "It's the general alarm. It means the city faces imminent attack. Autarch wants the Child Guard, *now*. And you'd better get back to your post or they'll be hanging you outside Traitors' Gate for desertion."

"Yes, sir," Keltan said. She sensed his hesitation, but it would have made no sense for a Watcher to say good-bye to the Child Guard he'd hauled home in disgrace, and he must have known it. She heard his footsteps run off down the hall.

Now she truly was alone.

The door swung wide and a Watcher stared in at her. "Good, you're dressed," he growled. "In the hall *now*."

Mara stepped out into the hall. She was the first of the Child Guard to do so, the others presumably having to don their robes, whereas she had slept in hers, but it did not take them long to muster. "Where were you last night?" whispered a girl, taller than her, who stepped in beside Mara, but Mara didn't dare answer and kept her eyes down. She couldn't even remember if they were the same color as Greff's. She dared not look anyone in the face.

In another moment it wasn't a problem. "Quick march," snapped the Watcher, and the Child Guard broke into a fast trot along the corridor. They went out, turned, followed another hall, turned again, climbed multiple flights of stairs . . . and emerged onto the landing in front of the tall golden doors of the throne room. Those doors stood open. They were ushered in.

The Autarch sat on the Sun Throne, though the sun was not yet up and so no light came through the glass behind the massive replica of his Mask that hung above the golden chair. Rather than blazing like fire, the eyes of that giant Mask instead were dull and gray.

The last time Mara had stood in the throne room she had worn the iron Mask that blocked her Gift, and the black basin that stood beside the throne had appeared empty. Now she could see that it brimmed with magic. But she could see more than that. She could also see that it could not be emptied of its magic, not easily: for the magic flowed up into it from underneath. *There must be a vast reservoir below the throne,* she thought. *Magic from the mine.*

Magic extracted through the pain and suffering and degradation of the unMasked.

She felt anger that she fought to hold down, though somehow it seemed disconnected from the anger she sensed inside the calm that now overlay her thoughts. *That* anger seemed to come from outside her, as if it belonged to someone else.

What's going on?

With the precision born of long practice, the Child Guard ranged themselves on the steps of the dais, each sitting on one of the blue cushions that rested on the white marble, much like the wolves had once ranged themselves around the Lady of Pain and Fire. Mara hesitated only a moment before seeing the space where Greff would be expected to go. She went to it and sat down on the cushion.

Now what?

More people came into the throne room: a half-dozen in all. One she recognized as Shelra, the Mistress of Magic, who had trained her in its use. Another wore a Mask of silver, like the Child Guard—but unlike the Masks of the Child Guard, this one was adorned with gems: blue on the forehead, green on the cheeks, silver tracing the entire periphery. She had seen such a Mask just once before, though the details were different. That would be the Guardian of Security, the replacement for Stanik, whom she had slain when her father had died.

These half-dozen men and women, then, must be the Circle: the Autarch's closest advisers, tasked with the day-to-day governance of the Autarchy. "Guardian Flinik," said the Autarch. "What exactly is the threat outside our walls?"

"It appears to be a bandit force," the Guardian of Security said. "All unMasked. Mostly men, a few women. We put the number at about a hundred."

"One hundred," the Autarch said. "And they dare to attack Tamita?"

"Ordinarily," the Guardian said, "they would pose little threat. But as you know," his voice trembled a little as though he feared what he had to say next, but he pressed on, "almost all of the battle-trained Watchers we have were sent north to deal with the rebel stronghold my predecessor uncovered the existence of. The messenger who arrived yesterday assures us the Watcher Army is aware of this threat and is riding south to meet it, but it is not here yet. If this bandit army is able to penetrate the walls, they could do much damage."

"*Can* they penetrate the walls?" asked the Autarch.

"Repairs are far from complete on the portion of the wall destroyed on the day my predecessor . . . predeceased me. The repairs have been slow. The bandits appear to be well aware of that fact. There is a risk." He paused. "A risk made greater," he finally continued, "by their unknown magical abilities. The reports from the messengers—of the complete destruction of the magic mine—are . . . worrisome."

Silence fell in the throne room for a long moment. Then the Autarch growled, "This cannot be borne. It is a direct affront to me and to my authority as Autarch. And therefore I will deal with it. Have your Watchers pull back, Flinik. They are to surround and protect the Palace."

"Your Highness?" Flinik said. "But that will leave the walls undefended!"

"No," said the Autarch. "It will not. This is an attack on the ordinary citizens of Tamita. And therefore the ordinary citizens of Tamita will defend the walls." He dipped his hand into the basin of magic at his right side . . . and Mara almost gasped out loud. She saw the magic pour into him, so rapidly and eagerly that the level in the basin visibly dropped even though she could sense more magic surging up like a geyser from the reservoir somewhere below them. But the Autarch did not hold it in himself. Instead, it went . . . elsewhere. She could feel it spreading out from the throne room as though the Sun Throne were the sun in earnest, casting its rays across the whole city. "Everyone but the Child Guard, leave me," said the Autarch. "I must concentrate. Flinik, array your forces as I ordered. I believe your doubts will be allayed before you even reach the wall . . . unh." The Autarch's eyes closed behind his golden Mask, and his chest heaved. The Circle exchanged glances, then fled. The throne room door closed behind them . . . *slammed* closed, as though shut in haste.

Muffled cries and thuds sounded beyond the door. Mara sensed, though from too far away for it to flow to her, the escape of magic from a dying man. *Hyram and Chell and Keltan were waiting for them. The members of the Circle have been killed or captured. So far, so good.*

But that wouldn't matter in the slightest if she could not cut off the head of the beast. She got to her feet.

The Autarch gasped again—and suddenly the Child Guard stiffened all around her, moaning as one, lighting up in her Gifted sight like torches, burning with magic which the Autarch drew eagerly to himself.

He has all that magic in the basin and the reservoir below to draw on, she thought. *Why does he need theirs?*

But she knew the answer. He didn't need ordinary magic, he needed *their* magic, the deep, raw magic of their young bodies, not to do whatever he was doing to defend the city, but to protect and restore his own aging body. Just like the Lady, sucking magic from the unMasked she had murdered in the mines, he lusted for power with no thought of the cost to those he tore it from, callously cutting short others' lives so he could extend his own.

The anger in her burned as bright as the Child Guard's bodies. She took a step toward the Autarch—

His eyes opened again behind his Mask of gold. "At last," he said. "At last."

And just like that, she couldn't move.

She looked down at herself. Red magic enwrapped her body, magic she could not touch, magic that had turned the air itself solid so that she might as well have been frozen in ice. She looked up again. "Did you really think," the Autarch said, the scorn in his voice sharp as a knife, "that I could be fooled by that crude copy of a Child Guard's Mask? I knew who you were the moment you entered the throne room."

"Then why didn't you kill me on the spot?" Mara said. She felt helpless and foolish and furious and guilty. *No guilt?* She had no *right* to try to move past her guilt. Once again, she had failed. Once again, she had made the wrong decision. Once again, people would die for her.

More shouts from outside the throne room. Mara could not see what was happening out there, but she could guess. The Sun Guards must be attacking, trying to fight through her companions to reach the Autarch. But the Autarch seemed unconcerned by the sounds of battle. "Kill you? Kill my old friend Arilla? The girl of my dreams?"

Arilla? The Lady of Pain and Fire? "I'm not—" she started to say . . .

. . . but then, suddenly, she *was*.

That strange disconnected bubble of rage wrapped in unnatural calm that had seemed so separate from her swelled like a bladder filling with water. It pushed Mara out of the center of her own mind, drove her to the edges, squeezed her into immobility, turned her into a spectator in her own brain. And suddenly, too late, she understood many things that had happened since she fired the crossbow bolt into the head of the Lady and Arilla's overwhelming power had rushed into her: the strange sense that she had in many ways become more like the Lady than ever before, the knowledge of the Lady's plans she could not remember how she had come by, the surprising ease with which she had altered the Masks of Greff's parents and Greff himself. The Lady's soulprint had not just *changed* her, it had *possessed* her. Some piece of the Lady survived in her body . . . and now it had seized control.

"*I think it is time to prepare the way for your final fate,*" the Lady had said. Was *this* the fate she'd had in mind? *Always* had in mind? Possession? To discard her own aging body in favor of Mara's young fresh one?

But she died! Mara cried silently. *I killed her before she could act!*

Not soon enough, apparently.

"I have dreamed about you, too," said Mara's voice, but it was the Lady who provided the words. "I have dreamed about how I would kill you, the many ways you would suffer before you died. And now here I am."

"Here you are," said the Autarch. "How is that working out for you?"

He stood then, and came over to where Mara waited, frozen. "We are so much alike," he said softly. "Variations of the same Gift. I cannot pull magic directly from the living as you can, but through my Masks I have that same power . . . as you see." He gestured at the Child Guard, each as stiff and frozen as Mara. "And clearly you, too, have thought long and hard about how to use that power to live forever. I had thought I could simply save this body," he gestured at it, "and I have done wonders with it, but I have known for some time that the ultimate solution is to take a new body. The difficulty, of course, is that that body must have the same Gift as ours, and that Gift is vanishingly rare. But then this girl came along." He reached out and caressed Mara's cheek. She would have shuddered at the touch if she had been able to move. "I allowed myself to be 'convinced' by the Mistress of Magic that she should be spared. I had thought to keep her around the Palace until I was ready to possess her. But that fool Stanik managed to let her escape. Thank you so much for bringing her back to me."

"You can't have her," the Lady said. "She is already mine."

"Arilla," the Autarch said softly. "You are only a ghost. Do you think I cannot tell? You are an echo of a fading song, a dying coal from a once-great fire. You are dead. I am alive. You cannot prevent me from taking her."

"We'll see."

"Yes," the Autarch said. "We will."

He reached up and took off his Golden Mask, revealing . . . not what Mara expected. He looked younger than he should have, when she knew he was at least eighty. The effect of drawing magic from the Child Guard, she guessed. Yet apparently it was not enough. He wanted her. He wanted to possess her. To become her.

As, it seemed, the Lady already had.

Was any of this plan mine at all? Mara thought. *Or was it all fed to me by this . . . ghost, this revenant, this remnant of the Lady?*

She tried to twitch a finger, move a foot, blink an eye, anything to prove she still had some control of her own body. But nothing happened.

The Autarch reached out and pulled the silver Mask from Mara's face. He tossed it aside. It rang like a bell as it hit the stones of the dais. "Beautiful as I remember," he said. He wasn't talking about the Mask. He touched Mara's cheek. "Unmarked. How did she manage that, when her Mask failed?" He thought for a moment. "Ah. Ethelda. She asked if she could attend in my place. I didn't know then that she was in league with the girl's father. I was worried that I was drawing too much magic too quickly from too many of the Gifted when I attended their Maskings, and that was why the Maskings were failing. I did not want that to happen to Charlton Holdfast's daughter. I wanted her to grow up to be my new Master Maskmaker." He smiled. "But things have a way of working out. This is much better. She has grown up to be my new body instead."

"Your city is under attack," the Lady's ghost said through Mara. "Your attention is divided. I know what you are doing. As I did with my villagers, you are using the young people who received the altered Masks in the past three years as your soldiers. You have been training them to fight and now you have thrown them at the unMasked Army."

"I will show these bandits," said the Autarch, "that the people of Aygrima will do whatever I ask of them."

"What you *demand*."

He shrugged. "It's the same thing, really."

"You cannot force me out of this body," the Lady said. "I am stronger than you could ever dream of being."

The Autarch laughed. "You still don't grasp the truth, do you, Arilla?" He leaned close, so close that his eyes were all that Mara could see and she could feel his hot breath on her lips. She longed to pull back, but she could not. Neither the Lady nor the magic holding her in place would permit it. "You're dead. It's about time you started acting like it."

And then the Autarch of Aygrima hurled his consciousness into Mara's mind.

It was all she could do to hold on to the tiny sliver of herself she still commanded. Like a spectator at a wrestling match, she looked on as the Autarch and the fading remnant of the Lady struggled for supremacy, for control of *her* body. It was clear to her from the moment the Autarch launched his attack that he would win. He had told the simple truth, after all: the Lady of Pain and Fire was dead, and the remnant of her, hiding inside Mara since the moment at the minehead when she had fired the crossbow bolt into the Lady's head, did not truly have the power of the Lady, because *Mara* did not have that power: not yet. The Lady had trained and honed hers for decades. Mara had barely even come to grips with the fact that hers existed.

And that was the Lady's undoing. The Lady was like a slippery eel, trying to evade the Autarch's hands, but he simply grew more of them, grasping and gripping, and she could not evade them all. Slowly, her control of Mara's body was wrested from her. The Autarch filled more and more of Mara's mind, squeezing Mara's consciousness down to almost nothing. A little more and it would be gone . . . and if that happened, she did not think it would ever return. The Autarch would have her. The Autarch would *be* her. And how many more decades could he . . . she . . . rule with a new young body, one with a greater degree of the Gift than he had ever had, but with all his accumulated knowledge of how to use that Gift?

Grute, all those months ago, had tried to rape her, and failed. The Autarch was succeeding, the violation more obscene, more repulsive, than anything Grute could have managed . . . and this time, she had no way to respond.

But through it all, her eyes were open, and her ears. She could hear the shouts and clatter of battle outside the throne room doors as her companions fought the Sun Guards. And she could see the Sun Throne, and the wall behind it, the tall glass windows brightening now as at last the sun broke the horizon.

She saw the door behind the Sun Throne swing open.

She saw Greff, still wearing his Child Guard Mask, step through. In his hand he held a dagger. He leaped forward.

He drove the blade into the Autarch's back.

The Autarch screamed, both bodily and in Mara's mind. In an instant he was withdrawing from her, rushing back to his own body. So intricately entangled with the Lady's soulprint was he that he took what was left of Arilla with him, both of them slamming back into the old body that had just been so violently injured. Mara saw an intense flash of white magic in the Autarch's eyes at the same instant that the magic holding her frozen and upright vanished. She dropped to her knees, raised her head to see the Autarch turn on Greff, who was staggering back, hand red with blood. The Autarch hurled scarlet magic into the boy's face. The silver Mask turned white hot in an instant, and Greff screamed, a horrible, high-pitched, inhuman sound, as his hair burst into flames and his ears burned to shriveled black husks. He dropped to his knees, scrabbling weakly at the Mask, and then fell lifelessly to his side, smoke pouring from his head, resting in a noisome pool of smoking grease and blackened blood.

But as Greff died, his magic slammed into Mara, who welcomed it eagerly, even though it burned her like the hot silver that had killed him. She gasped as her body filled with Greff's magic and her mind with his soulprint, still blazing with the hatred and determination that had driven him to his final desperate act.

All around the dais the Child Guard screamed, echoing Greff, as the Autarch, desperate for power, ripped it from their bodies. As one, they, too, toppled, whether dead or alive, Mara could not see. What she *could* see was the blade withdrawing itself from the Autarch's back, magic flickering around the wound as he desperately tried to knit together the damaged tissue.

In a moment the Autarch would have healed himself. He would turn on her again, and she would be unable to resist him.

But she did not give him that moment.

With the magic she had taken from Greff, she reached out for the only weapons at hand: the two Masks lying on the dais in front of her, silver and gold, hers and the Autarch's. She poured all her magic into them— and hurled them at the Autarch's head.

He had just turned back toward her, triumph on his face, his wound healed, the ghost of Arilla no doubt destroyed as well. And then that look of triumph was wiped away forever. The heavy Masks slammed into his chin. In a spray of blood and shattered bone and pulped brain, the Autarch of Aygrima was flung off his feet and backward, to thud, headless and blood-soaked and very, very dead, into the Sun Throne. For a moment his body remained upright in an awful parody of a seated king; then it slid down into an ungraceful bloody lump on the dais.

Mara expected the magic of the Autarch to tear through her like a hurricane. She doubted she would survive it. But though she felt the Autarch's magic explode outward from his corpse, none of it touched her. Like the radiating rays of the golden sun behind the dead ruler's throne, the magic, brilliant and blinding to Mara's Gifted sight, blazed out of the throne room in all directions. She could not see everywhere it went, but she could guess, for some of it impaled the silver Masks of the unconscious Child Guard . . . and with the sound of ringing bells, every one of those Masks broke in half and fell away, revealing young and pale faces.

It's over, Mara thought. *It's really over. All the Masks . . . everywhere . . . they're breaking. They're falling apart. The whole Autarchy, unMasked.*

It's over. We won.

She staggered to her feet. Greff . . . she could not bear to look at the awful ruin of the boy she had promised to save for his parents. He had died a hero, but she didn't think that would be much consolation to Filia and Jess.

Tears filled her eyes. She turned toward the throne room doors, intending to go out to see how many of her guard survived, to see what had happened in the city beyond, but before she could take a step from the dais the doors burst open.

A man in silver mail and white surcoat exploded through, a bloody sword in one hand, a bloody dagger in the other. He wore half a Watcher's

Mask, the bottom half having fallen away. More blood spattered his tunic, and dripped from a wound that had laid his cheek open, exposing the skull-like gleam of teeth. He charged Mara, screaming, sword raised. *He's going to kill me—*

Something hit him from behind and he went down hard. Whiteblaze leaped over him and stood between him and Mara, growling. The wolf advanced, teeth bared, and Mara, still in shock from what she had just done, what had just happened to Greff, reacted too slowly to what was about to happen in front of her. She had just started forward when the Sun Guard lifted himself and drove his dagger into Whiteblaze's side.

The wolf howled and turned white with magic as he collapsed, and Mara, screaming, took that magic and tore the Sun Guard limb from limb, painting the floor of the throne room red with his blood and scattered entrails. She scrambled forward on all knees to where Whiteblaze lay still as death, and buried her face in his bloody fur.

She was still clinging to him when something struck her in the back of the head and in an explosion of shock and pain she fell into darkness.

TWENTY-THREE
Outcast

FOR AN INDETERMINATE TIME, Mara bobbed in and out of consciousness, surfacing and submerging like a twig caught in a mountain stream, never fully escaping its icy clutch. At one point she thought she heard Keltan shouting. She heard the clash of steel. She heard a vast roaring sound like a mighty wind or an enormous crowd. Her eyes flickered open to see the carved wooden beams of the Palace's main-floor corridors passing by overhead. She opened them again to find herself in a bed and a woman in the blue dress of a Healer, though unMasked and with a strained, pale face, bending over her. She glimpsed the blue glow of Healing magic.

And then she slept.

Nightmares awaited her. She had absorbed too many deaths without the filtering effect of the black lodestone amulet. Old ghosts resurfaced: Grute, oldest of all, naked and headless; the Warden, throat ruined; the Watchers she had killed; the Lady, trailing blood as she dropped into the mine shaft; the Autarch, headless and bloody as Grute . . .

But the worst were those she cared about most. Her father, who in her nightmare just stood and stared at her, hangman's noose still around his neck, voiceless in grief and disappointment; Ethelda, who whispered over and over again, "Monster . . . monster . . . monster . . ."

And Mayson. Her best friend from childhood. The boy who had always wanted to be a Watcher, when none of them knew what that meant. She saw him lying wounded on the floor of the Warden's house, heard him trying to speak, "Mmmm . . . mmmm . . ." He had tried to speak her name, to save himself, to stop her from murdering him . . . and she had snapped his neck like a twig.

"Monster . . . monster . . . monster . . ." Slowly the whisper from Ethelda grew in volume and scope, until all her nightmare victims were gathered around her, repeating the word in unison. "Monster! Monster! Monster!" They closed in on her. She screamed, tried to wake up, but something was holding her asleep, holding her trapped in her mind, and she thought her heart would burst from terror and grief . . .

. . . and then she felt a familiar furry head under her hand, and terror bled away, the nightmare images flowing out from her like wine through the tap of a barrel, and she fell into a far deeper darkness where no dreams waited, one joyful thought following her down.

Whiteblaze is still alive!

The next time she came to consciousness it was to full wakefulness at last. She lay in a soft white bed, staring up at a ceiling that looked strangely familiar. For a moment she just blinked sleepily up at it. There was something on her face. *Why didn't they take off that silver Mask?* she wondered—then remembered that the Autarch himself had stripped her of her Child Guard Mask, and she had used it to kill him.

More memories rushed back. Whiteblaze . . . nightmares . . . Greff . . . why was she wearing a Mask?

She lifted a hand, trembling with unexpected weakness—how long had she been lying there?—and explored her face.

Horror filled her. She was not wearing the silver Mask she had made.

She was wearing a half-Mask, a Mask made of cold, pitted iron. A prison Mask, like the one the Mistress of Magic had placed on her when she had come to the Palace the last time, a Mask that blocked her Gift, prevented her from using or even seeing magic. And that ceiling looked familiar because this was the magically shielded room where she had trained with Shelra, the room no magic could enter or leave.

What's happening? I killed the Autarch! Why am I a prisoner?

She tried to sit up. The too-familiar room swam around her, but she managed to hold herself shakily up on her elbows. At the table by the fire sat someone she didn't know, though she had seen her briefly during her period of semiconsciousness: the Maskless Healer. "What's going on?" she said, or tried to say. Her voice didn't want to work, so it came out as a harsh whisper. "Who are you?"

The Healer's head turned sharply toward her. "You're awake!" She looked almost frightened.

"Yes, I'm awake," Mara said. She could feel anger rising within her—and this time it was all hers. The Lady was gone for good. She had felt her vanish into the maelstrom of the Autarch's fury and fear as he fled back into his own body to try to heal the wound from Greff's knife. The Lady's ghost had accompanied the Autarch's spirit to hell, or wherever demons like him went when they died, and good riddance.

But she was the one who had exorcised him, and the Lady, too, with Greff's sacrifice and the help of so many others. Why was she iron-Masked and imprisoned and blocked? "I asked you a question. Who are you? And why am I here?"

"I am Healer Chara," the woman said. "Lord Edrik asked me to . . . look after you. But I'm afraid," she hurried on, "I can't answer any more of your questions. I am to send word to Lord Edrik as soon as you are awake. I'm sure someone will come shortly." She went to the door, unlocked it, and spoke in a hurried whisper to someone outside. Footsteps clattered away. The door closed, and the Healer bolted it again. Then she turned back to Mara. "Now," she said. "How are you feeling?"

"Weak," Mara said. "And betrayed." She touched the iron Mask. "What the hell is this doing on my face?" *And why does she keep referring to Lord Edrik?*

"I told you," Chara said weakly, "I can't answer any questions."

"What *can* you do?" Mara said. She had to lie down again; her vision was showing an alarming tendency to close in around the edges. She took a deep breath. "Can you give me food and water, at least?"

"Of course," Chara said. "*That* I've been doing all along."

"I don't remember it," Mara said as Chara hurried over to a cabinet against the wall.

"You were awakened enough to eat but not enough to be fully aware of it," Chara said. "It is a healing technique for when the brain may be damaged and must have time to heal."

"You mean I ate even though I was asleep," Mara said.

"Essentially. Yes." Chara was putting fruit and cheese on a plate. She filled a mug with water from a clay pitcher, placed everything on a wooden tray, and brought it over to Mara. She placed it on the low table by the bed, and then said, "Let me help you sit up."

Still feeling horribly weak, Mara let Chara push pillows under her back until she was upright. She ate, her hands still shaking. "You're saying you deliberately kept me asleep?" she said. "For how long?" She looked down at herself. She was wearing a nightgown and covered by a blue blanket. *At least there's no diaper this time*, she thought, remembering another occasion when she had awakened after being unconscious for an unknown time. *But if they woke me up enough to eat, maybe they woke me up enough to . . .*

She decided not to ask.

"I don't think I should tell you how long you've been asleep, either," the Healer said. "Someone else will." She put her hand to her face, then drew it back again and gave a shaky laugh. "I can't get used to not wearing a Mask," she said. "I feel . . . naked."

"Can you at least tell me what happened to the Masks?" Mara said. "When the Autarch . . . died?" *When I tore his head off . . .*

"They broke. All of them. Everywhere. From one end of Aygrima to the other." The Healer shook her head. "It was terrifying. Worst for the youngsters, the ones who had been Masked in the past two or three years. We all knew there was something different about their Masks, different about *them*. Then when the unMasked Army started attacking the weakened part of the wall, they all dropped whatever they were doing and marched to battle. They were fearless, even though many of them came unarmed. Some of them came *naked*. The unMasked Army fell back. They didn't want to kill teenagers, though there were a few . . ." She swallowed. "It was bad. But when the Masks failed, those young people all screamed and fell senseless. Some of them died instantly. Others . . . still aren't themselves. A few are starting to recover. I was trying to help some of them when I was seized by the unMasked Army and told I had a new patient. They brought me to you. You had suffered a blow to the head. I made sure there was no permanent damage, but then they had me put you to sleep . . . or try to. You screamed and screamed as if suffering terrible nightmares. The young man . . . Keltan . . . suggested we bring you your wolf. Once you touched him, you finally went under completely."

"Whiteblaze," Mara said. "I saw him stabbed, I thought he was dead—" *And Keltan is alive, too!* A weight she hadn't even been aware of lifted from her heart.

"He very nearly was," the Healer said. "But I was told to Heal him as well."

"Where is he? Can I see him?"

"He was taken away once your nightmares subsided," the Healer said. "I'm afraid I don't know where he is now."

"And why am I awake now?" Mara said.

"I was ordered yesterday to allow you to wake up at last. I permitted you to rise from magical to ordinary sleep. And here you are." She blinked suddenly and pressed her lips together. "I may have said too much." Her hands went halfway to her face again.

"No Mask," Mara said. "No one will know." She touched the hateful pitted iron clinging to her face. "It appears I'm the only one still Masked in Aygrima."

"And so it will remain," said a new voice from the door, and Mara jerked her head around.

Catilla stood there, leaning on her cane of pale wood. She looked older than Mara remembered, older and yet somehow more fierce than ever, like an aging hawk still ready to fly to the hunt. Edrik was with her. The two of them came over to her bedside. "You've done well," Edrik said to the Healer. "Leave us for a few minutes."

"Yes, Lord Edrik," the Healer said. "Lady," she added with a quick bob of her head to Catilla. She gave Mara a faint half-smile, and then hurried out. A guard in the hall outside closed the door again.

"Lord?" Mara said. "Lady?"

"We have had enough of Autarchs," said Catilla. "But Aygrima still needs a ruler. Once it was the Kingdom of Aygrima. So it will be again." She nodded at Edrik. "In a fortnight, King Edrik will ascend the Sun Throne, and a new era of peace and freedom will begin."

"King Edrik?" Mara said. "Not Queen Catilla?"

"There is no point in a crowning a Queen who will not live out the first year of her reign," Catilla said. She coughed a little, and Mara suddenly understood.

"The cancer has returned," she said.

Catilla nodded. "Ethelda bought me time, and for that I am grateful, for I have seen the overthrow of the Autarchy and the destruction of the Masks and will see my grandson become king and my great-grandson Crown Prince. My father is avenged and his heirs will rule. I am content."

"I'm not," Mara said. She touched the iron Mask. "Explain this. Explain what happened in the throne room, and how I came to be a prisoner here." Her eyes narrowed. "And explain how *you* came to be here. You were in the north, days' travel away. How long have I been a prisoner?"

"Three weeks," Catilla said. "Three weeks have passed since you slew the Autarch and destroyed the Masks."

"Three *weeks*?" Mara couldn't believe it, though it explained her weakness. "What happened to me?"

Edrik regarded her steadily. "The unMasked Army fighters who you let into the city had orders," he said. "If you succeeded, and survived, you were not to be allowed to go free. You were to be subdued and brought to me."

Mara stared at him, feeling cold. "The blow to the head . . . ?"

"Hyram," Edrik said. "He took the task on himself because he felt he could judge the blow better than the others, who might have been tempted to simply . . . remove you." He made a sour face. "More of a danger than I realized. One of Chell's men let the Sun Guard through after the Autarch's death in the hope he would kill you. Chell slew his own sailor for that. Fortunately, you . . . dealt with that threat. Rather forcefully."

"And then Hyram knocked me out?" Mara felt more betrayed than she had any right to. Hyram had been infatuated with her when she'd first arrived at the Secret City, but his attraction had not survived her naïve betrayal of the unMasked Army to the Watchers. *I'm probably lucky he didn't kill me.* But she missed him as her friend. She missed those early days when Keltan and Hyram had been competing for her attention. It seemed years past though it had only been a few months.

So much had happened in so little time . . .

"Don't be too hard on him, Mara," Edrik said. He surprised her by the softness in his tone. "He was following our orders. He argued against them. He thought we were being unnecessarily cautious. He really didn't want to hurt you. He has been very concerned about you."

Mara didn't know what to say to that. *He didn't want to hurt me, but he still knocked me out.* "'Unnecessarily cautious,'" she repeated slowly. "You had me knocked out, and then put this Mask on me before I woke . . . you're afraid of me."

"Wouldn't you be?" Catilla said. "In fact . . . aren't you?"

Afraid of myself? Mara thought. She wanted to scoff . . . but in truth, she couldn't.

I am afraid. Afraid of my Gift. Afraid of what it means to be the only one left who has it. Afraid of where it might lead . . . where it already has led. So much death and destruction . . .

"I think you begin to understand," Catilla said. Her voice, too, was softer than it had been, with a warmth she had rarely heard from the old lady. "The Lady began as you are now, young, powerful, idealistic, trying to overthrow tyranny. But she became a tyrant in her turn, unable to resist the lure of her Gift, the attraction of control over others, the desire to live forever. I don't know that that will happen to you . . . but I don't know that it won't. And I don't believe even you can be certain."

Mara swallowed. "No," she said. "No, I can't."

"The new Kingdom of Aygrima must have time to rebuild without worrying about your power. Perhaps you need time to rebuild, too. And so we have Masked you, with the help of the Master Maskmaker: one last Mask before we burned his workshop to the ground."

Burned . . . "My old house?" she whispered.

"Yes," Catilla said. "I'm sorry. But it had to be done. We've ordered the destruction of all the Maskmaking shops round the kingdom, as proof that the era of the Masks has ended." She coughed again.

Anger poured into Mara, white-hot. She ached to tear the magic from the evil crone cackling at her bedside, tear her apart as she had the Sun Guard, burn Edrik where he stood . . .

She caught herself, horrified and sick. *The Lady is gone!* she thought. *Where are these thoughts coming from now?*

There was only one place they could be coming from. Within her.

Is Catilla right? she thought.

Monster . . . monster . . . monster . . . The chants of her nightmare visitors whispered in her ears.

She touched the Mask again. *Maybe this is for the best,* she thought. *Maybe I do need time to rebuild. Just like the Autarchy . . . no. The kingdom.*

"How long do I have to wear this?" she whispered.

"For as long as you stay in Aygrima," Catilla said.

Mara stared at her in shock. The anger lurched back to life inside her like a creature rising from the dead. "You'll make me wear it *the rest of my life?*"

"That's not what she said, Mara," Edrik said. "She said, 'For as long as you stay in Aygrima.'"

"You mean exile."

"I'm sorry, but we simply cannot risk having someone with your power active within the kingdom," Catilla said.

"But I can't remove it myself," Mara said. "Even if I leave Aygrima, it will remain—"

"No," Catilla said. "The Mask you wear is keyed to the magical boundaries of Aygrima, the defenses that protect us from invasion on all sides, set in place by the great Gifted creators of the ancients. Once you pass far enough beyond those boundaries, the Mask will fall away."

Mara found her fists had clenched. She eased them open. "So where am I supposed to go?"

"Prince Chell asked me to once more extend to you an invitation to travel with him to his home country of Korellia," Edrik said.

Mara's heart leaped. She'd thought . . . "His ships were destroyed. It will be months before—"

"For his men working alone it would have taken months to jury-rig one of his hulks into a sailable vessel, it's true," Edrik said. "But we have provided him with Gifted Engineers and a good supply of magic. He believes he can salvage one ship from the wreckage of the two in less than a month with their help. He has already traveled north with them and his surviving crew and officers."

"You're allowing other Gifted to travel and use magic freely?" Mara said a little bitterly. "I'm surprised you're not locking up *all* Gifted."

Edrik laughed. "Mara, just because we never had magic at the Secret City doesn't mean we hated it. It's Aygrima's greatest asset. Now that people are free from the Autarch's tyranny, the kingdom will blossom again, thanks to magic. Eventually we'll reach out into the outside world again and resume the trade in magic that once enriched us all." The amusement in his voice died away. "No, Mara. We don't fear magic. We fear *you*."

"Do not mistake us, Mara," Catilla said. "I am grateful for what you have accomplished. I'm in awe of it. I spent my whole life trying to find a way to overthrow the Autarch with my unMasked Army. Years ago I decided the task was hopeless, but I kept going through the motions, because at least we provided hope and freedom for those who found their way to us. When we first rescued you, at your father's urging, I thought only to use your nonmagical ability to craft believable Masks—a foolish scheme born of my own ignorance. I had no idea that by saving your life we would finally bring an end to the Autarch's tyranny. Yet in eight scant months you have achieved the task I set for myself when I fled to the Secret City . . . and failed at so spectacularly through decades of wasted time." She smiled sadly. "Mara, you are *dangerous*—dangerous now, and who knows how dangerous in the future? You're not even sixteen years old, and you have single-handedly slain the two most ruthless and powerful Gifted individuals Aygrima has ever seen. You may think you could never turn into a new incarnation of the Lady of Pain and Fire or the Autarch, and I pray that you will not—but you cannot yet know that for certain. More to the point, neither can *we*." Her smile faded. "After all, I never thought, when I was sixteen, I would turn into *this*."

"Why not just kill me, then?" Mara said bitterly. She spread her hands wide. "I am helpless before you."

"We are not monsters," Catilla said. "We fought to make this land better and freer. Executing the one who gave us the opportunity to do so would be a poor way to begin the new era."

"But you seem to think *I'm* a monster."

"I think you could be, yes," Catilla said. She looked at Mara steadily. "Don't you?"

No, Mara wanted to say, but she could not. Because how many times had she expressed to herself the same fears Catilla was expressing to her now?

"Live," Catilla said. "Live, and prove our mutual fears wrong. Go with Chell."

Mara swallowed. "What if . . . what if I do . . . become evil? If the Mask frees me as you promise it will, what will prevent me from simply returning and taking my revenge?"

"Once you leave," Catilla said, "the borders of Aygrima will be closed to you as they were against the Lady. She only broke through that defense with your help. I do not think you will find anyone Gifted as you are in the world outside our land."

Anger still bubbled in Mara, trying to break free . . . and oddly, that helped convince her. "All right," she said. "I'll go with Chell, to Korellia. I'll leave Aygrima." Her throat closed and it was a moment before she could speak again. "Do you . . . do you know if my mother is still alive? I haven't seen her since my Masking . . ."

Edrik shook her head. "I'm sorry, Mara," he said softly. "I asked after her, but . . . the Autarch's Watchers found her in the south and brought her back to the capital after your father's death and your escape. She was executed, in accordance with his practice of killing the entire family of anyone convicted of treason."

Executed. Mara's anger rose again, but this time directed at the Autarch. She'd had her revenge. He was dead and the Masks gone forever. But so were her parents. So were so many others. The anger dropped away into the old familiar seething turmoil of grief and guilt that filled the cauldron of her thoughts. Tears pooled in her eyes and slipped down the iron of the Mask.

There's nothing left for me in Aygrima, she thought. *Catilla is right. I'm too dangerous. Unstable. Aygrima needs time to recover from the ravages of people like me. And I need time to recover myself . . . if that's even possible.*

She raised her head. "I will go into exile with Chell."

"Good," Catilla said. "But you need not go alone. There are two others waiting to join you. They're outside. We'll send them in." She reached out a wizened hand and put it on Mara's arm. "I am sorry, Mara," she said softly. "I truly am sorry it had to come to this. But . . . thank you. Thank you from the bottom of my heart." Her eyes gleamed, and a single tear tracked down her cheek. She dashed it away with the back of her hand. "Damn old age," she growled, and turned away. "Come along, Grandson."

"Yes, Grandmother," said the presumptive King of Aygrima, and together they went out.

The door did not close, however. Instead, it filled with a boy and a large furry beast: Keltan and Whiteblaze.

Mara would have loved to have leaped up and run to both of them, but since she would have undoubtedly fallen flat on her face had she tried, she settled for reaching out. Whiteblaze bounded across the floor and licked her face enthusiastically. Keltan proceeded more sedately, probably because he had one arm in a sling and a bandage on his head.

"What happened to you?" she asked him, which wasn't the greeting she'd intended a moment before, but Whiteblaze had rather preempted the "enthusiastic kissing" option.

"Disagreement with Hyram," Keltan said. "After I saw him hit you over the head. I looked a lot worse three weeks ago and he looked worse than me. But he had backup, and I didn't."

"He was just following orders," Mara said. "If he hadn't done it, someone else would have . . . and probably harder."

"I know that now," Keltan said. "But I didn't wait for anyone to explain it to me. And it wouldn't have made any difference if they had."

"I'm just glad you're all right," Mara said. "I felt people die outside the throne room when the Sun Guards arrived . . ."

"Prescox and Lilla of unMasked Army. Three of Chell's sailors. Eight Sun Guards and four of the Circle," Keltan said.

"Antril?"

"Fought like a demon," Keltan said. "He's all right. We gave better than we got, but only because we had the advantage of defending the top of the stairs. Another few minutes and they would have killed us all. But then the Masks broke. Only two of the Sun Guards fought on. We thought it was almost over—and then one of Chell's men deliberately let a Sun Guard past, screaming at him, 'Kill the bitch for us!'" His voice shook with the memory. "Chell cut his own sailor down on the spot, and Hyram and I ran into the throne room, behind Whiteblaze. But you had . . . ah . . . dealt with the threat on your own."

Mara remembered exactly what she had done to the man, and swallowed. She ruffled Whiteblaze's fur. "And so here we are," she said. "Exile." She looked up at Keltan. "Are you really willing to come with me?"

"Not just willing," Keltan said. "Eager." He sat down on the edge of her bed and took her hand in his. "There's nothing for me here. I'd just be another soldier, unless I wanted to go back to the tannery . . ." He grimaced. "Not likely. And then there's the fact I'd have to serve under Hyram. Sooner or later I'd probably try to kill him . . . and since he's about to become the Crown Prince of Aygrima, I don't think that would end well for me."

"Wait," Mara said. "I just realized . . . does that mean Alita is going to be a princess?"

"If she marries him as they plan, then yes, I guess so," Keltan said. "And Queen one day."

"Her village will be so proud," Mara said. She couldn't feel any bitterness toward Alita, or Prella or Kirika. She hoped they all lived happily ever after, whatever happened to her. "When do we leave?"

"As soon as you're strong enough," he said.

"I'm already strong enough for some things," Mara said, and pulled him down to her.

The iron Mask didn't get in the way of kissing nearly as much as she'd feared.

◆ ◆ ◆

They left Tamita on a wet, blustery morning ten days later, escorted by half a dozen of the unMasked Army, who kept to themselves and hardly spoke to either Keltan or Mara as they rode north. Mara only looked back once, as they crested the ridge that would hide the city from them once they descended its northern side. The clouds were so low they dimmed the tallest towers of the Palace, where the blue banners of the Autarch had been replaced by banners of red and gold, the chosen colors of Edrik's soon-to-be-ennobled family. The half-repaired wall looked like a bruise from this distance, but already Gifted Engineers and workers were bustling around it, trying to have it intact in time for the coronation.

Mara was glad she would not be there to see the crown placed on Edrik's head, or the circlet of the Heir Apparent placed on Hyram's, or to see Edrik ascend the Sun Throne she had last seen splattered with the blood of the Autarch. The people loved him, or at least the *idea* of him, the great liberator who had freed them from the tyranny of the Masks. Her own role in that remained deliberately obscured from general knowledge.

She turned north again, and let Tamita sink out of sight behind them.

She'd thought to pay a visit to Jess and Filia in Yellowgrass, to tell them how bravely their son had died, but Catilla had forbidden it. "You've caused them enough grief," Catilla had said. "I do not think they would welcome you."

Mara couldn't really argue. *It's probably for the best.*

Indeed, Catilla had forbidden them from stopping at *any* villages, including Silverthorne, though Mara would also have liked to have told Herella how successful their Maskmaking had been. Instead they camped at night and rode during the day, eventually crossing out of Aygrima through the pass Mara had opened for the Lady scant weeks ago, and descending into the valleys north of the range, making their way to the Lady's village.

The place looked half-empty to Mara as she viewed it from horseback high above. Keltan had told her that the unMasked from the mines who had fled there had mostly gone south again the moment the Masks were gone. "And some of them," he said, "are going to pose a problem for Edrik. Many will end up in other prisons sooner rather than later." He sounded rather pleased by the idea.

Mara had insisted on coming this way, instead of riding to the Secret City and up the coast. "I will not go into the village," she had promised Catilla, "but I left some personal items in the fortress I would like to retrieve."

"And how do you plan to get into it without going into the village?" Catilla had demanded.

"I lived there for weeks," Mara said. "I know a way in I doubt anyone in the village will have found."

"Very well," Catilla had said. "But only with an escort."

And so, as darkness fell, Mara, Keltan, Whiteblaze and three of their guards rode down into the narrow ravine behind the mass of rock on which the castle perched. There Mara found the wolves' trail she had used when she had sneaked into the village without the Lady's knowledge, all those weeks ago. Together she and the others climbed up it, and crawled into the fortress through the low, hidden opening in the wall.

The castle had been sacked. The beautiful tapestries were torn and burned, the rich furniture missing or smashed, the pantry empty, everything of value gone. But none of that concerned Mara in the slightest. She led the way to the Lady's private chamber, found the loose rock the Lady had pried up in her presence . . . and took out the small chest containing the scrolls and books the Lady's father had retrieved from the Palace Library when they had fled Tamita, the ones that contained everything the scholars of old had learned about the rare Gift that she and the Lady and the Autarch shared.

She did not open the chest in the presence of the unMasked, and they, having been given no orders to interfere, let her take it without question.

The next morning, they continued their journey to the coast.

On a bright sunny morning they emerged from the woods onto the warm, stony beach that had been covered with corpses and snow the last time Mara had seen it. She had expected to see the wreck of *Defender* still keeled over on the beach where the Lady had flung it, with men working around it, but instead she gasped in surprise: the ship floated offshore, gleaming with fresh paint, sails neatly furled. The Engineers and magic sent from Tamita had indeed worked wonders.

Tents dotted the shore. Someone looked up and saw them, and gave a shout—and a moment later Chell himself came striding across the beach toward them. "Mara," he said. "Keltan." His gaze flicked to the wolf. "And Whiteblaze." He looked back at Mara. "I have been waiting for you," he said. "Word came that you had chosen to accompany us. I'm honored."

"Catilla left me little choice," Mara said. "But the truth is, I'm glad to be leaving Aygrima behind." She looked at the unMasked who had accompanied them. "Your task is done," she said. "Why don't you ride on home to your mistress?"

"Our task is not done until you are aboard that ship and sailing away from these shores," Hathar, the leader, said unsmiling. "We will remain in camp until that is done."

"Don't bother putting up your tents," Chell said. "We've been ready to sail for two days." He glanced over his shoulder. "Gifted Engineers are . . . amazing. Despite everything I had seen, I hadn't realized until now just how much we lost when we lost contact with Aygrima."

"Magic can be used for more than destruction," Mara said. "Or so they tell me."

Chell opened his mouth to say something, then closed it again. "I'll see you all aboard," he said after a moment's pause.

An hour later, Mara stood on the deck of the reborn *Defender* and watched Aygrima slip away, the tents on the shore blending into the hills behind them, which faded into the mountains, which were eventually lost in haze. After that, there was only the sea.

She slept a lot those first couple of days. Slept, and talked with Keltan, and made sure Whiteblaze was fed and watered and exercised. They had meals with Chell, but Chell said nothing about what would happen once they reached his homeland. Mara knew what he wanted—knew that he hoped her Gift could somehow be used in his kingdom's war against Stonefell—but he held his tongue, and for that she was grateful.

Early on the morning of their third day at sea, she stood on deck with Whiteblaze at her side, staring over the rail at a school of flying fish glittering in the sun. Lieutenant Antril stood on the poop deck next to the helmsman, but otherwise the deck was deserted, the night watch heading to their bunks, the day watch still at breakfast.

They were galloping along, a brisk breeze filling the sails. A bit of spray splashed Mara's cheek. She jerked back from the railing in surprise . . . and in that instant, the iron Mask suddenly and without warning dropped from her face, clattering into the scuppers. Whiteblaze sniffed it curiously, then sat on his haunches and grinned up at her.

She gasped and gripped the railing, waiting for a rush of magic, or anger, or memory, or madness . . . but nothing happened. She felt just the same. She loosened her grip and took a deep breath. Something fluttered in her chest like a bird released from a cage. *Hope*, she thought. *I think that's* hope.

They were many days from Korellia. Many days before she had to make any decisions at all about what she would do in her new life.

For now, it was enough that she was free of the iron Mask, that she had left all of Aygrima free of the Masks that had enslaved them for so long; enough that she had Keltan and Whiteblaze with her.

She could feel, all around her, the magic in the bodies of the sailors in their ship. But the sea muted it. She didn't *crave* that magic. She didn't *need* it. She could leave it untapped.

For the moment.

She went in search of Keltan.

Behind her, the last Mask of Aygrima, forgotten and discarded, rocked gently to the motion of the great ship.